ANATOMY OF A KILLER

Sam Jordan never lets emotion interfere with his work. He is a precise and ruthless killing machine, dealing out death for hire. But his last job had ended wrong for Jordan, and now Sandy is sending him out again—without a break, yet—to take care of someone named Kemp. Hell, he even has to case the job himself. The whole thing feels jinxed. That's when Jordan meets Betty, who works at the diner. To her he is Mr. Smith, a button salesman. But to Jordan, Betty is a sweet moment in his life, a safe haven. And that's where he makes his first mistake— he allows himself to feel human.

A SHROUD FOR JESSO

Jack Jesso knows that Gluck wants him out of the syndicate. Still, when Gluck sends him on an errand to find a missing guy named Snell for a shady client of his, Johannes Kator, Jesso doesn't figure it to be anything more than a test. He finds the guy alright— sick and rambling—but Gluck double-crosses him, and tosses Jesso onto a Europe-bound steamer with Kator's crew, their orders to kill him. Jesso quickly realizes that he holds the key to a big money deal in Snell's ramblings, information that Kator desperately needs. All he has to do to stay alive is keep Kator interested. It's a simple enough scheme—until Jesso meets Kator's beautiful sister, Renette.

PETER RABE BIBLIOGRAPHY

From Here to Maternity (1955)
Stop This Man! (1955)
Benny Muscles In (1955)
A Shroud for Jesso (1955)
A House in Naples (1956)
Kill the Boss Goodbye (1956)
Dig My Grave Deep (1956) *
The Out is Death (1957) *
Agreement to Kill (1957)
It's My Funeral (1957) *
Journey Into Terror (1957)
Mission for Vengeance (1958)
Blood on the Desert (1958)
The Cut of the Whip (1958) *
Bring Me Another Corpse (1959) *
Time Enough to Die (1959) *
Anatomy of a Killer (1960)
My Lovely Executioner (1960)
Murder Me for Nickels (1960)
The Box (1962)
His Neighbor's Wife (1962)
Girl in a Big Brass Bed (1965) **
The Spy Who Was Three Feet Tall
   (1966) **
Code Name Gadget (1967) **
Tobruk (1967)
War of the Dons (1972)
Black Mafia (1974)

As by "Marco Malaponte"
New Man in the House (1963)
Her High-School Lover (1963)

As by "J. T. MacCargo"
Mannix #2: A Fine Day for Dying
   (1975)
Mannix #4: Round Trip to
   Nowhere (1975)

Short Stories
"Hard Case Redhead"
   (Mystery Tales, 1959)
"A Matter of Balance" (Story, 1961)

*Daniel Port series
**Manny DeWitt series

ANATOMY
OF A KILLER
- - - - -
A SHROUD
FOR JESSO

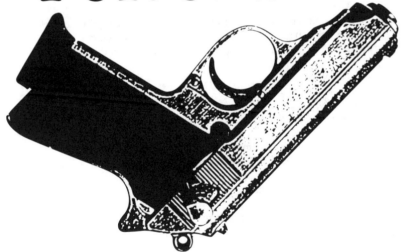

TWO MYSTERIES BY
PETER RABE

STARK
HOUSE

Stark House Press • Eureka California

ANATOMY OF A KILLER / A SHROUD FOR JESSO

Published by Stark House Press
2200 O Street
Eureka, CA 95501
griffinskye3@sbcglobal.net
www.starkhousepress.com

Exclusive trade distribution by SCB Distributors, Gardena, CA.

ISBN: 1-933586-22-2
ISBN-13: 978-1-933586-22-9

Text set in Figural. Heads set in American Typewriter.
Cover design and layout by Mark Shepard,
shepdesign.home.comcast.net/~shepdesign
Proofreading by Rick Ollerman

*The publisher wishes to thank Chris Nielsen and
Max Gartenberg as always for all their help on this project.*

First Stark House Press Edition: April 2008
0 9 8 7 6 5 4 3 2 1

NOIR AND GESTALT:
THE LIFE OF PETER RABE
BY GEORGE TUTTLE

Gold Medal Books discovered many talented novelists who could write hardboiled fiction, but in 1955, the editors felt that they had found its biggest discovery, Peter Rabe. On the cover of Peter's second novel *Benny Muscles In* (1955), their opinion is expressed: "Not since Dashiell Hammett and Raymond Chandler, who--under the guidance of that great editor, Joe Shaw--established the school of hard-boiled fiction, has a writer and a style come to the front with such brilliance and power as Peter Rabe. The editors of Gold Medal can remember nothing like it in the last quarter of a century."

Gold Medal Editor-in-Chief Richard Carroll believed that Peter could be a new giant in the mystery field, a status eventually obtained by fellow Gold Medal writer John D. MacDonald. But unlike MacDonald, Peter never reached that exalted level. Though he had a successful career throughout the 1950's and received high praise from the likes of New York Times critic Anthony Boucher, his success did not carry on into the 1960's. This article will try to explain what happened to Peter Rabe; why one of the most promising writers of the 1950's fell short of fame.

Peter Rabe died on May 20, 1990, of lung cancer, fifteen years after his last novel. In 1967, he felt forced to walk away from professional writing to become an Associate Professor at California Polytechnic State University at San Luis Obispo. Five years later, while still a professor, he returned to Gold Medal with *War of the Dons* (1972), and then after one more book under his own name and two under a pseudonym, he stopped writing crime fiction for publication. Peter loved writing and continued to write for his own amusement, but he quit attempting to sell his fiction.

The novels of Peter Rabe will give you little insight into the man. Unlike some writers whose stories are filled with personal feelings and experiences, Peter always keeps a certain distance from the characters he created, and the stories he told. His thrillers are almost all written in the third person and are not attempts to live vicariously. Instead, these novels are truly the theater of his imagination, and though Peter directs the action, he is not a participant.

An example of the distance that he maintained is revealed in the settings he used. He rarely set his novels in places where he lived, at the time, but instead, he preferred to use settings from his past and often used places that he had only known briefly. In *A Shroud for Jesso* (1955) and *A House in Naples* (1956), there is the Europe experienced as a child, updated to contemporary times. In *Stop this Man!* (1955) and *It's My Funeral* (1957), there are scenes from L.A., where he lived for a short time, during the early 1950's, while attempting to establish a career as a practicing psychologist. Peter's early novels (probably just his first two) were written while living in Maine. Later, Peter lived in Cleveland and in the scenic town of Provincetown, Massachusetts. By the late 1950's, Peter had moved to Europe. *Bring Me Another Corpse* (1959) was set in Cleveland, but by the time it was written, Peter was probably in Germany receiving treatment for a misdiagnosed terminal illness.

Peter grew up in the Germany of the 1920's and 1930's. His father Michael Rabinovich (Rabinowitsch, the German spelling) was a Russian Jew, who had immigrated into Germany so that he could study medicine. After attending the University of Strasburgh and being interned as an enemy alien during World War I, Michael moved to Halle where he enrolled in the Martin Luther University. There he met a secretary who worked in one of the departments, Elisabeth Margarete Beer. They were married in Halle in January of 1921. Peter was born November 3, 1921. A few months later, they moved to Hanover, in Northern Germany, where Michael set up a practice as a physician and surgeon. Two more sons, Valentin and Andreas, would follow about a decade later.

As a child, Peter learned to live with intolerance, even though he was only Jewish on his father's side (his mother's family was Lutheran.) One memory he shared, years later, with his daughter Jennifer was an outing in which he participated with a group of boys. At one point, during their hike through the countryside, they had to ask a local property owner for permission to cross his field. In response to their request, the man looked at the crowd of boys, pointed his finger at Peter, and said, "All of you can cross but him. Not the Jew."

As the Nazi movement grew, it became apparent to Peter's father, Michael, that it was no longer safe for his family to stay in Germany. One day, he was ordered to appear at the Gestapo office and was confronted with a huge file of transcripts of conversations he had had in his office with patients on politics. It wasn't long after this that, in October 1938, Michael and Peter, who was nearly the age for military service (or possible internment) immigrated to the United States, first settling in Detroit. Michael's brother, Robert Rubin, sponsored them. Peter and Michael stayed with the Rubin family while Michael took a course in obstetrics in Chicago and got his license to practice medicine. He later located a village named New Bremen that was settled by Germans and needed a doctor to replace a retiring one. Michael bought his office and telegraphed Peter's mother to come to

America. Peter's uncle, Robert Rubin, who had changed his family name, recommended to Michael that he do the same. The family name was changed from Rabinovich to Rabe ("RA" from Rabinowitsch and "BE" from Margarete's maiden name); hence Peter Rabinowitsch became Peter Rabe.

Peter, who could speak English before he came to the United States, adjusted quickly and soon enrolled into Ohio State University and received his bachelor's degree. After a stint in the Army, he attended Western Reserve in Cleveland, where he got his Masters and Ph.D. in psychology and worked as an instructor. It was while he was at Western Reserve that he met and fell in love with Claire Frederickson. She was five years younger than Peter, but like him, she was also a psychology major and she and her family had fled Europe to escape the Nazis.

An important fact about Claire is that she had a passionate interest in literature. She would sit in on the meetings that the graduate English majors held in the University's cafeteria. It was during these sessions that Claire became friends with Max Gartenberg. Claire introduced Peter to Max, a man who would later become a fundamental part of Peter's writing career.

Peter and Claire's relationship led to marriage, and after they'd finished their studies at Western Reserve, the couple moved to Bar Harbor, Maine, where Peter had received a post graduate grant from the National Institute of Mental Health and worked for Claire's brother, Emil Frederickson, at the Jackson Memorial Laboratory. Peter admired Emil and felt that Claire's brother was brilliant.

Despite his respect for Emil, he grew to dislike the work, which consisted of psychological experiments on animals. These experiments went against Peter's love of nature and respect for animal life. The research resulted in two papers: "Experimental Demonstration of the Cumulative Frustration Effect in C3H Mice" (The Journal of Genetic Psychology, 1951, 79, p163-172) and "The Cumulative Frustration Effect in the Audio-Genic Seizure Syndrome of DBA Mice" (The Journal of Genetic Psychology, 1952, 81, p3-17).

When the project was finished Peter and Claire traveled to Los Angeles where Peter set up a practice as a therapist. He quickly discovered that the market for a therapist in Los Angeles was sewed up by those receiving referrals from established psychiatrists. By August 1952, the Rabes returned to Cleveland, Ohio, where Peter eventually found work at a factory, but was soon elevated from a blue-collar job to writing copy, doing layouts and illustrating for ads. Around this time, Claire became pregnant. She gave birth to their first child, Jonathan, on April 5, 1953. This experience was the basis of Peter's first book, a book totally unlike the novels to come. This work was a humorous narrative, illustrated by Peter, about the trials and tribulations of childbirth.

Peter submitted the manuscript to an agent, who tried unsuccessfully to sell it, telling Peter it was not marketable. Peter was still unwilling to give up on the story, and since the agent had tried only book publishers, Peter decided to submit it to McCall's magazine. After waiting two months, he called McCall's and was told that they were enchanted with the story and planned to publish it.

The story appeared under the title "Who's Having This Baby?" in the September 1954 issue. After its appearance, Peter was contacted by Vanguard Press, who wanted to publish it as a book. To work out the contract, Vanguard recommended that he get an agent. So he contacted the agent he had used previously, the one who couldn't sell it, originally. The story was finally published in book form by Vanguard, in 1955, under the new title *From Here to Maternity*.

As all of this is happening, Peter happened to have a completed novel called *The Ticker*. It is the story of Tony Catell who steals a radioactive ingot of gold and is unaware of the deadly nature of his actions. Tony travels to sell the ingot and starts a cross-country manhunt. Of all of Peter's books, this one is more of a traditional thriller, rather than noir. The story has a hero, Jack Herron, and a clear, distinct resolution. It isn't an anti-hero story like many of his later works.

He showed the manuscript to his agent, who told him that she didn't handle those types of books, what the publishing trade called "blood 'n' guts" stories. So once again, Peter was on his own. He submitted the book to Gold Medal.

Meanwhile, Claire had heard that her old friend Max Gartenberg had formed his own literary agency. Since Peter would eventually need representation, she went to New York to see Max and ask him if he'd be interested in checking on the status of *The Ticker* and handling Peter's next book, *The Hook*. Max said, "Yes."

Max happened to have a friend at Gold Medal, an editor named Hal Cantor. He contacted Hal and was informed that Gold Medal was delighted with *The Ticker* and wanted to do more books by Peter. So Max offered them *The Hook*. Peter's career was off with a bang.

Gold Medal's excitement over Peter's work led Gold Medal's Editor-in-Chief Richard Carroll to look for a way to give this new author a big send-off. Carroll decided on getting an endorsement from Erskine Caldwell, one of the biggest selling authors in the history of publishing, and sent the galleys, with an endorsement fee to Caldwell's agent. But since Caldwell didn't have time to read the book and the agent didn't want to turn down the fee, his agent endorsed the book for Caldwell, with the words' "I couldn't put this book down!"

The Ticker was released August 1955, under the title *Stop this Man!*

When Peter visited the offices of Fawcett after the publication, he asked Carroll if he could have Caldwell's address so he could thank the famed author. In response, Carroll said, after a long pause, "Peter, do you know why Erskine Caldwell said,'I couldn't put this book down?' It's because he never picked it up."

The humor of the situation wasn't lost on Peter, who took the incident in stride. Endorsements were all part of how paperback originals were marketed. Peter accepted this and didn't resent Gold Medal for doing what it felt necessary to promote a book. Likewise, he took it in stride when Gold Medal changed the titles of his novels – when *The Ticker* became *Stop This Man!*, and when his next novel *The Hook* became *Benny Muscles In*.

Title changes were a standard operating procedure for Gold Medal. They saw a book's cover as the chief means of advertising a paperback and reserved in the contract the right to change the title to something more marketable. All of Peter's early novels had their titles changed. The only exceptions were *A House in Naples* and *The Box* (1962), though in the case of *A House in Naples*, the title was actually suggested by Max Gartenberg, Peter's agent.

Even though he didn't care much for the titles chosen (most were too crass for his tastes), he didn't let this color the fact that he liked writing for Gold Medal. He was intrigued with the type of situations dealt with in crime fiction. He liked the directness in which the characters reacted to one another and how the situations unfolded. These stories came easily to him and were well received by Editor-in-Chief Richard Carroll, who was very enthusiastic about Peter's work.

To write a novel, Peter would start with an outline. Using a clipboard and unlined yellow paper, he would write down the basic events that made up the plot. Once the outline was finished, he would work at the typewriter with the clipboard next to him, creating the story as he typed. He typed quickly and would only occasionally pause to light a cigarette, take a drag, and place it in the ashtray where it was usually allowed to burn out. He composed his novels directly on the typewriter, typing quickly and rarely rereading what he wrote.

During the mid-1950's, Peter's life changed for the better. His writing career took off, and he bought a summer cottage on Commercial Street in Provincetown, Massachusetts, a scenic town on the tip of Cape Cod. His family grew. A second child, Julia, was born on March 6, 1955, and later, another daughter, Jennifer(November 22, 1957).

In 1958, the success in publishing continued, but a complication developed. Peter started having health problems due to a stomach tumor. By July 1958, he received a report from a specialist in Boston recommending a gastric resection. After the procedure, a suspicious spot was biopsied and diagnosed as cancerous, and he was told that his condition was terminal.

As a result of the surgery, Peter lost weight and looked close to death. Peter's father made arrangements with the Ringberg Clinic, which specialized in alternative treatments for cancer. The clinic sits along Lake Tegernsee in Bavaria, Germany, and was run by Dr. Josef Issels. Peter moved his family to Taormina, Sicily, while he relocated to Germany. (Claire had no desire to revisit memories of Nazi Germany.) So Peter and Claire separated. While his family stayed in Sicily, Peter received treatment in Germany, hoping for the best, but preparing himself for the worst.

Soon after this happened, a second event occurred that would severely damage the writing career. Richard Carroll stepped down as Editor-in-Chief at Gold Medal Books, due to his own health problems. He eventually died on March 11, 1959. Carroll was one of Rabe's biggest fans. He thought Rabe could become a major writer of hardboiled thrillers, and Rabe might have if Carroll had lived. It's rare that a writer can find an editor who is truly willing to work with him. Carroll was that type of editor. He would let Peter know precisely how he felt about a novel. If a story had a weakness, Carroll would let Peter know where it fell short. In a 1991 interview (published Paperback Parade, issue 25) Peter described Carroll as "a very incisive and swift person, but he was open to dialogue. There was nothing particularly dictatorial about him. He was very explicit about what he didn't like, so, I liked working with him."

Peter's health had no immediate effect on his writing. Carroll's departure did. Knox Burger, who had been in charge of Dell's First Edition line, eventually replaced Carroll at Gold Medal. Since Knox had no previous ties to Gold Medal, he tended to favor writers he knew while working at Dell, authors like Donald Hamilton and James Atlee Phillips. This made things tougher for most of the old regulars, Peter included. Though Rabe sold several novels to Gold Medal while Burger was in charge, he didn't have the close relationship with Burger that he had with Carroll. Burger did think highly of Peter. Peter was one of the few writers from the Carroll era that Burger respected. He later describes Rabe, in a 1992 interview for Mystery Scene (appearing in issue 34) as one of "two or three very good writers I thought had been sort of mishandled by the previous regime." Burger seemed to think that all the writers under the previous regime were either hacks or mishandled. Burger's attitude did not mellow, over the years, particularly when paperback collectors and fans would ask him questions about David Goodis, Wade Miller, Lionel White, Bruno Fischer, and other writers associated with the Carroll years and would neglect to ask questions about Burger's pet writers.

Meanwhile in Europe, Peter's health improved. The reason for the improvement was uncovered when his father Michael double-checked

Peter's test results and found a major blunder. The results of Peter's biopsy had been switched with that of another patient. Peter's biopsy was cancer free. Michael telegraphed Peter the news. Soon after receiving the telegram, Peter left Germany, in July 1959, and returned to Sicily.

The separation and the emotional strain of this whole episode had severely damaged Peter and Claire's marriage. The whole series of events that brought them to Europe were not easy for either to handle. The fact that much that had happened was needless didn't help the situation.

In an attempt to salvage the marriage, Peter and Claire left Sicily and moved the family to Torremolinos, Spain, in the hope that the change in environment would help. It didn't. After about six months, Peter left for the United States, while Claire and the children stayed in Spain. Some time later, after attempts at reconciliation failed, they divorced.

Peter returned to America a different man. Many things had happened to change his outlook on life. First there was the illness that had been diagnosed as fatal, then the discovery that it was all a mistake, and finally, the split in his marriage and separation from his family. The man who returned to America in the early 1960's was not the same man who left, and it showed in his writing. In the sixties, Peter's style became less direct and more ambiguous. His sentences no longer had the crisp, simple clarity of his early writing. Peter explained the change in the 1991 Paperback Parade interview, stating that he had gone through "some very deep disturbances. Out of those disturbances emerged a man who no longer felt like writing that sort of thing."

As his writing style changed, so did the book publishing market, and unfortunately, it didn't change in his direction. The bottom dropped out of the paperback original market and a number of companies died or cut back on originals. Though Gold Medal stayed prosperous with a number of successful series like Shell Scott, Matt Helm, and Travis McGee, it found itself less interested in noir fiction. From 1961 to 1964, Gold Medal published only one new Peter Rabe novel unlike the previous four years when it published ten.

That one novel, *The Box* (1962) is a story about a man who crosses a crime boss and is punished by being packed alive in a box and shipped around the world. Max Gartenberg, who had heard of a similar incident from his cousin, a lawyer, gave the idea to Peter. It was one of his finest novels, clear evidence that his talent had not died.

In an attempt to weather this lean period, Peter started selling to Beacon, a paperback house that specialized in sexually suggestive literature. Beacon's trademark was a lighthouse and probably the greatest example of the use of a sexually subliminal image to market a product. Many paperback original writers who fell on tough times during the sixties, sold to Beacon,

Harry Whittington, Ovid Demaris, Michael Avallone, and Robert Turner to name some. It wasn't a high paying market like Gold Medal, but it was a paying market. At the time, Peter needed money.

The first book Peter wrote for Beacon was *His Neighbor's Wife* (1962). It's a good work of noir in the tradition of some of his best Gold Medal work, but it is unlikely that Beacon was completely happy with it. The problem with the book from Beacon's point of view is that it's centered on a criminal conflict, not a sexual conflict. Since they specialized in sexual-oriented fiction, it's doubtful they would have been happy with this novel. The book focuses on a hit-and-run accident and the psychological effects of the accident on the driver Martin Trevor and the passengers, his wife and another couple. Though the book has its share of sex, the sex is only a subplot, and hardly transforms the novel into the wife-swapping romp that the cover blurb promises. *His Neighbor's Wife* is a good book, but it's wasted on a publisher not interested in a psychological crime thriller.

Peter's next two novels for Beacon were more tailored to their need. *Her High-School Lover* (1963) and *New Man in the House* (1963) are the type of erotic thrillers Beacon is associated with, but not the type of book that Peter had interest in writing. Though not a prude, he had no desire to write novels based solely on sex. Peter was not proud of these efforts, and published them under the penname Marco Malaponte.

As Peter was trying to get his writing career back in order, he also tried to piece together his personal life. He met and fell in love with a blond Scandinavian beauty named Kristen, nicknamed Kiki, and they married. But the marriage lasted about as long as Peter's relationship with Beacon. They lived awhile in Spain, where Peter could be close to his children, and then moved to California where Peter and Kiki divorced. Little came of the brief relationship, though while Peter was in Spain, he developed a friendship with writer Lorenzo Semple, Jr., who would later join Peter in California, where they both tried to find work writing for television.

Television seemed to be the logical next step, since the paperback original market was suffering due to television. And though there was initial optimism, the optimism was quickly crushed. By June 1962, Peter writes in a letter from L.A. that out of ten TV script outlines he's sent out, only one has been rejected. The rest were all still under consideration including one for Hitchcock they'd asked he write based on one of his books. He also had a script accepted by the producer of the "Alcoa Hour." But later, both, the Hitchcock and Alcoa projects, were rejected by the sponsors. Interest followed by rejection characterizes Peter's career in television.

Around this time, Claire Rabe wrote a book called *Sicily Enough* (1963). The book was published in Paris, by Olympia Press. This short novel was later anthologized in The Best of Olympia (1966) and became a minor classic, receiving praise from authors Henry Miller and Thomas Sanchez. It was later reprinted with a collection of short stories by Claire, under the title *Sicily Enough and More* (1989). Claire is a totally different type of writer from Peter. While Peter preferred to maintain a distance from his creations, Claire's fiction has an autobiographical quality. The feelings and experience of the protagonists are intertwined with the author's, to the point that it's difficult to separate them. *Sicily Enough*, which is about a woman stranded in Taormina, Sicily, with her three children, mirrors many of Claire's experiences during her time in Taormina. It is interesting how Peter and Claire, who were so close, wrote fiction that is so radically different.

Throughout the Sixties, Peter continued to struggle. He roomed together for a short period with Lorenzo Semple, Jr. It was Semple who got the first big break when he landed the job of head writer on the *Batman* TV series. As a result of this break, Semple was able to send work in Peter's direction and Peter penned the episodes: "The Joker's Last Laugh" and "The Joker's Epitaph." Peter did other writing for *Batman*, but it was not used because of a format change in the series, the addition of Batgirl to the cast. Though Peter did other television work, the *Batman* episodes were the extent of his screen credits.

Peter moved regularly during this time, living in Anaheim, Hollywood, and Laguna Beach. He would occasionally take trips away from the West Coast. One trip was to Provincetown, and showed in an ironic way, that his readers had not been forgotten him. Peter's old home had sold, and he had come east to remove his things, and transport the bigger items, temporarily, to a friend's home, outside New York City. Unbeknownst to Peter, there had been a string of robberies of summer places on the Cape, and the police had a description of the car, a model that resembled Peter's. Peter finished what he had to do late on a weekend night, packed the back seat full of paintings, lamps, and other furnishings, and started out for New York. On the way, he was pulled over by a small town cop, who spotted the suspicious car full of what looked like loot, and Peter ended up in jail. Peter tried to reason with the officer, but the cop, who was also the jailer, kept stating that nothing could be done until the Justice appeared Monday morning. Eventually, the cop realized that he had read several of Peter's books and asked him to autograph one of them – but still the law was the law, and the officer had to keep Peter in the tank until Monday.

While Peter was trying to break into television, he continued to write novels. He created the Manny deWitt series for Gold Medal and wrote a novelization for the movie "Tobruk." To make ends meet, he also delivered newspapers, drove a taxi and did other odd jobs.

In 1967, Peter married Barbara Renard, whom he had known back at

Western Reserve University and had met again while in Hollywood. As a result of Barbara's insistence and the need for a steady income, he quit professional writing and reluctantly returned to the field of psychology. He obtained a teaching job at California Polytechnic State University at San Luis Obispo. They eventually bought a home in nearby Atascadero, California. Had it not been for Barbara, Peter might have stayed in writing and maybe roughed it out through the Sixties. As it was, teaching gave him financial security and a chance to be a father to his three children.

In the late 1960's, a little remembered actor/director, Peter Savage, bought the rights to A House in Naples and with producer Joe Justman, made a movie. The movie "A House in Naples" starred Pete Savage and his friend, boxer Jake LaMotta and was filmed in Italy. It had a limited release in 1969. Peter's agent Max Gartenberg, who saw the movie at a special screening, described it as awful, and said, "The negative is probably in somebody's warehouse, rotting away, which is the fate it deserves." At the time, the movie must have seemed like a disappointing final note to a once promising career.

Peter grew to love his work as a teacher. He renewed his interest in psychology and established a reputation as a respected Gestalt psychotherapist. But then his marriage with Barbara fell apart, and he gave writing another shot. The opportunity to be published presented itself when Knox Burger left Gold Medal and Walter Fultz took over. Walter provided a friendlier atmosphere for the old Gold Medal regulars of the 1950's and published Lionel White, Robert Colby, and others who had been frozen out when Burger took the helm. The result of this effort was entitled War of the Dons (1972) and became one of Peter's biggest sellers. It capitalized on the interest created by Mario Puzo's The Godfather. Rabe followed with another organized crime novel, Black Mafia (1974), a book in the tradition of his early gangster novels, like Benny Muscles In. In Black Mafia, an individual operator, a black man named Cutter, attempts to challenge the authority of the crime bosses. It's very much like the noir novels that first established Peter's reputation and was a fitting end to his relationship with Gold Medal, an end that was foreshadowed by the death of Walter Fultz and the hiring of a new editor.

Peter's last mass-market project was for the paperback house Belmont Tower. He wrote two novelizations based on scripts from the TV series Mannix. Both were published in 1975, under the penname J.T. MacCargo. Then Peter left professional writing, this time willingly. Things had changed in twenty years. There was still no one to replace Gold Medal's Richard Carroll, a man whose enthusiasm was an added incentive to stay in the business. Also, teaching was a much more stable profession than writing and a job where there were no concerns about changing markets or adapting to the individual taste of a particular editor, nor writing novelizations while waiting for markets to open up. Though he still wrote fiction throughout the Seventies and Eighties, he just no longer concerned himself with publication. He wrote for his own amusement.

As Peter made the transition from noir to gestalt, his life became more settled. As a professor of psychology, he had a greater control over his destiny. In 1971, he met Chris Neilson, a psychology student. Once again he fell in love, but this time he didn't jinx the relationship with marriage. Chris moved into his Atascadero home where they lived together until his death.

Still noir didn't abandon him. The dark images of Tom Fell (*Kill the Boss Good-By*), Daniel Port (*Dig My Grave Deep*), Jack St. Louis (*Murder Me for Nickels*) and anti-heroes of the earlier Rabe returned. During the late Seventies and throughout the Eighties, a following grew in both Europe and America for the old Gold Medal crime fiction and for Peter Rabe. In 1988, Black Lizard Books started reprinting Peter's books. He was surprised and flattered by this interest and deeply touched that he hadn't been forgotten as a novelist.

Peter career in noir was short. It started in 1955, soaring, only to crash and burn in the Sixties and then briefly resurrect itself in the early Seventies. When asked in the 1991 Paperback Parade interview, "Do you think if Carroll had lived longer that you would have stayed in the writing profession?"

Rabe answered: "I feel very sure that I would have become a better writer, a more consequential storyteller and may well have stayed in longer."

Possibly, if Carroll had lived into the next decade, Rabe would have made the transition from noir to a fiction style more marketable during the 1960's. Maybe, Daniel Port wouldn't have retired in Mexico or Rabe might have developed a series based on *Blood on the Desert* instead of creating the character of Manny deWitt. As it was, Peter Rabe did have a good life with Chris Neilson in Atascadero.

ANATOMY OF A KILLER

BY PETER RABE

1

When he was done in the room he stepped away quickly because the other man was falling his way. He moved fast and well and when he was out in the corridor he pulled the door shut behind him. Sam Jordan's speed had nothing to do with haste but came from perfection.

The door went so far and then held back with a slight give. It did not close. On the floor, between the door and the frame, was the arm.

He relaxed immediately but his motion was interrupted because he had to turn toward the end of the hall. The old woman had not stepped all the way out of her room. She was stretching her neck past the door jamb and looking at him. "Did you hear a noise just now?"

"Yes." He walked toward her, which was natural, because the stair well was that way. "On the street," he said. "One of those hotrods."

"Did you just come from Mister Vendo's room?"

"Yes."

"Was he in? I mean, I wonder if he heard it."

"Yes. He's in, and he heard it."

Jordan walked by the old woman and started down the stairs. She shook her head and said, "That racket. They're just like wild animals, the way they're driving," and went back into her room.

He turned when her door shut and walked back down the hallway. This was necessary and therefore automatic. He did not feel like a wild animal. He did his job with all the job habits smooth. When he was back at the door he looked down at the arm, but then did nothing else. He stood with his hand on the door knob and did nothing.

He stood still and looked down at the fingernails and thought they were changing color. And the sleeve was too long at the wrist. He was not worried about the job being done, because it was done and he knew it. He felt the muscles around the mouth and then the rest of the face, stiff like bone. He did not want to touch the arm.

Somebody came up the stairs and whistled. Jordan listened to the steps and he listened to the melody. After he had not looked at the arm for a while, he kicked at it and it flayed out of the way. He closed the door without slamming it and walked away. A few hours later he got on the night train for the nine-hour trip back to New York.

There was a three-minute delay at the station, a matter of signals and switches. Jordan sat in a carriage close to the front and listened to the sharp knock of the diesels. There was a natural amount of caution and care in his manner of watching the platform, but for the rest he listened to the diesels. In a while the clacks all roared into each other and the train left. Jordan never slept on a train. He did not like his jaw to sag down without knowing that it happened or to wake with the sweat of sleep on his face. He sat and folded his arms, crossed his legs. But the tedium of the long ride did not come. He felt the thick odor of clothes and felt the dim light in the carriage like a film over everything, but the nine-hour dullness he wanted did not come. I've got to unwind, he thought. This is like the shakes. After all this time with all the habits always more sure and perfect, this.

He sat still, so that nothing showed, but the irritation was eating at him. Everything should get better, doing it time after time, and not worse. Then it struck him that he had never before had to touch a man when the job was done. Naturally. Here was a good reason. He now knew this in his head but nothing else changed. The hook wasn't out and the night-ride dullness did not come. He set his tie closer and then worried it down again. This changed nothing. He saw himself in the black window, his face black and white and much sharper than any live face so that he looked away as if shocked because he did not recognize what he saw. The shock now was that this had happened. The thing with the arm had happened and he had never known that there was such a problem. Like a change, he thought. A small step-by-step or a slip-by-slip change following along all the time I was going, following like a shadow behind me. But it does not have my shape. The shock of seeing my shadow that does not have my shape....

He wiped his hands together but they were smooth and made no sound. He rubbed them on his pants, hard.

It was so bad now, he went over everything, the job, the parts of it, but there was nothing. All smooth with habit, or blind with it, he thought. So much so that only the first time, far back, seemed clear and real. Or as if it had been the best.

The small truck rode stiff on the springs and everything rattled. The older man drove and the younger one, behind in the dark, kept his hands tucked under his arms. The noise wouldn't be this hard a sound, thought Jordan, if it were not so early in the morning and if it were not so cold.

The truck turned through an empty crossing and went down an empty street.

Gray is empty, thought Jordan. He was thin and pale and felt like it.

"I'm coming up front," he said. "The draft is cutting right through me back here."

"What about the antenna? I don't want that antenna to be knocking around back there."

They had a spiky aerial lying in back and Jordan pushed it around, back and forth, so that it would lie steady without being held. The whitish aluminum felt glassy with cold. He crawled forward and sat next to the driver.

"How are you feeling?"

"Fine. Just cold."

"You should have worn more under those overalls. What you wearing under those overalls?"

"I'm dressed all right. I'm just cold."

"Jeesis Christ, Jordan, if you're dressed right..."

"My hands are cold. I can't have them get too cold."

The driver didn't say anything to that. He started to look at the younger man but didn't turn his head all the way. He caught the white skin on Jordan's nose and then looked straight ahead again. Why look at him?

"I just hope that antenna's all right back there. Is it jumping around there?"

"It's all right. The tool box is holding it."

"If that tool box starts moving though, I don't want none of them things on the antenna to get bent."

"It's all right."

The driver sucked on his teeth as if he were spitting inward. He looked straight and drove straight, sucking his teeth every so often. He would have liked it better if Jordan had talked back. But Jordan never did.

In a while the driver said, "I hope your hands are warm. We're here," and he rolled to a stop.

The driver got out toward the street and Jordan got out on the sidewalk. They closed their doors without slamming them, and Jordan looked down the length of the empty street, everything gray, except for the fire escapes which angled back and forth across the faces of all the apartment houses. The fire escapes were black and spidery, and the houses looked narrow and very busy with too many windows. But that didn't give life to the view either. It just made it look messy.

"You gonna give me a hand with this thing?" said the driver.

He had the back open and was edging the aerial out. The only thing that doesn't fit in all this, thought Jordan, is the sky. Everything's gray and the sky is blue. It's clean and far.

"You gonna...."

"You take the aerial," said Jordan. "You carry it and when you've got it out of the back, I take the tool box."

The driver didn't answer and they did it that way. They went into the third house looking like they belonged. They went up all the stairs, and then up the ladder which went from the landing to the roof. The driver climbed up first while the younger one held the prop antenna for him.

When the driver pushed the trap door open the wind caught it and slammed it back on the roof. Jordan held a dead cigarette in his teeth and bit hard on the filter.

In a while the driver looked back through the sky door and said, "Okay down there?"

"Yes." Jordan looked up to where the driver's head was against the sky. "Is it very windy?"

"Some. Pass me up that aerial. But careful now, feller."

He got the aerial and then he helped lift the tool box through, because it was large and awkward. It was not very heavy.

They crossed the roof, which was quite blowy, and the driver had to hold the aerial with both hands. They crossed from one roof to the next, stepping over the little walls which showed where the next building started. Then came the high one and they had to climb iron steps. A draft blew down at them and they could smell warm soot.

When they were up on the building the wind leaped at them as if it had been waiting. All the aerials on the roof and the one which the driver was carrying were whistling a little. The roof looked like a set with a very strange forest, thin trees after something terrible had happened to them.

"There's too much wind," said Jordan. "Christ, that wind."

The driver didn't answer anything. They passed a pigeon coop which was built there on the roof, and now the driver let Jordan walk ahead of him. He saw him look at the pigeons. Jordan was moving his head back and forth. All the pigeons were bluish gray, except one, which was speckled. All the pigeons sat in neat, fluffy rows.

Jordan walked to the parapet and the driver saw how the wind pulled the coveralls around his legs. The driver looked at that and the way Jordan humped over a little, holding the box, and he thought—this hotshot, this expert with specialties, he doesn't look very impressive.

Jordan looked back and told the driver to stand away from the pigeon coop; he did not want the animals to start fluttering around. They should stay as they were, in their rows.

"I'm holding this aerial here and if I step over into the wind...."

"Get away from those pigeons because I want them quiet."

The driver nodded. He watched Jordan kneel down by the parapet and said nothing. They feed 'em raw meat and pepper, he thought to himself, and this is how they turn out. The raw meat is all those dames, all those dames, and the pepper's the money. All that money. And this is how they turn out. Worried about pigeons.

But the driver was just a driver and understood very little of Jordan's work and what went into it.

Jordan opened the tool box and took out three parts. He snapped the barrel into the stock and he clicked the scope on the top of the barrel. Then he cowered at the rim of the roof and looked down into the empty street.

"Six forty-five," said the driver. He stood back on the roof and could not see the street. "Should be about now," he said.

Jordan did not answer.

"Anything yet?"

"Watch the roof," said Jordan. "Watch the roof and that door back there."

The driver did, but what he wanted to see was the street.

"You know it's that time now, and the only reason I'm talking—"

"Shut up."

It was the first job but Jordan already knew it would be better alone. No one along from now on. It was the first job, but already very private.

The driver heard the sound of a car and saw Jordan bunch and saw the rifle move up.

"Boy..." said the driver.

The wind leaned the aerial into his hand with a steady push and the aluminum felt glassy with cold. How does he do it, thought the driver. Hold still like that. I bet he was a monster when he was little. That's how he does it....

Jordan spat the cigarette out because the filter was coming apart in his mouth. And he could now get his head into a better position. He took a sighting, very fast, so the barrel wouldn't stick over the roof too long.

The cabby was getting out of his cab; he walked around the hood of the car, and went into the building.

Jordan pulled the gun back.

A good sighting. Fine scope. The double-winged door with the etched glass windows pointing up and the black line where the two wings of the door came together. The place that mattered. The hairline on the crack of the door.

For the briefest moment he felt that he would go out of his mind if he had to wait one instant longer because never again would any of this be so simple. Sight, aim, squeeze, check. How those pigeons stink. And the wind raising hell with the aim. Too much distance. It would have been better if they had told him to make a close play of it, planning it so he would be the cabby. But the distance was good. Everything small like a picture inside a scope and not quite real. And you simply sight, aim....

Sight now.

But let the cabby get by, let the cabby get by, for Godsake not the cabby. I don't know the cabby. Why squeeze on him.... But the crappy thoughts that came. I don't know the other man either.... Good, good, good. Where in hell was... Sight, aim... blink. The eyeball coming to a point. *Now....*

Big fat crack in the door. Sight, aim, *squeeze*....

Big fat crack out of the rifle, and *run*.

Not yet. Check it first.

Big fat blob rolling down the steps. Check it with the *scope*.

Tiny little hole in the forehead, and... gone. Making tendrils all over the forehead. And at this distance even the mess looks neat....

"Jordan...."

He looked back at the driver while he took the gun off the parapet. The driver stood in the wind and the antenna was weaving. He stands as if his pants were wet, thought Jordan.

"Okay?" said the driver. "Okay?"

"All done."

Click when the scope came off, click when the stock came off, other noises when the parts plunked into the box. That scope, he thought, won't be worth a damn after this.

Then they ran.

Which was just something in the muscles. Jordan felt the rush nowhere else, no excitement, and he thought, what did I leave out—what else was there?

When he ran past the pigeon coop the wildness stopped him. There were no more fluffy rows of pigeons, but now a mad and impotent beating around and a whirling around inside the wire-mesh coop and their eyes with the stiff bird stare, little bright stones which never moved with the whirl of fright around them. They beat and beat their wings with a whistling sound and with thuds when they hit.

Godalmighty if that wire-mesh breaks....

The driver was ahead and when he came to the end of the roof he looked back and saw Jordan standing.

"Come on!"

Sweat itched his skin on the outside and, looking back at Jordan, a sudden hate itched him on the inside. A little thing with a trigger, taking a minute, he thought, and this happens to him, the pale bastard. Standing there in a loving dream about pigeons, that they all should smash their heads on the wire, most likely. A little thing with a trigger and cracked crazy from it....

"Jordan. Come on!"

"Stop screaming," said Jordan. He left the coop and they went as planned.

"But if you're gonna...."

"Stop screaming. You feel the shakes coming on, hold them till later. Leave the antenna."

"I thought...."

"Leave it!"

The driver left it and turned to run.

"Wipe it!"

The driver wiped it. Then they left as planned.

Later Jordan watched himself, waiting for the shakes to catch up. But they never came. It's over, he thought, or it's piling up. Later he thought of the street, roof, scope-sight, everything. The shakes never came....

He sat in his seat and sat in his seat and blinked his eyes often because he did not want to go to sleep. I never sleep in a train and the job isn't over. When I get to New York it's over. Like always. Then I sleep, look up Sandy? No, and why anyway.... First I sleep, like always. It takes care of one or even two days. A big, thick sleep which always takes care of almost two days....

2

The patrolman always stood at the bar where it curved close to the door. He could turn his head and see a lot of the street or could turn the other way and look at the barmaid. There wasn't much to her or anything between them but the whole thing went with the uniform. The patrolman was young and got along well all around.

The place was chrome and plastic, which was uptown style, and in the window sat a pot with geraniums, because the bar was a neighborhood bar. The patrolman looked out on the street from where he was standing and said, "Here comes Sandy."

The barmaid looked at her watch; it said three o'clock. Sandy always came at three o'clock. He came through the door when the barmaid finished putting his beer on the back table.

Sandy was not blond. He had the name because it was simpler than his real one and sounded a little bit like it. The name was all right because it was friendly and quiet sounding. Sandy had very black hair and a very smooth chin. He wore a wide-shouldered overcoat of soft gray flannel. He wore this coat summer and winter. He had a hat on, dark blue, and he never took that off either.

The patrolman said, "Hi, Sandy," and Sandy said, "Hi, Bob."

"Hot even for August, isn't it?" said the patrolman.

"Yes. Hot." Sandy opened his overcoat and sighed.

"But good for business, huh? For indoor sports."

"I haven't noticed," said Sandy. "I don't think bowling is seasonal."

"I never thought of that," said the patrolman.

"Except for the air-conditioning bill," said Sandy. "I don't even like to think of that bill."

"I can imagine. Nine alleys is a big place to keep cool."

"Had your coffee yet?" Sandy asked.

Sandy asked this every day and the patrolman smiled and said the same thing he said every day. "No. I haven't," he said.

"Put Bob's coffee on my bill," Sandy told the barmaid, which also was part of this thing.

Then the two men nodded at each other and the patrolman watched Sandy go to his booth. He drank his coffee and thought that Sandy could not be too worried about his bowling alley or the air-conditioning bill in August. Sandy wears very nice clothes and has a beer every afternoon and never has troubles or raises his voice. Once Sandy looked up and the two men smiled at each other across the room. That's how the patrolman got along all around.

The phone rang at the other end of the bar and the waitress walked over to it. She went slowly because of the heat. She fluffed her blouse in front and did it a few more times when she got to the end of the bar and then picked up the phone. She put it up to her ear and then put it down on the bar. "For you, Sandy," she said, and walked back to the patrolman.

Sandy looked across at the girl but did not move. She said, "For you," again, and then Sandy got up and said, "Crap," but low so that nobody heard it. When he had picked up the phone he said, "Who is it?" and the voice answered, "Meyer."

"What're you calling here for?"

"Don't waste my time, huh?"

Sandy had his bowling alley on the east side of town, and Meyer had a restaurant an hour's drive north where the guests could look down at the Hudson. The two men rarely met because everything was well organized, and phone calls were even more rare. Meyer was the bigger of the two and sometimes he called.

"There's a man in from the Coast," he said. "With a message."

"Why call here? We got a regular way of...."

"He's new. His name is Turner, the new errand man, and I told him to meet you at the place where you are."

"That was smart. The way I run...."

"It's arranged. I'm just telling...."

"You keep interrupting me, dammit."

"You got nothing to say," Meyer told him. "And this is rush."

Sandy moved the phone to his other hand. Then he said, "With that much of a rush, let him handle it from the Coast. And if it's a heavy job, I don't know if I can furnish right now."

"Talk to Turner about it, will you?"

"Listen, Meyer. I don't run a store with shelf goods, you know that?"

"You run what's been set up. What's been set up is for us to furnish the service, anywhere, and stop thinking like a neighborhood club."

Sandy looked across at the patrolman and the girl working the bar and while he did that Meyer hung up. Sandy hung up too, without any show at all, and went back to his seat.

"In the last booth," he heard the patrolman say. "The gentleman with the hat."

When Sandy looked up he saw the patrolman leave and saw a short man with a round belly come toward him. Turner was suffering from the heat and his suit hung in folds. He looked all folds, except for the belly which came out smooth like an egg.

"I'm Turner," he said. "I was told...."

"I know. Sit down."

Turner sat down and sighed.

"You want a beer?" Sandy asked him.

"Yes. I think a beer would be nice."

Turner slid his rear around on the seat and did not look at Sandy. He disliked this kind of booth. The circular table seemed to want to slice into his belly, and the seat was like a curve on a track and gave no feeling of comfort. Then came the beer and Turner watched the girl pour from the bottle. He watched her hand on the bottle, an uninteresting hand but something to look at for the moment.

"You water the geranium today?" Sandy asked the girl and she said, "Yes." And then, "Lou does, in the evening."

After she was gone Sandy waited a moment, waiting for Turner to talk, but Turner did not look up. He was moving his glass up and down on the table, making rings, and then he took a swallow of beer. Sandy did not want to wait any longer.

"So?"

"Yes. Well, we got this job."

"I know. What details?"

Turner picked his beer glass up again but then did not drink. He put it down again and said, "Do I tell you? What I mean is...."

"I'm not the headman," said Sandy, "if that's what you mean. But you talk to me."

"Yes. Well, you know I just run the errand."

"I know."

"What I mean is, you're not the one who does the job, are you?"

"No."

Turner looked at his glass again. There were little webs of foam all around the inside. "Do I talk to the man who does the job?" he asked at the glass.

"Just tell me about it, will you?"

Turner did not make clear to himself whether he wanted to see the man whom he would actually send out on this job, but instead stayed uneasy about all this which he blamed on the newness of his work.

"I thought this was rush," said Sandy.

"Yes, well, there's this hit."

Sandy put his face into his hands and rubbed. He said through his fingers, "All right, so there's this hit. Come on, come on."

"Yes. The job is this old guy, name of Kemp. Big once, on the Coast, and...."

"I thought he was dead."

"No, no. Just out, you know? But now, we just got this, he's going to move. He's been in touch with a new group, something new in Miami, and with what Kemp knows and with what these new ones have in mind about our organization...."

"Where is Kemp?"

"He's in Pennsylvania. The rush is, we know he's going to move, in a week even, the way it's been figured, and the rush is to get this done now, while he's still sitting down and has an everyday routine. And while he's without organization, living retired like with an everyday...."

"You said that." Sandy took a cigar out of his pocket but did not light it. He only looked at it and then put it away again. "I don't have anybody," he said.

"What?"

"I said...."

"What do you mean you...."

"Stop yelling, will you, Turner?"

Turner shut his mouth immediately and then wiped his head. He did not have much hair and suddenly the sweat on his head was tickling him like crazy. And this errand job. He had thought there would be a clear-cut matter of bringing a message, explaining things with the details he had been given, and that would be his work. Perhaps he would also see the man whom he sent out on the job, but he had not thought of any other kind of excitement or anything, really, which would involve him. He did not talk loud again, but with a fast edginess which was almost mean.

"They say now. I just bring the message and the message is now. And you're set up for this thing, is the way I got the picture. Why in hell...."

"Now when?" said Sandy.

"Now, like today. Like now!"

Sandy nodded and looked across the bar and out of the window.

"Everybody is that busy?" said Turner. "How can it be that everybody in a big layout like you run here and that Meyer...."

"Not everybody is busy," said Sandy. "But I can't send just anybody."

"What is there, for Christ's sake? You get a finger that can bend around a little old trigger...."

"Why don't you shut your stupid mouth, Turner, huh?"

Turner said nothing and picked up his glass. There was a little warm beer left at the bottom and he drank that down without liking it.

"Retired or not," said Sandy, "Kemp is a pro. And special."

"Naturally. That's why."

"And there's three kinds for jobs. There's the nuts, there's the dumb ones, and the ones who are special. What you need is special."

"Special? All I...."

"They got a lot trained out of them and a lot trained in. That leaves out the nuts, which we never use, and that leaves out the dumb ones, like your finger around a little old trigger."

"They said now, is all I know, and that we got nobody for it on the Coast. They said now and your outfit is the one to furnish."

"I know. I'm trying." Sandy folded his paper up and stuck it into his pocket. "I got just one right now to fill the bill. But I got to ask him first."

"*Ask* him? What you got, prima donnas?"

"No. And not machines, either."

3

Jordan did not expect to be met at the train nor was it the order of things to run into each other in public and acknowledge it. He ignored Sandy and the man with him and kept walking. This impressed Turner as exciting.

Turner had a notion that eyes tell a great deal about someone. He was able to read a great deal into somebody's eyes. But it did not work in the case of Jordan. The man just looked. He did not squint, dart, hood, sink his eyes at or into anything, and he seemed to carry his head simply to balance with the least possible strain. The face was tilted up a little; he had the neck and head of a man who is thin. Though Jordan was not thin. He had a slow step, like a thin man, but that might have been because he was tired.

When Jordan walked by, Sandy said, "I got the car outside," and Jordan said, "Okay," and kept walking.

They all walked together or they did not walk together, depending on who was thinking about it. There were a lot of people coming and going. Turner was in a light sweat.

He felt nobody else was sweating. He felt nobody else wore a coat and hat—as did Sandy—and nobody carried a suitcase—as Jordan was doing. And my God if that suitcase should snap open, what might fall out...

When they all got in the car Jordan sat in the back seat alone. Sandy turned once and said, "Hi," and Jordan said the same thing. Then Sandy faced front again and drove away from the curb. He drove back and forth through Manhattan waiting for Turner to talk. But Turner did not get to it. He looked out the rear window a few times, and once he saw that Jordan held a dead cigarette and he offered a light. But this did not start anything either. Jordan said no to the light and Turner said nothing else.

"He's from the Coast," said Sandy after a while. "He runs errands."

"How do you do," said Turner. "How are you."

"Thank you, fine," said Jordan.

"His name's Turner," said Sandy. He did not give Jordan's name.

Turner had a moment of sudden panic, now that the man in back knew his name.

"I'm driving around so you can talk," said Sandy. "Yes. Very good. You went through a yellow light."

"It's a job," Sandy said over his shoulder.

"Yes. Would you like a fresh cigarette?" Turner asked the back.

"What did you want?" said Jordan.

"Well, yes. It's about Kemp. You know Kemp?"

"No."

"No? Well, it's about him. Sort of special."

"What's special?" said Jordan.

This gave Turner a nervous fit of the giggles, as if Jordan had been making a joke. Jordan had not meant anything like that. What was ever special, he had thought. It upset him to be thinking about this at all. He felt nervous and squinted. I'm tired, he thought and rubbed his face. What's special? I'm tired. That's why these crappy thoughts.

"It isn't special like being tricky," said Sandy. "It's nothing like that. Just it has to be done right away."

"I just got back."

"Yes, well, but this is about Kemp," said Turner and when Jordan did not answer, Turner thought he should now explain as much as he could. "Kemp was—I mean, he is the Kemp who organized, when was it.... I think it was twenty-five years ago, he's the one.... You know, he's the only one left over from that time, before the new setup shaped up, and the decision I'm talking about was made on the Coast... You sure you don't want a light?"

"He means Kemp's got to go," said Sandy.

"Well, yes," said Turner.

"I know you just got back," said Sandy, "but the way he puts it, there's no time."

"He hasn't said anything yet," said Jordan.

Turner giggled again because he could not stand the remark from the back. It was barren and had to be filled with something, and there had been just enough impatience in it for Turner to build that into a terrible threat.

He stopped giggling and would now tell the whole thing so he could not be interrupted.

"This Kemp has been all right for a while, since retiring, living around here and there, not much money or anything, but enough to live around here and there, not too open, you understand, because of the type of background...."

"I don't need any of that." said Jordan.

On the train, coming back, Jordan had sat with his shock, but then it had gone away. A thing like the arm would not happen again. If something like that should happen again it would not be like the first time, it would be without the surprise, and then there was always the trick he knew, a flip-switch type of thing, where he split himself into something efficient. Put the head over here and the guts into a box and that's how anything can be handled.

He had settled this, and then he had sat for the rest of the time, almost into New York, but the train-ride dullness had not come. He had tried to unwind, until he had found out there was nothing to unwind.

This too had happened without his having known it, like seeing his shadow which was no longer like his own shape.

There was nothing to unwind. What had wormed at him had been something else. He was dreading the nothing, between trips. The job was now simpler than the time in between.

Jordan dropped his cigarette to the floor of the car and said, "All right. I'll do it, if it looks all right."

Sandy took a breath and kept driving. He nodded at Turner to go on.

"Well, yes," said Turner. "That's the job. Watch the light, Sandy."

Sandy pulled the car over to the curb, stopped, looked at his hands. He kept them on the wheel and talked without looking at Turner. "Maybe if there's no red, green and yellow lights, Turner, and happy motorists driving home from the movies and tired cops dreaming of a cool beer, you think maybe you might get to the cottonpicking point if I fixed all that for you?"

He got out of the car and slammed the door before Turner could answer and walked to the corner into a telephone booth.

Turner sat and said nothing. He was afraid Jordan might be as wild and nervous as the other one seemed to be.

After the call, Sandy drove to an address which was not far away. It took only a few minutes, and the apartment was on the sixth floor. Far away from the traffic, thought Sandy, and close enough so there would be no more of this sweaty stuttering in the car.

The man who opened the door looked young, well dressed, and a little worn out. A gold chain clinked on one wrist, a gold watch ticked on the other, and he knew Sandy and Jordan. He did not know Turner but smiled at him. He had a vague smile for almost everybody.

Sandy said, "Thanks, Bob, much obliged," and the young man said, "Nothing, Sandy, anytime," and when Jordan walked by he grinned at him and said, "Sam boy, you're looking good."

He closed the door after everybody and said they should go right ahead, straight ahead to the door at the end of the hall. Then he took Sandy's arm and watched the others walk down the hall.

"You going to be long?"

"No. But listen, Bob, if it's inconvenient...."

"No, no, no." He did not talk very loud. "I just meant, I got these people coming."

"We can be out...."

"Just a party, Sandy. Just a party. Besides, you know everybody."

Turner opened the door at the end of the hall and said "This one?" and

the young man said to go right ahead and then talked to Sandy again.
"Who's your friend?"

"Business. He's all right, just business."

"Jordan business?"

"Yes."

"Oh."

"I'll have everybody out in ten, fifteen minutes."

"That's all right. That's all right. Party'll be over there, see? Three rooms away, so take all the time."

"Okay, Bob."

"When you're done, if you want to join—"

"Fine. Maybe."

"Bring your friend, you know?"

"Fine."

Then Sandy went through the door and the young man closed it behind him.

The room had a bed with bare mattress, a night table, dresser and chair. It all looked new but there was much dust. The air in the room smelled of dust.

Turner sat down on the bed, Sandy took the chair, and Jordan stood with his back to the window. He did not look at Sandy and he talked to Turner, so they would get into the business.

"Are you the spotter?"

"Huh?"

"He wants to know," Sandy told him, "if you did the leg work on this thing. Where Kemp lives, where he goes, what time he gets up, that kind of thing."

"Oh! Oh no. I just run errands. I always just run the errands," he said to Jordan. "Sandy knows that."

"All right," said Jordan.

"I always just...."

"All right."

But then Jordan was sorry to have interrupted because Turner, he thought, might take a long time now. Why do they send a creep, he thought. Why does he sit there and think I'm a ghoul?

"Tell me the next thing," said Jordan. "What have you got from your spotter?"

"Got?"

"I don't think there was time," said Sandy. "Is that right, Turner?"

"Yes. There wasn't any—"

"Let me get this," said Jordan. He took his hands off the window sill and wiped his palms. "You mean this thing hasn't been cased?"

"Well, yes. I mean, it hasn't been. I was trying to explain plain before, in the bar, you remember? I was going to tell how this came up sudden, about Kemp getting into it again, and ready to cause all kinds—"

"When will I know?"

"When what?" said Turner.

They could hear the front door being opened and people laughing.

"Jordan can't work," Sandy explained, "unless he's got something to work on."

"Yes. Of course." The sounds from the corridor distracted Turner. He now wanted to be done. He had seen this man now, Jordan, he had felt various strange sensations, and he now wanted to be done. Somebody in the hall said, "There's no ice in the bucket."

"Kemp's got to go within a week, at the outside," said Turner. "And nobody's done any casing."

Jordan took a new cigarette out and put it into his mouth.

"So we thought," said Turner, "you would do your own casing."

There was barely a pause and Jordan said, "You must be nuts."

On the other side of the door the hall was empty now, and there was no noise any more to cover the silence in the unused room. Turner smelled the dust. He thought he might sneeze. Then he said, "Well?" looking at Sandy. "Well, what is this?"

The problem was, Sandy knew, that Jordan had just come back from a trip. He was not sure what Jordan did after coming back from a trip nor had he bothered to think about it because Jordan was worked in well and no point thinking about anything beside that—unless there were signs. But there were no signs about Jordan. But the thing now was, he was asked to go right back out which was not usual. Always watch it when it wasn't usual.

"Sam?" he said.

"What?"

Jordan had a match in his hand, playing with it. I think he does sometimes play with a match in his hand, thought Sandy, which means nothing. And he's tired. The thing now, talk personal. We have known each other some time. Make it personal and I know how you feel.

"Put it this way, Sam. Here's a job, four-five days at the outside, in a place with no special angles—medium-size town, nobody knows you, nobody's looking. And there's Kemp with an everyday routine, same place for breakfast, same place where he takes a walk every day. There he is, not expecting, with no organization—and you go in there. I know you're getting rushed out close to the last job, but when you come back you'll get extra time, extra dough. I've mentioned that, Turner, and that's all there's to it. Okay, Sam?"

Jordan struck the match. "The same man," he said, "who goes out to do a job, doesn't also go out there and do his own casing."

"Why?" said Turner.

"When he noses around," said Sandy, "talks to people, he gets seen. That is what he means. That's what you mean, isn't it, Sammy?"

It was so plain, Jordan did not even bother to think about it. It kept him from thinking about something else: that he had never—very carefully never—been in any touch whatsoever with the man who was a job. Except for yesterday's accident. And that, of course, he had thought about quite long enough.

"How big is Penderburg?" Sandy asked.

"You know San Bernadino?" said Turner.

"Jordan," said Sandy, "you know San Bernadino?"

"No."

"Give another example."

"Well, I don't know any other example. It's small, what I mean is, not any too big. What I mean is, you wouldn't stick out right away, just walking down the street. But the way I get it, small enough to get a line on a man who lives there and does the same thing every day. What I mean is, that's how I got the picture. You see it?"

"Talk to Jordan, not me," Sandy told him.

"You see what I mean, Mister Jordan?"

Jordan nodded. He had lit the match and let it burn out, and he had put it down on the window sill. He nodded and played with the matchbook.

Say no to all of it. First, an impossible job, after that, the long stretch of nothing. Say no to all of it. I can't do it.

"It stinks," he said.

Sandy looked down at his shoes and then he got up. He got up with a quick snap in his movement and then walked to the window and back to his chair. Naturally, he thought. Naturally when he does his trick he thinks about nothing except how to set his mark and then blow. He doesn't know if the guy is important or anything. A hell of a lot of these worries don't touch him and "it stinks" is all he knows. No time for a beer is all he knows.

"All right, Jordan. What is it?"

"What?"

"I said what is it, is something bugging you?"

"Maybe," said Turner, "he means he can't handle it."

Sandy gave the fat man a brief look and said, "That kind of talk don't cut any ice with him," and then he looked back at Jordan. "So answer me."

Jordan, of course, had nothing to answer. He did not like Sandy's tone, which was enough reason for him to shut off the topic, and the topic—aside from that—was not a talking matter at any time.

"So why did you say it stinks and you won't take the job?" Sandy asked.

"You know it stinks, that kind of setup."

"That's why I picked you and not some fluttergut jerk."

"That kind of talk," said Jordan, "doesn't cut any ice with me either."

"Maybe there's more cut to it, if I tell you this looks like you maybe got the shakes?"

"You can stop talking crap," said Jordan. "You hear me, Sandy?"

I've got him, thought Sandy. Like everybody he's got to be perfect and don't-mention-the-shakes-to-me. Nice. I've got him. And then Sandy pushed his point.

"If it isn't the shakes, then why get prickly about it?"

Jordan shrugged this time. What had made him sensitive was the word and everything it implied. The shakes themselves were not bothering him, though Sandy could think so, if he wanted.

"Or is it something else?" Sandy said, and while he did not know it, he had Jordan again.

"No. Nothing else."

"What then? I want to hear this."

"You can stop riding me, Sandy."

"I'm not riding you, I'm asking a question. I want to know why missing your in-between break shakes you up enough so you can't take on the next job."

"Nothing like that shakes me up."

"Then what does?" Sandy kept at it.

"Nothing does."

"So why is it no?"

"Don't take that tone with me," said Jordan.

It meant different things to everyone in the room. Turner thought the next thing might be a shot. Jordan thought, this will change the subject. It better change the subject, because some things are nobody's business. And Sandy thought nothing. He carefully dropped every thought because Jordan talking this way was not usual.

"You going on this job or not?" he said quietly, the way Jordan had talked.

Before he asks again, thought Jordan. Before he stirs up what I just found out myself. About the change having crept in.

"I'm going," Jordan said.

This means no change, Jordan thought. This means there was nothing important, and he struck another match and this time lit the cigarette he had in his mouth.

After that it was cut-and-dry business and Sandy stayed out of it. He felt there was nothing else that he needed to do.

"And bring two more glasses," somebody said in the hall, and a door slammed. Jordan took the cigarette out of his mouth, knocked the coal out of it on the window sill, put the dead butt back in his mouth. "So whatever you've got," he said to Turner, "let's have it."

"And the beer," somebody said in the hall, and the door slammed.

Turner made the bed squeak and smiled. "My," he said. "A beer would be nice now, huh?" Then he pulled folded papers out of the inside of his jacket. "Well now," he said, and put the sheets down on his knees.

Jordan sniffed, smelling dust.

"First of all," said Turner, "the name. You got the name, right? Do you want a piece of paper and my ballpoint to write all this down?"

"No."

"Yes. Now. Thomas Kemp. Same name he uses now. And the town is Penderburg. Address—" and he looked at his paper, "505 Third Avenue. He-he, they got avenues."

"What does he look like?"

"What does he look like? Here you are. I brought this shot. This picture, I mean," and he held it out.

Jordan took the small photo and looked at the old man in it. The old man sat in a chair in the sun, garden hedge behind him, and smiled. He had all his hair, Jordan saw. Maybe kinky.

"Is he gray?"

"Gray? Just a minute.... Yes. Sort of streaky."

The sun was bright, and Jordan could not tell much about the man's eyes because of the black shadows. Small eyes perhaps, but then Kemp was smiling. Lines in his face. From smiling? He looked fit, and built chunky.

"When was this picture taken?"

"When was this—let me think. Let me think what they said.... This year. It happens he's got a daughter in L.A., and the way we got this picture, knowing he was going to visit her, we went...."

"I don't need to know that."

"Oh. That's right."

Jordan gave the picture back and then leaned on the window sill again. "Tell me more about where he is now. What he does."

"Yes. And I better mention this," said Turner. "Kemp's got a bodyguard."

Sandy exhaled with a sound which he covered by tweaking his nose, as if something itched him there. He sounded busy, very preoccupied.

Jordan did nothing. He had a matchbook in his hand and was playing with that but he had been doing that anyway. The bodyguard thing was a technical matter. He had no reaction to it, except technical interest. "What kind of bodyguard is he?"

"What kind? What do you mean what kind?"

Jordan looked at Sandy and Sandy explained it. "Is he just a punk or has he got training, Turner?"

"Well, he carries a gun. He hangs around all the time and, you know, watches."

"You didn't answer," said Jordan, and Turner, who very much wished all this were over because he had nothing else to say and what else was there anyway, having met Jordan and seen all there was to see, started to giggle again.

"I mean, he carries a gun all the time. *You* know. That kind."

Sandy sighed a slow sigh. Then he said, "In Pennsylvania. Where they dig coal. And he's got a gun all the time. *That* kind." Suddenly he slapped his hands on his thighs and started yelling. "Are you making this up as you go along, Turner, like maybe working up some kind of a comedy routine, or is this supposed to be the report that'll lay out this Kemp or whatever?"

"I—what I mean..."

"Shut up!" Then Sandy sighed again. He stretched back in his chair and said to the ceiling, "Of all the jinxed-up, screwed-up deals that I've ever seen."

Turner squeaked the bed.

"Jordan," said Sandy. "You getting anything out of this?"

"Yes. A few things."

He had a name and a place, and there were two men. He was startled by Sandy's anger, just as Turner was, though for other reasons. He was impressed that Sandy had spoken up like this, though he wished he had not used the word jinx. And now, maybe, they could break up this meeting and Turner would leave, and perhaps there would be some time to have a beer somewhere, but without Turner.

Turner said that he was sorry there was nothing else, and why couldn't Sandy take a reasonable attitude about this the way his friend there, Mister Jordan, was taking it, and the only thing about the bodyguard was, he did not seem to be there because of Kemp's maybe getting active again, but had been there with him for some time. "You know how those older ones are," said Turner, "those kingpins, always having somebody hanging around. You know what I mean?"

"No," said Sandy. "I don't."

"He means habit," said Jordan.

There was a knock on the door and the young man stuck his head in. "Oh," he said, and smiled at Sandy.

"Yeah," said Sandy. "We're almost done."

"I didn't mean...."

"That's all right, that's all right," and he got up, stretching.

"Maybe a drink?" asked the young man.

"Now that," said Turner, "would be a fine idea," and he bustled his papers around and stuffed them into his pocket. "As a matter of fact, there's a drink I know, what you do is...."

"Not right now," said Sandy. "Later." Then he looked at Jordan and said, "Finish up."

"I'm done," said Jordan, "unless Turner here...."

"No. I got nothing else."

The young man in the door raised his eyebrows at Sandy, and Sandy nodded at him. "Okay," he said. "We're done."

Then the young man opened the door enough to come in and leaned against the door frame. He smiled at everybody and waited.

"You're looking fine," he said to Jordan. "How you been?"

"Fine. Thank you."

"But tired, huh?"

"Yes. Some."

They all stood around while Turner took his papers out again to refold them, and while Sandy put on his overcoat. Jordan was chewing his cigarette. The party sounds were much clearer now, and with music.

"Tell you what I'll do," said the young man. "How about a drink before you go, huh, Jordan?" and he ran off down the hall before Jordan could answer.

The three men in the room stood around while the young man was gone, and Sandy wiped dust off his pants. Turner said how hot it was and wouldn't a drink be the ticket now.

The young man came back with one drink, which he gave to Jordan. "Happiness," he said.

The drink was straight bourbon with ice, and Jordan kept a mouthful of liquor and let it burn. It distracted him while there was nothing to listen to or to say. He heard the young man say, "How about it?" to Sandy, and Sandy answered, "Who's here?" It was, Max is here, you know Max, and his brother, you know him and his bunch, you know, that crowd, nice. And Sandy said that would be nice and Turner started talking about his special drink again.

Then Jordan thought about his own affairs, just briefly, there being time and need to think more about all of it later. Vague job, which was the kind needing thought ahead of time. Bad having to case Kemp himself, almost as bad as having to touch somebody afterwards. But that made sense. No superstition in that. No jinx. Not casing was caution and not touching was hygiene.

Turner had already left the room. Jordan swallowed the liquor and wiped his face. Then he put the glass on the window sill.

"You didn't finish," said the young man.

"That's all right."

"You want my car to drive home?" Sandy asked.

"No. I'll take a cab." Or, no. Maybe I'll stay, he thought. "Who's here?" he asked, and walked to the door where Sandy and the young man were standing.

"Nobody you know. Not well, I mean. There's Max, I don't know if you...."

Just vaguely, thought Jordan. I probably know everybody there, just vaguely. Then he said, "That laugh just now. That sounded like Lois."

"Hey, yes," said the young man. "That's right. You know Lois."

"You want her?" said Sandy. He held a cigar in his hand and was licking the end with his tongue.

And the young man was off down the corridor again. There was music and talk buzz when he opened a door down the hall and then just the mumble again when he closed it.

"When are you leaving town on this?" Sandy asked.

"I'll make it tomorrow. Middle of the day."

"Need money?"

"No. We can work it out afterwards."

"You're not dropping over tomorrow, before going out?"

"No."

The buzz getting big and then the mumble and the young man came back.

"Gee, man, I'm sorry. She's with what's-his-name, you know, Fido's brother."

"I don't know his name," said Jordan.

"Well, you know how it is, he brought her." He smiled and went away.

Sandy took Jordan's arm and they walked down the corridor all the way to the end.

"I'll call that Ruth for you," he said. "I'll call her from here."

"That's all right. You don't have to do that."

"What's a phone call?" Sandy opened the front door.

Jordan said good-by and, "In a week or so..."

"Yuh," and when Sandy closed the door Jordan thought, who in hell is Fido's brother....

4

He took his suitcase out of Sandy's car and walked back to the main drag. There he hailed a taxi and took it to a place three blocks from his building. He walked the three blocks and smoked a whole cigarette.

He had a room for sleeping and for keeping his clothes. He shut the door, walked to the dresser, bending a little when he walked past where the light hung from the ceiling. He took a clean shirt out of the suitcase and some underwear, and put them into a drawer. He had dirty laundry in a little bag, and he dropped that on the floor. Then he closed the suitcase and put it into the closet. He carried a gun and put that away in the place where he always kept it. Then he sat down on the bed and closed his eyes. He sat like that for a while but could not decide whether he was tired.

She came down the hall to his room, and he knew who it was by the steps. Then she knocked on the door the way she was supposed to and he let her in.

"Hi, Sammy. How's business?" and she laughed too loud.

She went past him, to the night stand, bending a little when she passed where the light hung from the ceiling. She put her purse on the night stand and said, "You got the bottle, Sammy?"

"I forgot," he said.

"Now, Sammy!"

He did not want to leave the room again but he did not want her to leave either. "Wait five minutes," he said and she said, "Naturally, Sammy," and laughed again.

He left and went to the liquor store on his block. If she looks around, he thought, she'll find laundry, that's all.

When he came back with the bottle she was standing and dressed as before, holding the purse against her belly. When Jordan had closed the door and put the liquor bottle next to the bed, she was still standing and holding the purse as before. She clicked the catch and the purse jumped open. So did her smile.

Jordan put money into her purse and she snapped it shut again.

He sat down on a chair near the bed and picked up the bottle, holding it in his lap. He worked the cap off the bottle while the woman undressed.

"You been out of town, Sammy?"

"Yes."

"You just come back?"

"Why do you ask?"

"Because I'm flattered," she said and laughed. She sat down on the bed which made metal sounds under the mattress.

"You're sitting on your hat," he told her.

She pulled it out from under her and said, "Damn it to hell. Damn it to hell, will you look at that!"

"I—you want me to buy you a new one?"

"What's the matter? You don't like me to curse?"

"I ask you, if you want me to buy you a new one, I'd buy you a new one."

"Don't talk crap," she said.

He did not answer and watched her roll down her stocking. She rolled down one but not the other. The other one she pulled off, making it look like a skin hanging down.

When she was naked she lay down on the bed and made a long, end-of-the-day sigh. Then she held out her hand.

"So give it here," she said.

He gave her the full bottle, and she put the neck into her mouth. After the first swallow she gave a little shudder, but none after that. She took a rest and then drank more every so often.

"Sammy?"

"Yes?"

"What you looking at?"

He had been looking at the window. He could not see anything there because it was night outside but the position had been easy on his neck.

"Just that way," he said.

"That way? You can't see out, that way."

"You ever ride in trains much, Ruth?"

"No," she said. She said nothing else and drank.

Jordan took out a cigarette and held it in his teeth. He did not know what else to say either.

"What you looking at, Sammy?"

"I was looking at your feet."

"Jeesisgawd." Then she said he should start taking his clothes off.

He held the cigarette in his mouth and watched her drink. The bottle gave a spark every so often, depending on how she moved it in the light. The spark from the glass was the brightest thing in the room. Then she put the bottle on top of the night stand, doing this just with her arm and without moving anything else. Her eyes were closed now and she lay still.

He got up, took his jacket off, pulled the shirt out of his pants. He unbuttoned the shirt. "How you feeling?" he asked her.

"Just fine, Sammy."

"Tell me something."

"What?"

"Why come here?"

"Why not?"

"That's it?" he asked her.

"Huh?"

"Why you come here, is what I asked you."

"Because nobody wants me either." And then she laughed hard again, without opening her eyes.

5

He had her the way it had been with others, not much difference any-where and when she left, it's a shame, he thought, but it's of no particular importance at all. Though he knew that it could be. It could matter that the woman left him, or that she stayed. However, as at other times where he needed to know how he would feel ahead of time, he had the trick. Where he clicked over to knowing where everything was—head over here, guts over there in a box—and kept only what he could manage. It was like looking at himself under glass.

When he had learned the trick is hard to say, but he had known it already when he had come to New York. The point is that he used it.

It was the worst in him, he felt for a while, and then he felt it was the best, for being so useful.

When he came to New York he lived with a relative whom he had never grown to know and who never knew him. The relative was an old woman and Jordan was no longer a child, and if they wanted anything from each other, it would not have been easy. He slept and he ate at her house and on Saturday, if he had money, he gave her some of it. He and the old woman never had any friction, which was the way Jordan managed it.

He worked on the East Side loading boxes in somebody's shipping department, and later he set pins in one of the nine alleys at Bandstand Bowling. Sandy had hired him and was somebody who always wore a hat. And an overcoat, most of the time.

After work, Jordan hung around the way it was done. They did not hang around the candy store, which was the place for younger ones, but outside a bar. As if they might all have come out of the bar or were thinking about going in, though not anxiously. They were six or seven, looking bored, even about Jordan who was new and when it was not clear yet how he fit in.

Jordan seemed no different from the others except the bully thought Jordan might be different. Who's who was important to the bully, because of his constant worry over matters of prestige.

"California, wasn't it?" said the bully.

"Yes."

"But you didn't say why you lammed out of there."

"I didn't lam. I just left."

"You left a long way. Why New York?"

"It was a place to go," said Jordan.

"Always wanted to see the bright lights, huh?"

That was not what Jordan had meant. New York was a place to go and so it just happened that way.

"So how do you like the bright lights?" And the bully spat in the street. As he spat he saw two men coming out of the night club, so he did it again.

"I don't know," said Jordan and looked at all the steps coming down out of the brownstones.

"Not good enough. That what you mean?"

"I wasn't...."

"You got uptown habits, huh?"

"Which?"

"You cop a feel or a lay or a candy bar, ain't good enough for you, is what I mean."

It was not good enough for the bully, which was what he had meant, but Jordan was only concerned with having no friction.

"It's all right," he said. "I got no kicks."

"That you don't," said the bully and laughed. "That you don't." They all laughed with him, at Jordan, but it did not lead anywhere because Jordan did not take it up.

This meant to the bully, Jordan was going to be easy, though the puzzlement was that Jordan did not seem to care how he looked. The bully did not understand this. It needed demonstration.

"Except for that job you got," he said. "That's great kicks, isn't it? I mean, you set 'em up and somebody keeps knocking them down."

Jordan did not answer. Maybe he could leave.

"And working right up alongside the boss. Yessir," said the bully and laughed.

"You don't have to act that way," said Jordan.

They saw that he wanted to leave and all of a sudden there was a ring around him.

"You know Sandy, don't you?" said the bully.

"Yes."

"But he don't know you."

"Why should he?" said Jordan, but the evasion made the bully that much more insistent.

"Why? Don't you watch the breaks?"

"All I'm doing there...."

"Is working up to setting two alleys instead of one, right? I mean, ambitious."

"Sure," said Jordan. "Sure."

"You know Jay?" asked the bully. "No. He left before you come in. That boy now, there was ambition."

"Listen. I want...."

"Shut up," said the bully. "I'm telling this story."

They all waited for Jordan to say something, or do something, but he held still.

"Like, working alongside Sandy is big time, didn't you know that, Jordan? Like, take Jay. He does this and that for Sandy, and that once, he runs an errand. Fifty bucks to run a parcel up to Harlem, that's all. You didn't know Sandy does other things, huh?"

"No," said Jordan, he didn't know anything about what Sandy did.

"Jay takes the fifty, runs the errand, opens up the parcel on the way. Know what was in it? I said, do you know what was in it?"

"No. I don't know what was in it."

"Half a grand, feller. Half a grand in sawbucks and singles."

"All right," said Jordan. "So Sandy is big."

"That's right. And there you are setting up pins and marking time for retirement, is what I'm talking about. But you know what Jay did?"

"All right. What?"

"Jay kept it. I got robbed on the way, he says, but he kept it." Then he said, "Jay was from California too. Looks like some in California aren't so dumb like some others, huh, Jordan?"

"Where's Jay now?" said Jordan.

"I don't know."

Jordan turned away, looking for a way to leave the ring. "It looks to me," he said, "that guy wasn't so smart after all."

They all thought about that for a moment, what might have happened to Jay or if Sandy might have done something to him.

"But smart and scared ain't the same thing," said the bully. "You smart or scared, Jordan, huh?"

"Depends when," said Jordan and tried to leave again.

They would not let him through. Somebody came out of the night club, and somebody stood on the fire escape of the house opposite. Jordan saw this and felt how cut off he was and that it could not be worse.

"But I want to know something," said the bully. He took Jordan's arm, thumb hooked into a muscle. "And you don't answer me straight."

"Cut it out," said Jordan, and tried to get his arm away.

"You smart or scared, Jordan. Which?"

"Just cut it out," said Jordan, but it came out dull because he felt dull now. And when Jordan did not give the bully a good opening for the next thing to do, the bully went ahead without the opening. "I'm going to ask you again and you show me...."

Jordan walked to the alley in the middle of all of them and then, against a brick wall, he got his beating.

It was painful, and a weird kind of fight, because the bully was running it. He ran it as a demonstration. He was big enough to keep Jordan well checked but the whole thing was just vanity fodder. That's why it took long, and so gave Jordan time.

Jordan, of course, fought for different reasons and did not even understand the other's delays.

He kicked the other one in the shin, when the time came. He now had five seconds or more to turn the fight his way, to make his demonstration. There were a number of ways, delaying and painful, to keep up what the bully had done so far. The other one was now doubled up and his face free for the moment.

Jordan grabbed his hair, held on; then his knee came up. The bully's jaw made a wooden sound. Jordan let go of the hair, let the head drop, watched till the other one fell flat on the ground. Finished.

Jordan stepped back. He looked at the others standing there, but they did not move. And the one on the ground was done. It felt so right that for one moment Jordan felt almost upset.

The others started to leave, walking sideways and with their hands in their pockets. They kept looking back until Jordan caught on.

At the mouth of the alley, by the wall, was a man. He wore hat and overcoat and he slowly walked up.

"Well," he said, and stopped by the one on the ground. "I've been watching you." Sandy looked up and then at the one on the ground again.

"Broke the jaw, I think."

Jordan wiped one hand across his mouth and said nothing.

"How'd you do it, Sam?"

"Do it? You mean, how did...."

"So quick. You were like a heap of clothes up against that wall, and then this."

"I was watching for it," said Jordan.

"How's your eye?" said Sandy.

"I think it's closing."

Sandy nodded and then he took Jordan's arm. They walked out of the alley, past the night club, and into Sandy's bowling place. They had left the one on the ground where he was, and Jordan did not remember about him until now.

"I think that guy back there could use...."

"Forget him. He's got buddies."

"I know."

"I got a drink for you, in my office."

"I just thought...."

"You got buddies?"

"What?"

"I said, have you got buddies, so after he would have been through with you, they'd come down to that alley and pick you up?"

"I wasn't thinking like that. I don't think it's got anything to do...."

"If you want to go, go," and Sandy went into the bowling alley. "But you did that good," he said over his shoulder.

Jordan stood alone on the street and watched Sandy go. The door made a loud hiss and when Sandy turned inside and disappeared, the door slowed pneumatically and the slit got very small.

There's nothing in the alley any more, Jordan thought, and besides, that was finished. And there's nothing on the street this time of night, and even too late for a movie.

Sandy had stopped at the counter with the cigars and the cash register. He was leaning one elbow on the glass top and looking at the door. He gave a brief smile when Jordan came in and then said nothing else till they had walked to the back of the counter and into his office.

"What I wanted to ask you," said Jordan, "was what you meant before when you said that I did that good?"

"Sit down. You must ache all over. Want that drink?"

"No. Thank you." But Jordan sat down.

"What I meant was you finished it neat. Not like that punk there. You did it neat and pared down, just enough for what was needed. I better get you some stuff for that cut...."

The reason Jordan stayed was because Sandy was paying attention. Jordan did not get all Sandy had said, except for the point that Sandy was pleased. And when Sandy asked again how he, Jordan, had done it, Jordan did not know the right answer, though he got close to the point when he said he had been waiting his chance. He had been watching the fight almost like standing next to it.

"That's maybe the only way you could take the beating," said Sandy, and later added, "That's the best way to do almost anything. Keeps you clean."

But the point always was that Sandy kept paying attention, and everything Jordan did in return, was for that. Not for more attention, but as the natural pay for the one lonely favor. Jordan knowing that the other one kept him in mind.

In a while he ran one or two fifty-dollar errands, and a while later he sometimes went out of town. Get a line on where this man goes, and what the house is like where he lives. Sometimes other details. Jordan cased without knowing what for, and when he learned what for, the shock was quite brief. Sandy spent time with him and the shock was brief. And if Jordan let the worst in him get honed to a fine finish, that's how he bought Sandy's concern.

Once he bought a lighter and had it engraved. It was for no special occasion. When he picked it up he left the store for the bowling alley, though he changed his mind about that on the way. Little changes had started. Jordan no longer worked on the alleys, so he should not really hang around the place very much any more. And for other reasons which made sense.

He did not go to the alley but at a quarter past three went the extra block to the place where Sandy had his beer and read the paper. He could see Sandy through the window of the bar, in back with the telephone. When Sandy hung up, Jordan went in.

He sat down in the round booth where Sandy sat. Nice and round, he thought. Like for playing cards or talk with a beer.

"What are you doing here?" said Sandy.

"Nothing. How you been?"

"Fine, I guess." Sandy put his paper down and asked Jordan if he wanted a beer.

"No. Here. Look at this."

He took the small box out of his pocket and when it sat on the table he took off the top.

"Like it?"

"Nice," said Sandy. "Nice."

The lighter was shiny as if it had never been touched and it lay on a very white cotton bed.

"Did you want something special, Sammy? Because I'm waiting for a call any minute."

"It's for you."

"What, this?"

"The lighter. For you."

"Is that right," said Sandy.

He gave Jordan a smile and picked up the lighter. The chrome got a fat fingerprint on it, and while Sandy wiped at it he looked at the phone. "Very nice lighter," he said. "Can you see the time up on that wall?"

"Three-twenty," said Jordan.

"What's this?"

"Three twenty, going on...."

"I said this. This here," and he put the lighter down on the table. The sound went clack.

"Inscription," said Jordan. "I had it inscribed."

Sandy did not say anything. He knew his reaction to all of this, but the right words were not ready yet.

"It says," Jordan went on, "from Sam to Sandy."

Sandy gave the lighter a spin and waited till it lay still again. It spun so fast it whirred. Then it lay still. "That's too bad," he said.

"Too bad? Did you say too bad?"

"From Sam to Sandy. What kind of junk is this?"

Jordan, to save himself, had an impulse to laugh and to say yes, junk it was. But he did not say that. He felt rotten to have thought it, to spit on all the effort that had gone into doing this thing. And besides, the thing was for Sandy, and why didn't he know this?

"You got to cut that crap out, Sam." Sandy looked at the telephone.

"Listen," said Jordan. "Listen here. I got that for you. I just thought of it and got you this gift. What are *you* talking about?"

Sandy did not like his tone. It imposed on him. The whole crappy thing did, the lighter and Jordan. He gave a quick look at the phone, no help though, and then he had the words to make good, sharp sense and to get rid of this problem.

"You don't come to the office any more every day. You don't go and sit in just any bar any more when you and me have a beer. You don't do one or two dozen things because I tell you you don't, because there's sense behind it, and because that's part of the deal. The deal is you're special. The deal is...."

"Don't try to pat me on the head," said Jordan.

"Shut your mouth and listen. Maybe this way it sinks in: You don't talk about the work you do and you don't breathe a word about the work you're working up to doing. But you think about it. You think about it all the time till you got it stuck in your bones. I'll use the square word, Jordan, like the squares would say it: You're bad, Jordan, and you're building to do the worst thing." Sandy took a breath as if he had been shouting. Then his low voice got pointed and sharp. "So for the good of the company, Jordan, and to keep away trouble, don't you put your name and my name right next to each other!"

"You're making a thing...."

"Shut up. You don't engrave it, you don't say it, you don't...."

"All I did was bring you a present. I didn't bring it to the precinct station, I brought it to you."

"I'm talking sense and business, Jordan, not personal crap. I'm telling you...."

"I don't know why in hell you're so jumpy," said Jordan. He picked up the lighter and started to drop it back into the box.

"Gimme that," and Sandy grabbed for it.

Jordan let him, because the lighter was Sandy's.

"I'll get rid of that thing and don't you ever...."

"What did you say just now?"

Sandy did not answer. He watched Jordan's face and with intentional slowness he dropped the lighter into his pocket and folded his arms.

"You going to keep it?" said Jordan. He did not like the sound of his voice. I know him best, thought Sandy, and from where does he pull this crap all of a sudden. And if it's serious, once and for all....

"Get the hell out of here, Jordan. I'm expecting a call."

Then Sandy waited, while he stared at the bar, because he was badly worried for one long, stiff moment, when it struck him that he did not know Jordan very well.

"You going to throw away that lighter?" he heard.

And if he says yes, Jordan thought, what am I going to do...?

"Yes," said Sandy. He rubbed his mouth.

Jordan tried his trick but it did not work. He was hating Sandy's guts. He tried his trick again but what interrupted was a tired feeling and a tired thought. And if I walk out, then there's nothing either....

"You can take it to a jeweler," Jordan said, "and he'll grind the words out for you."

"Yes."

The phone rang and Jordan said, "There's your phone."

Sandy nodded and got up. "Where you going to be tonight?" he said.

"I'll see you tomorrow," said Jordan and walked out.

Nothing else happened, which meant Sandy got his way. And nothing showed with Jordan, because he was special.

6

Penderburg looked homey and neat. The houses were red brick with gingerbread porches; there were big elm trees along the streets, and most of the week there was little traffic. Quiet streets and some even pretty. But the town sat in a valley of a most unnatural ugliness. The hills around the small town were geometric. There was a round hill of mining waste north, a long one with camel's hump south, and a third one had a sharp tip and a conveyor going up the side. The conveyor was dribbling rock and shale, and from a distance the long machine was like a stiff-legged insect leaning up the side of the hill. The two older hills were gray and the new ones showed black shimmers. When it rained, they all shimmered.

At nine in the morning, when the sun shone and everything looked like small-town summer, Jordan drove into Penderburg.

The dead hills, he thought, made the sky look out of place. Hot shale hills and little brick houses and only the big sky didn't fit.

Then he looked for everything which was important. He found 505 Third Avenue very quickly, an old apartment house with three stories and the trees in front reaching all the way up. There was an empty lot on the other side of the street, an old empty lot, with trees. Under the trees was a diner, made out of wood. Behind it a gray grass railroad spur, the hill dry in the sun, and also gray grass between the sleepers.

There were no other three-story buildings on the street. One-family bricks, frilly woodwork, a little tower worked into the side, blue shirts and white shirts on the lines in back.

He drove to the shopping square and started from there. It went, hotel, bus depot, church, porched houses, gray hill. Then back again. This time, railroad station, police station, bars, bowling alley, porched houses, the other gray hill. Next, movie house, porched houses, railroad sidings, warehouses, fence along mine, black hill. The highway went around this one. And the last tack not much different, with the other movie, other bars, dance hall Saturdays Only, gas station, gas station, state highway and out.

By late afternoon Jordan knew what was important. He knew streets and distances, how to come and go. He drove out of town and ate in a roadhouse which was five miles away.

He did not eat because he was hungry but because it was a way to spend time. He had to spend time.

He thought, I'll wait till the evening. I never work in the evening, because of the light, rarely in the evening, but what comes now is not the real job yet, the right part, but the wrong part which I have to get out of the way, I never work in the evening, which is always the dead stretch of time waiting to get done, but this time I have this thing to do and it will fill up the evening.

He cajoled himself like that and stroked his jumpiness so it would lie still like a cat. He waited till dark, which came late at that time of year, and drove back to the square in town. He left the car there and walked.

Warm and dark under the trees, he said. Leaf sounds up there, like something swarming. I'm nervous and paying attention to unimportant things.

The apartment house had lighted windows which showed in no special pattern. That one is Kemp's, or that one is Kemp's, or none.... Jordan stopped at the entrance and looked past the door frame at the mailboxes inside the hall. He did not go in, he just looked in.

T. Kemp, it said. There was a newspaper in the box. Jordan went across to the diner.

There was a waitress behind the counter, and there was a man sitting but Jordan could see only his back. He could see that the waitress had a round face and moved slowly, and the inside of the diner was probably hot. The man wore a cap on his head. But Jordan was not really looking at him, or at the waitress, but now felt the gravel under his shoes. He stood in a tree-dark place outside the diner and heard the leaf sounds and felt the gravel points under his soles. He started to curse but interrupted himself with a quick breath. I've felt gravel before. I've watched before, standing like this, and have spent time before like I did today, laying everything out. And Kemp is in town, I know that; his name is on the box on the other side of the street, I know that; I know everything ahead of time, not counting the details; how it will end, not counting the details; and even that the back sitting there at the counter is not Kemp, and this relief now is fake. Relief is always fake.... He stopped himself and felt the gravel under his shoes.

The man at the counter got up and was not Kemp. He was too young. When he came out of the diner he was whistling and kept doing it all the way down the street.

Jordan felt no change. He had known that ahead of time, too. Then he went into the diner because he could not stand it to think back and forth any more.

The girl was at the sink and looked up when Jordan came in, but only to say good evening. Then she looked down again and washed dishes.

There was too much paint in the place. The diner was very narrow, with counter, stools, tiny booths, and circus paint everywhere. Red counter, green swivel seats, blue booths, trims and borders and thick colored paint.

"You wait just one second? Or you in a real hurry?"

"No. Go ahead and finish up."

"If you're in a real...."

"No. I'm not."

She kept making soap-water sounds and then splashes when she dipped into the rinse, and once she looked over at Jordan but he did not look back. She had started to smile but he had looked away.

It would be easy to say more now, something about take your time, there's no hurry.

She used her forearm to wipe hair away from her face.

Or something about how hot it is.

Her hair was very light brown and her bare arm was very smooth.

I can say nothing about that. There is nothing to say. I will have to talk to her because it is that kind of job, the kind I have never done before and should not be trying. What I do best has nothing to do with people.

"I'm ready now," she said.

He told her coffee with cream and two doughnuts. He had no idea why doughnuts when she bent down at the counter and wrote the order on a pad. He thought two doughnuts are good. I can stay longer.

She wrote slowly and, bending over, her head was close to Jordan. He thought he could feel the skin-warmth coming from her, especially from her hair. The hair fell forward again, the way it had done at the sink, and she was so close, if she doesn't brush the hair back again at the sides.... Jordan put his hands in his lap and worked his fingers together. They felt thick with heat and stiff with it. She has almost an empty face, he thought, and that's good.

"You want plain or powdered?" she said.

Jordan felt the draft on the back of his neck when the door opened, and if that's Kemp I won't have to talk to the girl at all....

"Sugar," said the man, "two black and two all the way."

He wasn't Kemp either. He had a shorn head and a big waist which might have been all muscle. He grinned with gold in his teeth and smelled of grease.

"Stop it," said the girl.

The man laughed and straightened up again after having tried who knows what, thought Jordan, because I wasn't looking. I wasn't looking when she put the cup in front of me, because here it is with the brown coffee smell lifting up to my face and I'm sweating. Naturally. It's hot in here. Naturally.

The girl put the four containers on the counter and said, "That all you want, Davy?"

"Well, mam, if you really want to know, chicken, I could think...."

"Don't talk like that, Davy." Her face didn't change at all when she said it, and it seemed she just looked at the man because he was there. Then she said, "You want plain or powdered?" and looked at Jordan.

"If you really want to know, chicken...."

"Stop talking like that, Davy."

"Plain," said Jordan.

"And yours is forty-eight cents," she said to the trucker.

"How you been, chicken?" He worked change out of his pocket and grinned at her.

She put two doughnuts in front of Jordan and said, "Fine, Davy."

The trucker put half a dollar on the counter and said because she was such a sweet chicken all around she could keep the change. He felt that was very funny, allowing two cents for a tip, and left it that way till she had picked up all the cups. Then he reached over, when it looked as if he was going to leave, and poked a quarter into the kerchief pocket on her uniform. This, he felt, was even funnier, and the only thing spoiling it for him a little bit was that she didn't slap his hand away or move back or say anything he could use for a comeback.

"Thank you," she said. He went out with his cups balanced on top of each other and laughing, to make the exit fit the rest of the act.

The girl leaned against the service board behind her and folded her arms. "Him and his manners," she said.

Jordan moved his face to show he was listening but the girl wasn't looking. She was stooping down a little to catch her reflection in the black window opposite, and with one hand she patted a wave in her hair. Then she fluffed it up again because of the heat. She could have been alone there. She sighed and folded her arms again. Where her uniform went over the round of her breast she had written Betty on the white cotton. She must have written it looking down at herself, thought Jordan. The script was that uneven.

"He must come in often," said Jordan.

"What?"

"Your friend."

"Him. Huh," she said.

Then he did not know how to go on. He put his head down over the coffee and drank some. Do you have many steady customers coming in here? Like Tom, maybe, my friend old Tom Kemp.... The questions felt wrong and stiff. He would say them stiff. Even hello and good-by if he had to say it now.

"I never seen you here before," said the girl. "You just coming through?"

"Yes."

He watched the light make patterns on top of the coffee. The light slid. He watched it and hated not having said anything else.

"Most of the time all the same people come in here," she said. "That's why I was remarking."

But Jordan did not pick it up. He thought of the plain matter of fact in this, how much simpler the other part of the job would be....

"But they're not all like Davy," she was saying.

"You don't like him?"

"He stinks."

Jordan had no idea how to react to that, so he said nothing. He had not expected she could be this definite.

"You know the kind that thinks they own everything? Well, he's like that. And I don't like it."

"I don't like that either," said Jordan.

"Like there was no other way to get along, you know? Well, there's lots of ways to get along."

"Of course."

"Like being friendly." She looked at the opposite window and frowned at the dark glass. "I'd like that to happen sometime."

She was talking too much and Jordan felt bothered that he was letting her. What she said did not bother him, he felt, just the waste of time.

"Do all your customers live around here?"

"I'd like to know what's wrong with being friendly, you know that?"

She's dull, he thought. One thing at a time. I can ask her about Kemp and not worry too much how she will take it.

"I don't think anything is wrong with that," he told her. "I often think the same way." He said it easily because he did not think about what he said. He felt it was small talk.

"Some do," she said. "Some live around here but some just work down that end a ways. The yard and the depot."

One thing at a time and one after the other. He was not worried about her. He also envied her.

Jordan felt the draft again and then saw dirty pants. The man sat down two seats away, and when he hit the seat he gave a great sigh. Jordan could smell the liquor.

"Without anything," he said.

"They drive a truck," said the girl, "and right away they think they got to be like a truck theirselves, you ever notice that?"

"Black and hot," said the drunk and the girl got the coffee.

The best thing, now that this drunk is here, I pick her up later, thought Jordan. He felt some ease and smiled at her when she turned. It was easy and she smiled back.

Some miners came in and ordered things off the grill and a kid came in to take something out to the car. There was talk and the girl was busy, and Jordan bent over to finish his coffee and doughnuts in peace. After a while he said, "How much is the bill?" and after that, when she would pay attention and look at him when he gave her the money, then he would ask her when the diner closed for the night.

"Onion like always?" she said, and the man next to Jordan said, "Same way, Betty. Don't rush."

She slid dirty dishes under the counter, which made a great crash; she put coffee on the counter, two cups, and turned back to the grill right away and put a raw hamburger patty on top. The raw meat hissed and steamed.

"Pass me the sugar, would you?"

Jordan thought he might smoke one more cigarette and drink one more cup of coffee.

"Would you reach me that sugar bowl over, please?" and this time Jordan knew that the man was talking to him, because his hand was on Jordan's shoulder and he pointed across at the sugar bowl.

"Yes," said Jordan. "I'm sorry."

He picked up the sugar bowl and watched the girl turn around with the plate of onions and hamburger. She said, "I already put sugar in your coffee, Mister Kemp," and she put the hamburger down on the counter. Jordan put the sugar bowl down again.

Everything shrank.

The man in the next seat said something else. "Thanks just the same," he said, and put his hand on Jordan's back once more, heavy and forever, but Jordan sat it out by not moving or breathing, though in the middle of that, from somewhere, he said, "That's all right," and then the hand was gone.

"Thirty-five," said the girl.

Kemp, next to Jordan, was eating his hamburger.

"Did you want to pay?" said the girl. "I thought you said you wanted to pay."

Jordan did not want to talk because he did not know what would come out. He picked his cup off the saucer and smelled the tar smell of the cold coffee.

"Another cup?" she said.

She took the cup and Jordan held the small piece of doughnut he had left. He bit into it, moved the piece back and forth over his teeth, felt the dryness of it and how it lay in his mouth like something which did not belong there. It stayed dry. He would never be able to swallow it. He put his hand up, slowly like everything else, and let the piece drop out of his mouth and into his palm. He put the doughnut into his pocket and left his hand there, too. The doughnut was still dry like a stone but the inside of his hand was wet, and his face.

"It's awful hot here," said the girl and put the fresh coffee down in front of him.

Jordan's shoulder and arm hurt and he would soon have to take his hand out of the pocket.

"Here," she said. "Here's a napkin."

"What?"

"Here's a napkin. Wipe your face."

She put it next to his cup and left. Jordan felt upset with gratefulness for the napkin she had offered, and for leaving him. He got weak, which relaxed him.

Then he took a deep breath. It was not good and deep but better than before, sitting with his hand in his pocket. It was much better now and in a moment I'll look at the man in the next seat and then leave.

The man next to him lit a cigarette and sighed the smoke out of his lungs. When he had chewed up the hamburger he had sighed the same way, to show how good it was. Jordan leaned away a little and looked.

This was Kemp. Same man as in the photo. Jordan looked at him as if he were a photo. The hair was coarse and tight-curled, one wire hair over the next wire hair. The temples were gray and white, but nothing distinguished. Creases ran out from Kemp's eyes, as if he were squinting into the sun, or were laughing. Jordan did not look at anything else. Kemp was too close.

"Does Paul want anything?" asked the girl.

Kemp turned on his stool and his face swung past Jordan. "Anything for you?" said Kemp.

There was a man in the booth behind and he answered, "No. I'm fine."

Somebody went by and out the door, and Jordan used that to turn and let his eyes go past the man in the booth.

The one in the booth looked at Jordan as if he had been looking at him all the time. Jordan swiveled back and stared into his coffee.

That was Kemp's man. Jordan knew this without any thought, wasted no questions on it. And that blank look had been intentional. He looks that way to cover, or because he is waiting to be provoked....

"You aren't sick, are you?" said the girl. "The way your face is wet."

"No," he said. "I'm not sick."

"Maybe it's the coffee. You been drinking a lot of coffee today?"

"Yes. A lot," said Jordan.

"Listen," said Kemp. He leaned closer so that his elbow touched Jordan. "There's no hangover that's been took care of with coffee yet," and he looked into Jordan's face and smiled.

"I just drank too much coffee," said Jordan. He put his hand into his pocket to pay.

"Or you might have something coming on," said Kemp. "All those things feel the same, when they first come on."

"Nothing," said Jordan. "I'm all right."

"But like that doughnut," Kemp kept at it. "Something does ail you, I figured. You spat it out, didn't you?"

When I kill him, thought Jordan, I'll kill him for this.

Just the drunk was left now, and Kemp with his man in the booth.

"You been driving all day?" asked Kemp.

"Yes."

"I thought so. I thought you looked like it. Salesman?"

"Yes. Traveling salesman."

"What you selling?"

"I have various lines," said Jordan.

"Like what?"

"Buttons."

The drunk down the counter laughed. "I couldn't help hearing that," he said. "Did I hear buttons?"

"Yeah, he said buttons," said Kemp across Jordan's face. "You got something against buttons?"

The drunk just laughed.

"You know something?" Kemp said to Jordan. "If there's anything I can't abide it's a bastard like that laughing like that."

"Now you hush up," said the girl to the drunk.

"I don't care what a man's doing," said Kemp, "long as he does his job right and is good at it. That's how I feel."

The drunk laughed again.

"Listen," said Kemp close to Jordan's face. "Go over there and clip him one."

"No," said Jordan. "I don't care if he laughs."

"Go ahead. If there's anything I can't abide...."

"No," said Jordan. "Besides, he's drunk."

"Maybe that's why you should hit him now. While he's drunk."

Paul said this from the booth, where Jordan could not see him. But he's looking straight at my neck, thought Jordan. He's sitting very still, waiting, the punk talking, waiting for a fight that won't cost him any effort.

"Harry's leaving right now," said the girl. She walked over to the drunk and said, "He's leaving right now. You hear me, Harry?"

"Well, mam, I was done anyhow, Betty, but if the button gentleman over there...."

"Please, Harry. I don't want trouble. Why does there always have to be trouble—"

The drunk got up and gave Betty's arm a pat. He laughed again when he walked past Jordan and then he went out the door. Nobody said anything after that and Jordan got up and put a bill on the counter. He could hear the sound the bill made when the girl picked it up and behind him was a sound from the booth, Paul scratching. Kemp sighed and watched Jordan stand at the counter.

"Good rest tonight," he said, "and you'll be all right." If he doesn't stop talking to me, thought Jordan, if he doesn't—

"You got a place yet?"

"No."

"Listen. Don't go to the hotel. That hotel...."

"There's two," said Paul.

"Don't go to any of them."

The girl said thank you when Jordan gave her a tip.

"You want a nice room?" said Kemp. "How long you going to be here?"

"Couple of days," said Jordan. He thought about it and said, "Week, at the most."

"I tell you about a nice room," said Kemp. "Now this here, this is Third."

"Yes."

"Next block that way is Fourth. You go to Fourth and the up-and-down sort of catticorner from where I live—I live right there, see the building?"

"Yes," said Jordan. "Right there."

"Well, catticorner from there on the Fourth block is this up-and-down with a sign says Rooms. You go there and ask for Mrs. Holzer and tell her I sent you. My name's Kemp."

"Kemp," said Jordan. "Yes."

Kemp held out his hand and Jordan had to take it. He had to shake the hand and then had to give a name. He said his name was Smith. He wanted to give a better name than Smith but shaking the other man's hand was making him stiff and dull.

"You go tell her I sent you, Smith," and then Kemp and his man got up and walked out of the diner.

When the diner was empty Jordan stood there and wished nothing had happened and he could start now. The girl was at the sink and her back was turned; she wore a white dress but with skin tone showing through where it lay close on her skin. Jordan watched the stretch folds move in the cloth and then he turned away. Jinx job, he thought. I met him and nothing gained.

When Jordan opened the door, the girl looked up and said good night. Face empty, he thought. Doesn't want anything.

7

There was always a half-hour slump that time of night when she would sit down for a moment and do nothing. If I smoked, she thought, I would now smoke a cigarette. She drank a glass of water and listened to the neon sign hiss in the window. The red, which was a beer-bottle shape, flickered. Then she finished her water, cleared the counter, washed the dishes. Next she swept the alley between booth row and stools which was always the time when Mr. Wexler came in.

He came in without saying hello because he was the owner. He looked wrinkled under the light of the ceiling and all his joints looked like big knots of bone. This showed on his hands, wrists, down the bumpy bend of his back.

The first thing he did was to walk by the girl too close. The side of his hip, like a shovel, pressed along her buttocks. He always did this and she said nothing. He went around to the back of the counter and drew black coffee for himself. He sat down and watched the girl sweep.

"You got crap on your uniform."

She looked down at herself and there was a coffee stain near her belly. She nodded and swept again.

"I want this place clean. That includes you."

"Yes, Mister Wexler."

He watched her belly and sucked coffee over his gums. "You working here, girl, I don't want those Rabbit Town habits to show."

Wexler was born in Penderburg and so was the girl. An outsider would say the girl was born in Penderburg, but Wexler, and more like him, said she was from Rabbit Town—where the families had nine children, where the chickens lived under the porch, where the coal truck never went in the wintertime because the shale hill ran down to the backyards. In Rabbit Town they used pickings from among the shale.

I hope he burns his gums, she thought. He knows I don't live there any more.

"You call the man about the neon sign?"

"Yes. He wasn't in, Mister Wexler."

"He wasn't in." Wexler held his cup as if he were drinking, and watched. He could see her back and wished she would turn around. "I thought you know him personal," he said.

There was nothing for her to answer. He thinks Rabbit Town when he looks at me and that means one thing to him. He tries it out every night.

"You see him around, don't you? Next time, tell him about the sign."
Wexler slurped. "Or ain't there absolutely no time at all for talk?"

"I don't want you to talk like that, Mister Wexler, please," she said.

Wexler laughed. She had turned around now and he just sat for a while.

"How's your sister?"

She wanted to say, which one, stalling him, but that had never worked
before and only helped him along.

"The one in Pittsburgh," he said. "She still doing all right?"

"Yes. I guess so."

"I mean she's getting on, I mean older than you. That's a point in her
business, no?"

She hit the broom on the edge of a booth and on the next sweep caught
it again. She felt awkward; she felt she could do nothing, and she felt in
her throat that she wanted to cry. He was old and filthy and worse than
any of the other things he always talked about.

"You didn't clean the grill," said Wexler. "When you're done sweeping,
do the grill before rushing out of here."

She worked the sweepings into the dustpan, and after she had gotten rid
of that came around to the back of the counter to clean the grill.

"Where you going to rush to when you rush out of here, Betty?"

"I'm going home to sleep," she said. "I'm tired." She worked the pumice
stone back and forth on the grill and the scrape covered just some of
Wexler's laugh. His laugh and the scrape went into each other as if they
were the same thing.

She heard him cough and get up. Every night.

"You got to turn the gas off when you pumice the grill," he said.

Other times it was: You're leaning into the gas cocks and pushing them
open, or, You're leaning into them and pushing them shut. Every night.

Then he came over where she worked on the grill and put his hand on
the gas cocks and left it there. He left it there, waiting for her to get close
to his hand.

"I'm going to get a bigger fan put into that flue here," he said. He stood
and looked up into the hood over the grill and let his hand wait. The girl
saw little sweat dots on Wexler's scalp.

"That's enough with the stone," he said. "You can wipe it now."

When she reached for the rag she felt his hand, the bones in it, on her
thigh.

"Mister Wexler, please—"

"What please, what?"

That was his mouth talking and his face looking smily but the hand was
something else, was a secret between him and her, and she should respect
the rule of that game.

She moved back with his hand staying on, clamping a little.

"This don't get you pregnant," he said.

Then he always let go at that point and laughed a chicken sound.

She moved back to finish the grill and kept her head down and away so she could not see him. That, she thought, is a horrible thing to say to me. A horrible thing, period. And I'm not going to listen to that much longer. I won't have to listen to that once I leave and it won't be much longer.

The thought was nothing angry, nothing with threat tone in it, because she thought this often and it was really a plan. It was where this side of the horizon and the mythology on the other side ran into each other. She would leave Penderburg sometime, which would leave Wexler and so forth behind. This made sense and absorbed her.

There was more, of course, but vaguely. To get married. To stop working in a while and then just husband and home. But this part was certain and ordained and did not need hoping.

"When you open up tomorrow," said Wexler, leaving, "call the dairy and cancel the sherbet order. Nobody around here eats sherbet."

She said, yes, Mister Wexler, and went to the closet where the bucket was, and the brooms and her dress. She squeezed in there to take off her uniform. And when I leave I can say I wasn't just a waitress but had other responsibilities. Orders, and so on. So that part doesn't worry me, but I first got to leave.

She changed and looked forward to the walk home. Slow, because tired, slow, to make a nice walk. Outside, the night hung warm. She liked that.

When he walked away from the diner he thought the air might change and feel lighter the farther he went. He walked fast, walked by his car at the curb, towards the square with the closed stores. Nothing changed. It's like glue sticking to me. Jinx job. I'll start over. Tomorrow.... But the thought of waiting that long gave him no comfort and there had to be something he could do so it would not be as if he were delaying the job. I'll walk back and look at the building. Then I check the mailbox position in the hall or maybe the number on the box in the hall and what have I done today then—I've found out where Kemp lives in that building. And nothing else happened today. Let's say that.

But if I had walked out with them when they left the diner, walked across with them and up to Kemp's room.... He dropped that thought with a great deal of satisfaction, reminding himself he had not been carrying a gun. He didn't work that way. He only carried a gun by plan, not by habit.

Jordan walked back, away from the square. It got darker down the street and he noticed there were no longer the leaf sounds overhead. Unimportant. Where does Kemp sleep? He looked at the building on the other side of the street and the same, and as bad, as sitting with him again, and what was he like? Nice. Tepid word which left out a great deal, but Kemp, sitting and talking, you might say was nice. Not if he knew who I was. Or worse yet: not if I were working for him, did this work for him, not then either. Would he say, go to that rooming house and mention my name to Mrs. Holzer?

Jordan looked at the building on the other side of the street and imagined nothing. Building with Kemp inside, Kemp-target.

"I think he'll be in bed by now," he heard.

Jordan held very still, waiting for more. Or, if I moved now, it would be so wild I could tell nothing ahead of time about what might come next....

When he did not turn, the girl Betty stepped around so that she could see him better. "I mean Mister Kemp," she said.

"Ah," he said. "I guess so."

The girl did not know what to say next. He talked so little. Or when he talked, he said nothing to invite a reply.

"I just meant," she said, "you were standing here, I saw you standing here, looking, and I thought you were looking for him because of that room. I thought maybe you had forgotten where Mrs. Holzer lives."

She made it very easy for him. I don't have to open my mouth and she helps, he thought.

"You want me to show you?" she asked.

"That's all right," he said. "No. I'll wait till tomorrow."

"Oh. You were just walking."

"Yes, back and forth."

"Ah," she said. "Yes. It's nice out. Better than daytime even."

He looked at her and her face struck him the way it had done once before. It holds still, he thought. The way a view out of a window holds still for you. There is a landscape and you look away and when you look back again, it is still there.

"I myself like it very much," she said. "Walking. This time of year."

The most harmless thing he did that day, he started to walk, knowing she would walk along. They went down the street.

"I just want to tell you," she said. "I think you were very nice before."

"What?"

"When you didn't take it up with that drunk, that Harry I'm talking about. I noticed that."

"Oh," he said. "What else was there to do."

"No, you were nice about it, not making trouble. I noticed that and I think you were very decent."

He did not react to this but instead thought quickly of a very good reason for this walk with the girl. Ask about Kemp and his habits. End of the jinx day, starting over like this. She's easy and I feel no effort. She is effortless like a view from a window. And I'm Smith, which leaves no problem between us.

Jordan felt invisible, a very fine, powerful feeling, invisible except to the girl next to him, and there was no harm in that.

"Your name's Betty?"

"Yes. Elizabeth. But that's too long, to write on the pocket."

"Yes." He looked at her, at the front where the name had been, and when she noticed it she put her hand up for a moment, feeling self-conscious.

"You got far to go?" he asked her.

"No. Just that way, past the square, maybe ten, fifteen minutes. Of course, I walk slow. I like it, in this kind of weather. You like it?"

"Yes I do."

They walked past his car but he did not want to say anything about it. He took a cigarette out and put it into his mouth. He said, "You have to walk fifteen minutes?"

"But I don't mind it. I just mind it when I'm very tired or when the weather is bad and then I just wish I had a car. Why don't you light that cigarette?"

"I don't smoke much. Just hold it like this sometimes. You want one?"

"But then, if I had a car, I wouldn't go home, I mean straight home either, you know? I'd take a drive. I don't smoke, thank you."

"I have a car," said Jordan. "Back there."

"You do?" and she looked back where he had pointed. Then she said, "Of course you would. You're a traveling salesman, I forgot."

"Yes," he said. "That's right."

"You must be sick of driving."

He took the cigarette out of his mouth and then put it back in and gave a little bite on the filter. "Would you like a ride, a short ride?"

She nodded and said yes, she'd like that. She didn't want to go home yet but ride with the window open, and did he have any idea what it's like working in that diner and none of the windows open ever. They got into the car and she told him which way to drive out of town where the country was the nicest. He knew the way because he had checked it so carefully during the day though he did not remember about the country being so nice.

He leaned across her, pushing at her a little, and rolled the window down for her and then straightened up again. She smiled at him and thought, if I knew him better now I would like to say something to him but I would hate to be wrong, saying something nice, and would not want to hear him answer with something clever. She knew about one kind of clever talk, having heard it often, and what it meant, a time-killer before the hands on her and then sex. As if she were stupid and did not know what came next and needed leading around by the nose first, with the sex work suddenly upon her like an accident or a total surprise. And that was stupid too and added a false haste to everything, something she did not like.

When it seemed Jordan had forgotten about the window already and was driving out of town, she said, "That was very nice of you, thank you, about the window."

"What?"

"About remembering I like the window open, a ride with the window open," and felt awkward after saying it.

There was a roadhouse ahead on the highway and Jordan slowed.

"You want to go in there?" she said.

"No. But I thought some beer—I'd bring out some cans and we can have it in the car. Driving."

"Yes," she said, "that would be nice." She thought it was fine of him to remember that she liked to ride but said nothing this time.

He got a six-pack and a key and, when he came back into the car, put all of it in her lap. Then he drove again.

"If it were always like this it would be all right, you know that?" she said.

"How do you mean?"

"Here's your can. Watch the foam."

"Thank you."

"Warm like this, I mean. Like this evening. You know where it's warm like this all the time?"

"Where?"

"In Florida. My girl friend in Florida she's been writing me. And she mentions it too. You ever been in Florida?"

"Yes," he said. "Once."

"You mean on business?"

"Yes. That."

"What's your name?" she said. "I don't mean Smith, I mean the other one."

He held the can awkwardly and spilled beer on his pants. "Sam," he said after a while.

"What a Bible name you have. You know, I can't picture anyone buying buttons in Palm Beach, can you?"

"I never was in Palm Beach, I was in Miami Beach."

"That's where my girl friend is! Make a turn here, Sam. This road."

He turned where she showed him onto a country lane. It went up a little. It was hard to tell anything else because of the darkness.

"She lives in Miami Beach?"

"If you go slow now I can find the spot. Little slower."

He drove more slowly and looked at her leaning out of her window.

"She works in a stand where they sell juices. You know those juice bars they have in Florida all over? She works in one of those, squeezing juices. Here it is."

"Here?"

"Stop a minute."

They were on the top of a rise where the lane got wide enough for the car to pull off to one side, then the rise dropped off again and Jordan could see nothing but the night there. He stopped the car for the girl and she leaned on the window sill and looked out.

"This, I bet, is a lot like Florida," she said.

"Where?"

"Turn the lights off."

He turned off the lights and after a while he saw a little better in the darkness.

"That's the beach," she said. "You see the lights?"

Somewhere down below he saw a curve of light and perhaps it looked the way a beach might look at nighttime.

"Penderburg is over that way and this is the Number Three Conveyor. We just call it that, the Number Three Conveyor. It goes up that new shale hill. Did you ever see tile roofs?"

"See what?"

"Like in Florida, you know? Those tile roofs with the round-looking tile."

"Spanish tile roofs."

"Spanish tile. That's what my girl friend calls them. There. You can just see them there."

He moved closer and when he put his head next to hers he could see the work sheds by the mine. They were made out of corrugated tin. The overhead light in the yard showed the geometry of the tin and from the distance it might have been what she wanted it to be.

The girl had a soft odor, something like soapy water.

"And when I've saved enough," she said, "I'm going down there. To Florida."

Not from soap, he thought, because it isn't an odor of chemistry. It's skin. He remembered the look of her arm with fair skin, showing no texture. He did not touch her arm or look at it now but only thought about the way it had looked.

"I've never been there," he said, "except on business."

It struck her that he had said the same thing before, and talking as little as he did, that he had repeated himself. She turned her head to look at him. She did it slowly because he was close and she did not want to bump into him, bumping noses, perhaps, which would be terrible. She leaned her head against the post of the door and she could see mostly his eyes.

"It must be terrible," she said, "seeing all those places and it's always on business."

She saw his eyes move so they no longer looked at her and then he looked back at her. "It's the first time I've thought of it," he said.

She wished she were not holding her can of beer. She could do nothing with it, he being so close.

"And now I don't want to think of the places at all," he said.

She wished she did not have the beer because her fingers would be cold and perhaps wet, and she wanted to touch the side of his face. He looked down so that she could see only his forehead and could not tell what he was looking at. She sat still and heard herself breathe.

"I want to go someplace sometime," she said, "because I don't have to. You feel like that, Sam?"

The worst times are between jobs, he remembered.

"I'd even like to come to Penderburg sometime. After I've left, I mean, and am living elsewhere. Come here and just walk through the streets and have nothing to do and look at things."

She saw him reach over to the window and drop his beer can out. It made a thunk on the ground because it wasn't empty.

"Is that how it is when you get to a new town?" she asked him. "When you go to a new town on business?"

"When I go to a new town on business," he said, "I don't even see the new town. It could be the place where I was before. It's all the same. The job is always the same."

He then did a strange thing, lifted his hand and put his fingers over her mouth. It was a quick motion but did not startle the girl because he moved smoothly.

"Though why this is not the same," he said, "I don't know."

He felt her mouth under his fingertips and that she slowly kissed them.

It's different, he thought, because I'm not yet on a job. This is like the time in between, dead time usually. He did not know that it was much more different than that. He put his head down and his face into the side of her neck and his hand on her. The girl dropped her can of beer and held still for him. He did not wonder about the difference now, that he was not really with her because he was between jobs, but that he was with her because he had run from one.

8

He took the girl home very late at night, and then he drove out of town again and slept in the back of his car. It was part of the original plan. Nothing else had been part of the original plan, and he felt disturbed and superstitious for the rest of the night. In the morning he drove into town and stopped at the bus station. He shaved and washed some in the rest room and after that had breakfast at the counter which was in the station. It did not occur to him to go back to the diner because that was something else entirely and this was a different day. The sun shone early, and Jordan walked across the square where the old men already sat under the trees and where a farmer unloaded produce in front of a store. Jordan went to the end of the square where he could see the length of Third Avenue.

He did not feel uneasy until he saw someone come out of Kemp's building. He was doing the part of the job which he did not want, the part which showed him who the other one was. But the man at the building was not Kemp. Jordan turned back to the square but did not know where to go. He did not want to lose sight of Kemp's building.

There was a store window with bolts of cloth and two dummies wearing flower print dresses in it. This store might buy buttons, he thought. One dummy had a foot off the ground because the limb had not been screwed in all the way. Jordan turned away, not liking the sight. That was when he saw Paul. The man stood by the curb, watching Jordan.

"Don't go away," he said.

He had his hands in his pockets and one foot up on the curb and his head was tilted because of the sun. Paul looked easy and very uncomplicated. Once he ran his tongue over his teeth.

"Been selling any buttons today?"

Jordan put his hands into his pockets but it did not feel relaxed. He took his hands out again and let them hang. This was more natural for him. He stood like that and gave Paul a slight smile. Paul was a familiar thing. He was nothing new, he was nothing important; and if he should become part of the job, it would be a side issue.

"No," said Jordan. "I haven't sold any yet."

"How come?"

"I'm still casing."

"Casing? Button salesmen do casing?"

"I learned the word in the movies. I go a lot. Do you go a lot?"

Jordan took a cigarette out and turned it back and forth in his fingers.

Paul was watching that. Then he said, "What?"

"Do you go to the movies a lot?"

Paul did not know how to take that, because everything of course had an angle. And he did not remember Jordan this way. He had a fixed notion of what a man might be like who sells buttons and who backs out of a fight. Paul came up with a formula and said, "What's it to you?"

"Nothing. Where's your friend Mister Kemp?"

"Kemp? Why?"

"I see you, I think of Mister Kemp. You know, that's how I met both of you."

But the answer did not please Paul. It did not relax him because it was his job not to be relaxed, and for a long time this rule had been the only reminder that he did have a job and was important.

"For a button salesman you ask an awful lot of questions that don't have a damn thing to do with buttons, you know that.... What's your name?"

"Smith."

"Smith. That's right. I never knew there were any real Smiths."

Jordan did not take it up and the tone did not bother him. He had his tack now and was working.

"I wanted to see him. That's why I asked. Where is he now?"

"He's busy."

"I wouldn't want to bother him."

"Then why see him?"

"I haven't found the house he was talking about last night. To rent a room."

"I remember where he said it was. I got it all clear in my head because Kemp knocked himself out explaining it straight. How come you don't remember a simple—"

"I was thinking about something else."

For a button man, Paul thought, this one is mean. He's untrimmed mean, the thin-nosed bastard, but before Paul was ready with his answer for that, Jordan turned, walked away.

Now, Jordan thought, he's got to follow.

"Hey—" and when Jordan did not answer, "Fourth is that way," said Paul. "There's nobody going to rent you a place here on Third." Then he was next to Jordan, keeping pace. "And the diner's run by an old man this time of morning."

"I'm going to see Kemp," said Jordan.

Paul prickled with irritation and could not think of a good thing to say. "*Mister* Kemp to you, button man." It did not come up to the mark. "And he ain't up," said Paul.

"Good. Then he'll be home."

"Button man—" The bastard is walking too fast. "Not up for you, button man."

"You his nurse?"

"Yeah. I'm his nurse."

But Jordan kept walking without giving an answer, and Paul kept on walking and did not talk any more either. Jordan felt he had learned what he had to know. Kemp's muscle took his job seriously. He was through bantering and was coming along. Whether or not he knew that it was serious made little difference, because unless he, Jordan, could shake the man later, it would come to the same thing. The little fat man from the Coast might have bought himself double service.

In the hallway of the building Paul would not say where Kemp was living. This one, thought Jordan, might be worse than he looks, because he is stupid and trying to make up for that with his stubbornness. Jordan looked at the mailboxes and then went to the third floor. Window at end of hall, runner on floor, fire escape to the back, card on door, *Thomas Kemp.* Jordan knocked.

He had to knock because Paul was standing there with him and it would not look innocent to walk away now. He knocked again which would seal it that he had to stay.

Kemp was up. He opened the door looking rumpled, and half of his face had lather on it. This made him look different from Kemp in the photo and Kemp last night in the diner, almost like somebody Jordan did not know.

"Well, lookee here," said Kemp. His smile looked clownish because of the foam. "Smith, wasn't it?"

There was one room, and a door to another one. Bed, sink, other things, lived-in clutter.

"Come in."

Jordan came in and Paul closed the door. Kemp kept smiling. There was a foam glob on his upper lip and he blew up at it. There was now a large nose hole. "Been working this early in the morning?" said Kemp.

Then he went back to the sink and Jordan did not have to say anything, except no, he hadn't been working yet. Kemp shaved and looked into the mirror and said Jordan should wait just a minute and find a seat.

There was just one chair and Paul sat in it. He had his legs crossed and dipped one foot. Every time Kemp scraped, Paul dipped his foot.

"He was real anxious to see you," said Paul.

"Oh?" Kemp grinned into the mirror. He worked the razor around the grin. "What for, Smith?"

"I couldn't find that room last night," said Jordan.

"You remember telling me...."

Kemp splashed and rubbed water all over his face and made a blowing sound into his hands. Then he used a towel. When Jordan looked up it was again Kemp's face with the squint lines by the eyes, the grey hair, young man's grin. Jordan rubbed his nose and looked out of the window. "I can come back when you've had your breakfast," he said. "Or if you'll tell me when you're free, when you don't have anything to do during the day...."

"I'll take you now," said Kemp. "How's that?"

It wasn't any good. Jordan nodded, but it probably would be no good going with Kemp because it would not help Jordan to find out how Kemp spent his day. He knew when Kemp got up and had an idea when he went to bed. And that Paul hung around all the time. It might have to be enough. Or he would have to go with Kemp and talk more.

"I can take him," said Paul. "Why should you bother?"

"No bother," said Kemp. He put a jacket on and pulled up his tie. Then he grinned into the mirror again, from very close, to see what his teeth were like. "I take a walk anyway," he said. "Before breakfast. Ready?"

They walked down the street with Paul following the two men. Jordan watched a garbage truck creep down the street. Because there were trees all along, the truck was in and out of the light.

"Business any good in town?" Kemp asked.

"I don't know yet. I haven't tried yet."

"Kind of slow, aren't you?"

"Yes."

"You know something? I've never seen anyone have a cigarette habit the way you do. Holding it that way, unlit."

Jordan threw the cigarette away and Paul, in back, laughed.

Kemp said, "Where you buy your merchandise, Smith?"

"In New York."

"Good profit?"

"It's a job, Mister Kemp."

"But the investment is low, isn't it?"

"I don't know," said Jordan. "Over the years, it isn't low."

This time Kemp laughed and they walked a while without talking. Then Paul said, "You're going the long way."

"I know," said Kemp. "You mind, Smith?"

"No. I don't mind."

"It's a nice day," said Kemp. "That's why."

Jordan looked at the mountain of shale which started on the other side of the railway tracks. "There aren't many places to walk here, if you like to walk."

"It's okay. I just walk on the streets. Like this way, and then around to Fourth street."

"You take this walk every morning?"

"Yes. I'd walk more, except Paul isn't much for it."

"He always comes along?"

"We're kind of together," said Paul.

"Yes," said Kemp. "Except we part ways on the movies. Christ, him and those movies."

Jordan waited for more but nothing came. "You don't see the same movies?" he said.

"I don't see any. Just Paul goes."

"This burg can drive you nuts," said Paul.

"Won't be long now," said Kemp. He sighed and looked up at the trees.

There was more talk but it meant nothing. There were niceties with the landlady who said she favored young men who came to town on business and Jordan paid for a room, one week in advance. Then the two men stayed with him while Jordan walked to the square for his car, and then they passed him again on their walk back, while Jordan was taking a suitcase into the rooming house. Kemp just nodded and walked by but Paul stopped and watched.

"That's damn little luggage for a salesman," he said.

"What I use for business," said Jordan, "is in the trunk of the car. I don't need that in my room," and then he went inside.

Upstairs, he sat in his room for a while. He sat near the window which opened on the house next to him, a yard with a chicken coop, and in the distance, the back of Kemp's apartment. It was ten in the morning and Jordan did some of the routine things.

He laid out toilet stuff, but not all of it. He laid out enough to make an impression, but he did not leave his hairbrush out or his razor. They were things which carried traces of him and which he would not want to leave behind. The toothpaste was new, the toothbrush was new, and the razor blades. He left those out but he wiped them. He put some shirts on a chair and they were new too. They had no laundry marks and they were not his size.

He had a twenty-five caliber target pistol and a thirty-eight Magnum. For the Magnum, because of the racket, he also had a silencer. He looked at the guns for a moment and thought that the smaller gun would be all he'd need. There would be time to aim and no need for a big slam. The target pistol would still make less sound, even counting the silencer on the Magnum, though he worried a while about the pitch. The report of the target gun had a high pitch, where the Magnum didn't. The Magnum was louder, but with the silencer it did not sound like a gun shot so much. Jordan could not decide and locked up the suitcase. He would think about it and decide later. This did not make him nervous. This was part of the craft.

He put the suitcase into the closet, locked the closet. He left the room and locked it. He drove partway out of town where all the filling stations lined the road. He filled the tank at one, got oil and air at another. In a garage one street over he had all the spark plugs changed because he did not like the sound of the motor in idle. He had the points cleaned and asked for a battery check. The battery was new but the check was routine. One cell needed water.

He drove out of town a short way and ate lunch on the road. He did not want to run into Kemp or Kemp's man any more. After lunch he smoked a cigarette and looked out of the window. There was a potato field and some cows behind a fence to one side. The sun was high and bright now.

He went back to his room and slept for two hours. When he got up he washed his face and then sat by the window. He clipped his fingernails and he chewed on a cigarette. After he had looked out of the window a while, he noticed that the coop down below was not for chickens. There were pigeons inside.

He lay down on the bed again, got up a short time later. He looked at the new tube of toothpaste, at the shirts, and once at the suitcase in the closet. He sat down again, by the sink this time. He had the window in back of him and watched a drop from the faucet. It was mid-afternoon and the waiting was worse than the job.

He made tiny turns on the head of the faucet and tried for a rate of drip which was just before the point where the drops slid together to make a thin stream. Between that time and evening he managed this twice.

"Those were lousy french fries," said Kemp.

He lay down on the bed and put his shoes up on the baseboard.

"I said those were lousy french fries."

"Yeah. Yeah, they were," said Paul.

There was an evening wind and the curtain moved. Paul hitched around in his chair so that the curtain would not reach him.

"You read that magazine yesterday," said Kemp. In a while he said, "Paul."

"Yeah?"

"You read that magazine yesterday. How often you read the same thing before you get it?"

Paul put the magazine down and pulled a cigarette out of his pocket. He did not take the pack out of his pocket but just one cigarette.

"I was looking at the pictures is all."

He lit the cigarette and picked up the magazine again.

"It's quarter to seven," said Kemp.

"Huh?"

"What in hell's the matter with you, Paul?"

"Nothing." He sighed and looked at his cigarette. "Those were lousy french fries," he said.

Kemp pulled his legs up and pushed the shoes off his feet. Then he dropped them on the floor. "It's quarter to seven. You'll be late for the movie." "Yeah. The movie." Paul stretched in the chair and said, "I don't think I'll go. I wanna read this magazine."

"Ohforchristsakes," said Kemp.

Paul looked at Kemp, waiting for more, but nothing came.

"What's the matter with you," he said. "Why you riding me?"

"What's the matter with *me?*"

"Yeah. If I wanna sit here and read a magazine...."

"You can't read."

"Now listen, Kemp—"

"You listen. You go to the movies. You go to the movies and just figure it's going to be maybe one more week like this and no more. So go to the movies."

"What are you gonna do?"

"I'm going to think about you sitting in the movie, for God's sake! Now beat it!"

"Listen, Kemp—"

Kemp groaned. Then he said Paul shouldn't put on so and how much worse it would be if he, Paul, had to make a living selling buttons, for instance, instead of resting his butt in a movie and being able to look forward to a very bright future in no more than a week or so.

"You know what I think of that guy, don't you?" said Paul.

"He's not your type is what you want to say."

"He's a creep."

"Leave him alone. Rest yourself."

"Did you ever see any of the buttons he's selling?"

"No. Buttons are very small."

"Now listen, Kemp. I been trying to tell...."

"You're going stir crazy," said Kemp. "Go talk to Betty."

"Listen, Kemp. You ever see a salesman before what never brags about his loot or the territories or what in hell they brag about all the time?"

"We're no customers is the reason."

"I been trying to tell you...."

"Go to the movies."

"You know something, Kemp? I wouldn't buy nothing from him, you know that? He—what in the hell is the word—he don't come out. You know what I mean?"

"Shy?"

"Shy? He ain't shy, man. I don't know what but he ain't that way."

"No," said Kemp. "He isn't really shy."

"So? Like I been telling you!"

"Go to the movies, Paul."

Paul gave up. He did not want to talk any more about something which he wasn't certain about, and he had no way of dealing with Kemp when he took the tone of the older man.

"I'm going to the movies," Paul said.

"Why, how you think of those things?"

"What are you gonna do?"

"Spend the evening, Paul. I'm going to just waste it away."

"You staying here?"

"Yeah, I'm staying here and I want to stay here alone!"

"All right," said Paul. "I'm going."

He left. He felt less sure about everything than before, and for a moment he stood in front of the house on the street. He looked up the street and down the street but not as if looking for something but like one who did not know what to look for and feeling sullen about it. His good will had been insulted. He could not tell Kemp about it but he would make somebody feel this. Go sit in the diner? He looked across and saw the girl Betty through the windows in front. To hell with her, he said. Go to the movies and to hell with all this. I'll go to the diner with Kemp afterwards. Like always. And the button man might even be there. Go to the movies now and then the button man. That's the ticket. The evening all planned and no problems about any of it. Sit in the dark in the movie, that's no problem, and later the button man, in the diner, that'll be just as good.

Paul walked down the street, toward the square, and he even felt something like interest. He did not think he had seen this movie before and that would mean almost two hours of entertainment. The street was dark and the square up ahead was lit up. Maybe the movie would be something funny. Maybe a cops and robbers thing and he'd laugh while the yokels sat there with the kiss of drama all over them. Or a big, bad syndicate thing, he'd laugh.

He was late for the movie but he stood near the ticket booth for a moment and looked at the girl behind the glass. She thinks she's a movie star. She looks at everybody like they're a scout and treats everybody like they aren't. She's going to rot here. She's going to have a white-eyed miner for a husband and ten slug-colored babies. He said nothing to her when he bought his ticket because ignoring her hairdo and make-up would be even worse. Yessir, he thought, this is the life I'm getting away from.

"I give you enough for two tickets, honey. Where's my two tickets?"

"Oh—I thought—I didn't see anybody...."

"Gimme two tickets, honey. One seat's for my feet." He bought two tickets and laughed. Then he saw Jordan.

Paul walked a ways into the movie because he hadn't quite realized anything yet but then he stopped and looked out again.

The button man. The creep son of a bitch on the side of the square, standing there with that wet butt in his mouth. And no sample case either. Going home? Not going home. He's thinking about going into the movie to beef up his life for the evening. Not the movie.

Walking. Who's the button man? Nobody knows the button man, not even Kemp. What I don't like I don't like and the button man fits into that dandy.

Why Third. Who does the son of a bitch know on Third? Betty. Everybody loves Betty.

And me with two tickets paid for in my pocket and creeping after the button man loving Betty. Who'd love a thing with a wet butt in his face....

Son of a bitch, he's cagey. If he don't act like a stranger in town. If he don't act like he didn't know Betty from nothing, with his back to the diner and looking the other way. Who does he know?

Kemp.

To sell Kemp buttons, and he don't carry a sample case. To ask about renting that room and he's got it rented already. To hang around and be a pain in the neck because who in hell is anybody with a name like Smith....

Not Kemp? Just a walk, then, which is worse yet. The button man takes a walk where he knows people on the same street and he doesn't stop to see either of them. He doesn't stop to see either of them because he doesn't like to be followed. Just for that....

Then Paul kept his distance and stayed in the dark to see what the other one would do. He watched Jordan go to the end of the block and turn down the street which joined Fourth. Paul didn't follow. He crossed by the apartment building, through the back, past the pigeon coop and he stood in the dark drive where he could see Jordan come down the street.

Have a word with him now? He's thin and a button salesman but like Kemp said, not really shy. Not really a button salesman, maybe....

He watched Jordan open the trunk of his car and take out a suitcase which he took into the house.

Time to go through his samples? That is the same suitcase he took into the room that same afternoon.... Leaving, then, staying....

Jordan came out again very soon and got into his car. What a sweet-sounding motor, thought Paul. What a weird thing to watch somebody move, not know what the man does, and to dislike the son of a bitch right from the start and then more so the less he made sense. With a sweet-sounding motor like that he drives like a funeral....

Slow enough to walk, thought Paul, and he walked. He rounded the corner to Third when Jordan's car crept up to the apartment building. There it stopped.

Paul started to run.

And this time the bastard saw me for sure, thought Paul, because why should he take off like that. A type like that and he takes off with the tires squealing. That don't fit, Smith don't fit, the buttons don't fit.... He ran to the lot where the diner stood and where his car was parked. He jumped in and then he thought that son of a bitch should hear this—the kind of noise he, Paul, was making; how the motor let out a scream and the gravel shot out and the whine when the car hauled over and into the street. And that's all for you, button man....

And now he's running and he's driving as if he knew the road and the countryside well. He's running from me hell-bent-for-leather.

When Paul realized this he stopped wondering who Smith was; he stopped turning it back and forth in his mind if he was salesman, or grifter, or a man who had come down to wheedle a deal, or had come casing even, because now the other one ran and Paul after him with never a doubt he would make it. And if I can't talk to him, he said to himself, then you will, Anna-Lee, and he squeezed his left arm into his side so he could feel the holster.

The car up ahead didn't cut speed at all when it turned. It leaned so heavily into the turn that Paul held his breath for a moment. Then he braked very sharply because he didn't know the road which the one up ahead was taking. Black top and two lanes and plenty of bumps. The two tail lights up ahead bounded up and down. Break a spring, you bastard, but nothing else. I'll break the rest for you, button man....

Then the car was gone.

Paul gunned and had to fight the wheel when he came into the bend of the road and what pulled him through, so it seemed, was the sight of the red lights up ahead again. Steady as.... He had stopped, that's why! Slammed into the side of the road with one door hanging open, with the lights still on, with one front wheel almost hanging over where the embankment dropped off and the bridge railing started. Why the door open? He fell out that way. Why had he been running? Because I was after him.

Paul grinned and stopped his car so that it slammed down on the frame. "Smith?"

He could look down the embankment but at the bottom he saw only dark.

"Smith? Hey, button man!"

"Yes?"

He thought he could see him now, down by the culvert which went under the bridge.

"Come on out!"

He could see Smith standing there and that man would have looked the same had he stood on a street. Smith looks weird standing in weeds up to his knees.

"Don't be scared, boy. I come to buy buttons. Smith?"

"Yes?"

"Where are you?"

"Here."

"I got all night, Smith. You hear me?" and he moved toward the bridge so that his shadow stretched out ahead of him.

Smith doesn't move. No sir, but now he does. Back, he does, and afraid of my shadow. Yessir, that one scares....

"Smith, little buddy, can you see me clear?"

"Yes."

"Oh my God, you sound all choked up."

This time no answer. Oh my God, how I hate the bastard.

"Little button buddy, here I am. For a sample—"

Then it spat so fast, Paul barely heard all the sound that went with it.

Oh my God, oh my God, how I hate, he thought, and was finished.

9

High angle shot, thought Jordan. Chest or head? Hard telling, with the headlight glare making false borders around his shape, and the foreshortened angle.

He put the gun in his pocket and climbed up the bank, through the dry weeds.

With the kind of jerk he had given, I think it was chest.

Paul, on his back, was dead, of course, and the jacket had slid up into bunches and the pants had pushed up to his calves. How that always happens. Chest. Like I thought.

First, Jordan moved the cars. He moved Paul's car to the other side of the bridge and well onto the soft shoulder. He turned the lights off and left the key in the ignition. Then he walked back and moved his own car to the other end of the bridge, also well off the road. This way, the cars would not alarm any motorist.

Jordan got out of his car and after he had closed the door, leaned against it for a moment. Dark and hot and I'll lean here for a moment and then go back. The rest can be as simple as it's been so far, because it needs no planning, because all I have to do is grab him by the back of the jacket and drag him down to the culvert. Done.

Jordan walked away from the car and back to the bridge.

But he's lying on his back and can't be grabbed by the back of the jacket.

Jordan held out his hand for the railing and when he touched it—he knew he would touch it—gave a start.

He's dead, so don't worry. This almost made Jordan giggle, though he did not let himself. It stayed a sharp, fluttery tickle in his throat.

Jordan slowed on the bridge because he could now see the body on the soft shoulder.

Though this is not a job as jobs go. None of it fitting the habits. Everything I do now is with the props gone. That new.

He worked his hand along the railing and walked like a blind man. He could see well enough now, but did not want to.

And even the job as jobs go hadn't been all that good. It had gone easily, because of the habits, but the habits had not been quite good enough for all that was needed. For instance, he thought, and then, for instance, again. I'm calmer already, he thought. But I got him at the right time for the best light but not at the right time for the best drop. He should have stood closer to the edge so he'd drop down the incline all by himself.

Jordan stopped. He could see it lying there, crabbed out with arms and legs the way they always do. He would now have to touch it.

His scalp moved on his skull, and he thought he could feel his skull tight and hard over the inside of his head. He had an upsetting image—all of him curled soft into the inside of the skull. But it's the second time. This is not the first.... He started to sweat, thin and quick, when he saw that it was worse now and not easier.

Then he moved because it became impossible to do nothing.

Jordan bent down and touched. He thought about the time after this time, all done with this, never again this, and so registered very little of what he was doing or what the body was doing, but the worst moments came through.

He touched the jacket high up and yanked. A dead arm swung around and hit Jordan's ankle. After his gasp the breath came out of Jordan's throat, shocking him with the sound because it was like a giggle. But his throat felt all right after that, without the strain in it.

I won't drag him down, I'll roll him down. I'll do that and between now and the moment when I touch it again a headlight will swing around the far bend, and I'll have to let all this go and just run, just run.

But he only thought this and suddenly scratched his head where sweat tickled him and for a moment he was just scratching—nothing else—and after that he had his feelingless calm again, out of nowhere, but the way he was used to it. He only worried for one split second about the quick switches that went on inside him, but that thought never got anywhere because then he touched again.

He dragged like a dog worrying a bone. When the body was over the edge Jordan let go with a quick jerk of his hand and kept jerking his hand like that, through the air, a little bit like a conductor with temperament. Because the body wasn't rolling. But the quick pizzicato beat kept up Jordan's speed. The dead arms and legs made contrary motions; Jordan kept worrying the thing like a bone, down the bank, through the weeds, feeling intent and all right about it because all the worry was in his hands. What he touched, how much he touched, where. And when he pushed it into the culvert, which took perhaps two minutes, he counted time by the number of times he pushed against bone instead of flesh.

Done, back through the weeds which were pulling at him. He kept wiping his hands and then wiped them with the weeds. They were not wet but brittle and dry and Jordan, wiping over and over, cut himself. Up the bank, job over. And how quick and clever the whole thing. It had probably been spite to start with—Paul following him by the movie—but then it was the plan working. It was good to know about plans working. Going down Third, drawing Paul after. Stopping at Kemp's place, getting Paul all riled up. Then the fast walk around to Fourth—Paul already there, having cut through a lot; then moving the suitcase to give him time and to mystify him, then the slow stunt with the car so he could follow on foot, and then driving off fast when Paul showed up again near Kemp's building.

Jordan worked up the incline to the highway, rehashing things this way, something he had never done. Job over.

Though this was not yet the important one.

Before the haste went out of him and left just nervous splinters, he rushed all the rest. He drove the dead one's car a little ways down the next lane and from there up a path which went to a spent quarry. Jordan knew it was there, drove Paul's car there, and left it. Jordan was not concerned with eliminating all trails but only with working for time. They would find the dead one and they would find the car. He worked for one day's leeway, and the trail would lead nowhere.

He ran back to the highway and his haste didn't change into something else until he sat in his car and knew what he would do next. There was all this momentum but it now turned sharp and clean. Clean like routine. Kemp was next.

Jordan drove back to town, sitting neat and still. He sat with his head on top of his neck like a stopper on top of a bottle. Fine. Everything fine now. Finish it....

He went through Third and saw a light where Kemp's room was. He drove past and turned through the square, doubling back to Fourth. To pick up his suitcase in the room and then finish. He parked and when he went across the street he went fast and kept his hand on his pocket. The Magnum was heavy and Jordan did not want it to swing. Then would come Magnum in suitcase, target pistol for job, suitcase in trunk, drive to Third, check target pistol in front seat, car on street pointed the right way, up Kemp's building, finish it.

Jordan opened the door to his room where the light was on and then everything became very slow. The brain, the movement of the door closing, the door *thunk* when it closed, even Kemp. He sat in Jordan's chair, looking slow, and he held Jordan's other gun.

"Ever use one of these?" he asked.

Jordan stayed by the door and the weight of the Magnum in his pocket was so great that he felt his right shoulder ache and thought Kemp must notice any moment.

"You don't look well, Smith. Why don't you sit on the bed?"

Jordan walked to the bed and wasn't aware of any muscles moving in him. He was only aware of Kemp telling him to sit down.

And this is the payoff for Paul, he thought. This is the payoff. Not for the job he had done, but for having done the job wrong. He had touched him afterwards.

"Jeesis," said Kemp. "You can smell pigeons all the way up here. You mind if I close the window?"

"There's a chicken coop down there," said Jordan.

"No. It's a pigeon coop. Hear 'em fluttering?"

"I thought it was a chicken coop."

"No. Mind if I close the window?"

"Go ahead," said Jordan.

Kemp smiled and closed the window behind without changing position. With one hand.

"That's better. Come on, Smith, relax, huh?"

"I can't," said Jordan.

"You're no salesman, are you?"

Jordan did not answer. He shifted a little on the bed and sighed. It was a natural sigh.

"And Smith yet. What a handle to pick. Don't you know about Smiths?"

"No."

"There aren't any." Kemp laughed.

The Magnum wasn't so heavy now because it was resting on the bed.

"Make it easy on yourself, Smith, why don't you."

Jordan nodded and put both hands down on the bed. It did not relax him but it would be more efficient.

"I'm not saying you're dumb all the way, or *that* obvious, and maybe I just spotted you, Smith, because I got some background. That surprise you?"

"I am surprised. Yes."

"Take your coat off, why don't you?"

"Thanks. No."

"Okay."

Kemp looked at the target pistol in his hand and didn't say anything for a moment. Jordan crossed his legs for position so he could lean on one elbow.

"And loaded yet," said Kemp. "This," and he nodded the gun.

Jordan finished leaning down on one elbow.

"You like this type?" Kemp asked.

"What?"

"This kind of gun," said Kemp, "means one or the other to me. Either hobby, or business."

"What do you want from me?" said Jordan.

"'Fess up, I guess. Instead of me getting it out of you."

Jordan. shrugged, which brought his right hand where he wanted it for the moment.

"I think I'd like this kind myself," said Kemp. "Very accurate, isn't it?"

"If it's balanced good."

"Is it?"

"For my hand."

"I noticed it's top heavy for me. You got a long thumb?"

"Yes."

"Figures." Then Kemp sighed. "Look," he said, "I'm just talking around to make you feel relaxed. Honest, Smith."

Jordan put his right hand on his hip and when there was no objection, he did relax. He relaxed into a balance which was like a steel spring balance.

"I mean it, Smith. Put it away."

He leaned forward and held the gun out. Jordan was not prepared. He was so set that he felt the Magnum might go off if he moved even a little.

"You won't say it, I'll say it, Smith. You're on the lam, aren't you?"

It took almost as long to get back to normal, thought Jordan, as it had taken him to get set. He straightened up with a pain in his back and he reached out for the target gun so that it felt like slow motion.

"Well?" said Kemp.

"Yes. You're right."

Jordan took the gun and turned it to look at the clip. The butt was empty and he held a cold gun.

"I took it out," said Kemp, "because I'm afraid of guns. Imagine that thing goes off in here. Bad for both of us." He pointed and said, "I left the clip in your suitcase."

Jordan tapped his knees with the long barrel and then he tossed the gun on the bed. He felt exhausted and didn't want to try figuring moves any more. Not for the moment. Not after all this.

And the Magnum was out. The silencer was in the suitcase and the racket would be too much. After that, even if the gun went off like a normal gun, after that he would have to run with half his things left in the room because all he would have time to grab would be the new tube of toothpaste on the dresser, a shirt of the wrong size, meaningless things like that.

Nothing now. He just wished Kemp would leave.

"So tell me, Smith. Who do you know?"

"Nobody. I don't know anybody who makes any difference," said Jordan.

"You know me."

"Kemp. That's all I know. Just the name."

"Well, let me tell you a little."

"Listen. I just as soon you wouldn't. I mean it, Kemp."

Kemp raised his eyebrows and watched Jordan sit on the bed. He thought the other man looked suddenly tired.

"I just meant for an introduction. Just a talk, Smith...."

"I don't want to talk."

"...to see if there was something for you and me in it."

"What?"

"Maybe there's a job. Maybe I can use you."

"Ohmygawd—" said Jordan, and rubbed one hand over his face.

"Well, maybe not," said Kemp. He got up and scratched under one arm. "I didn't mean in this town, if that's what you meant." He walked to the door and stopped there. "Just think about it, huh, Smith? Before you blow town, come over and see me. Okay?"

"Yes," said Jordan. "I will."

10

After Kemp was gone Jordan locked his door from the inside. He took his jacket off, so as not to feel the weight of the Magnum. At the closed window he looked at the black glass.

I'm not built for this and I'm not trained for this. It comes to the same thing. I know so much and no more and it isn't enough. Or there is always something worse. It comes to the same thing.

Then he turned away from the window because he was beginning to notice his reflection. He packed, the way he had planned it, and he started all over the way he had planned it, because he really did not know anything else.

On Third he parked in the lot next to the diner, heading the car the way he wanted. He thought about leaving the motor running but decided against it. There was light in the diner. There were two other cars in the lot, and somebody friendly might turn off his key, take it out, bring it into the diner for safekeeping maybe. He turned off the motor, put the key in his pocket, stuck the target gun into his belt and buttoned his jacket. If the silencer would only fit the pistol he would have liked that. It was a margin of safety. This was now a job for margins of safety.

He crossed behind the diner where the garbage cans stood, and a cat ran away. The cat made a potato roll over the ground and he picked it up. It was a big, raw potato and he took it along.

At Kemp's door he knocked.

"Paul?"

"No. Smith."

"The door's open. Come on in."

Jordan went in and closed the door behind him. Kemp was on his bed, dressed, shoes off, a paper across his middle. The paper went up and down with his breathing. Kemp was lying down and stayed that way. This is a bad angle, thought Jordan. The radio next to Kemp was playing mood music.

"Well now. You're looking better." Kemp turned the radio down to a mumble and smiled from his pillow. "You come for the job?"

"I got a job."

"Christ—"

Jordan had the gun out and he worked the potato over the end of the barrel.

"Smith... Wait a minute. Let's talk...."

Jordan didn't talk. In the movies there is talk, for the drama. Jordan worked without drama. Or there is talk because there is a grudge. There was no grudge.

"Smith, just lemme...."

"Sit up."

"Yes, I was gonna say, lemme sit up—"

"Go ahead."

While Kemp sat up Jordan took a stance. He never fired from the hip because when he fired he was never on the run. He aimed straight-arm and only the potato bothered his aim.

"For God's sake—"

The voice was hoarse as if it had the worst kind of cold and after that type of sound there was often a scream. Jordan did not want that and would have been ready if the potato did not interfere with balance and sighting.

"Smith... I ask... I beg—"

Dull sound, slightest recoil, potato spraying all over. Kemp's head snapped back and went *thunk* on the headboard. Mood music mumble. The hole was high and the blood was just filling it. Black in the light.

A drawn-up knee collapsed and the leg dangled a little and Jordan was going down the stairs.

When he got out on the street he stood for a moment and took a deep breath. He thought that the air was just right. He himself felt right and he felt finished with the job he had come to do.

A young couple came down the dark street and Jordan turned his head away out of habit. He crossed the street to his car and noticed that the diner was dark. He got into his car, feeling right and finished. When he put the key into the ignition he noticed that his hand was shaking.

He did not know why it was shaking because everything felt right now and he was done. He took the gun out of his belt, wiped the end of the barrel across his pants because the metal was wet from the raw potato. He wiped and wiped and then he put the gun under the seat. He started the motor, got into gear almost immediately so that the car jumped and the motor died.

It was not his habit to drive this way. He had a routine with the car where he started the motor, nursed it in idle, then got into gear and took off, smooth and gentle-footed.

While he started over again he thought about everything, thinking too much. At first, way in the beginning, the work had been hard, with everything effort. When that became better, a job was achievement. After that, a job was smooth habit. That had been most of the time now and had felt like the final thing.

He took off the way he was used to it, except faster. There was a man by the letterboxes inside the vestibule. He had a lunch bucket under his arm and was getting his mail.

But this time, thought Jordan, there was this. He was done but his hand was shaking. He was done but he drove too fast. If more of me were shaking, he thought, I would know why I'm feeling this way. Just my hands are shaking, so it's nothing. A fine job up in that room.

What upset him now was that he was thinking about it at all.

He drove through the square and took the street at the other end which went out of town.

Maybe eight minutes since, he thought. That's three more than planned.

What upset him again was not the loss of three minutes but the thoughts he had about a job which was really well done. This felt indecent.

On the other side of the street someone was walking and then turned up to a house with no lights in the windows. The porch light went on and Jordan saw the girl from the diner. She still had her uniform on and was carrying, a purse over her arm. She went into the house while Jordan passed.

He kept driving because he was now nine minutes off. Yes, yes, yes, and such a fine finish after that godawful thing on the bridge and then under the bridge. I would hate, he suddenly said aloud, to leave here without such a neat thing done like the Kemp job.

The voice shocked him and the thought—that there had to be thought about any of this—shocked him so that he held the wheel hard, rocking on it. The wheel gave with the rocking, the springiness keeping the rocking motion going. Jordan kept nodding back and forth. What now, what now, he kept thinking, what more, what more now. It's done, it's done— double everything, because it went with the rocking. All the props gone out from under, he thought, all the props I never knew had been there, like don't talk to him, don't touch him, don't know him too well. But they *don't* mean a thing, and his thinking got loud again, because I *did* finish....

But he did not recognize himself. He stopped rocking because it made him sick, and he stopped thinking, because that made him sick. He was able to stop thinking because it was easier just to feel the confusion.

She wouldn't think anything like that about me. Her dumb face knows everything and I'm Smith and sell buttons. Her dumb face doesn't care if I'm Smith or sell buttons. She never once mentioned anything like it. She mentioned that I am a gentleman. Jeesis. She mentioned that she likes a quiet man. "You want me, Sam? You want me, Sam, and you don't talk around it. I like that."

She can't be all wrong, he thought. She must know something. She's dumb which just means there's no confusion, and if she says now, Sam, you look fine and not shivery like one day ago—she can't be all wrong. He swung the car into a U-turn and drove back toward town.

He knocked on her door, and she said, "Who is it?"

"Smith."

"Who?"

"Sam. You remember me?" he said through the door.

"Oh, Sam! Come in!"

Jordan went in and closed the door behind him. Betty was on the bed. She had a housecoat on, her shoes were off, and there was a magazine lying across her middle. The magazine went up and down with her breathing. The radio next to her bed was playing mood music.

She said, "Hi, Sam," and, "You know, you're looking ever so much better." She smiled from her pillow and turned the radio down to a mumble.

Jordan let go of the door knob behind him and felt his hand tremble. He did not move away from the door but leaned against it. He began to tremble all over. He did not move, not his eyes or anything, except for his trembling.

Her smile faded a little and then just went away. She raised herself up on one arm and stared at him. "Sam," she said, and then, "Sam?"

She got off the bed slowly and then she walked toward him and came all the way over. She did not say anything else or walk faster but when she was up to him, she slowly put up her hand and laid it on the side of his face. "What is it, Sammy?" she said.

He leaned his face into her hand and closed his eyes. He had to explain nothing, do nothing, and could just stand this way while the girl came closer and put her face next to his. "Come sit down, Sammy," she said. "You'll be all right."

He sat down in the chair she had and was not trembling any more. She brushed at his lapel and said, "How did you ever get raw potato on there. It's just like raw potato," but Jordan was not trembling any more and what she said and did had nothing to do with before any more, with the use of a raw potato. The girl was concerned over his suit and she was concerned that he should sit and rest. It meant that.

"You're not used to the heat," she said and opened his tie and collar a little. "Or is it something else?"

"It's that," he said, "and also something else. But you don't have to worry about it, Betty. It's nothing for you to worry about."

She sat on the arm of his chair and looked down at him. "Are you sick?"

"No. It's something hanging on, but I'm not sick. Really, Betty."

She thought he does not look sick. A little worn, perhaps, needing sleep, but he's all right. He said so and he smiles.

"What do you need, Sammy? Can I do something?"

He took a cigarette out and asked for a match. He puffed on the flame and then he sat back in the chair and looked at the girl and the room.

"I'd like to stay a moment," he said.

"Of course, Sam. You mean, you're leaving?"

"Yes. I'm done here."

"Ah," she said. "You've done your business. Was it good?"

"I'm done," he said. "Yes."

She got up and went to the bed. He watched her lean over the bed and straighten the cover on it. He liked watching her do this. When she straightened up she brushed some hair back and he thought it was a beautiful gesture.

"I'm sorry," she said, because he was looking at her and she felt that her housecoat looked old. She looked down at herself and straightened the front.

"I like you in that," he said. "Really. I like you better in a housecoat than in anything else."

She felt it was nice of him to say this and she made no other remarks about it.

"Can I give you something?" she said, "I don't have a real kitchen, but iced tea, something like that. I can give you something simple like that."

He said that he liked iced tea and then when she said there was a can of sardines and some crackers, he said he liked that, too. He watched her in her housecoat, opening and closing the icebox she had, making the iced tea and getting the sardines out on a plate and the crackers. He would not have stopped for any of this somewhere else but he felt calm and well watching her bring all those things and sitting with him afterwards, eating.

"I'm glad you came over before leaving," she said. "That was very nice of you."

"I like seeing you, Betty."

"I think you were very nice, I mean, the times I've seen you."

"I have to go," he said. "It's a shame."

She nodded a little, nothing serious, and put the plate and crackers away. "Maybe, if you come through here again..." she said.

"Yes. I would look you up."

"Or maybe if you ever get to Miami. You know, I expect to be in Miami sometime. I told you."

"Yes."

"It's warm like this all the time, isn't it?"

"The sun shines and there's a breeze from the ocean and nights it's warm. If there's something blooming," he said, "you can smell it, night-times."

He knew nothing like this about Miami, having been there on business only and having finished in a very short time, but he thought all this might be true and he knew that she liked hearing it.

Then she gave him the address of her girl friend in Miami and said if he ever got there and if she herself got there sometime soon....

He went to the door and she stood with him for a moment and brushed at his lapel.

"Well," she said, and smiled.

"Thank you," he said, just so.

He kissed her on the side of her mouth and stroked her back.

"I've liked you," she said. "Good-by, Sammy."

"Good-by," he said, because this was a short daydream, and he did not want to do anything to change it or to see it become impossible. He stroked her back and felt her hands on his arms.

"If you want me," she said next to his face, "I mean, before you go. Before you have to go, Sammy...."

They went back to the bed and she turned off the lights and the radio. Then she helped him with his tie and shirt buttons. Then he undressed her, moving as slowly as she.

11

Everything being different, Jordan did not drive back the way he had planned. He left town going south, instead of taking the north way; he doubled around on new roads, replanning the routine, and when morning came he was still in the country and not going straight back on the turnpike as he would have done had all this been the old schedule. None of this was upsetting to him because the job was done and the rest, afterward, had been a matter apart from the job. In the morning he stopped at a hotel, went to bed, slept for twelve hours. It was a deep, dull sleep, with only a moment of thinking just before he dropped off. Her one-room place, with a bed and a corner for cooking on a hotplate. Frill curtains, which had looked new and cheap. Housecoat, and the girl moving around him. Had been reading a magazine on her bed. It had been like coming from work, resting, watching her do housework, then sleeping together.

Having been trained to a very special point, pathetically ordinary things had become Jordan's peace.

Sandy leaned on the glass counter and looked down at the cigar. He reached into the case and watched his hand take a panatela and when he had it in his mouth he looked across the bowling alley. He especially watched alley six and seven where the Kantovitz Kats and the Burns Machine Company were playing tournament. A man with the white and purple shirt of the Kats came to the counter and asked for three cigars.

"You got any money on this, Sandy?" and he nodded back at the alleys.

"No. I don't gamble."

"Too risky for you?" and the man laughed.

"That's right," said Sandy and gave the man his cigars. "Who's winning?"

"They are."

The phone rang under the counter and Sandy reached down without looking. He put the receiver to his ear and said, "Yeah?" After that he listened for a short while, then said, "No," and hung up.

"They're winning," said the man in the shirt, "but not because of any superior ability. It's the balls. They got tournament balls and we got all kinds. I think it makes a difference."

"I told you I'd get you the new ones. You could have ordered...."

"Sandy, we don't got that kind of dough."

"I can't go any lower. I'm giving them to you for what it costs me anyways."

"Sandy, with your kind of connections you can get 'em for less than they cost. You know that."

"I got no connections like that. I don't make anything on them as it is. Honest."

"I believe you." The man lit his cigar and said, "Business is tough."

"That's right."

The phone rang again and Sandy picked it up as before. He said, "Yeah," and then, "Yeah," and hung up. He wouldn't have minded standing at the counter some more and talking, but he pushed himself away and said, "Gotta run. I hope you guys make it."

"We won't. But think about those balls, will you, Sandy?"

"I will. I'll check around," and then he went to the back for his hat and overcoat.

Sandy had to drive for about fifteen minutes. He tried to go faster, because in the heat the draft helped, but there was a great deal of traffic. He drove with one arm on the window and let the draft run up his sleeve.

Maybe Venuto can help, he thought. He owes several favors and knows Dryer Supply. Maybe he can get the balls at manufacturer's price, and why not. He owes several favors.

Sandy turned off the thoroughfare and went through the wholesale district. Drygoods, then papergoods. There were trucks and semis parked on the street and angled into alleys.

Because I hate to see somebody lose all the time, thought Sandy. Nice, strong outfit like the Kats, why should they lose all the time, just because of no-good equipment.

He parked with two wheels on the sidewalk and two in the gutter, which was the only way traffic was able to pass him on the street.

He went into a store with the windows painted black half way up and inside nothing but storage space. The place had the dry smell of a great deal of paper. There were tall stacks of it all around, wrapped in brown packages. Sandy went past one side of a shelf which divided the long place in two. The other side of the store was the same as the first, except that there was a desk and a bulb hanging over it. The desk and the bulb were surrounded by paper packets so that the space looked like the inside of a box.

"Hello, Bass," said Sandy.

"Sit down."

Sandy took a chair next to the desk and said, "Christ, how can you work in this place?"

The other man didn't answer. He was bald and squat and the suit he wore didn't fit the place. It was dark flannel, cut up to date, and his shirt was a fashion pink. His bald head was very smooth and his face had heavy lines.

"Well?" said Bass.

"Nothing. I would have called you."

"He ever been late before?"

"No. Not unless he calls. He hasn't called though." Bass took his ballpoint and made zigzags on an order blank.

"I want you to send somebody down there."

"That's no good. I never do that, at this kind of time, and especially with a burg like this Pender—what was it?"

"You just said it. Penderburg."

"Yes. For all I know the whole place is popping. You should get a paper. I'm sure they got a local paper."

"You just said it, that it's a burg. Where'm I going to get a paper from there?"

Sandy shrugged and looked at the stacks all around. "Maybe the car broke down," he said.

"His car ever break down before, on a job?"

"No."

"Maybe something else broke down." Bass looked up and asked, "How long you had him?"

"He's all right. I see him all the time."

Bass looked at his ballpoint and then at Sandy. Sandy shook his head.

"No. He's been fine. He's quiet, kind of, but that's all."

Bass shrugged and got up. He stretched his back and said, "How quiet is fine?" Then he looked at a crack of light between the stacked paper packets, where a window was on the other side. "Meyer is on pins and needles and says I should call you over and get you to explain this thing. And what you're going to do about it."

"Frig him," said Sandy and he got up. "I got things to do."

Bass turned around and watched Sandy go. Bass was just the man in the middle and the less he had to do with this the better.

"I meant to ask you," said Sandy and he stopped by the door. "You know Venuto?"

"Who?"

"Never mind," said Sandy and then he left.

He stood by his car for a moment and watched a semi snake up to a loading platform. And if Venuto can't do anything, maybe I'll ask Schultz. I hate to see those Kats lose all the time.

"Hey! Sandy!"

He turned and saw Bass in the door to the paper place.

"He just called your place."

"From where?"

"He's in town."

"Where in town?"

"He left word you should call him at the number you got. You'd know where."

"Okay. I know," and Sandy got into his car.

"Wait a minute. Call him up and tell him to show at Meyer's place."

"When?"

"Now, damn it. What are we running here, anyways?"

"A business. What else?" and Sandy drove off.

Meyer's place had terraces and glass walls in the dining rooms, so that the weekend trade from the city could look at the hills in comfort or out at the river. This was not a weekend and the big dining room was locked up. Meyer walked back and forth on the dance floor, and when he looked up he did not see the rolling view outside the large windows but all the empty chairs and tables.

Meyer did not look like a restaurant owner but perhaps like a man who sold houses. He was small and his clothes looked untidy, the kind of untidiness which says there are things more important than clothes. Meyer had a face like a hawk.

The first car which drove into the lot brought Bass. He parked in line with the other cars; he went into the bar and had a drink next to the other guests. There were not very many. They were mostly women having an afternoon drink, and they talked about maid and gardener problems.

Bass went through the door which said *Gentlemen* and from there out through another door which said *Gentlemen.* That way he got into the dining room.

Meyer nodded at him and Bass nodded back. Then Bass sat down at a table and looked out of the windows.

Sandy and Jordan came in by a different way. Not even Meyer had noticed when they had driven up. They came in through the empty terrace and only Sandy said hello.

They all sat down at the empty tables and since there were so many tables, everyone sat at a table by himself. A bug was beating itself to death on the sunny side of the terrace; for a moment there was no other sound.

Meyer looked at Jordan but all Jordan did was look back. The two men did not know each other well. Then Meyer drummed his table a few times and twitched his nose. "All right," he said. "Done?"

Jordan nodded.

"How come you're late?"

"There were two of them."

"The guard too?"

"Had to," said Jordan.

"How come we didn't hear sooner?"

"Because I just got back."

Jordan took a cigarette out of his pocket and put the filter between his teeth. He held it like that, looking almost as if he were grinning.

"All right," Meyer said again. "I want to know more. Something here isn't regular."

"What more?" said Jordan. "You want his head on a platter?"

Bass looked at Sandy and Sandy looked down at his fingernails. Meyer looked shocked. Then he said, "All right. Jokes. All right. But you never been late before. What kept you?"

"I never had to do my own casing," said Jordan.

Bass had thought Jordan would say something else. He thought the natural answer would have been, I never had to kill two on one job. But Jordan said nothing else. He had closed his eyes, sighing, but kept holding the cigarette in his teeth like before, teeth showing, as if in a grin.

"I want to know more about it," said Meyer.

This is as bad as doing the thing, thought Jordan. And screw Meyer. Hold that talk. Better not say "screw you" to Meyer.

"More?" said Jordan. "What are you, a pervert?"

After that Jordan lit his cigarette, and everyone watched him doing it because it was the only thing that was happening. When Meyer talked again, he sounded carefully slow, almost uninterested.

"Something ailing you, Jordan?"

"I'm fine."

"You sound like you need a rest maybe."

"I don't want a rest."

"Oh."

"There's a point," said Bass, "when a man doesn't necessarily know that he needs a rest. Like when I get to the point—"

"Not the same thing," said Jordan. "I don't sell paper, you know that?"

Jordan smoked and looked at Bass because Bass happened to be most in line. Then he looked away from Bass and watched Sandy. Sandy was getting up and walked to the table where Jordan was sitting. He bent sideways a little and looked down at Jordan's suit.

"How come it's all buttoned, Sam?" he asked. "With this heat and all, Sam?"

"How come you wear an overcoat all the time, Sandy?"

Sandy said, "Because I'm a little bit nuts," and then he reached over and patted Jordan on the front where his stomach was.

He did it with the back of his hand and his big signet ring made a hard sound when it tapped.

It took less than a second, Jordan slapping the hand out of the way, and

he looked immediately the way he had looked before, but all the others—
shocked with the suddenness—did something. They sat up more, touched
tie, shifted seat.

"Since when," said Sandy, "are you carrying a gun, Sammy, while not
working?"

Jordan said something filthy, which was almost as much of a shock as the
other thing, his sudden slap.

The bug on the terrace had changed his sound. He wasn't bumping any
more but just buzzed. He was on his back, the way it sounded, buzzing.
And they could all hear the phone ringing. It was someplace far away and
somebody picked it up almost immediately. Meyer looked away, at a door
in the back, and everyone waited. Then he got up and left the big room.

Jordan had worked the coal out of the end of his cigarette and watched
it smoke itself out in the tray on his table. The dead stub was in his mouth.
Sandy asked Bass if he knew Schultz and when Bass answered no, he did-
n't know any Schultz, Sandy explained he was interested in buying some
bowling balls. This sounded like nonsense to Bass, coming from Sandy, but
Bass didn't feel detached enough to make anything of it. Then Meyer came
back.

He had a newspaper in his hand and sat down where he had sat before.

"Business call?" said Bass.

"That was Sherman." Meyer put the paper on top of his table. He looked
down at it, and talked that way. "I don't think you know Sherman. Just
somebody runs errands for me."

"How about it," said Jordan. "We done?"

"He just called," said Meyer, "I should look at the afternoon paper."

He leafed through it and said, "Only page nineteen."

Jordan got up and dropped his butt in the ashtray.

"I haven't slept much," he said.

"Sleep on this," said Meyer. "Kemp's alive."

12

"For a minute there," said Bass, "I thought he was going to pass out."

All three of them stood by their tables and looked out at the parking lot where Jordan was driving by and out to the highway.

"He just got pale," said Sandy.

"But *that* pale."

"You know, professional pride."

"Let's go to my office," said Meyer and he took the paper along.

They still had the view like before but the room was smaller and Jordan was no longer there. It changed the mood between them—nothing to do with feeling better or worse—but a change from a big room to a small room, a change from four people to three, a change of sitting closer together now, all to one side of Meyer's big desk. If there had been a stove, they might all have sat closely around it.

"What do you think?" said Bass and looked at Sandy. "I want to hear what's in that paper."

Meyer nodded and looked at it again. "He's alive, in a hospital. Duncaster County Hospital, says the article."

"Is that the county where that burg-something is located?"

"Sherman's finding out. What it says here, somebody downstairs got riled by the radio blaring—Kemp somehow upset his radio maybe, when he wasn't dead, and that radio kept blaring there on the floor."

"Maybe Jordan had turned it up on account of the shot," said Bass.

"No. He doesn't do that," said Sandy.

"I was saying," and Meyer rattled his paper, "the guy from downstairs says he went up to Kemp's door, after midnight sometime, and after knocking and knocking he tried the door and went in."

"And?" said Bass.

"And what? He found Kemp there. What else?"

"How'd they know it was Kemp?"

"Yeah. That's a nice one. Gunshot, so naturally cops. Just a minute," and Meyer looked for a paragraph.

"Here: *A search of the victim and his room offered no identifying information, and beyond the landlord's contribution of his tenant's name, nothing else could be learned about the victim. Only on the basis of a fingerprint check was the victim's full identity established several hours....*"

"He wouldn't talk?" asked Bass.

"It says here he's out. It says here—just a minute—it says he's in critical condition and in a coma. And partial paralysis, one side."

"Can he talk that way?"

They didn't know. They thought maybe he would die and if he did not die, maybe he would still not be able to talk. They knew nothing else. Only that Jordan had missed.

"Anything about the other one?" Sandy wanted to know.

"No. Just that there must have been another occupant in the apartment. They're looking for him."

"I hope Jordan did him right."

"He said two."

"He also said Kemp was done and he isn't."

They sat and smoked. Meyer folded the paper and looked at the two others. Then he looked only at Sandy. "What's he been like?"

"Like?" Sandy looked from one to the other and didn't know how to say it. "You know.... Just, I guess, normal."

"What I mean is...."

"He's never missed before, if that's what you mean."

"He shoots good, is that right?"

"Sure."

"Then why not this time?"

Sandy did not know what to answer.

"Here Kemp was lying in bed. The article says, he fell out of bed. Here he's in bed. Jordan walks in with his gun. No distance to worry about, nothing. He does a job and misses."

"Maybe somebody walked by in the hall outside," said Bass.

Sandy shook his head. "First of all, that wouldn't throw him. Second of all, he wouldn't fire."

"Does he use a silencer?"

"So what? He can hold the gun in his foot and not miss."

"All right," said Meyer. "So it's nothing like that." He sucked air through his nose and then coughed it out. "So let me ask you this. The way he was acting before."

"Getting pale?"

"No. That's normal. Before that."

"Professional pride."

"Whatever. I mean before that. The way he talked all of a sudden."

"He was tired. Like he said."

"He ever been like that before?"

"No.."

"He ever been tired before?"

Sandy shrugged. He crossed one leg over the other and shrugged again. "Ask him."

"That's what I'm talking about. I did and you heard how he got with me. Nasty."

"And the gun in his belt, remember?" said Bass.

Sandy got out of his chair and went to the window. He looked at the view, put his hands in his pockets, took them out again. Then he turned around.

"Look. He's an investment, you know? Think of it that way."

"I'm thinking he's maybe a liability."

"Just give it a little time, will you?"

"Maybe Kemp will die," said Bass, as if that made any difference.

Meyer didn't bother to answer. He looked at Sandy and then he closed his eyes.

"What I'm saying is, you're responsible."

Sandy got annoyed and put his hands back into his pockets. He pushed them deep as if looking for a coin.

"I never liked the whole thing from the start, Meyer, I told you that. You don't send a gun out doing his own casing and you don't send 'em out an hour after they come back from another job. I told you that, Meyer."

"What's so tough about casing?"

"How in hell do I know? All I'm saying is, you don't...."

"He gets paid good, don't he?"

"Yeah. He gets paid good," said Sandy and then he did not say anything else because he did not know how.

Meyer got up, walked around the desk, leaned his rear against it.

"I'm sending a man down to check this thing out."

Sandy put on his coat. "I'd leave it lie," he said. "It's too close to the time when they're looking the hardest."

"And give the fuzz all over that Penderburg the time of their lives running a hot trail?"

"Jordan doesn't leave a trail," Sandy said but felt foolish for having said it as soon as it was out. Nothing was quite so sure any more, about Jordan.

Meyer did not take it up. The point was too obvious. But he said, "There's only two things which are the worst with the kind of operation we run. First, if a gun misses. Which has happened. Second, if he leaves a trail. Which I hope hasn't happened. The first is bad enough because it leaves one too many who can talk his head off, and the second is worse because the trail leads to us. They catch one man, that's one less man. They catch wind of an organization, that's everything down the drain." Meyer got up and sighed. "So I'll handle that end. Penderburg. You check out Jordan."

"I'll look him over," said Sandy and went to the door.

"And let me hear tonight."

"What?" said Sandy. "Tonight what?"

"How he is. What you think."

The trouble with Meyer and his kind, they handle things like there are no human beings in it. "He'll sleep all afternoon," said Sandy. "I'll look him over tonight."

"Your Wednesday afternoon routine can wait," said Meyer. "You check Jordan out now and to hell with everything else."

Sandy did not argue. Meyer was being a bastard about this, rushing things because he was nervous, and running it as if there were no human beings in it. Jordan wasn't going to run amuck if unattended this afternoon, and Sandy's own Wednesday routine also would not throw anything out of kilter.

"All right," said Sandy. "Unless he's asleep."

"Check him out," Meyer said again.

"All right."

"Because if Kemp doesn't go on his own, Jordan will have to finish it."

Jordan was not asleep but sat in his room, by the window, and looked at the building opposite. He could see the flat roof line and the flat-line windows under that. On the windows he read Optic Supply Co., Central Dental Supply, and after a skip of one black window, J. S. Mackiewisznitz. What Mackiewisznitz sold Jordan did not know. This was time in between. Jordan sat and looked at the building opposite.

This was not time in between. Jinx job. There's no time between jinx jobs because when the jinx hangs on the job's never over.... Maybe Kemp will die by himself?

Jordan took a small pair of scissors from the shelf over his sink and cut his nails. Then he put the scissors back, gave a twist to the faucet by the sink, sat down again.

This was clearly not time in between like the other times. I'm waiting too much for what will come next, he thought. It feels lousy. Talk to Sandy? No. He says less than I do. Jordan thought about Penderburg, then the girl, and could not keep the two apart. It made him feel irritable. He sat and looked at the building opposite and his mood jumped back and forth, from screamy to dull. He got up and twisted the faucet again, which hurt his hand. The two have nothing to do with each other. She, one thing that happened, finished and clean. The job, one thing that happened, not finished.

When the knock came on the door Jordan asked who it was and when he heard Sandy's voice he opened the door. He had a brief moment when he knew that he did not want to see Sandy now but when that made no immediate sense, Jordan acted like always; quiet, wait what he says, and what might he like.

"Not sleeping, I see. How you feel, Sammy?"

"Why?"

That was not acting like always. Jordan knew it, but not till it happened, and Sandy knew it, but did not want to give it weight. He laughed and said, "Was a stupid question. You're not sleeping because you're not tired and that's how you feel."

Jordan nodded and closed the door. Screamy and dull, back and forth. But I slept good last night....

"Leave the door open," said Sandy. "First off, we get your dough, okay?"

"First off?"

"Sure. You just got back and we'll have a beer, huh?"

"Oh," said Jordan. "Yes."

"We'll drive down to my place and you wait in the bar down the block and I run over and get the money."

Jordan thought, yes, there it is again, and I almost forgot. There's so much for you, Sam fellow, and no more. You don't show your face here, and we don't talk to you there, and with all the money you're making, why kick?

In the meantime Jordan did not answer, though he always answered when Sandy said the usual things. That's conversation. But he did not answer, this time, which was the first sign, and one which Sandy missed.

They drove to Sandy's neighborhood and stopped at a corner. Sandy pointed and said, "You wait in the bar there while I run over and get the money."

"That's all right," said Jordan and did not get out of the car.

"That one," said Sandy. "Don't you want a drink?"

"You got a bar in your alley," said Jordan. "I'll have a drink there."

"You mean, go along?"

"And to get my money."

"Sammy, I think...."

"You think what?"

Now, of course, it was clear. The boy should be asleep, thought Sandy. Natural, to get irritated. And if I push this fast and he goes home to sleep, it won't ruin the afternoon's routine. Meanwhile, better keep him in harness.

Sandy stopped in front of his bowling alley and said, "You're not going in with me. That's just sense."

"Nobody knows me here any more," Jordan said. "That's just sense," and he got out of the car and walked into the building.

Sandy watched Jordan go in and did nothing. He was not sure if there might not be a scene. But after this, starting right now in private, I'll have to show that son of a bitch how to get back in harness. He went after Jordan who was waiting for him at the counter with the cigars.

"The office," said Sandy, and went to the back of the counter.

There was a man doing paper work in the office and Sandy told him to get out for a minute. Jordan closed the door after the man and Sandy went to the small safe. He didn't open it but turned around.

"Give me that gun, Sam."

"I'm not carrying a gun," said Jordan.

He looked at Sandy and Sandy looked Jordan up and down. He walked up to him when Jordan took one step back. The desk touched him from behind and Jordan sat down on it.

"I'm not carrying a gun," he said again and then he smiled. "And if I were, Sandy, do you think you could frisk me?"

He's playing games. The bastard is playing games with me, as if he and I didn't know each other!

"Sandy," said Jordan. He wasn't smiling any more and his voice was low. "I don't want to act like you and I don't know each other. I'm just, it's just that kind of time. Coming back like this, the deal sour..." and he opened his coat so that Sandy could see there was no gun anywhere. "Okay, Sandy?" he said. "Okay?"

But Sandy missed it. The switch was too fast for him, and the afternoon ruined for him, and Jordan better get back into harness.

"Don't pull a trick like that on me again," he said and turned away. "Come over here and get your dough."

He kneeled by the safe, opened it, took out a green box which he put on the floor. He hadn't heard Jordan's steps but then he saw his shoes next to the box. He didn't see Jordan's face and didn't know that Jordan had almost said, I don't want the money, and when he did hear Jordan talk it was games again.

"Are you in a great hurry?" Jordan said.

Sandy missed the tone because he was tense. "Yeh," he said. "That guy outside is my auditor and I pay him by the hour." Then he opened the green box.

Jordan went down on one knee and Sandy counted out fifties and hundreds. He put them on the floor next to the box and snapped the box shut again.

"Pick it up," he said. "Come on."

"That was four," said Jordan. "I get eight."

And if he's edgy there's one way to remind him what this is all about. "Kemp isn't dead yet," he said.

"One of them is."

"He doesn't count. You know that."

"Kemp's almost dead," said Jordan. "Or as good as dead."

"Don't argue with me. Take the four gee."

But Jordan was not interested in the money. He was interested in arguing.

"It was eight."

Sandy hitched himself around and leaned on one hand. "He isn't dead yet. But he will be. Like you said. Now listen. If he doesn't go by himself," Sandy watched Jordan and thought his face tightened up, "then you go back there and get done with the job."

At first Jordan did not answer. He looked down and watched his hands fold the bills double and then he put the bills into his pocket. He rubbed his left eye with one finger.

"Who said that?"

"Meyer."

"And you?"

"Me too."

"And all that brings the other four gee?"

"Right. Like I said."

Sandy locked the box back into the safe and the two men got up. "Clear now?" said Sandy.

Jordan brushed at his knees.

"You got all of this clear the way it's going to be?"

"We'll see," said Jordan.

Sandy said nothing. He had heard Jordan give wrong answers, or no answers at all, but he had not seen Jordan be cagey before. The pressure gets all of them different. This one argues. Nasty talk. Bound to happen with an unfinished job. Best thing will be, he goes back to that Pender-place, gets it done, puts some vinegar in it. Did the job cold and not liking it, that was the trouble. Sandy sighed.

"Well, what are you going to do with all that dough, Sam?"

"I think I'll spend it. Wouldn't you?"

Now it's glib. Whole afternoon shot and it's talk on top of that. I'm a grease monkey and this bastard is engine trouble. Overheated engine trouble.

"Let's go and have this beer," said Sandy.

"That won't cost much."

"You want the beer or don't you want the beer?"

"Aren't you worried?"

"Huh?"

"Worried. Who might see you with me, and in the daytime."

"Jeesis Christ, Sam, will you lay off that idiot talk?"

Jordan laughed. Sandy did not like that either, not that sound, the way Jordan was doing it, but the case was a clear case of nerves and maybe the whole thing would solve itself if Jordan felt he should go home and to bed. But Jordan did not want that. He wanted the beer they had been talking about and to relax in the meantime, talking. That's what it did for him, he said. It relaxed him to be talking.

They left the bowling alley and drove to a place called the Dawdler's Bar. There were several places, like this bar, where Jordan could go, or Jordan and Sandy could go, and there would be no problems about it. They drank beer in a booth and Sandy put coins in the juke box. Jordan faced the other way, toward the street side, and where the sun slanted in he could see dust move in the light. Then he watched the juke box which had colored lights dancing and spiraling, and after he had watched for a while he discovered the system. The flickers and spirals repeated themselves every three-quarters of a minute.

Sandy thought about Jordan's four thousand dollars and what he would do with it if he had just earned it. Sandy had no idea what he would do.

"Another round?" he said.

"No."

"You say no?"

They had not talked, sitting there, and now the talking was not any easier than the mute part before.

"Let's go to Monico's," Jordan said.

There were several places, such as Monico's, where it was not all right for Jordan to go. Sandy might go there, or perhaps someone like Meyer, a different echelon when it came to the social. Jordan was not known there, which was as it should be, and he was not wanted there, which only made sense.

"They're closed," said Sandy. "It's afternoon and the place is still closed."

Sandy said other things, much more to the point, but Jordan did not even get nasty again. He got up and said, "Are you coming?"

"But it's closed, damn it."

"Are you coming?"

"Of course I'm coming."

"Then we'll get in, won't we?"

They got in. A man in shirt sleeves came to the door; when he saw Sandy through the glass of the door he opened up and said, "Hi, Sandy." He did not know Jordan and just nodded at him, a little bit puzzled.

"You see?" Sandy waved at the low room, dark with none of the lamps turned on. "Closed. Get it? Nothing."

Bar, with the bottles shrouded under a long, white sheet, empty tables, empty chairs, empty bandstand in one corner. Frescoes with goats and minor gods capering, grape garlands, looking dumb and useless with nobody looking at them.

"You're a little early," said the man. "They're still rehearsing."

Sandy did not say anything but Jordan said, "Still rehearsing? Where?"

So they went to the back. They went through a smoking room where you could hear the toilets going off and from there to a room in back with the stage one length of the wall. There were couches, easy chairs, little tables. All the seating equipment faced the same way.

"You want a drink?" asked the man. "Frank isn't here to mix up anything but if you want a bottle...."

"Bring the bottle," said Sandy. "Hell yes. I was going to say bring the bottle."

"Bourbon, wasn't it?"

"Hell, yes, bourbon."

The room was dark except for what light came from the stage. The stage wasn't lit for effect, just efficiency. The footlights were off and the two overhead lamps made a dull yellow light on the row of girls who stood on the stage listening to the thin man with the longish, elaborate hairdo. He had black hair, and wore a white shirt, black pants, white socks, black shoes. He explained the dance.

The girls wore almost anything, but very little of it. Jersey striped this way, jersey striped that way, blue shorts, red shorts, leotards, heels. They all wore heels. The piano went thumpety thump and some of the girls did something with one leg and the hip.

"*That's* it," said the man with the hairdo. "Work it *through*. On the thumpety *thump* you got to work it *through*."

"Mary and Jack," said one of them. "It's less work lying down."

"*Pu-leeze!*"

It was not very hard because it was not really dancing. It was mostly display. And they were all built alike and for the same thing.

And maybe this isn't a bad turn at all, Sandy thought, because the place is dark and won't open for hours and by then he'll be out of here. He hasn't slept much and isn't used to much liquor. He didn't like hearing about having muffed the job and less, maybe, having to finish it. This'll tire him out....

"The second one from the left," said Jordan. "That's Lois, isn't it?"

"Yeh, that's Lois."

From the distance she looked like all the other ones. Round rear, smooth thighs, and the standard-sized breasts.

"That why you came here?" Sandy asked.

Jordan had not even known that the girl worked in the Monico. "Yes," he said. "That's why I came here."

"Listen, Sam. You remember I told you she and Fido's brother...."

"But she works here."

"What's that got to do with it?"

"Nothing," said Jordan. "And that's why I'm looking."

Jordan got up before Sandy could stop him and walked to the stage. He stood at one end of it and watched.

"Who's he looking at?" said the girl next to Lois. "You?"

"Legs," said Lois and when the piano went thumpety thump she was late with the thing she was supposed to do.

"*Pu-leeze!*"

They all started over.

"You know him?" asked the girl.

"Once."

"Who is he?"

"You don't want him. He's with Sandy."

"Gee—"

"*Pu-leeze!* You are not coming *through!*" The man with the hairdo glared and then he yelled, "Like *this!*" and did the coming through thing better than the line-up had done it.

"I'm sure he's looking at you."

"He can go to hell."

"*Stop!*"

The piano stopped and all the girls stopped. All the bosoms went up and down, because of the exertion and all the girls stood on their long standard legs, one straight and one cocked.

"*What* did you say about me?" asked the man with the hairdo.

"I said you did that *well,*" said Lois.

"Because I *practice.*"

"Dry-run Charley," somebody said, and there might have been envy in it.

But the man with the hairdo did not take it that way and got venomous. He said how more vertical dancing and less horizontal dancing might get them much farther than they thought because a good dancer might even get married some day and last a lifetime.

Jordan stood to one side of the stage and looked at the cigarette in his hand. He felt no interest in the Monico any more and wished he were somewhere else.

"And now, *positions.*"

They all complained and did very badly on the thumpety *thump,* and in a while the man with the hairdo gave up and said rehearsal was over. All the girls walked off the stage and some of them looked down at Jordan and a few of them looked farther back into the room. Sandy must be up, thought Jordan, and walking this way.

"All over," said Sandy behind him. "Let's go."

Jordan caught the relief in the voice, and he caught how Sandy looked at the stage and how Lois looked back. What a keen, idle memory, Jordan thought, remembering that pitiful time, that once in her apartment.

"There's a back to this place, isn't there?" he said. "For more business."

"Sam, I've told you and you got eyes to see this place isn't open for...."

"How's Lois?"

"Lois."

"Yes. How's Lois. She like the work?"

Sandy looked away and held his breath for a moment. The problem was now that the matter was partly personal, a much harder matter than just dealing with Jordan, important property. But think of it that way: he was property, and because of a wrong job and no time yet for relaxing, in a funk. A matter of discipline. Nothing personal.

"That why you came here? Lois?"

"You asked that before," said Jordan. "You remember asking me?"

"All right, Sammy. All right." He told Jordan to wait for a minute and went to the back part of the place, the part Jordan had talked about.

Behind the door next to the stage was a corridor with a long line of doors. There was faint, artificial light, and a faint, artificial odor. Powder, perfume. Behind the first door Sandy could hear the girls talking, a chatter without any words and as uniform as their looks when they worked on the stage.

Sandy knocked on the door and when somebody asked, who is it, he said his name and then the door opened. The room was full of tables with naked bulbs; the girls were sitting around putting on faces, taking off faces, and some were changing clothes.

"I'll be right out," called Lois.

Sandy waited in the door and when Lois came she smiled at him. She still had her jersey on, and the shorts, but was barefoot. "You got rid of him?" she asked.

"No."

"No? You can't stay?"

"Close the door."

She came out into the corridor and closed the door.

"He wants you," said Sandy.

"Crap," she said. "Oh crap." Then she noticed how angry Sandy was, how he had one eye squinted smaller than the other and how he kept pulling one cuff of his shirt.

"Is the bouncer here yet?"

"I don't know. But if it's Benny's day, he comes early. He might be here now."

"That would be nice," said Sandy. "If it's Benny, that would be just right." Then he told Lois he would look for the bouncer and she should go down to room three in a while and not worry about it, and how she should behave. Then he went to look for the bouncer.

Benny was in the linen closet where he hung up his clothes and changed into his tux. He also had a mirror there, to check how the cummerbund looked and how his hair was arranged.

"Don't you knock?" he said. When he saw it was Sandy he wished he had said something stronger.

"I got a job for you," said Sandy.

"I'm working for you? Since when am I...."

"You know Jordan? Guy works for me?"

Benny put his hands on his hips and then let them hang again. Then he put them back on his hips. "So?"

Then Sandy told him. Benny did not like Sandy any better now than at any time, but he said, "Sure, feller. Anything to keep the club clean and for decent folk."

Then Sandy went back to the room with the stage, where Jordan was waiting. He stood by the footlights, on the wrong side of them, and the room was much darker now. More lights were turned off and nobody else was there.

He looks like somebody asking for a job, thought Sandy. The way he stands there and waits. The picture was neither quite true nor did it satisfy Sandy. For the first time that he could remember his picture of Jordan was mixed up. It used to be Jordan, shy and quiet, then less shy and much more quiet. Now this. Now this ill-fitting, sharp-sitting way of his, where nothing matched, where the meanness came from nowhere, and it showed that Jordan did not know what to do with it.

"Well? You want her?"

Jordan turned and sucked breath through his nose. "Yes," he said. "Why not?" and they walked to the door in the back.

It had sounded like a real question. It would have surprised Jordan had he gotten an answer, but he would have been grateful for an answer. He felt so little at the moment, he wished somebody would say something to him.

The room was number three, with big drapes over a window and a big pillow pile in one corner. There was no bed, just the vast pillow pile with two low seats next to it and a small table. There was a radio and Jordan sat down by the table and played with the knobs. He got a sudden loud blare of music and turned it down too far so that it only murmured. What a lousy sound, he thought. There's no sound as lousy as that mumble, and he clicked it off.

The girl said, "Hi, Sam," behind him and closed the door. She still wore the same things as before, the little shorts and the jersey with stripes stretching around her. She went to the pile of pillows and sat down on it.

"You see that cabinet back there?" she said. "There's liquor in there. And fixings."

"Oh. You want some?"

He acts like a hick, she thought. She crossed her legs and looked at him without smiling. She did not remember him being so slow.

He got a bottle, two glasses, and poured.

"No," she said. "Not for me. For you."

Jordan sat down on his seat and watched the liquor make a commotion inside the glass. He swirled the glass and then took a small sip, as a gesture.

"I watched you dance," he said.

"How'd you get in?"

He looked up, but not for long. He watched the liquor in the glass. "How've you been, Lois?"

"Fine."

"Ah. That's good." He looked up once and saw her scratching behind an ear. He looked away again, because she had not smiled.

"Well," he said, "you like it here?"

"Huh?"

"You like it? What you do."

"What kind of a question...."

"When did you get up today?" he said.

"What kind of a question is that?"

"Just, I just wondered," he said. He gave a small, interrupted shrug. "Just in general. How you spend a day."

"I work and I sleep. Like everybody."

"And it's like that all day, full with it?"

"Jesus, Sam, what are you talking about?"

"Just a question. Normal question. Not everybody does the same work and has the same day."

"That's right," she said. "And how's yours?"

He took a drink and then blew air through his lips. "I don't work all the time. I don't think I work as often as you do."

"Why, you creepy son of a bitch!"

He looked at her, blinked a few times. Then he took a cigarette out and lit it. "We're just talking," he said. "Spending time. Why get sore with me?"

"Because you asked for it?"

He looked at the smoke make a spiral at the end of the cigarette and then he shook his head. He smiled and shook his head.

"What you come here for?" she asked.

"I know. You don't want me and how do I take it. That what you asked?"

This time he looked up and smiled at her and she hated his face. She could say nothing.

"And how do you take it, sitting here with me?" he asked this time.

She felt vicious but had a rule against that, so it sounded prim. "If you're going to do a thing well you got to perfect the right habits. Good work habits. And that's how I can sit here with you."

He took a hot drag on his cigarette and talked the smoke out. "There aren't that many habits," he said. "There comes a point and no habit will do."

It was getting too serious for her and nothing was getting done. For a moment she wondered why he had come but she had work habits and thought she knew. But so far, nothing accomplished....

"Why don't you forget about work," she said and made a smile.

He looked up too late for the smile but he saw her lean back on the pile of pillows and stretch out. She did it well. When she did this, it said, when I lie down you want to lie down.

"Sit here," she said. "I can't see you."

"That's all right," said Jordan. "I'm fine."

Her work habits won't do her now, he thought. It's a painful sight.... He was done and he wanted to leave. The professional part which would come next did not interest him and he did not want to watch the girl become more forced and he himself awkward.

"Sam?"

"Yes."

"Come on." He did not answer right away and she lay on her back, listening for something else. It's time, she thought. Goddamn all of them. "Come on, Sammy," she said again.

This time she sat up and pulled off her jersey.

Like peeling a fruit, he thought, a smooth-skinned fruit. She sat in a small, white brassiere, the red shorts, and then she arched to unhook herself.

"You still have your shoes on," he said.

She held still for a moment, letting it grow that she was being used, misused and insulted. Then she yanked one shoe off and threw it at him.

"You lousy son of a bitch!"

Jordan leaned out of the way and got up. He felt depressed and felt wrong for having stayed this long. He got up and went toward the door but the girl was in the way. She was loud and foul, very loud, and would not let him pass. She screamed insults at him with a high timbre as if calling for help.

Jordan put his hands on her arms to move her out of the way. He felt wrong and depressed. "We just talked," he said. "And it wasn't any good."

"Damn you," she yelled, "damn you, you bastard creep," and the door jumped open.

There was the bouncer, small-hipped with cummerbund and farther back in the dark hall, Sandy was there, and talk, talk, talk, sharp and fast to fit all this. And why, thought Jordan, why....

He got in one good punch; it felt like a good one, in his arm and shoulder, but suddenly the girl was silent, they all were, and it killed all of Jordan's intent. Sandy back in the hall, looking, the girl back by the wall, looking, Benny as close as he needed to be, looking, looking, concentrated and cold. Is that what they see—like Paul, or like Kemp—is that what they see, when I step up to them? No. The bouncer does this for love—I've *never.* I never knew they disliked me this much....

Jordan got beaten badly. He had doubled over and had started to cry though nobody saw this because of all the smear on his face and the method in general. Sandy was dim in the hall but was the only one Jordan saw in the end. This was perhaps due to the angle. Then Sandy walked away with the girl. Benny—as a fact—hardly mattered.

13

"Can you make it?"

He could make it. He got up and stood. Sandy let go of his arm and held out a wet rag. "Wipe yourself."

Jordan wiped and gave the rag back.

"Can you make it?"

"Why? Why was this—"

"Rule of the house. The bouncer thought...."

Jordan did not hear the rest because he was not listening. *I did not know they disliked me this much.*

"Can you make it?"

"Sure."

"Can you drive?"

"Sure."

"Here. Here's the keys. Take my car."

"Sure."

"Maybe I should drive you home?"

"Sure. I mean, no. I'm sure no."

"I got something else to...."

"Sure."

When Jordan was in his room he sat on the bed for a while and felt the pain start. He went to the sink and had a very hard time opening the faucet because he had shut it so tight earlier. He washed and it started to hurt more.

He saw that it was fairly dark outside and that soon he would go to sleep. He felt strangely comfortable with his pain because it was strong and concrete. That way, he did not think. But he did a few things, step by step and uncomplicated by thinking, even without any clear, urgent feeling.

He walked along the wall, down the stairs, to the drugstore at the counter where he bought a styptic stick. At the adjoining counter he bought one envelope and a stamp. In the back, on the shelf for the telephone books, he wrote on the envelope, putting down as much as he knew: *Betty. Diner on Third Avenue. Penderburg, Pa.*

He took a bill out of his pocket and put it inside the envelope. He stamped, sealed, and dropped the letter into the mailbox outside. *Was it five C? I think it was five C.* He walked home. He worried about the money, and why five C instead of one. *Who was she? Why not more. A grand. He* went to his room and, on his bed, fell asleep almost immediately.

One week later Kemp was still alive. And they had found Paul under the bridge, in the culvert, because of the smell. It was now a gang killing with solution imminent and the guard around Kemp in the hospital was heavy. Kemp stayed in a coma but breathed inside his oxygen tent.

Jordan stayed in his room, on the bed, and sometimes he loosened the faucet a little so that he could watch, by turning his head, how the drops came slowly. He cleaned his guns a few times, in order to concentrate. He knew how to make a proper job of this, a good craftsman's job, though it meant more than that. And I'm going to tilt right out of my mind if I don't hold on to the few things I know.

But it did not help. What he knew felt jinxed. What he knew for these days were things he had never paid attention to before: the bedsheet wrinkled under his back, the stain on his towel from washing his face, the morning noise, noon noise, and evening noise three stories down on the street. He liked the noon noise best because it was one car, two cars, one laugh, two voices, all distinct from each other. He never looked at his ceiling, because it made him feel flattened and small. Once or twice, it seemed, he had a fever.

He called Sandy from the drugstore, for information. There wasn't any. There had been no change.

"How's your head?"

"Much better. Thank you."

"Where you calling from?"

"The drugstore, here at my corner."

"When you called yesterday, you called from the same place?"

"Yes."

"Now listen to me, Sam. Stop making these lousy calls from the same place all the time if you know what I'm talking about. There is... Stop interrupting. There isn't a thing gained by these calls you keep making except maybe you get spotted once or twice too often. First news, I get word to you."

"Sandy, I can't just...."

"You loused it up. Not me. And stop calling."

"It's been over a week. There's got to be some...."

"When Meyer decides what next, you'll hear about it. Listen, I got a tournament on."

"How's Lois?"

"What you say?"

"Good-by," and Jordan hung up.

He stayed in the booth for a while, turned to the blank wall. A line of sweat moved down his cheek, and he stuck out his tongue to lick. He would not call Sandy again. The upsetting thing was how it came over him, how a faint sting happened and next he would say something which he had not thought up ahead of time. Stupid things, without feeling to them. How's Lois....

He called Bass. He had no difficulties with Bass but also learned nothing. Bass did not like to be called by Jordan, he had no information, and he said all that. He said, "If you call here again I'm going to do something about it."

"How are you?" said Jordan. "Are you all right?"

"What?"

"I won't call you again," said Jordan, and hung up.

Next day he called Meyer. Jordan ordered a hamburger at the drugstore counter and while it was on the grill went to the booth and called Meyer. Meyer was not easy. Jordan had to call three numbers and with the third one he had to wait a while till the girl went to see if the call was wanted. Jordan ran his tongue around the inside of his cheek, where a cut wasn't healed and it tasted like metal. He spat on the floor and put his foot over it.

If he says Kemp is dead, that will change everything. It will mean time in between like always. No. It'll be Sam Smith this time, Sam Smith doing between-time vacationing. The thought pleased him though he had no idea where he might go.

"Hullo?"

"Meyer?"

"Yes, who...."

"This is Smith. I...."

"What?"

"Jordan. I meant Jordan. I said Smith because...."

"Who in hell gave you leave to call here? Don't you got any better sense than...."

"The reason I said Smith...."

"Shut up!"

Jordan did, feeling patient. The dullness of patience was something new he had learned. He had not needed patience before.

"...be sure you'll know before long what's what, if anything happens. Meanwhile, there's nothing. And meanwhile I want nothing from you!"

"I mean, is there no plan?"

"Didn't you hear what I said just a minute ago? And we don't do this kind of business on the phone, damn your crazy head!"

"I've got to know...."

"You sit tight and wait like the rest of us!" and Meyer hung up.

Jordan forgot to stop for his hamburger and walked out on the street.

The sun shone and he thought he might get a new room, with a new view, and more sun perhaps. I might spend more time there. Sam Smith unemployed. He watched himself walking past a store window and thought he looked like anybody. But if no one believes me, how can I be somebody else? Paul thinks I'm Smith and he's dead. Kemp thinks I'm Smith and doesn't count. I mean, how can you talk to Kemp, down under in the oxygen tent. What's Betty's last name...?

14

"When I think of it," said Jane, "when I imagine I have over four hundred smackers—you know what I'd do?"

"There's a customer," said Betty.

"Where?"

"The short one there. The little boy," and she pointed to where the head stuck up over the counter.

"And I bet he wants orange juice."

"Orange juice," said the boy. "A small one."

Jane got the orange juice and Betty looked out the stand to the other side of the street. There were planted palms, there were convertibles moving, and some of the buildings across the way had Spanish tile roofs. There was sun over everything and the beach was behind the next block.

"I was saying...." said Jane.

"But I told you, honey; I told you right when I came when I told you all about it. I said, Jane, some of this is for you."

"Let me finish," and Jane folded her arms, leaned against the cooler, and looked up at the coconuts which hung on strings and had faces on them. "If I had that money," she said, "you know what I'd do?"

"No," said Betty, very patient.

"I'd go to Oregon, is what I would do, for the apples. I want to see nothing but apples and forget all about oranges."

Betty had heard that several times before but she smiled. "It's nice here."

The other girl didn't answer that and then they had customers.

After a while they sat down on their stools and Jane smoked a cigarette. Betty drank orange juice.

"You know what really kills me about this?"

"About what?" said Betty.

"About all this," and she swept her arm over everything: stand, juicers, street, traffic, palms, sunshine. "The sticky fingers," she said. "I got these constantly sticky fingers."

"Oh. From the orange juice."

"Just say juice, Betty. The other goes without saying."

They had customers and didn't talk for a while. Betty had a small pain in her back, from bending down into the cooler.

"It's four o'clock, honey," said Jane. "Don't forget your doctor's appointment."

"It's only fifteen minutes. The last time I walked it, I got there...."

"You know what I'd do if I had a doctor's appointment, let's say an appointment at eight in the evening? You know what I'd do at, let's say seven in the *morning?*"

"You'd worry about it all day."

"Ha. At seven in the morning I'd call the boss, and I'd tell him—"

"You got a customer, Jane."

She got to the office in time but then had a long wait. After the doctor she took a long walk and when she took the bus into Miami she got off at the wrong stop. It was almost dark when she got to the rooming house and she walked slowly. There was a palm tree next to the house and she could hear the leaves scraping.

"Honey?"

She stopped on the porch steps and saw Jane on the swing. The swing clattered when the girl got up and Betty saw Jane dressed to go out.

"He's here," said Jane.

"What?"

"The one, you know. The one you been telling about."

All Betty said was, "Gee—"

"He don't look rich."

"What's he look like?"

It sounded one way to Jane and was meant another way by Betty. It had slipped out that way because she could not remember his face too well.

"I don't know. Pale, I guess."

"Oh."

"You better go in now. He's been there an hour." Jane put the strap of her bag over her shoulder. "I won't be back before two."

"You don't have to do that, Jane."

"Are you kiddin'? 'Bye now," and she started down the steps. "Wait a minute, I almost forgot!"

Betty stopped in the door and waited. Jane came close and then, "What did the doctor say, honey?"

"Three months."

"Three? Was it him?"

"How could it be?" Betty went into the house.

She could not tell whether he seemed especially pale because the light was almost gone in the room. She saw him get up from a chair and come toward her. When he was close she saw he was smiling.

"Remember me?" he said.

She had the feeling, for a moment, that she did not.

"What a question, Sam! Why, what a question!"

She thought he would want to kiss her but he did nothing. He stood there smiling and she was still struck by that. His smile was a stretch of his face, though this did not make a false smile but only an awkward one. He was embarrassed, she felt, and it embarrassed her. She stepped up quickly and gave him a kiss. He gave her a kiss and straightened up again. He deserves more, she thought, and knows it, but he is a gentleman.

"I guess you got the money," he said, "didn't you?"

"It was you, wasn't it, Sam?"

"Surprised you, huh?"

He was still smiling, as if trying very hard. The girl reached up with a small gesture and stroked his face. Then she turned away. She went to the couch and sat down there. "Sam," she said, "come and sit with me, Sam."

She looked down into her lap when he sat down next to her and so could not see him at all. "I don't know what to say, Sam." She smiled, but did not show him her face.

"I don't either," he said.

She leaned over to the side of the couch and turned on the radio. "Have you eaten yet?" she asked him. "What I mean is, did you just come to town, Sam?"

He did not answer because the radio was coming alive and he leaned across her and snapped it off. When he sat up again and saw her face, he quickly smiled again. "I don't like it," he said. "I'd rather talk to you," and after that, after there was more silence, he said, "even if we have nothing to say."

Then he took her arm in his hand and held it. "I've just come to town," he said. "Yes."

"I think it's wonderful that your business...."

"I came just to see you."

She pressed her arm against her side, to give his hand a squeeze. He could smell the slight acid odor of orange peel.

"What's your last name?" he asked her.

She was very startled and laughed.

"Mine's Smith," he said. "I've come to see you."

"Evans. Elizabeth Evans."

"Mine's Smith," he said again, and then he took out a cigarette which both seemed to end this conversation and also to make it a point of importance.

How nutty, she thought. We both should have laughed about this name thing because actually, it could be funny.

"Now we'll eat," he said.

She was glad he had brought that up because it was a topic and something to do, and she said since coming to Miami she had not been out yet at all and so didn't know where they might go.

"I'd like us to eat here," he said. "I don't mind waiting. I'll sit and watch."

She did not mind that either though she was sorry she had nothing special. Peas from a can, and there were hot dogs, there was...

"It's all right," he said. "Whatever. Put your housecoat on."

"What?"

"Put your housecoat on. You're home."

She laughed and he smiled back and in a way, she thought, what he says just sounds strange at first but then really isn't.

He sat on the couch and by turning his head he could see the head of the palm outside the window, the one which kept rattling its fronds. The window had the same curtains which he had seen before in the girl's Penderburg room. Jordan, as he knew he would, felt well now. He sat, looking at everything, the room with the curtains and the used furniture, the girl moving back and forth in the kitchen alcove, and while he saw mostly her back he also felt that much more at ease because of that. As if they had known each other a long time and had no need for the special. He saw nothing cheap, common, crummy, or little, nothing of the pathetically small in his choice of an evening; he saw none of that because it was not there. It was not there, because the pressure and effort which had brought him this far had been so sharp and tremendous.

She put ice-water in glasses next to the plates, which was a restaurant habit, and she served him first and kept watching his plate, which was no habit at all but was natural. After eating they had instant coffee, and they talked about how quickly she had left—two days after he had sent the money—and about how long he could stay this time. He would tell her, he said, he would tell her soon.

She pressed no point, though she asked personal questions. Why shouldn't she, was Jordan's feeling. I'm Smith. I am out of town a lot, because I travel on business; I come home here between times, because I have time in between.

The evening was dull, slow, warm, and harmless. That way, it lasted and lasted.

It gave Betty time to think of a number of things. Four hundred, she thought, maybe four hundred is enough. If I knew him better. I might ask him about it, tell him about it. He might even help. He's a gentleman, really. He's gentle.

When Jane knocked on the door it was not two yet. But there had been nothing for Jane to do after the movie was over and she'd thought: It's my room as much as hers and who is Smith anyway. She knocked, with a lot of purpose, and then she called through the door.

"That's all right," Betty called back. "Come on in." And when she's in, Betty thought, she's going to say something like, how are you two lovebirds, or something.

"Well, well, well," said Jane. "How are you two bugs in a rug?"

Jane was the only one who laughed, though Jordan got up from the couch and said something about Jane might want to sit there, and Betty said, wouldn't it be nice to have some iced tea.

She made iced tea, and Jane sat down on the couch and told Jordan to sit down next to her. Then she talked a lot, touching her hair, hiking a strap, peeling the lacquer off one of her nails. But she watched Jordan all the time and tried budging him in various ways. It's a good thing, thought Betty, that he's calm and a gentleman, or I would feel badly embarrassed for Jane.

"So, how you doing?" said Jane. "I mean, in your business." Her voice had a splash sound and was too loud.

"Fine," said Jordan. "Nothing special."

"You down on business, Mister Smith?"

"No. Just a visit."

"Oh. You salesmen. I bet everybody else thinks you're down on business, huh?" and when he did not answer, "Buttons, isn't that what you told me, Betty?"

"Yes," said Betty from the sink.

"Is it a good business, Mister Smith?"

"No. Not very."

"Oh, I bet you're just saying that, Mister Smith, aren't you?"

Jordan got up and went over to the sink. He gave the faucet a twist and then went back to sit down again.

"Well, I do beg to differ," said Jane, "about the way you interpret your business, because I do happen to know about that generous gift you sent Betty. It made Betty very happy, didn't it, Betty?"

"Yes, very. You want me to put lemon on the table?"

"You know what I'd do, Mister Smith, if I got a gift like that from an admirer? I'm not saying I got an admirer, you understand, but...."

"You'd go to Oregon to see the apples," said Betty.

"Well, that was very funny. You haven't got the tea strong enough, I don't think. Tell me, Mister Smith, are you married?"

"No."

"Ah! But divorced."

"I've never been married."

"A woman hater!" and she laughed with a clickety sound. "Is he a woman hater, Betty?"

What had been there for Jordan was thinning out. It was thinning out into an embarrassing daydream. A time in a hot room with a view of a dusty palm in the next lot, and the girl by the sink talking flat and about something hard to remember. He would remember everything Jane was saying.

"Tell me, Mister Smith, what's the name of your company?"

"Don't you want your iced tea, Jane?"

"Betty, you keep interrupting. Tell me, Mister Smith, will you come often? Is it one yet?"

"Yes, it's one," said Jordan.

"You must hear this program! The Two Sleepy People, and it's the swooniest...."

"Leave it off."

"What?"

She had the radio on and Jordan got up and clicked it off again.

"You mean you don't like music, Mister Smith? And I thought, right from the start when I saw you, Mister Smith, a sweet, quiet gentleman like...."

"Leave."

"What did you say?"

"Leave. Come back tomorrow."

"Why, you must be out of...."

"Here's ten dollars. Go to a hotel for the night."

Jane got up and when she stood up she started to laugh, loud and straight into Jordan's face. *"That's* a switch! What do you take me for giving me money and telling...." She stopped talking because she did not really feel brazen any more, watching Jordan. He was somebody else now...

"Boy," she said. "These button men—" and gagged on it with a sudden jolt when Jordan hit her in the face.

It hurt, but above all she was frightened. He said, "Get out," again and she ran. She heard him say, "Don't you ever say that to me," and she nodded her head, nodded her head, while trying to get the door to the hallway open. He grabbed her arm to make it hurt and took her out to the porch where he turned her around, toward him. "Git," he said. "Git and don't mess what I've got."

He snapped her around toward the steps and she almost stumbled. Then she ran.

Jordan did not watch her but went inside. He went to the table and picked up a glass of iced tea, and while he drank it he looked all around. All like before now. Only Betty is frightened. He put his glass down and went up to her and put his hands on her face. "I want you here," he said. "Not her."

"But, but you hit—"

"I've never done that before." Then his face changed, and before she could see what it meant he moved very close, put his head next to hers. "Don't be frightened. Please. Don't be frightened...."

She suddenly knew herself to be very important, that nothing else mattered between them, except what he felt about her. She took him into the

next room, left the light on in the front room, left the light off in the bedroom, stood still when he took off her clothes. She waited next to the bed
while he got undressed, and when they lay down together they lay still for
a long time. They made love once and then lay together because he did not
let her go.

15

He sat in the plane and sometimes moved his head so he could feel the cool blow of air from the vent overhead and sometimes he looked out of the window, at the clouds below, though with not much interest. A commuter does not look out of the window with much interest. Smith, leaving Miami for New York, where Jordan worked. It would be all right. The apartment, the pieces of furniture, pots and pans, and the girl there, happy with it. It would be all right. Jordan is a good provider.

In New York it was too warm and the sky slate-colored with rain hanging there. By the time Jordan got out of the taxi in town he felt wet under his shirt and his palms were wet. He also felt a stiffness in his neck. He watched the taxi drive down the street and hated the sight of the street and the car leaving.

He went into the drugstore but stopped on the way to the telephone booths to sit down at the counter. He looked at the booths every so often and drank a large glass of orange juice. Then he went to the back and placed his call.

His neck hurt with a slight stiffness and the phone was slippery in his palms. Maybe he isn't in. No. He'll be in. This isn't Wednesday afternoon. Tomorrow is Wednesday. He listened for the ring and felt nervous thinking about things that did not matter. Was Kemp dead by now? That mattered.

"Bandstand Bowling."

"Is Sandy there?"

"Just a minute." It took a little time and then Sandy said, "Yuh?"

"This is Jordan."

Sandy did not answer right away and Jordan could hear the hollow sound when the pins get hit.

"Where in hell you been, you sonofabitch?"

Jordan moved the phone to his other hand, wiped his free one on his pants. "I was out of town."

"Ah. You were out of town."

"Yes. Time out. Between time."

"Between time. You didn't know, maybe, this thing wasn't over, this thing was hanging fire and you were supposed to hang around?"

"I got to relax sometime. You know?"

But Sandy cut Jordan off. He thought there might be explanations next and that did not interest him.

"You know the trailer place," he said. "Meet me there. And leave right now."

"Listen, Sandy. What's developed? You know."

"Get off the phone and get over to where I said I...."

"Just tell me."

"I will," and Sandy hung up.

What it means, thought Jordan, what it means.... He got out of the booth and pushed the folding door shut behind him. Kemp is alive.

The jinx hangs on. But Jordan, you're a good provider and who else is going to keep Smith alive? Think of it this way: The first time in Penderburg was a job on Paul. Done. And the second time in Penderburg will be a job on Kemp. How do you shoot a man in an oxygen tent? Won't that cause an explosion?

Jordan walked four blocks to the place where he kept his car. He carried his overnight bag, since he had not yet been home, or as if on a job. Jordan the good provider and how else am I going to keep Smith alive....

On the Jersey side, before Newark started, was a house trailer lot on the side of the highway. There were two or three lots like it, and secondhand car places in between. And garages and gas stations. Like everybody is going to take off, thought Jordan. Like everybody organized to kill their time in between. Jordan pulled into the lot which said Trailways in neon, a big neon sign which showed green-fluorescent against the gray daytime sky.

The man at the office shack bent down to look and then he straightened up again and looked out at the highway. Jordan drove to the back where the two-axle house trailer stood with the sign in the picture window, *Another Trailways-Safari-Leisure-Time-House Sold to a Happy Customer.* Sandy was in the open door. When he saw Jordan he stepped away from the door.

The inside smelled of linoleum and plywood. There was a rubber-blade fan on the kitchen sink blowing air to the living-room area. All the windows had drawn, flower print curtains. The couch under the picture window was covered with the same curtain print. The formica table was bright red and yellow. A determined cheerfulness everywhere.

Sandy stood away from the fan and was smoking a cigarette. He rarely smoked cigarettes. Meyer sat on the couch. His bald head seemed grimly bald with all the prints and the color around. His sharp bird-face looked hungry. There was a young man in the bedroom passage whom Jordan did not know. The young man rubbed one shoe against the back of his calf and then looked at the shine.

"Where were you?" said Meyer.

"Short vacation."

"Sit there," said Sandy. "You face is dripping."

Jordan sat down in the chair but the fan draft was like a sheet flapping against his face. He got up again and wiped his hands. And going back to Penderburg isn't going to be the worst thing at all. It's end of jinx time and means Jordan the very good provider, keeping Smith alive....

"I got you over here," said Meyer, "so you can catch up on the news."

"What do I do?" said Jordan.

"First you should listen," said Sandy. "Wipe your face."

Meyer said, "Kemp is dead."

Jordan wiped his face. "Kemp is dead?"

Nobody said anything to that except the young man in the bedroom passage. The silence embarrassed him and he snickered. "Jeesis," he said, "the man of steel."

"Well," said Jordan. "Well, well, well," and then he coughed to cover the squeak in his voice which he was sure would came any moment. "Jinx time to jig time," he said. "What do you know...." Then he laughed. It was not a funny sound and he stopped it very soon.

He did not know how to be just glad. And he did not think that the men in the trailer would understand if he laughed. He allowed, "Well, well, well," again and, "I must say, yes sir, that is something."

"Will you shut up a minute and listen?" said Meyer.

Jordan took a deep breath and took a cigarette out of his packet. He rolled it back and forth between two fingers and said, "Certainly. What else is there?"

At that point he squeezed the cigarette too hard and the paper split open. It annoyed him that his fingers should do something which he knew nothing about ahead of time.

"So listen close," said Meyer. He leaned his arms an his knees and talked straight at Jordan. His voice sounded somewhat like a cough. He was not sure he was reaching the other man and was straining. "Kemp's dead and never said a word."

"Good. Fine."

"Just listen, Sam. Will you?" said Sandy. Then Meyer went an again, the rasp in his voice sounding close to anger.

"Dead without a word, like I said. Fine. And the bodyguard, when he started to smell, he didn't lead anywhere either. Fine. Standard. They talked to the landlady where you stayed and she has an idea you got black hair and look dangerous. Like it should be. And now, if you please, they're still not done."

Jordan put a cigarette into his mouth and held onto the filter with his teeth.

"Since when," Meyer yelled suddenly, "since when you been whoring around on a job, Jordan?"

"You say whoring around?"

"Because they're looking for that bitch!"

Jordan sat still and did not worry very much. He knew much more about this girl than the men in the trailer and what was true above everything was that the girl Betty did not fit or belong into any of this and therefore Jordan could not get excited.

"Sherman," said Meyer. "Get on that phone again."

The young man in the bedroom passage pushed away from the wall and went out of the trailer. Sandy and Meyer watched him leave but Jordan was looking down at his hands. They were quite dry now, he noticed. His face felt dry too.

"They find her," said Meyer when Sherman was gone, "they find her, Jordan, and what do you think's going to happen?"

"I don't know," said Jordan.

Sandy gave a quick look over, then turned away again. He did not like the tone Jordan had used, and the dumb words. He knew Jordan was not dumb and he had never seen him act sullen.

"You don't know!" said Meyer, and he looked back and forth between Sandy and Jordan. "You come back and don't know if the hit took or not. You don't know any better than to go out and make time with some lay while you're out on a job. And you don't know what's going to happen to you once they find that woman and tell her who's been laying her between business assignments! What do you know?"

"She doesn't know my name," said Jordan. He said this because it was the most important thing at the moment. That the girl knew Smith and nobody else knew him. That was important.

"Who else in Penderburg paid any attention to you, Jordan?"

"They're dead."

"And she's alive."

"But they haven't found her," said Jordan. "Isn't that what you said?"

"But I'll tell you what they know. She left town. She took off for Florida. She'd been talking about that for a long time and she bought a bus ticket that way."

"Where in Florida?" said Jordan. He was not too keenly interested because nobody here knew anything that was important.

"She's got a girl friend in Miami Beach and they're looking for her."

"Have they found her?" and Jordan looked across at the dry faucet.

"Sherman's checking again."

"They won't find her."

"What? What do you know about this?"

"Nothing," said Jordan. "I just mentioned my feelings."

Meyer jumped up with his bald head turning red. "Feelings? What in hell has any of this got to do with feelings? What's a cut-and-dry job got to do with your lousy feelings? Now you listen...."

Sherman came back into the trailer and Meyer yelled at him. "Well? What?"

"About the same," said Sherman. "What they got new is she's seen this guy before leaving, this button salesman by the name of Smith. They think maybe...."

"*Smith?*"

"Yes. Smith."

"You gave the name *Smith?*" said Meyer and leaned toward Jordan. "Will you explain to me sometime, sometime when there's peace and quiet, how you came to pick such a clever, such a damn clever name like the name Smith?"

"It wouldn't mean anything to you," said Jordan.

Meyer had no time or patience to get this answer straight and besides it was crazy impertinence anyway. If they didn't need the son of a bitch so much.... "What else," he said to Sherman. "Come on, come on."

"And they think maybe Smith is it, or at least worth looking at, seeing he shows in town, is buddies with Kemp, Kemp gets his, and...."

"We got all that. What *else?*"

"And now they got that this girl friend in Miami, in Miami Beach, works in a juice bar. One of those orange...."

"All right, all right. Orange juice bar. What else?"

"They're looking. They got the Miami cops on this thing, but of course there's a hell of a lot of those juice bars all over Miami and Miami Beach."

"All right." Meyer got up and pushed the yellow and red table out of the way so he could walk straight to the door of the trailer. "You take it from here," he said to Sandy. "You talk to the wunderkind." Then he snapped around at the door and looked at Jordan. "You remember her name?"

"Yes."

"You remember her face?"

"Yes."

"Like she's going to remember yours, Jordan. So get her quick, Smith." Then he meant to get out. He made a disgusted face and meant to get out of the door.

How Jordan got to the door so quickly was not clear to Meyer, but Jordan was there, very close, holding the door so it would not open and his face with a clamped look.... But the strangeness of his face could just be, Meyer thought, because I've never seen him this close. And then all Jordan said was, "I've never done a job on a woman."

After that Jordan let go of the door and stepped back and perhaps none of this had really happened, thought Meyer, and just everything about the son of a bitch is a surprise to me. How Sandy gets along with this creep is beyond me....

"Come outside a minute," he said to Sandy. Meyer frowned and left the trailer.

Sandy went out after Meyer and Sherman and when he looked up at the sky he thought it might rain any minute.

Meyer had his hands in his pockets and stood away from the trailer a ways. Sandy went over there.

"You saw that just now?" said Meyer.

"What?"

"When he held the door shut."

"I saw that. He held the door shut."

Meyer did not know how to put it. And what Jordan had actually said had not been anything special.

"You mean the nerves," said Sandy. "The way he's jumpy."

"Maybe you call it jumpy," said Meyer. "I don't know."

Sandy, when it came to his handiwork, felt a certain loyalty, or at least felt something like that, because of the effort he had put out over the time. Jordan, because of strain and an unorthodox job, had been fairly jumpy, but now with the end of it soon, with the girl out of the way, there would soon be no more of this. Besides, Meyer should stay away and keep his browbeating tactics for his office help.

"I keep wondering," said Meyer, "if we're making a mistake."

"Jordan goes out on this! He's the only one who knows the girl by sight."

"Sure. That's reasonable. Is *he?*"

"Damn it, Meyer, you keep riding this thing. You keep riding it without knowing the first thing about it. I've spent enough time...."

"You've never seen him crack up before."

Sandy lost his temper because Meyer was interfering where he had done none of the work. He kept his voice as low as he could and anger made him sound hoarse. "When he cracks I know it. When he gets quiet and doesn't say a thing, then I start worrying. When he goes under, believe me, I know how his type turns out: he'll fold, crawl in a corner, and he'll shiver there."

Meyer waited a moment and looked up to the sky. Might rain any minute, he thought. Then he said, "So let us all give thanks that he's prickly and offensive. And that he's all yours." Then Meyer turned and walked away.

16

When Sandy came into the trailer Jordan was at the kitchen counter. He was leaning there and his hand was on the faucet.

"There's no water in there," said Sandy.

"You never know."

Sandy closed the door and then he asked Jordan if he could bum a cigarette. Jordan said, "Sure," and gave him one. Then Sandy smoked.

"Well. You heard the man."

"Who's idea was it?" asked Jordan.

"Idea?"

"That I should go after her."

"It just came up."

"It was yours," said Jordan. "I think it was yours."

"All right. So it was mine."

"Sandy, it's not a good idea."

Sandy inhaled too deep and felt it burn way down. "You can relax," he said. "After this one, you can relax."

"You could send another man down and I'll give him a hand. I got an idea how to get to this girl, to this Betty, and the other man can do it as fast."

"That doesn't make any sense," said Sandy.

It made a great deal of sense to Jordan, how he would handle that kind of arrangement, and what he would save. Jordan felt weak, suddenly, when he thought about all he would save....

"Sandy. I'm asking you," he said.

Sandy did not like the tone, since it confused him. He said, "All this over a lay?" and thought it would change the mood. It changed nothing.

"Please," said Jordan. "Please, Sandy. I'm asking you this."

The silence was too thick after that and the face Jordan showed—Sandy squinted, blew smoke, threw his cigarette into the dry sink. Mushy! If his goddamn face doesn't look soft and gone.

Sandy got mad. He had one thing in mind, had one picture about this, and there had never been cause before to change what he thought and for sure this wasn't the time for any changes on his part. Soft and hard was the scale here. You go soft; how to fix it? Go hard. He talked fast and spitty with his excitement and with no time to watch how Jordan reacted.

"Soft and hard," he said. "That's what I'm talking about. You go soft, you fix that one way, fellow; you fix that and go hard. You been mushing apart

at the seams piece by piece, Jordan; piece by piece, the way I've been seeing it. Over not getting your break when you came back from the last trip,
over going out on a job with a little switch in the routine, over getting a
lay which was maybe the nuts, just compared to the last one, and so help
me, Jordan, if I ever seen a punier set of bad reasons, a more laughable,
crappier little bunch of bad reasons, so help me I don't know when that
might have been. Jordan!"

"Yes."

"You follow me, Jordan?"

"Yes."

"You don't follow through on this thing, I don't know what's going to be
with you. I don't know how you're going to make it and I don't know if
you're going to make it at all. But I know one thing, you son of a bitch, and
so do you! Once I don't know any more how you're panning out, that's
that, feller! That's that!" His throat hurt and he took a deep breath. He
talked low now, and relaxed after the shouting. "That would be that, Sam
Jordan, and you'd never make it again."

He sat down. He wiped his mouth, feeling wetness, and added what this
was all about. "What happens to your type when they're through, we don't
have to discuss that."

"Of course," said Jordan.

What Sandy had listened for had finally happened. "Of course," Jordan
had said with his voice and the shortness like always. He's come around,
finally, thought Sandy. It was so much what Sandy expected, he missed out
on the way it had happened.

Jordan, at some point, had stopped listening to Sandy. He was done listening.

Then they left the trailer. "Why in hell doesn't it rain," said Sandy when
they walked over the lot.

17

They saw each other once more that day, when Jordan was packing in his room and Sandy dropped in. He stood around and watched Jordan pack and was satisfied how he did it.

"You're taking three guns?"

"Sure."

"I didn't know you always took three guns."

"I take one when everything's certain. I take two when there's a choice but it isn't all clear. The third one is nothing. It's just a twenty-two automatic."

"So why...."

"Cats have nine lives. I have three guns."

Sandy grunted something but did not say any more. He wants three guns? Let him have them. Or nine lives, if he felt that was an advantage.

"I got your four gees for the Penderburg job," he said. "You want it now?"

"Drop it in the suitcase."

Sandy dropped it in the suitcase and watched Jordan take things out of drawers. "Where do you keep your dough, in a bank?"

"No. I got a place."

"Oh. Smart."

"Oh yes."

Then Sandy sat on the bed a while longer and watched how Jordan packed his suitcase so neatly.

"You're taking the plane, aren't you?"

"Eight-ten, National, flight two-seven-one."

"I know that one. I never liked it because it gets you there in the middle of the night."

"I like that."

"Yes. I see where it makes sense. You starting in on this right tonight?"

"Yes."

"So maybe I'll hear from you tomorrow."

"That's right. Wednesday."

Sandy felt relief hearing all the concrete parts of the planning and see-ing the right, sensible way in which Jordan packed. He felt there was no more for him to do, which was true enough, and he left. Jordan closed the door after him and went back to his suitcase.

He took garters out and snapped them around his calves. He took the twenty-two back out of the suitcase and hooked it under one of the garters

where the elastic had a gimmick sewed on for the purpose. In the beginning, some time back, Jordan had worn the small gun this way, because he
had felt like a beginner. It had served no other purpose and in a while he
had stopped. Quite a while back.

He took the roll of hundreds and fifties and opened the bills up. Then he
climbed on a chair and took the end cap off a curtain rod and pulled out a
very tight roll of bills which he had kept there. He combined all the bills
and tucked them into a place inside his suitcase.

When he left his room there were some shirts left in one drawer, new
shirts and not his size. There were also unused razors in a sealed cello-
phane wrapper and a full can of shaving lather. He himself always used
cream.

At nine that evening Jordan left the plane at the Washington airport.
Washington, D.C., was even hotter than New York and it was not raining
there either.

Benny liked the job and he even came to work early. He walked into
Monico's ten after four when he knew that rehearsals were over, and the
first thing he did was to go to his cubicle where he changed into the black
pants, dress shirt, and cummerbund. He liked what the cummerbund did
to his shape and for that reason always left the tux jacket off. He left it on
the hook until later and walked out into the corridor.

It went one way to the stage and the other way to an exit door with a
red light. That was required by law. The door led to a walled yard and the
wall had an alley on the other side. Like the weekly ice, this door was for
protection, though the weekly ice went regularly and was enough. Nobody
used that door. Benny passed numbers five, six and seven. The next door
went to the dressing room. It was open and all the girls were inside. They
sat at their tables with the lit-up mirrors and some were farther back
where the shower room was. When Benny stopped at the door he smelled
the creams and the lotions.

Like a court eunuch, Benny had a number of privileges. He had the run
of the corridor and the rooms all along there, and after rehearsals he liked
to walk into the dressing room.

He took a cigar out of his shirt pocket, walked through the door, and
watched himself coming in on one of the mirrors. "Hi, girls, hi, girls," he
said.

They answered or didn't answer, depending on where he was looking.

"You're getting fat," he said to one of them.

And she said, "You keep looking at it while I'm sitting down, so naturally."

Lois came in from the shower room and had a big towel over her shoulder. She wore that and the shorts and had washed her hair. Her head was down and her hair hanging over her face. "What a whoozy masculine odor," she said. "I bet Benny has brought his cigar."

Some laughed and Benny laughed and he had in mind to say something clever. Lois said, "Hold the dryer for me, Benny?" and sat down at her table.

He pulled up a chair, close to hers, and plugged in the dryer. "Cut it shorter," he said. "It'll dry faster and show more." He looked at her bent head and her hands fluffing her hair. When she made the right movement he could see her bare front.

"She can't," someone said two tables down. "It's got to, after all, be longer than Evelyn's."

She pronounced it Eve-lyn, with a long e, and they all laughed about the dancing instructor.

"What a name for a guy," said Benny. "I can't get over it."

"It's British. Over there they got this same name for the men and women."

"A lisp don't make him British."

"But his father's a lord."

"Eve-lyn's no lord, he's a lady," and they laughed again.

Benny watched Lois fluttering her hair and he watched her elbows. He had an idea elbows showed true age when nothing else might in a woman, especially with the ones here. He bent down a little, trying to see the girl's forehead. That was another revealing part. Forehead, and sometimes the eyes.

"Benny?"

He straightened up and said, "Yes."

"I feel a draft," said Lois.

"Naturally. I got this dryer trained straight at you."

She threw her hair back and kept her face turned to the ceiling. Benny turned off the dryer and the room was quiet.

"On my legs, Benny. I mean a draft on my legs."

"Maybe it's the hall door being open."

Lois picked up a brush and went through her hair. She dragged it and whipped it through and Benny watched.

She had put the towel down on the table. "You want me to blush, Benny?"

"Blush? I'm just looking."

"I don't like eyeballs touching me, Benny. Be a sweet and close that door?"

"Sure," he said, and got up. He went to the door and looked out in the hall. He saw no doors open there and felt no draft. "I don't feel nothing," he said.

"I don't feel it any more either," said Lois, but when Benny came back, she thought of something else. "Get me my robe, be a dear, on the bathroom door?"

He looked behind the door and told her it wasn't there.

"I left it in back last night," she said. "I think I left it in number three."

"Okay," he said. "Okay."

He walked down the corridor which had dim little sconces along the two walls. They made a gray, spotty light in the passage, meant as thoughtfulness for the customers. Benny had to go almost as far as the exit door because three was in the rear.

Inside he switched on a light because the curtains were always drawn, and then he switched on the light in the small bathroom where he found Lois's blue robe. Like a telephone booth, he thought, and looked at the tiled cubicle. When he switched off the light there he heard the door in the hallway open.

"You want to catch a cold?" he said and watched Lois come in.

"My compact," she said. "Did you see it in there?"

She had the towel around her shoulders again but took it off when she came toward him. She turned and held her arms back and Benny helped her on with the robe.

"It's in this pocket," she said. "Never mind."

"Oh good," he said. "Then I don't have to leave right off."

"Never mind, Benny."

But he stayed where he was and left his hands on her. He slipped them around her, to the front.

"Benny, please," she said and tied the cord at her waist.

"Huh?" he said next to her ear. "What do you say, Losy, huh?"

"Benny, let go. I feel like something in a window, in a store window, I mean."

"You don't feel like it to me."

"For heaven's sake, let go, Benny. You're like a baby."

"Listen, if you think I'm like...."

"No."

"How about it, Lois?"

"I can't. You know he's coming any minute."

"That's all I need. A minute."

"Ask Sue. You know he's coming any minute."

"To hell with Sue and to hell with him. You know what I think of him."

He let go of her and she fixed her robe. "What did he ever do to you?"

"Nothing. And he never will. There's just some I like and some I don't like is all. How about it, Lois?" and he stepped up again.

"Please, Benny. Not now."

"Later?"

"All right. Later."

"Before showtime."

"All right. Then."

They were done with the topic and thought of other things.

"You going to use number three?" Benny asked.

"Might as well. Turn the radio on, will you, Benny? I'm going back for a minute to get my mules."

She left number three and Benny stayed in it. The next thing Lois ran into Sandy, he coming one way in the hall and she going the other.

"Hi, sweets," she said. "Go on back. I'll be just a moment."

"Number three?"

"Sure. Three," which was the part Jordan heard.

Sure, three, he thought, and I don't see a one of them. One across the way in the room where everything happens, one down the hall, and one just a ways beyond that one. Jinx job. Here he comes. What a shadowless corridor with those nasty, dim lights. Here he.... Now. Poor, shadowless Sandy and wouldn't he jump with fright if I reached out now and touched him.... Touched him? Nobody touches that one. Poor Sandy. The cigar though, I could drill that cigar straight out of his face or straight into his face and he'd know that, of course, he'd know that and would worry about it. Jeesis Christ, what happened to my cigar, that kind of thing.... Turn. Nice, big back going into that door. Number three, where I got it, number three, where the.... Now? But the girl might still be down the hall and the noise she'd make would be too much to bear. They scream so with that ten-mouse scream piercing straight out of their gullet..... Good. That's a good light in that number three workroom over there. Christ. They got the radio going. Jinx job. Easy, Jordan. You're the provider, Jordan, and how else keep Smith alive? What else but this, Jordan, what else did he teach you and what else is there now but to do the best thing you know how, Jordan, to keep Smith alive? Can't have Jordan walking around trailing a corpse behind him, some dead Smith corpse hanging down and getting tangled with what Jordan might call a clean job of providing.... Goddamn that radio mumbling. Door closed. Now. Corridor empty. Now. *Now!* Ohmygod how—what is it? How whatever it is hurts. But it's going to be clean. Very clean when it's over. Smith there, Jordan here, dead jinx, clean all over.... Now, provider....

As soon as he pushed the door open to number three, Jordan, clean, was the professional. He didn't even hate anybody or want anybody. He was fast and barely visible and never lost his head once though he saw the jinx job setup with the first glance through the door. Two of them and the radio going and a drip faucet sound from farther back.

But he did not have to touch a thing, just look, do it, be done, end of jinx job. There was Benny's big back, there was Sandy by the opposite wall, there he was pouring liquor into the glass on the table and the radio behind, that mumbling mood music over everything.

Sandy straightened up, looked up, and smiled. He's never smiled at me this way, and the last thing he'll do is smile at me just that way. Now. And he fired.

He felt clear and good as soon as he had done it and before Benny could turn Jordan was no longer there. Jordan had had his glimpse, which was all the touching he needed, the smile looking at him, the smile gone absolutely, then Sandy leaning, and the mess on the wall behind Sandy's head.

Clean job, good provider, dead jinx, Smith breathing a sigh. Jordan closed the exit door without slamming it and ran.

18

He ran because he was in a rational hurry. There was this much time and this much to do and to make all of it fit it meant fast now. No haste, but fast. Fast was clean and haste was messy and now, of course, everything was finally clean. And this for the final touch, a present for Smith.

Jordan stopped walking when the Forty-second Street library was exactly opposite. He stopped to give himself time to calm down.

Not a present for Smith, but like a present for Betty. It would be: I give you this absolute Smith, this absolutely real Smith, Betty; look at me in black and white, Betty, so absolutely clear cut and right; hell, we could even get married. Jordan laughed and walked into the library.

He sat down in the newspaper room and held a paper. At seven, as always happened, Caughlin walked in. Jordan let the old man sit down and then waited another few minutes.

Caughlin, like his habits, was always the same. He had a brown overcoat on, long and large, which had one button high up in front. The button was closed so that the shirt would not show. The shirt was an undershirt. Caughlin took his glasses out, brushed white hairs back over his skull, started reading. He never looked right or left when he read, which made him seem stiff-necked or stolid.

"Evening, Caughlin," said Jordan.

Caughlin waited till the other was sitting. Then he looked sideways and back at his paper again.

"Good evening, Jordan," he said. "Why me?" and his Adam's apple starting bobbing. There was no sound when Caughlin laughed, just the Adam's apple bobbing. "Am I a job or do you want one?"

"I need one."

"Murder in the Reading Room," said Caughlin, and seemed to be laughing again. "Corny, isn't it?"

"Stop the crap, Caughlin."

"And start the music."

Jordan said nothing because everybody knew the old man was crazy, though this was to say nothing about his work. His work was expensive and could not be touched.

"I need everything from the bottom up," said Jordan, "and I need some of it right away."

"What name?"

"Smith."

This time Caughlin laughed with a sound. A man at the next seat looked up from his paper but Caughlin, who rarely turned his head, kept on laughing and paid no attention. When he was done he looked down at his paper and talked again.

"I'd be ashamed to sell you something with the name of Smith, Jordan."

"But it is Smith. I'm saying, it has to be Smith. Birth certificate, car registration, insurance, driver's license, social security. Samuel Smith."

"Too many esses."

"What?"

"Sounds like a superior job."

"It is."

"And who's paying for it?"

"I am."

"I thought you said it was a job, Jordan."

"Damn you, stop digging," he said. He was glad that the old man did not look up and would not see the mistake show in Jordan's face. "I get reimbursed for it," said Jordan, "which is the new way we got of handling things."

"Ah. There've been changes."

"You seem the same."

"Permanent, superior quality. When do you need this?"

"Jinx time."

"What was that, Jordan?"

"Jig time, jig time. I mean now."

"I can't get it for you all in one day. What do you need first?"

"The birth certificate."

"Ask the impossible, and it costs extra."

"Caughlin, come on. This is rush."

"Easiest way, Jordan," and Caughlin never changed his face, "is for you to go out and do a job on a Smith and then bring me the papers so I can fix them up."

"You going to keep horsing around here with that nut talk, Caughlin, or do I get this job done?"

"Murder in the Reading Room."

It's part of the price. You buy from Caughlin and part of the price is the digging and squirming he does like a worm and you better take it.

"What do you need the things for, Jordan?"

"I'd only lie to you."

"All my customers do. But they all say something."

Jordan said nothing.

"Need it that bad?"

He needed it so badly, Jordan felt suddenly on the point of tears or a scream, he did not know which, both Smith and Jordan screaming why all this....

Because a wife can't testify against her husband, it struck him. That's why. I'm Smith and I marry her, for that good reason. The scream went and Jordan felt right again, admiring the quick lie he had made. He knew full well he was lying, the same as he knew there was no Smith and no Jordan, but it worked well that way.

"Smith is an easy name," he said. "You've got to have something on file that I can use."

"I do," said Caughlin. "Needs a little work, but is a good birth certificate."

"You son of a bitch, why didn't you say so in the beginning?"

"I like to talk," said Caughlin.

"I want it tonight," said Jordan. "Get on it now so I can have it tonight."

"Too expensive."

"Come on!"

"Four thousand, counting your hurry."

The price for Kemp.

"And the driver's license," said Caughlin, "that's for nothing."

The price for Sandy. I mean, speaking of money, thought Jordan. He said, "I got five hundred with me. You get the rest when you're done."

They went outside and stood on the street. It was still light but the street lights went on. Caughlin said something poetic about that and then he said he wanted the five hundred.

"At your place. I want to see the merchandise."

"I got to fix it a little."

"I know. I want to see what you're going to fix."

They walked through a small park where the bums sat in the warm evening air and from there down a street with tall office buildings which were all shut for the day. The street was quiet and empty because of the hour.

"This one," said Caughlin, and they went into an alley between two buildings and from there through a steel door into the furnace room. There was a dry heat in the basement room and just one bulb burning near the panel which had to do with the heating and the air-conditioning system.

Caughlin lived behind that room. He lived in an enclosure with a good door, but the room behind turned out to be no room at all. It was like a bin. There was no window, but there was one diagonal wall with a hatch on top where the coal used to come through when they had heated with coal.

The floor was covered with newspaper and the walls were glued over with newspaper.

"I'm in the news," said Caughlin. He said this to everyone who came in there and it sounded automatic. Some of the papers on the floor lifted gently at the edges when Caughlin closed the door.

There was a cot, a table, a closet—nothing else would fit into the place. In the closet were a great number of things, dirty laundry at first sight. Caughlin rummaged around in the darkness and came up with a sheet of paper.

"This one," he said.

It looked all right. It made Jordan forty-five years old but aside from that it was a good document.

"Make me younger," said Jordan, "and for the first name, make it Samuel."

"That's your name."

"Yes."

"All amateurs do that. Like they're afraid to let go altogether."

Jordan laughed. He could let go Jordan and fall into Smith and he could let go Smith and fall back into Jordan. It was that kind of forever situation and he felt there was nothing neater.

"When?" he said.

"I can change the name easier than the age...."

"Naturally," said Jordan.

"Age," Caughlin finished off but did not seem to feel interrupted. "But to do both of them...."

"Just the name. Leave the age. When?"

"Tomorrow. Early."

"Tonight."

"I'll work all night."

"Do it faster."

Caughlin shrugged and took the five one-hundred-dollar bills Jordan held out. "Between twelve and one tonight," he said. "Come back here."

Jordan nodded and went to the door.

"I admire the calmness of a worker like you," Caughlin said behind him.

Jordan stopped, and turning to look at the old man, he tore some of the sheets on the floor.

"In the face of loss and disaster," said Caughlin.

"Like what, Caughlin?"

Caughlin sat down on his cot and made the springs squeak a few times, to fill the silence. Then he said, "I see where Sandy is dead."

He did not creak the springs again and the only sound was Jordan lifting his feet carefully, so as not to tear paper again. Then he leaned against the door. "You know that?" said Jordan.

"Don't you?"

"How come you know that?"

"You think all I do is read the papers?"

"No," said Jordan. "I know you don't."

It would, of course, not be in the papers because what went on in the back of Monico's rarely ever got beyond a known circle. But a shadow man like Caughlin, of course he might know.

"I know you knew Sandy," said Caughlin, "but did you know Benny?"

"No."

"The one who did it. The one who does bouncing at Monico's."

"Who did it?"

"Benny. The one who does bouncing at Monico's."

"Well, well, well," said Jordan, or his voice said it while he listened to it. "Why?"

"For the hoor what fingered him. I don't know her name."

Jordan did not say Lois or anything for a moment. Then he said, "That's no reason."

"Of course not," and Caughlin laughed. Then he said, "You sound like the one who did it," and laughed some more. "Like what Benny said."

"Like what Benny said?"

"He said, 'That's no reason. Even a guy I don't like I wouldn't do in for a hooker.'"

"He said that, did he?"

"But they got him."

"They?"

"Who else, the cops?" Caughlin laughed again.

The way this is handled, Jordan knew, was by the private justice department. He knew about that part. He put his hand on the knob of the door, wanting to leave. "They done with him?" he said.

"I thought you might know about that," said Caughlin. "Considering your line of work."

"Stop digging," said Jordan. "Would I need to be Smith for a routine like that?"

"When they're done with him, will you let me know?"

"I don't even know where they're keeping him."

"Shor's Landing," said Caughlin. "Will you let me know?"

"Why?"

"I'm morbid," said Caughlin. "Why else know anything?"

"I'll be back midnight," said Jordan. "You be here and be done with the job."

He left that way, saying no more than he always did, Jordan all harnessed and held neat with his habits, avoiding the busy streets because that made sense, but done thinking about problems because they had all been settled.

Even Caughlin the talker didn't worry him. While I'm in town he'll be busy; when I'm in Miami, let him talk. Oh the sense of it, Jordan thought, and even with Meyer with a nose like a pointed question, oh the ease of the answers, if he should ever ask. I thought you were in Miami? I needed the stuff from Caughlin. I thought you had a job on this what's-her-name? Her name is Mrs. Smith and a wife cannot testify against her husband. And besides, she won't. She won't. No, she won't. How come, Jordan? Because Smith takes care of that.

He walked, neat, clean, and all settled, and had time for the other thing.

He thought, what a beautiful, warm evening with nothing to do. With Jordan having time in between and Smith, getting shaped up to perfection. Jinx dead, he began, hours late, but completely, to appreciate the right thing he had done.

The first job ever that had not been a job, and the beauty of it, he kept thinking. Done like a job, that Sandy thing, but with a first-time feeling of ripe satisfaction. Well, of course, it had been necessary, but it was beautiful too. Sandy, had he lived to know it, would agree and would say, Sammy, I'll pay you double. Not that he didn't pay, of course, for Sandy always meant money. Dear Sandy, yes how well he paid, always and from start to finish.

Nine o'clock and more time to go.

And, for instance, Lois now, I even wouldn't mind her. A true time-in-between girl if I'd only known it sooner.

But while Jordan felt free now, he did not feel foolish. He did not go to the Monico or even waste time on the notion. Maybe next time I'm back in town and between Jordan and Smith time. This is between Jordan and Smith time, but that does not mean I should be foolish.

Ten o'clock and more time to go and Jordan, very sensible, agreed with his thoughts that he might spend the time out of town.

He stole a car and drove to the Jersey side. He took his first ride through a warn night and with no need to go anywhere. He even whistled.

Eleven o'clock and below the dip was Shor's Landing. This shows, he said, how perfect everything can be, because it is.

Shor's Landing was a line of docks on a little lake, a line of lights hanging between tall posts, and a restaurant—more lights—where woods started again, and cabins—few lights—where woods came from the other side.

The pine needles breathed out a nighttime smell and the band at Shor's Landing made nighttime music. Everybody dancing, thought Jordan. It's not bedtime, just nighttime.

These must be lovers, thought Jordan. This cabin is dark like the others but with two sleepless voices.

This one? Empty. Shor is not renting too well.

And in this one a fisherman, with ear plug and nembutal to make certain he'll be up fresh at five in the morning. And he has a belly, as I can tell by the snore.

Ah yes. This one by the door with a cigarette. Glow and fade, glow and fade, nervous in the night and wishing he were somewhere else. Who wants to sit by the door of a cabin with the music someplace else and the bed taken up and the holster making a heavy patch of black sweat.... What did Sandy used to pay for that type of job, ten fins?

Jordan walked up to the cabin and asked the man for a light. Before getting the light he kicked the man under the chin, because the man sat low on the stoop and the method was soundless.

The screen door creaked and Jordan thought, I bet Benny thinks this is it.

He was on the bed, as expected, tied up, as expected, gagged and sweated. Jordan knew this ahead of time because the method was standard.

After that, standards having nothing to do with it; Jordan turned on the light by the bed and smiled down at the man.

"I bet you think I'm it," he said.

Benny could not talk but he got it across with his eyes and the worm-bunched wrinkles on his forehead. And he wetted his pants, though Jordan did not know this.

"I'm not," said Jordan. "This is me, in between time."

He took the pillow out from under Benny's head and put it over his head, on his face.

God, I don't want him to suffocate, Jordan thought, and pressed the twenty-two into the pillow and fired.

Then he picked up the pillow to see if the shot had been all right, but because of the feathers glued down all over he was not too sure. He put the pillow back, and the gun, and did it again. Soft, muffled thud, and this time Benny did not jerk. Jordan went by that.

Almost twelve and I better hurry. He turned off the lamp and left the way he had come.

And even though he was in a hurry there was no jumpy tension in the way he felt. All was new, all was fine, Smith being done up to perfection back in town, and this, Jordan knew, was the first time ever, the first in-between-time job, only done out of idleness.

19

Meyer, because of all that had happened, was still at his desk in the middle of the night. Then he got two phone calls one after the other.

"Mister Meyer, how are you?"

"Who in hell...."

"Not well, I notice, not too well."

"Do I know you?"

"Not directly, but just the same. This is Caughlin."

The nut. And how did that forger get this number? "Would you buy a birth certificate with the name of Smith?"

"Listen! My name's Meyer which is bad enough, but if I should want your merch...."

"Not you. I meant that just for an example. For a fact though, this is for somebody else."

I'll wait. For a minute I'll wait, thought Meyer. Caughlin is a talker but with his prices he is not all nut.

"For who?" said Meyer.

"Whom. You mean, whom."

"Goddamn your crazy...."

"Please, Mister Meyer. You know I always end up serious."

Meyer said he was sorry and would Caughlin hold the phone for a minute. He put his hand over the receiver and said, Smith, Smith. Then he yelled at the door, "Come in here a minute," and Sherman came in.

"That Penderburg dame," Meyer said, "who did she say was her button salesman?"

"Smith. That's the name Jordan gave."

Meyer nodded and bit his lip. "When did Sandy say Jordan left for Miami?"

"Sandy's dead."

"I know that! Preserve me—" Meyer said to nobody and then he screamed again. "When? I asked you, *when?*"

"Last night sometime. I think he said...."

"Call National and Capital and whoever else flies the Florida run and check out on his flight. Jordan or Smith. Where he got on and got off."

Then Meyer talked to Caughlin again. "You still there?"

"Mister Meyer, the price just went up."

"Yeh. Sure. Listen. Your Smith customer, when is he picking up?"

"That isn't free information either."

"But he isn't picking up in the next half-hour."

"Mister Meyer, the way I earn pin money...."

"I know. The price just went up. My point is, Caughlin, I want to call you back."

"Why?"

"Half an hour."

"You don't think it's important?"

"That's why I want to call back in half an hour."

"The customer is paying four thousand dollars. You still think it isn't important?"

"You gave that away for free, didn't you, Caughlin?" and Meyer hung up.

If he needed Caughlin, and Meyer thought that he did not, then he would call back for sure. And at that moment the phone rang again.

"Caughlin," said Meyer, "when I say half an hour...."

"Hey—is this Meyer? Let me talk to Meyer."

"Yes?" said Meyer, because the voice sounded sick.

"Benny's dead."

"*What?*"

"This is Ferra, you know, Ferra. I got hit on the head, I mean got jumped here at the Landing, and then Benny is dead."

Meyer groaned through the whole story, through the whole thought that the Sandy thing made no sense now, not that the Benny thing made any sense either, except haywire sense, if there was such a thing. He hung up and went into the next room.

"I got this," said Sherman, "there's no Jordan anywheres, but a Smith took the eight-ten National flight out as far as Washington."

"D.C.?"

"Yes. That."

"So?"

"But his ticket was paid into the International at Miami."

Meyer nodded and went back to his desk. He picked at some papers there and then walked to the dark window.

He thought, Sandy once said if that one goes he'll be crawling into a corner and whimpering...

Then Meyer walked back to the other room and laid it out to Sherman what he wanted done.

When Jordan turned into the street with the office buildings, there was one lighted place, right at the corner, and after that came the dark street. He walked past the hamburger place with its bright, steamy windows, and when he passed the door somebody said, "Psst"

Jordan did not stop or look around because the sound made no sense to him.

"Mister Smith."

This time he stopped and the hate in his sudden movement was automatic.

"If you'll just turn around slowly, Mister Smith, you'll feel ever so much better."

Caughlin stepped out from the crack between buildings and walked with his stiff head held straight, facing front. He walked to the hamburger place and said, "You should follow me."

Run. Put the scream of fear into a very fast run.... That was how much everything broke in on Jordan, as if nothing good had ever happened before and nothing good was hoped for in any future....

"Wait," he said and grabbed for Caughlin's arm. Caughlin stopped immediately and tried to smile Jordan's motion away.

"You son of a bitch," said Jordan. "What? What happened?"

"We should go into the restaurant so that...."

"I'm going to kill you bone by bone, old man, bone by bone if you're double-crossing me—"

"Jordan, please. It's more complicated than that."

"We're going to your basement, old man."

"That is precisely, Jordan, precisely why I am here. To tell you about that. And you must get off the street."

Jordan let go of the arm and when he looked down the dark street he realized that he himself stood in a bright shaft of light. He pulled Caughlin again, away from the door and into the shadow. Caughlin talked now without being pressed any more.

"They're in the street," he said, "and I think it's for you."

Jordan looked and saw nothing. Then he saw a car pull away from the curb at the end of the block, pull away slowly, and the lights going on only later. But the car was going away, not coming closer.

"You don't mind being seen," said Caughlin, "but they do."

"More," said Jordan. "Tell me more."

"It's very complicated. You can let go my arm." But Jordan did not and Caughlin tried again. "It has to do with raising the ante."

"You said four thousand. If you...."

"I know. It didn't work."

"We're going to the basement."

"No. I'm trying to tell you, by way of help, if you can believe that...."

"I want the paper, old man, I must have the paper!"

"The double-cross is," Caughlin tried again, "that by way of double-crossing me in a matter of business, there's a stakeout for you which I am trying to counteract, counter-cross if you wish, as a pure matter of ethics and because you're my only true paying customer, though that isn't the whole...."

"Who? Who is there?"

"How redundant...."

"They're all dead, except you."

"Meyer knows," said Caughlin, and Jordan, with a great, sudden tired-ness thought how wrong he had been that last time.

The between-time idleness job. What a strange, wrong thing to have done. Like a—like a killer. Jordan felt ill and leaned by the wall.

"Now, the point I was delicately trying...."

"The paper," said Jordan. "Come on."

Or Jordan the provider, even he would not be worth anything any more, without the paper to make Smith.

This has got to be, got to be; he kept going on, and pulled the old man down the street.

"This one," said Caughlin and stopped by the big door which showed the bulb in back over the elevator and the narrow hall leading there.

"The basement door you showed me is down the alley."

"I should want to check first, Jordan. For heaven's sake, if I were you...."

"All right, all right—"

Caughlin kept knocking on the glass door for a while till a man came out of the lighted elevator. He limped and kept craning his neck to wake up. When he stopped by the door and saw Caughlin, he kept craning a while and then opened up. "I thought you was downstairs. Ain't you supposed to be watching the furnace?"

"It's summer time," said Caughlin and went in.

"I meant was, ain't you supposed to be watching the blowers because of that air-conditioning trouble up on the third?"

"Yes, yes, yes."

"And why ain't you using the back way, like you're supposed to?"

"Door slammed shut."

They all went down the hall, to the lighted elevator. "And who's this here? You know you ain't supposed...."

"Air-conditioning expert." Caughlin looked at Jordan and said, "Good, huh?"

"You mean you gonna take the elevator? Why don't you...."

"How I hate a whiny old man," and Caughlin took Jordan past the ele-vator to the back stairs. "Sometime when you have nothing to do, Jordan, why don't you, just between times...."

"Damn you, shut up!"

The door to the staircase hissed a little when it swung back and Caugh-lin took Jordan one flight up. "While I go and check," he said, "I'll leave you...."

"Wait a minute."

"Jordan. Please. You're worth four thousand dollars."

"Three-five, Caughlin."

"Why, of course, three-five. And as a token of my you-know-what," he put his hand into his pocket and took out a card. "A beauty, isn't it?"

It was a bona-fide driver's license, state of New York, for Samuel Smith with a local address. "Take it."

Jordan took it. "I need that other paper," he said.

"Now you admire this while I go and check," and Caughlin left Jordan in the dark, first-floor corridor where a firm had fixed easy chairs, scenic photos, and its advertising in a restful manner. Jordan watched the door hush shut and sat in the dark with his hand on his belt. In a while, because of the long wait, he pulled the Magnum out and held it.

Caughlin did not go all the way down to the basement. He stopped on the ground-floor landing where the pay phone hung on the wall and dialed his number again. Meyer, he felt, should have his one more chance.

Meyer, said Sherman, had gone to bed, and when that and some questions did not stir the old man into any worthwhile talking, Sherman said, go to hell, the deal's off, and he should go to bed too.

Caughlin drew his resigned conclusion, looked down the wall to the basement door, and then sighed. I'm a coward, he said, and why change now? He went to get Jordan then, so that they could go to the basement.

"There's nobody down there," he said. "Come along."

"How do you know? Just by walking in?"

"The truth is, I didn't even walk in. I called my informant and got the all clear."

"You're scared."

"I know. Are you?"

"Yes," said Jordan, and though it shook Caughlin and made him gape it was now too late for anything else because they were down at the door. "I want the paper," Jordan said again, and Caughlin pulled open the metal door.

One of the air-conditioning motors was humming. "Usually," said Caughlin, "the light by the furnace...."

At that point, he got shot.

Caughlin spun and pitched into the railing which ran down the cellar stairs and Jordan tossed himself flat on the floor. He heard, "Got the wrong one—" and then, "but I think both of them—" He did not listen to all of it because he spun on the floor where he lay halfway through the basement door and with a hip shot blew out the bulb back of him in the stair well.

Now both sides were in the dark.

The motor hummed and it took him a while to hear anything else. And then I'm going to get the paper... He then heard a short scuffle which was way in the basement and while that went on Jordan got off the floor. He stood up on the cellar landing and let the door hiss shut behind him.

There was a useless shot, because Jordan was no longer in line with the door. While the shot still twanged back and forth on the concrete, Jordan bumped into the fire extinguisher next to the door. He yanked it off the hook.

"Hey—" someone said in the basement. "Hey, you think he's still here?" Jordan spun the wheel on the extinguisher and tossed the cylinder off the landing. When it bounced into the basement the sound was a fright.

Two quick shots, useless.

Then the thing lay there in the dark and just hissed.

Jordan said nothing, the two down in the basement said nothing.

"Hey—" and then, "Jeesis in heaven what *is it?*"

"I don't know. Just shut up, I don't know—"

After that Jordan told them, "It takes about one minute. If you think you got the guts, put out that fuse." The thing lay there in the dark and hissed.

"—Fuse?"

"Shut up," said the other one. "Shut up, shut up—"

"Forty seconds maybe," said Jordan.

It hissed.

"Hey.... Hey, you up there!"

"Thirty maybe."

"Hey you up there, you're Jordan, ain't you Jordan?"

"What good will it do you?" said Jordan. He licked his lips in the dark and wiped his free hand.

The hiss changed then, because the pressure was going down.

"For godssake answer up there, will you please?"

"Turn the light on," said Jordan, "and I'll stop the fuse."

"Okay. Now hold...."

"You shut up you shut up," said the other one.

"Fifteen and Geronimo," said Jordan.

"*Wait!*"

"Toss your guns where I can hear them clatter," said Jordan.

One clattered, by the foot of the basement stairs, the other one didn't. The other one fell on top of the dead Caughlin, but Jordan knew it was there.

"Okay, you got them. Now just hold it, Jordan, do you hear?"

Jordan got ready to see in the sudden light, and the bulb went on.

There was a big, foamy puddle of white on the floor and the fire extinguisher in it, still burbling a little. The two men in the light were just staring. It gave Jordan good time to come down the short stairs, and as soon as he was there he shot first one and then the other. They both got identical holes in the forehead and were dead when they hit the floor. And then the rush was on Jordan again and he jumped over the men and ran to the back of the furnace. Back there. Caughlin's door was locked.

Reason had nothing to do with it, just a wish strong as his will. He pulled, wrenched, rattled the door and said hoarse things. He lost his senses, found them, lost everything he had ever learned, got it all back at the wrong moment, lost one hope after another, turned into worm, rat, idiot, rage, hate splinters, baby panic, a gasp in no air....

But he would not go back up the short flight of stairs to where the Caughlin corpse lay, and turn it over and touch it for the key....

And then the footsteps came down the other side of the basement door, they went limpedy-limp, and the easiest thing in the world, Jordan thought, when he shows in the door now.... The old man from the elevator pulled open the door and came in, gaping, standing a split second away from being dead. He made one more limpedy-limp— That's an idleness standing there, said Jordan, and I *know* better....

One more sick tired drag on the door and Jordan ran. He gave up and ran with mouth open, voiceless, because the wail in him got all used up with the running.

20

She said, "My God, Sam! What happened to you?"

He sat down in a chair in the room she had furnished and was ready to tell her what he had meant to do, what he had done instead, how confused it had left him, that she, Betty, was the only thing in all this that had never confused him, and that he thought this is what he had wanted all the time.

Later, he thought, after a breath. What he said was, "Nothing. It's all right."

"But—but honey, you looked like you *ran* all the way."

"I rented a car," he said.

She laughed and said she liked his sense of humor. She came over to him and ran her hand through his hair. "You have an accident, Sam?"

"Yes. A real one."

"Bad, honey?"

"I don't know yet. But it shook me."

"Well, you just tell me later," and she went to the front window where she pulled up the blind. "I didn't know you were coming, Sammy, or I would have fixed up something. Did you notice the new couch I bought?"

"Close the blind, Betty."

"Close it?"

"No. Leave it open. So I can look out." He got up and looked out. He looked across the porch of the bungalow he had rented for her and up and down the street full of late sunshine. No palms here, but there was Spanish tile on the house across and Betty had liked that.

"You don't want to eat now, do you, Sam? You don't look...."

"No."

She came over and wanted to lean against him but he changed it into something else, holding her, so she would not lean into the gun.

"You look," she said, "you look almost a little older, or something."

"No sleep," he said. "It's been very hard sleeping."

Then she took him into the bedroom and wanted to help him off with his coat. "No," he said. "I'll do it," and she laughed again and said that was just like him, not to accept a little consideration.

"No," he said, "it's not that."

"Not that?"

"I will, in a while," he said. "But right now I'm not yet done running."

She did not understand that and laughed this time for that reason. "Sam," she said. "Look what I bought in the meantime."

While she went to the chest of drawers, he put the gun in the closet and hung up his jacket there.

"Look. And just today. Just as if I knew you were coming." She held the fine spun nightgown up and moved it back and forth in the air. "Like it?"

"Yes," he said. "I like you *very* much."

He sat down on the bed and she said, "Oh, Sammy. You're so tired you don't know what you're saying."

He did not correct her, because he was tired.

"You going to stay a while this time, Sam?"

"Yes. Really."

"How nice that will be, Sam. How nice."

"Yes," he said, and stretched out on the bed.

"You want a nap before eating, don't you, Sammy."

"Stay here."

"If you want me to."

"Yes. Stay here."

She sat down on the bed and he laid his hand on her thigh. She put her hand on his and gave it a small push. "You're not wearing a housecoat," he said.

"Well, I wasn't, I mean...."

"No, stay here."

She stayed and then he said she should put on the new nightdress she had bought.

The sun was going outside and part of the time while she undressed he closed his eyes and just heard the sounds she made with cloth against skin. Once a car got louder down the long block, but Jordan was so worn he did not tense till the car had gone by and then he relaxed again.

"I'll lie down next to you," she said.

They lay like that and Jordan almost went to sleep. But he did not want to lose knowing that she was there, and the darker it got the more he listened for other things.

She moved against him and he stayed awake. He moved his hand over her and felt her skin in the places where he liked to feel it especially. They lay like that and touched only in a few places and she thought, should I tell him before or should I tell him after. He is so friendly now....

"Sam?"

"Don't move away."

"I wasn't going to."

"Stay like this, Betty, and I'll talk to you."

We'll talk, she thought, and this is a good time to tell him.

"I tried and I tried," he said, "but not all of it really came off. It's mistakes that happened, wrong things along the line, but what I did wrong, Betty, my faults, I mean, they—I don't know, Betty, I don't know how to say it..."

He said, more, with the worry pushing him, the worry about not being able to keep Smith and Jordan apart, the new awful thing which he had never imagined, but the girl wasn't listening then. She felt a quick panic.

"Are you trying to tell me you're married?"

"Married? Hell no," and he sat up, trying to focus.

She had heard how shrill she had sounded and how it must have struck him. She thought before I lose my courage I must speak. "I remember you said no once before, Sam, but you were acting so strangely, and here I have this important thing, this worry on my mind, and if you say so, Sam, of course I...."

"What?"

"I'm going to have a baby."

He said nothing but she felt his quick move and she panicked again. "I mean, you got to take that into consideration, Sam. You got to remember I sit here all alone and only you know where and I got this worry..."

"Baby?"

"Yes."

"Who says?"

"The doctor said so when I...."

"When?"

"Three months now."

He jumped off the bed and wiped his mouth, staring at her. Dark now in the room. He had talked and asked all the last things from sheer confusion but that was done. Clear now.

"Three months? From me?"

"Sam, Sammy. I didn't mean—what I meant was, was something else. What...."

"Shut up." I'm rattled, he thought, and then said it, "I'm rattled. Shut up for a minute—"

She lay still and confused and he thought that face there, I have never seen anything emptier. What is there.... Except for the lie she tried, the lie with the baby.... One lie in back, that was Sandy; one lie in front, staring empty.... Easy, try it easy like Jordan does this, and he stepped back almost into the closet. Smith gone now, he thought, but don't give up Jordan. And no between-time kick, on-the-run kick any more. And my God, he thought—and there was a sound in his throat—what is left now....

The light snapped on.

The man nodded his head and nodded the gun at Jordan.

"Wasn't she supposed to be dead?"

"Sam! He's got...."

She stopped when the killer walked farther into the room, and when Jordan moved over where the killer wanted him.

"Where's your gun?"

Jordan nodded at the closet.

"Ah," said the killer, and left it to lie there when he saw it on the shelf. Then he turned all the way back to the room.

"A shame," he said. "She could have stayed in one piece if I could have gotten you elsewhere. But now she's going to see this."

Jordan sank into the chair behind him and his breath came with a paper sound.

"I think I'll do her first. Real shame," and he lifted the gun the way Jordan would do it. Outside a motor raced loud. He took a stance the way Jordan did when he was not on the run.

The girl gagged when she saw the gun come up to level, and she understood nothing when all that stopped.

Jordan, the way he hardly ever did, squeezed from way low and the killer seemed to draw up his shoulders. When he fell, Jordan was over him, looking hard for the little hole which did not show clearly because of his clothes. He held out the little twenty-two and made a hole where he wanted it. He felt nothing.

When the girl made a hoarse sound Jordan looked up. He felt rattled and confused, Smith-Jordan confused. He looked at her drawn up on the bed and said, "Don't be afraid, Betty. He's dead."

Then he ran out. He saw the car by the curb, motor revving, but when he ran out on the porch he thought better of it and pulled back. So the car took off.

He stood on the porch and watched the car go. He was not so confused that he did not know what came next. Next would come the same thing, the same thing again, with only one finish to it. He knew the routine. He felt heavy and still. One more run, he said, one more run. Not for long now, but for just a little.

He ran back into the house and into the bedroom.

"Betty....."

"Please!"

"Quiet, Betty, quiet quiet. Here now, get this on."

"What are you—who are—"

"Nonono. Forget that. Sam Smith. Remember? And the buttons." He held the coat to her but she stepped back into a corner.

"Betty, please," he said, "Betty, please. One more run is all, Betty sweet, one more and it's over. When you're gone and it's over, they won't want you any more."

"What are you—"

"He said so, remember? Before he was dead. Here, the coat."

She put it on, so he would go away. When she had it on he pulled money out of his pocket. "Now this, Betty. Stick it here, in the pocket," and he held the thick roll out with two hands.

"No. I won't touch...."

"Betty."

"You're some filthy kind of...."

"Please," he said, talking slower now. "Please don't quarrel."

He put the money into her pocket and she held still with fright.

"You come now," he said. "Here, shoes. Then we go. Run, I mean."

She put the shoes on and he rushed her. He left his jacket where it was, but was not so confused that he did not take the Magnum. He put it in the place under his belt but moved it into the pocket when he saw how she looked at it.

"Please," he said again. "Don't quarrel," and he ran her out to the street.

He ran her to the car at the corner and when they were inside he drove fast and skilled. For a while they sat next to each other like that without talking, he not talking because of all he was thinking. What there was of him and the things he had done, so that she would know the bad and the good of him, and what he had wished would have happened. But he did not know enough about any of it and the confusion kept him from talking. She sat still too, so he felt that she felt the same kind of things, and was kept from talking. Once he reached over and made a light stroke on her arm. Her fright kept her silent and stiffened.

Her fright made her keep step with him when they ran into the airport; and when he found a ticket for a plane which left in five minutes; and when he rushed her last through the gate and said something she did not understand....

He latched the chain across the empty gate and watched the plane swivel slowly and then move slowly with a big roar. It moved out of the light and in a while it will fly off, he said to himself.

He felt no need to watch that. And he did not remember where her ticket went. Just that the girl had been.

They picked him up again in town and they had him when he went into the bus station. He had gone into the station because there were people. Then he saw the three men and knew immediately.

They shot him against a wall with a summer schedule behind him, and that got torn too.

It felt to him as if he sat on the floor a long time, and for one very bad moment a sudden, great wildness almost tore him open, like pigeons beating around inside a wire-mesh cage and even their eyes with the stiff bird-stare turned wild with glitter.

But he made that all go quiet again. He could not see any more and wished he had said more to the girl, had told her some things he had done, so that she would know the bad and the good of him and he would not be just a blank.

He had a great deal of pain and then died.

When the policeman turned him over, he found one driver's license which said Smith and another one which said Jordan.

"Must be Jordan," he said. "There aren't any Smiths."

The End

A SHROUD
FOR JESSO

BY PETER RABE

Chapter One

The Constellation swung close to the ramp, coughed a few times, and stopped. There was a second or so of silence, then the clatter of the wheeled ramp, the door swinging open in the flank of the plane, the passengers making noises of hello and good-by. They filed out in a fast line that seemed to knot for a moment when it hit the cluster of reporters at the bottom of the stairs. Then the line pushed through and left the reporters in a happy circle around the blonde with the baby face. She slung back her mink to show more of the real thing and the flash bulbs started to wink. The baby face smiled, fresh and pretty, and the girl looked for all the world as if she'd just had a nice hot bath.

Jack Jesso pushed by the crowd that stood around the girl. He gave her a short look, remembering the back of her head. He'd been looking at it ever since L.A. He looked at the rest of her now, but all he could think of was a hot bath.

When he got to the baggage counter, nobody was there but the attendants and a stewardess holding a clip board. Then the rest of the passengers came through. It got really hectic when the girl with the open mink came by, but Jack Jesso wasn't paying any attention. He rubbed the black stubble on his face and kept looking at the door that led to the taxi stands. After a while he was alone again. He looked at the clock over the reservation desk, picked up his brief case, and went to the phone booth. By the time he got his party there was a mean squint around his eyes and his voice sounded clipped.

"This is Jesso. That you, Murph?"

"Hi, Jackie. I'm sorry about—"

"Why aren't you over here?"

"Jackie, I'm sorry I couldn't—"

"I sent you a telegram two days ago. That's enough time for anybody to get off their can and do a simple trick like showing up at the airport. I'm taking the bus in. Meet me at the First Avenue station."

"Listen, Jackie, I was gonna come out, honest, but—"

"First Avenue in an hour. Be there."

"But Gluck didn't—"

"Gluck?"

"Sure, Jackie, I'm trying to tell you. He said no."

There was a pause. Jesso looked at the clock again, then turned to the phone. "First Avenue at eight," he said. It sounded straight and normal, but he smashed the receiver on the hook as if he were hitting at a face. The receiver missed the cradle and clattered down as far as the cord would let it. Jesso walked out of the booth. The phone dangling in mid-air like the arm on a slow clock.

By the glass door that led to the outside he almost ran into her. She was holding both doors by the handles, holding them together so the doors wouldn't swing, and she looked at him through the glass.

"Smile, Jackie, or I won't let you out."

Jesso stopped close to the door and looked at her through the glass. "Open up, Lynn."

She looked into his face. She might have kissed him if the glass hadn't been there. "Smile or I won't let you out, Jackie."

He felt irritable. He wished Lynn weren't there. "Open up, Lynn. I'm in a hurry."

He hadn't smiled once, but she opened the door. Lynn looked like the blonde from the plane, except that her face wasn't babyish. Even with the glass door gone now they stood apart; Jesso because he wanted it that way, Lynn because she couldn't help it. She looked at Jesso a while longer, but when he started to go she grabbed him by the arms and kissed his chin.

"You're back," she said. She tried to smile.

"So what?" He took her wrists and pushed her hands down. "Lynn, once and for all, go away." He tried to make it sound even. "I'm in a hurry, Lynn. The bus."

Then she started to talk fast. "But I brought the car, Jackie. I called you and called you and then I got Murph, and he told me you'd been away. So I came out to pick you up, Jackie." She laughed. "I always seem to be trying to pick you up."

He didn't make a joke of it. "There's nothing to pick up, Lynn."

She suddenly turned. "Look, Jackie, the bus is leaving." She watched him. He looked angry. "I'll give you a lift. I brought the car to give you a lift. Murph said—"

"All right. Come on. I'm in a hurry."

They found her car and she drove.

"Why such a hurry, Jackie?" She kept her eyes on the road.

Jesso lit a cigarette and didn't answer. At least he was getting a lift.

"Jackie, why always a hurry when I see you?... Jackie? Don't you remember the way it was?"

He threw the cigarette out of the window and turned to the girl. He looked tired. "Look, Lynn, once more. I remember how it was and it's not that way any more. And there's your answer." He leaned back in the seat, rubbed his hands over his face to make the stiffness go away. "So get off my back, Lynn." He talked through his hands. "Stop acting as if I was the only man in the world."

"You were the first," she said.

He groaned, turned to the window.

They drove without talking for a while and then Lynn got busy with the traffic and that killed some more time without talking. Jesso looked at her from the side. A beautiful profile. A beautiful profile all the way down. Even sitting in the soft seat of the car she looked poised, distant. That's how she'd looked the first time. She'd been that way. She sounded finishing school and looked North Shore and touching her was like a brash, strong move against the thousand things she had and he had not. That's how it felt, at first, and then she gave. Even that was good for a while, but then it all turned into putty. There wasn't a thing that she could give him any more. She came to his side of the tracks, she started clinging, and Lynn was through.

"Jackie?"

He looked ahead and folded his arms.

"Why didn't you let me know you'd gone to the Coast?"

"Business. Wouldn't interest you."

"Vegas?"

"What's the difference?"

"We met in Vegas. You were there on business that time, Jackie, and then Tahoe. You took me to Lake Tahoe."

He sat up. His voice was controlled. "Lynn, listen. I got nothing against you. And I got nothing for you. Learn that, willya?"

The way she took it, without ever showing a dent, made him feel as if he wanted to break something. He took a deep breath and kept staring ahead. It would go away in a minute. It would go away, get indifferent, just the way it always had with Lynn, and with who knows what their names were.

"I can wait, Jackie," she said, but he wasn't paying attention any more.

She pulled up to the bus terminal and Murph was standing there. He kept hitching his pants over his belly, and now and then he wiped a handkerchief over his bald head. When Lynn's car rolled up and Jesso got out, Murph ran up to carry the brief case.

"Thanks for the lift," Jesso said, "and good-by."

"Not good-by, Jackie."

"Good-by." He straightened up and had his back turned when the car took off. Murph reached for the brief case.

"Hi, Jackie." Murph grinned. "That little Lynn girl—"

"Where's the car?"

"You know, she's been calling ever since—"

"Come on, Murph, where's the car?"

Murph started moving, but it didn't stop his train of thought.

"You know, Jack, I always say once you get one of them—"

Jesso held the man by one sleeve. "Keep it clean, Murphy."

"Jeese," Murph said, and then they got to the car. They didn't say another word until Murph swung the car into traffic on Fifth Avenue.

"Turn off and take the parkway. I'm not going to Gluck's."

"Jeese."

Jesso lit a cigarette and offered the pack to Murph. Murph didn't want one.

"I oughta tell you, Jackie. Gluck wants to see you right off."

"Take the parkway."

"Jeese, Jackie. Gluck's the boss!"

"You know what he can do?"

"Heh. Just this morning he said the same about you."

Jesso leaned back and tried laughing, but he didn't really feel it. Gluck wasn't going to be laughed off. Gluck was still the boss.

"So let's have it, Murph. What's his beef this time?"

"His beef? Nothing. Just you. Like always."

Jesso curled his mouth under, as if he wanted to give his face a stretch. "Like always, like always. How long's that bastard been in? A month, two months? That's always? You know how long I been here, Murph?"

"Sure. You been—"

"From the beginning! And no trouble all along the line. A neat little setup, right here, and nobody big enough to buck it."

"It sure was neat, Jackie. Remember when Delancy tried to muscle in, and—"

"Delancy was small time. We were big enough for the syndicate to want a piece." Jesso sat chewing his lip, thinking about the time the syndicate wanted a piece. They could use a man with his local connections, they said, a man as big as he was and all on his own. They gave him a wire service and they asked him how to handle local problems. Sometimes he told them. Most of the time he just got things done the way he knew how, fast, no fuss, no ass-kissing, and nobody left to ask any questions. They liked that and Jesso went his own way. And then one day he saw how big the organization had got, bigger than one man, bigger than Jesso. They were sweet as pudding when he found that out. They were so sweet they sent him a man to help with the details, because big time needs big-time organization, they said. It needs the individual touch—and that was Jack Jesso. It needs a smooth-looking front—and that was Gluck. And when they trimmed up the whole big beautiful setup, with wire service, numbers, and a piece of the water front all tucked in neat little pigeonholes, with dummy companies and tie-ups to the Coast and hell knows where else making a net like a spider, then Gluck was in and Jesso was out. "We need you," Gluck said, "but now do it my way." He didn't say "or else." He was too oily for that.

"Jackie," Murph swung to the right lane of the parkway, "I can still cut off and get to Gluck's place without—"

Jesso gave Murph a look as if he were going to spit. "The bastard can wait. I set up the Vegas deal a week faster than he could have done it."

"That's what he's beefing about, Jackie. That's just what—"

"How can a pig beef?" Jesso pulled the hat over his eyes and tried to sleep.

So Murph just drove. He turned off the parkway before they got to the George Washington Bridge and wound up the hillside to the apartment houses. When he stopped the car he tried once more.

"Look, Jackie—"

Jesso got out of the car. It was ten in the morning and the white sunlight on his face made him look all used up.

"Take the brief case and give it to Gluck. I'm going to bed. Be back here at seven and tell Gluck I'll see him after nine tonight."

He walked around the car and into the apartment building.

There was a barbershop off the foyer. Jesso saw that the place was empty and walked in. The barber jumped up from behind his paper and beamed. "Why, Mr. Jesso! I'm glad to see you back from the Coast. Shave today? Haircut?"

"Shave is all."

Jesso sat down in one of the chairs and stretched out. He liked sitting in a barber's chair. The barber started to lather up. "You don't have a tan, Mr. Jesso. I thought when people went to the Coast—"

"Just business."

He stretched his head back and closed his eyes. The pose made his face change expressions; it was a blanker, smoother face now. The barber finished and jacked up the backrest. "How about a trim, Mr. Jesso? Just the edges?"

"Go ahead."

The barber flicked his scissors around. He flourished his hands like a conductor. "A remarkable head of hair, Mr. Jesso."

He was right. The hair was thick and black, cut short so it stood up like the nap of an expensive rug. When the light hit the hair just right it looked like velvet on top.

"Massage, Mr. Jesso? To relax—"

"I'm relaxed." He got up and paid.

"Manicure, Mr. Jesso?"

The girl had wheeled her tray in, nudging it with one thigh. Jesso watched her do it, then looked at her face.

"Give me fifteen minutes," he said. "You know the suite number." He walked to the elevator.

After his shower he put on a bathrobe and fixed himself a drink. He felt tired, but it was pleasant now. It was the kind of tiredness that feels good.

There was a knock on the door. Jesso put his drink down and turned.

"The door's open," he called.

The girl from the barbershop came in, pushing her cart with the manicure stuff. She was smiling the way she'd done before. She closed the door and came across the room. She left the cart where it stood, because Jack Jesso never took a manicure in his life.

Chapter Two

Boss Gluck had a tower place in the Wells Arms and it wasn't easy to get there. First there was the doorman and then there was the desk in the foyer. After the ride in the elevator came the tower foyer and another desk. Behind the suite door marked B-2 was a room with couches and a kid who kept his hat on all the time. He had a phone with buttons. Then there was a big guy dressed like a butler, and he took you through the doors into a neat little place that didn't have anything but a chair and an ash tray. After that came Boss Gluck. If it was important, Boss Gluck got up from behind his desk in the room with the terrace, took the visitor through a door with a drape, and sat down in the little cubicle where the filing cabinets stood.

It took Jesso no time at all to get to the room with the ash tray. He stood by the chair, walked to the window, went back to the chair, and sat down. He was lighting a cigarette when the door opened. Jesso threw the cigarette in the ash tray and got up again. But it hadn't been the door to Gluck's office. The butler was back, holding the door wide so the two men could pass. The tall one came first, looking anonymous in a black ulster and a stiff hat. The short one followed in step. He seemed stout but walked with a spring and made sharp little sounds with his heels. He wore black, too, with a Persian-lamb collar folding wide over his shoulders and down the front.

They stopped in the middle of the room and Jesso watched a fast ritual with gloves, hat, scarf, and overcoat. Holding the stuff, the tall one bowed to the chair, and before Jesso had taken all of it in the stout one was sitting down.

"You're welcome," Jesso said.

No answer.

"My chair is your chair," Jesso said.

The tall one took off his hat and looked around.

"If you will take these," he said. He held out the clothes over his arm without even looking as if he were waiting.

Jesso took the bundle and watched the man remove his coat. "You're welcome," he said.

When the tall one draped his coat over the rest of the stuff on Jesso's arm, put his hat on top, and turned away, Jesso started to get the picture. He hefted the load and made a laugh.

"Bundles for the Bowery don't get picked up except Monday and Tuesday. Today is Friday."

Nobody laughed back. The tall one stood next to the chair like a standard bearer. He ran his hands through his long hair and then folded his arms over his chest.

"What I mean to say is, perhaps it doesn't show, but I haven't got my moth bags and clothes hangers along."

Jesso looked from one to the other, making an expectant face. He still thought it was funny. He stepped close to the squat man in the chair and leaned down confidentially.

"Now, Bean Pole has said his daily words and I'm not going to be unfair to him. How about it, Porker? You haven't talked yet."

But Porker looked right through him. His small white hands lay peacefully in his lap, and Jesso was surprised at the hands, because they were so different from the bull neck and the thick face of the man. His skull was shaved to a stubble except for a full-grown patch over the forehead, and that patch was arranged in a fat shiny wave.

"I'm gonna count till three," Jesso said.

The heavy face turned slightly to the tall man, turning with a muscled twist of the neck as if it were going to creak any minute.

"You may hang up the clothes," said the tall one. Jesso noticed the precision in the voice.

"One," he said.

"Your conduct will be reported, at any rate."

"Two."

For the first time the squat man's face showed interest. He had very light eyes and they traveled from Jesso's feet to his head, as if the man were thinking of buying a side of beef.

"Ready or not," said Jesso, looking at the light eyes. There was something else about them. The way the man's nose was tilted, it looked as if his eyes and nostrils were all in one line. The long upper lip and thin mouth finished the picture. Just like a porker.

"Three," Jesso said, and he dropped the clothes on the floor. The man in the chair didn't move, but the tall one started to scramble. He was halfway across the room before Jesso knew how he got there, and then the man started to crouch. It wasn't as if he were preparing to jump. It was more scientific. Jesso saw the shoulders hunch, the long arms held still, one hand held higher than the other. Those hands stayed open, the fingers stiff. Jesso pushed away from the wall and started to lean. The man's face didn't tell him a thing, just cold, light eyes and the lips bunched hard over the teeth. Jesso couldn't figure why the man looked like murder or why dropping his lousy coats should bring on all this seriousness. But he wasn't going to stop and argue. He got set for the rush, leg ready, because once Bean Pole was close enough he was going to get it where it hurts. When the man started to dip on his feet there was a snap. Somebody had snapped his fingers.

Bean Pole straightened up abruptly, turning to his buddy in the chair, who snapped his fingers once again and pointed to the clothes. Bean Pole was picking up the overcoats while Jesso was still standing there. Then he relaxed.

"Boy," he said.

Nobody answered.

"Boy, that's training," he said.

Bean Pole was holding the coats neatly and the squat one in the chair looked as if he weren't even there.

"And no whips, even," Jesso said. "Just snapping the fingers. Tell me, Porker—" but then the door to Gluck's office opened.

But it wasn't Gluck and it wasn't for Jesso.

"Mr. Johannes Kator," said the butler, and the man in the chair and the tall one with the overcoats moved as one. The heels made sharp little clicks. Kator went first, then Bean Pole. Jesso and the tall one looked at each other, but it didn't mean a thing. Jesso was thinking that he didn't like Johannes Kator at all.

They came out again before ten minutes were up, which was just about as long as Jesso was willing to wait. So when the two men came out, Jesso walked through the open door before he was called. It was the kind of thing Gluck didn't like.

But Gluck didn't show it. When the door banged shut and Jesso walked across to the desk, Gluck turned to look and he was ready with his smile.

"Greetings, boy." He took the dead cigar out of his mouth and tapped it. "Make yourself comfy for a sec, huh?" Gluck carried a folder to the room with the filing cabinets. He had a flat-footed walk, probably because of the weight he carried in his rear, and he made a grunt each time he took a step.

"You shoulda waited outside," he said when he came back. Then he sat down and the jowls around his face made a quick shimmy.

"I waited. What in hell did you think I was doing out there besides waiting?"

"Now, Jack boy, let's act like buddies. You and me—"

"Stop licking, willya, Gluck?"

"Jackie boy, what's eating you?" Gluck put the dead cigar back in his mouth.

Jesso didn't answer right away. He held it for a minute because it wouldn't do to buck Gluck all the time. Not when it wasn't important. Save your strength. Ignore the bastard, just the way Gluck knew how to ignore the things he didn't like. It wasn't easy to figure what he liked and what he didn't like. Most of the time he took just about anything as long as he could call a man his buddy boy. And then somewhere along the line buddy boy would get the shaft.

"You know why I'm boss and you aren't, Jackie boy?"

The cigar came out and there was a friendly smile.

"No," said Jesso. "You tell me, President."

"I will," and the cigar went back. "Because you don't know people, boy. You never studied how to get along. Take me, for instance."

"Don't. Don't put yourself out, Gluck. Just keep the secret."

"Like right now, boy. You're riled because I let you wait."

Jesso lit a cigarette and tossed the match at the ash tray. He missed. "Now I know why you're president and I'm the punk around here. You know everything. So now let's talk about Vegas. You read the stuff and papers I brought back?"

"No." Gluck smiled. "I didn't have to. On account I read minds." He sat back and gave Jesso a wink.

"You're not doing so hot, Gluck, or else you'd be reading right now you should stop clowning around." Jesso got up and ground his cigarette out. "Let me know when you're ready for a cabinet meeting, Gluck, about Vegas and so forth. Or better yet, go out there yourself next time and don't send a flunky." He turned to the door and then he heard Gluck's chair creak.

"I didn't," said Gluck.

Jesso stopped. That was another thing about Gluck. He always got the last word or the last lick. And once Jesso turned around there would be jolly old Gluck swishing his cigar around. Jesso turned and went back to the desk. He put his hands flat on the top and leaned.

"How did you mean that, President?" He sounded calm as hell. "You mean you didn't send a flunky or you didn't send me?"

"I didn't send a flunky." Suddenly Gluck wasn't smiling any more. "So you shouldn't have gone there, Jesso."

Gluck hardly ever insulted a man in a straightforward way. And he hardly ever had a lit cigar in his mouth. Gluck was lighting it now and he never even blinked when the strong smoke crawled up around his face.

"Sit down, boy. I want to talk about Vegas."

Jesso didn't sit. He pushed himself away from the desk and thought about walking around to the other side, where Gluck was sitting, and starting out by grabbing lapels.

"This is important. It's all about you, Jesso."

Jesso sat.

"You goofed, Jesso."

But this time Gluck made no impression. Jesso never goofed unless he knew about it.

"And I'm taking the time to explain it to you because in this new setup, you working for us, you can goof and not know it. You haven't got the background to know it."

Jesso kept still because Gluck was making sense.

"Who told you to go to Vegas, Jackie boy?"

"Nobody."

"So you goofed." Gluck sat back and started smiling.

Jesso sat back too. He took his time lighting a smoke, and this time he didn't toss the match, but placed it in the tray as if he had nothing else on his mind.

"Gluck," he said, "there's two things I don't like. One, I'm not working *for* you. I didn't before you came, I'm not doing it now. Two, I don't goof. We been after a tie-in with those two clubs in Vegas for a long time. Those two were outsiders and we wanted in, right? They been using our bonding company, the money outfit that started right here with dough I put out long before you ever came along. We put up their bond and they never came across with their percentage off the tables. Now, you know I want in, I know you want in. So what did you and your glorified bookie friends do about it? Nothing. So I did. I don't horse around sending messages on business stationery. I go out there. We're in for a cut on those clubs right now. What would have taken you another year I did in twenty-four hours. And that was yesterday."

"Bravo," said Gluck, but he wasn't smiling. "And now I tell you why you goofed." He squeeked his chair around and lit the dying butt again. "Let's not talk about your taking off without my say-so. With you, I'll overlook that. Let's talk about what Limpy told me. Limpy called from Vegas and says you're there seeing Buchanan and that sidekick of his. You're seeing them about the percentage from their clubs. Next thing, you're ready to leave town, the percentage guarantee all settled in your favor—and Buchanan in the hospital."

Gluck paused, trying to make an impression. Jesso just sat, because it didn't mean a thing to him.

"You roughed him up!" Gluck yelled, and it came so suddenly that Jesso wasn't sure he'd heard it right. "You caused a stink, you lousy moron!"

Gluck sat down again, and except for the color of his face he looked as settled as before.

So did Jesso. He crossed his legs and said, "Say that again, President?"

"This is the deal," Gluck said, and for once he talked straight. "We do things in a new way around here, and that includes you. We don't roughhouse, we don't attract attention, we don't act like hoodlums in a gang war. It's big business all around, which means be nice, do what you're told, and when you shaft a guy you make him like it. Understand?"

"Sure. But that's not for me, President."

Gluck sighed. "You know, you're asking for it, Jesso."

"What?"

"The boot."

"Try it, Gluck," and Jesso smiled.

"Not me, buddy boy. The syndicate."

Jesso just laughed.

"What if I asked you to fade, Jackie boy? Blow, scram, never come back?"

Jesso shrugged. "I wouldn't go. I got some interests to protect."

"That's what I like to hear, boy." Gluck looked friendly. "I like to hear you're interested in your skin and that it's all tied up with us."

"So?"

"So you can stay. Like on probation."

This time it stung. Jesso got out of his chair like a shot and slammed his hands on the desk.

"Gluck, you sonofabitch, try pushing me! Just try." Jesso's voice was like a knife. Then it sounded foolish to him, because it wasn't really Gluck that mattered. It was the spidery web of one big clique that nobody ever saw, a thing much bigger than one man. He stood still, waiting.

"You listening, Jackie boy?"

"Yes, sir."

"I got a job for you."

"Thank you. I got one."

"An easy job, Jackie boy, but it's like probation."

"Like what? Apologize to Buchanan?"

Gluck laughed. "We wouldn't do that to you, boy. This job is easy."

"What?"

"I'm farming you out."

Jesso got tense. He had to hold on, bide his time, stall them long enough to get his things in order. The syndicate might look polite, but in the end they handled things just about the way he did. One fast punch, or push, or shot, and the problem was solved. For good.

Jesso sat down again. "What job, Gluck boy?"

"They want you to find a man. That's all."

"How much?"

"Twenty grand. For me, not for you."

Gluck sat back, obviously hoping that Jesso would bust something. He watched as Jesso's neck swelled and the eyebrows made a sudden line grow down the middle of the forehead. But Jesso didn't do anything else.

"I won't do you the favor, President. I won't goof," he said. "I'm a good little boy taking his licking." He took a breath. "Who's the outfit?"

"Here's the card with the address." Gluck handed it over. "Just an address, Jack boy, and it isn't an outfit."

"No name, even?"

"The name's Kator," Gluck said.

Jesso got up and went to the door. "I'm going to do you the favor, buddy boy," he said. "I'm taking that job."

Chapter Three

Kator had a suite in an uptown hotel and Jesso got there at eight in the morning. If Kator wasn't out of bed yet, that would be fine too.

The tall guy opened the door. He took the card Jesso had brought, and that was all. He hardly nodded when Jesso wished him a good morning.

"Remember me, friend? The clothes tree."

"This way, please."

"How's Porker, friend?"

"Mr. Kator is waiting."

The next room wasn't large, but Jesso didn't see Kator right away. He sat hidden in a high-backed chair, his small hands folded in his lap. The thick neck was wedged into a stiff collar, and Jesso had to walk around the chair before he could see the man's face. Then Kator was out of his chair with an easy movement.

"You are Mr. Jesso," he said. He held out his hand. When Jesso took it he was surprised by the strength of the grip. "Now that you will be working for us temporarily, please be seated and listen closely."

Kator might just as well have left out the "please." His voice was clear, machine-like. The English was so perfect that Jesso was sure that Kator spoke another language, one that he must like much better.

Jesso sat.

"Now that you are working for me, I will give you all the necessary leeway to do your job. However, I require a report of every step you take. The nature of your job and my interest in its outcome—"

"What's the job?"

"Did you understand my instructions?"

"Sure, Kator. Sure. What's the job?"

Jesso had been talking fast. The way he was starting to feel about Kator, it helped to talk fast.

Kator pulled up his chair and turned his head right, then left. The stiff collar made a scraping sound on his neck.

"A member of my organization has disappeared. You are to find him, Jesso. His name is Joseph Snell. He is, in fact, hiding out from me, apparently under the impression that I wish him ill. I know he is in New York. However, I do not know how long he will stay here. You can see it is imperative that he be found quickly. Those, in brief, are the facts. Find Joseph Snell, inform me of his whereabouts, and your job is completed."

Kator stopped.

"That's it?" Jesso lit a cigarette.

"Yes. How do you propose to start?"

"I'll start with you. What's your business?"

Kator blinked. "I fail to—"

"If I don't know what your boyfriend Snell's been doing, how can I look for him in the right places?"

"It will be sufficient for you to know, Jesso, that I am a businessman. A businessman with far-flung obligations, and Joseph Snell is one of my associates."

"Why do you want him?"

"Mr. Jesso." Kator turned his head with that slow squeeze of the neck. "I will tell you what you need to know, and I will decide what you need to know. I regard any questions as impertinence."

For a moment Jesso forgot all about Gluck and what might happen. For a moment, he forgot that he was in the middle of a squeeze and that it would take more than a punch or a push or a shot to get it all back to where he wanted it. Then he held still. He leaned back in his chair and blew smoke slowly. He concentrated on just that, and Kator. What got him was the way Kator had said it. He had said it just so; not to be insulting or to act big, but just so. Because Kator felt he was talking to a bug. There probably wasn't a man on this earth that Kator didn't think was a bug.

Jesso kept sucking on his cigarette. When he figured his voice was going to be steady, he leaned forward again.

"I'm going to ask what I need to know. I'm not a divining rod, Kator, but I got the job to find your flunky, and as long as I do your gumshoeing for you, you open up and answer. Or get someone else."

Kator sat still, waiting.

"Who's Snell?" Jesso asked.

"An associate of mine."

"Why's he hiding?"

"I remind you, Jesso—"

"The hell with that!" Jesso was up now. "Let me remind you of something. If Snell's on the lam because you're gunning for him, that's one kind of job. If he's got something you want, that's another. I wanna know if he's laying for me ready to kill, or ready to argue, or just lying there scared stiff." Jesso took a deep breath. "So let's have some answers."

"Joseph Snell is most likely scared stiff, as you call it, and I want him found because I must speak to him." Kator raised his small hands and put the fingertips together. "Whether he is likely to take a shot at you, that is something you may tell me about after you've found him." Kator shifted in his chair. "Now then, what else do you need to know?"

"Has Snell got any friends in town?"

"Really, Jesso. We've explored that angle."

"Has he?"

"No. He has been with me for a number of years. We met in Europe and his ties in the States were severed long ago."

"How long?"

"The early thirties. In fact, he used to know a man called Bonetti. I mention the name because you and this Bonetti are in a similar—uh—field."

Jesso started to pace the room. "Hell, Bonetti's dead. He died— Wait a minute."

Jesso had forgotten about Kator and Gluck, about the stupid way this punk job had been thrown at him. He wasn't thinking of any of this because now he had started to work. Jesso went to the phone and dialed long-distance.

"Give me Las Vegas, the Sagebrush. I want to talk to Mr. P. Carter.... Yeah, person to person. And call me back." He gave his number and hung up. Next he called Murph, who was repairing the carburetor on one of Gluck's cars. Murph got the call in the basement garage.

"Murph? Jack. Listen. Put out the word I want a guy that's on the lam. He's from out of town. His name's Joseph Snell, might be using his own. Now, this guy's an outsider, and—Kator, what's Snell look like?"

Kator had been watching without a word. He gave an involuntary start. "Short, thin black hair. His hands tremble, a condition he has. Eyes blue and somewhat protruding. He—"

"That's good enough. Murph? Listen," and Jesso repeated the description. "Call the usual places and let me know when you hear something, Murph.... To hell with his carburetor. Let him get a mechanic.... No, right now, and get to it."

Jesso hung up. He stared right through Kator, and there was a concentrated frown on his face.

"Do you propose to conduct your search from my telephone, Jesso?"

"Why, you short of money?"

"I'm trying to appraise your methods."

Jesso put his hands in his pockets. "Look, Kator, why'd you come to Gluck for this job if you don't think we can do it?"

"I didn't. It was Mr. Gluck that suggested the arrangement."

"What?"

"You are surprised? My original business with Gluck had to do with other matters. I have a ship in the East River and my business required special docking procedures, and Mr. Gluck's—uh—unique influence over docking matters—"

"You mean Gluck dreamed up this job in the first place?"

"No. The job was there. I mentioned my efforts to find this associate, and

Mr. Gluck suggested that you might help."

Not until then did it occur to Jesso just how badly Gluck wanted him out. That grinning bastard even went out of his way to hunt up a bum job for Jesso.

The phone rang, but Jesso didn't move. For a moment he felt pushed into a corner, squeezed from every side by Gluck, the thing he stood for, the big, invisible strength of the syndicate.

"Jesso, the phone is ringing."

He reached for the receiver and said, "Yes, hello." It sounded a little sharp.

"I am ready with your call to Las Vegas. Go ahead, please."

"Hello. That you, Carter?"

"Jackie, how are ya? You're hardly home and already—"

"Listen close, Paul. I got business. You remember Bonetti?"

"Bonetti?"

"Yeah, yeah, Bonetti. Twenty years ago. You're old enough to remember."

"Oh, Bonetti! Sure, I remember him."

"You knew him pretty good, didn't you?"

"A little business here and there."

"So listen. He had a punk in his crowd called Snell. Joseph Snell."

"Never heard of him."

"Sort of short, popeyed."

"Never heard of him, Jackie."

"All right, all right. Snell was in his crowd, though. Who's still around that Snell might know?"

There was silence for a moment and then Carter said, "Bonetti's dead."

"I didn't ask that, damn it!"

"There was Pickles, but he's on the rock."

"Bonetti had a brother, didn't he?"

"That's right. But, Christ, he must be seventy or something. Besides, he never hung around much. Did the fencing, is all."

"And kept a hideout for the boys, didn't he?"

"That's right. But he must be over—"

"Never mind. What happened to him?"

"Christ, Jackie, I wouldn't know."

"Who would? Think, Paul."

"He had a daughter. Cook's the married name."

"Here in New York?"

"I think so. At least, five years ago I remember—"

"O.K., Paul, thanks a million."

Jesso hung up. He turned to Kator, who had lit a cigar and stood by the window watching Jesso.

"I need a phone book, Kator. Manhattan first."

"To your left, in the drawer." Kator rolled the cigar between his lips and watched Jesso.

There was a long string of Cooks, and Jesso felt disgusted before he started. Then the phone rang. "This is Murph. May I speak—"

"It's me, Murph. So?"

"I checked around by phone, Jackie, and so far nothing. Nobody's seen anything like that Snell guy around. And I meant to tell ya, Jackie, Gluck came down and the car wasn't ready. So I tried to explain to him how you—"

"To hell with Gluck. What else?"

"I sent a few guys checking the flops and got some names for you. Names of guys what used to keep a hole in the wall for special guests."

"Let's have it."

"Well, there's that farmer Cook, out near Nyack."

"You say Cook?"

"Yes, Jackie. He's in New Orleans right now, due back in a week. Then there's Murrow, Able—sometimes, anyway—another Cook, Jenowitch—"

"That's enough. Stay at Gluck's place and I'll be right over."

"O.K., Jackie, but I wanted to tell you, Gluck was sore when his car wasn't—"

"Forget it. And wait for me."

Jesso hung up. This job was going to be over so fast that Gluck was going to have sleepless nights thinking of bigger and better ways to get under Jesso's skin.

"Where are you going?" Kator was still by the window.

"To find your man. I'll phone you."

"Just a moment." Kator was in the middle of the room when Jesso turned. "You will take one of my men with you. As I explained to you earlier—"

Jesso stopped at the door. He made it short. "I work alone. Send one of your monkeys and you won't find your man for weeks. I'll see to that." He slammed the door.

Chapter Four

The other Cook lived in Brooklyn. After Jesso had taken Murph's list, he decided on the Cook in Brooklyn first. Murph had finished with the carburetor in the meantime, so Jesso took Gluck's car.

The address was a store that said, "Notions." The dim insides hung full of dusty dresses, and everything looked twice as cheap where a naked bulb made a glitter on the boxes of fancy buttons. When Jesso came in, a fat woman with an apron over her coat was scratching a fingernail over the plastic eye of a button. "No, thanks, dearie, it ain't what I want," she said. Her other hand dropped something into her pocket. "No, dearie, this ain't the right color," she said, and left through the door.

The other one didn't look any better. She watched Jesso walk up to the counter. When the glare from the bulb hit his face she said, "What do you want?"

"Buttons," Jesso said.

She patted her hair. It was a rumpled gray and she kept patting it as if that were going to make a difference.

"The buttons I'm after are blue. Popeye blue, Mrs. Cook."

She stopped patting. "How'd you know my name?"

"Your father told me."

She leaned her face closer and Jesso saw wrinkles stretch in her neck.

"You're lying. He ain't left the back in years." She straightened up again and folded her big arms. "What do you want, copper?"

Jesso laughed. Then he stopped and put his hands in his pockets. "Where's Bonetti?"

She still look rattled. "Who's that?"

"Your old man, in the back. He ain't left the back in years, you said."

She was stupid. "Who's Bonetti?" she said again.

Jesso shrugged and walked through the curtain in the back. It was even darker there. He stumbled over an empty carton that lay on the floor and hit his leg against a sewing machine. Then he stood still, trying to get his bearings. Tissue paper crackled under his feet and there was a smell of burned coffee.

"He's a copper," the woman said from the curtain.

"Oh, no, he ain't."

Jesso turned, looking for the cackly voice. Then he saw Bonetti. He sat all sunken in a wheel chair, his old man's jaws chomping in a constant tic, and there was a big .45 in his hand. It trembled a little, but the aim was good enough.

"Call the police, Ann," Bonetti said.

Jesso kept his hands down, turned slowly.

"Go ahead, Ann," he said. "Gluck's going to like that. And Snell."

But Gluck didn't mean a thing to Bonetti and he ignored the name Snell.

"Go on, Ann," he said. He kept working his jaws.

Bonetti's daughter stepped around the sewing machine and grabbed the phone off the hook. "Police," she said.

When she was connected with the police she gave her name and address, and asked to have a man sent out right away, because her daddy had caught a prowler and was holding a gun on him. She hung up and turned to Jesso. "Smart guy," she said, and worked her mouth the way her father was doing it.

"That's right," Jesso said. He stood still and watched the old man's gun. The muzzle was making short, trembly arcs, the safety was off, and one bony finger held the trigger the way it ought to be held.

"Lemme reach for a smoke," Jesso said. He waited for an answer.

"See if he's clean, Ann."

"He's clean," Jesso said, but the woman started to pat his sides, without ever getting in the way of the gun.

"So smoke," Bonetti said.

Jesso lit up and let them watch. He could tell they were getting puzzled.

"You know you made a mistake, don't you, Bonetti?" The old man didn't answer. His daughter poured a cup of the coffee that Jesso had been smelling and the old man started to slurp.

"This'll ruin your setup, Bonetti, once the cops have been here."

Bonetti just slurped.

"You should have asked my name, Bonetti."

"And get a lie."

Jesso sighed and took an elaborate puff on his cigarette. "I thought you might feel that way, Bonetti." Then he leaned against the sewing machine, finished his cigarette, and just waited.

When the cop came charging into the store and through the curtain, nobody turned.

"That's him," Bonetti said, pointing with the gun.

The cop stumbled over the paper carton and knocked against Jesso. He grabbed him by the arm and held his .38 against Jesso's side. "What's he done? Who's preferring charges?"

Before Bonetti got his mouth open, Jesso turned his face to the cop.

"Nobody's preferring charges," he said.

There was quite a pause when he was through.

Then Bonetti flicked the safety and put the gun down in his lap. "I am," he said. "Breaking and entering."

"Pops is balmy," Jesso said. "We're old pals having a chat. Then his mind starts to wander, you know how it is," and Jesso moved to shake the cop's hand off his arm.

But that didn't come off, either. The young cop was a rookie and he wasn't getting any of this. He grabbed Jesso's arm and yanked.

"You resisting arrest, buddy?" His face came close.

"Heavens, I wouldn't!" Jesso said. He grinned back at the cop.

"So don't make suspicious movements," the rookie said, and he waved his gun up and down.

"Before you shoot, Officer, I got a confession to make." The cop waited. "Ever hear of Jack Jesso?"

The cop had, but he didn't like being snowed. He turned back to the old man, but he wasn't any help either. Bonetti had heard of Jack Jesso too. Bonetti sat still, waiting for the rookie to carry the ball.

"So what?" said the rookie. "I also heard of Jack Rabbit. Now move, buster. You, lady," he nodded at Bonetti's daughter, "better come along to the station."

But Jesso didn't move, and the woman didn't move. Old Bonetti waved his hand at her and the woman stood still, waiting for somebody to make up his mind.

"I got more to confess, Officer," Jesso said. "It'll save you the trouble of facing up to a false-arrest charge."

"Who'll charge false arrest?" the rookie yelled.

"I will," Jesso said. "Me. Jack Jesso."

The cop stepped back. "Stick out your hands," he said, and he fumbled for the handcuffs under his coat. He still held the gun in the other hand.

Jesso folded his arms. "I'll save your job for you," he said. "One phone call, rookie, and I save you your job."

"Don't move," said the rookie.

"Or I'll bust you back to civilian."

"Stick out those wrists."

"You don't hear Pops preferring any charges, do you?"

That was true. Bonetti hadn't said a word. He was chomping his gums and trying to look sly.

"One phone call, rookie, and the whole thing's forgotten."

"Don't move," said the rookie. He had started to sweat.

"I'm standing still," Jesso said. "You make the phone call. What's your precinct?"

The rookie told him.

"Call and ask for Captain Todd. Tell him I want to talk to him."

Jesso could almost see the wheels going around in the cop's head. He would be a fool to let this go by. Either way, how could he lose?

The cop made the connection and then Jesso took the phone.

"Ed? Jesso.... Fine, fine. Listen, a man of yours asked me to call, for character reference, sort of. Tell him who I am and so forth.... No, just a mix-up.... No, no. Just a real alert kid. Wanted to make sure there was no mistake. Some loony called the cops thinking I was going to steal his wheel chair.... No, honest. Here he is." Jesso turned to the cop and gave him the phone.

It didn't take long after that. The rookie hung up, holstered his gun, and put the handcuffs away. He gave Bonetti a dirty look, kicked the paper carton out of the way, and left. When the front door banged shut, Jesso walked over to the wheel chair and took the .45 out of the old man's lap.

"Nothing like a cop for a character witness, is there, Bonetti?"

The old man coughed. "How should I know who you was? You shoulda told me who you was."

"And get told I'm a liar," Jesso said. He tossed the gun on the sewing machine. "Where's Joe Snell?"

"Look, Jackie." Bonetti came wheeling across the room. "I gotta make a living. I never yet crossed a customer."

"There's no convincer like an honest cop, Bonetti."

The old man squirmed in his chair. He rolled the wheels back and forth as if he were trying to twist them off.

"What are you worried about, Bonetti? You know I haven't got a gun."

"All right." The old man sounded peeved. "Take him down." He nodded at his daughter. "He only paid in advance till tomorrow."

Bonetti's daughter led the way through another room, into the kitchen, and stopped by a chipped piece of linoleum on the floor.

"Pick it up," she said. "I ain't so young any more."

Jesso picked it up and then the trap door underneath. The woman climbed down the stairs, grunting each time she took a step. She waited for Jesso in the basement.

It stank. It wasn't just the mold and the dead air, but other things too. Behind a coal bin, in a thing like a storage closet, there was a cot under a dim window.

The first thing Jesso saw about the man was his eyes. They glittered like the buttons upstairs.

He lay on the cot, face up, and he was mumbling without ever moving his lips.

"He's sick," Jesso said. "Has he seen a doctor?"

The old woman made a motion with her mouth, turned, and went back up the stairs.

The man on the cot was lying as before. His bony head looked white and his hair started far back.

"You Joseph Snell?"

His eyes blinked and he started to chatter.

"Look pal. I'm not getting a word of this," Jesso said.

"They can't wait," the man was saying. "Can't much longer. I told him. Kator knows it."

"You're Snell, all right." Jesso leaned closer. "You wanna glass of water?"

"But you gotta have both. I got it, I got it. Honeywell—You were sixteen, my village queen—" he started to sing.

Jesso picked up the milk bottle at the foot of the bed and sloshed the liquid around. It was water.

"Here, take some." He held the man up by the neck, forced the bottle through the man's teeth, and poured. Snell started to drink. His eyes focused suddenly and he sat up. He spat out the water and pushed the bottle away.

"Did you hear?" he said. "A beauty. Man, such a beauty!"

"Yeah, what a kid."

"What a prom," said Snell, and he shook his head. Then he slumped back again and stared. "Honeywell," he said.

"I know. Certainly." Jesso put the bottle down.

"Honeywell high! Honeywell high!" The man sounded excited.

"Look, Snell—"

"Honeywell high, Honeywell high!"

"Sure, what a team. Good old Honeywell High."

"Good old Honeywell High," said the man, and his sick eyes weren't looking at anything.

Jesso tried to get through once more, but he had to give up. He went up the stairs into the kitchen, and left the trap door open. In the room with the sewing machine he found Bonetti and his daughter.

"Take him some coffee," he said. They stared at him. "Take him some coffee."

He watched the woman take a cup of the stuff to the kitchen and left. There weren't any customers in the front; just the buttons with the sick glitter.

He took his time driving back to Manhattan. The job had taken barely half a day. Kator could wait. And Snell, he wasn't going anywhere with that fever. The noon traffic was heavy across the bridge, but Jesso hardly noticed. He thought of Gluck once, good old anxious Gluck with the convention smile, biting his fingernails, hardly able to wait for Jesso to throw the job and give Gluck his chance to make his move. All by the code, too. "You goofed, Jesso, and out you go. We can't afford dead wood," or some fine phrase like that. Gluck had a surprise coming.

But the thought didn't give Jesso any real kick. He kept crawling with the traffic, not minding it, because right then he didn't feel like going anywhere fast. Maybe a drink would pick him up. Maybe a short trip South and to hell with Gluck and his schemes. Or a woman, if he had a real woman.

He stopped the car in the Fifties and walked across the street to the bar. There was a lot of carved oak and antlers and brass-buttoned leather. Aside from that, the place was almost empty. The barkeep was eating a corned-beef sandwich, and when he saw Jesso he took one more bite and reached back for the bottle of Scotch.

"Been out of town?" he said through a mouthful. Then he pushed Jesso's double across the bar.

Jesso paid and sat down.

"Where's the cool, beautiful blonde?" said the barkeep.

"Don't talk with your mouth full."

"Lynn, wasn't it?" The barkeep took another bite. "Been here a few times. Nary a drop she had, just looked. You two busted?"

"You will. Any minute now," Jesso said. He took his glass and went to a table. He sat down and watched the fat shine of the sunlight where it hit one end of the oak bar. At first he thought about Lynn, because the barkeep had mentioned her and because she used to come here with him. He'd brought her here because he liked the place, not because it was especially good for a twosome. She got to like it too. She started to like everything he did, in the end.

Jesso sipped his double and tried to think of Lynn. But it was just a game, because he was so completely through with her that there was nothing to think about. One of the brass buttons on the leather chair opposite kept shooting a light in his eyes, so Jesso shifted. Another chair with brass buttons. Nothing but buttons all over the place. Like that poor bastard in Bonetti's basement with two fever buttons for eyes. Jesso wondered what Kator might be after. It couldn't be friendly. Kator was too big and Snell was too small. Just about the kind of setup Gluck would have liked. Gluck big, Jesso small, and the chase was over. Jesso sipped and felt the Scotch work up behind his eyes. Nothing like Snell was going to happen to him. Not Gluck or Muck or who knows what was big enough to make that happen to Jesso. He took a big breath, as if testing whether there were still enough air around. That felt better. Right then even the thought of Gluck didn't bother him, because actually Gluck didn't mean a damn thing to him. Gluck was a small bug in a big web and he thought everybody else must be the same. Jesso blew smoke and watched it drift away. That's what he thought of Gluck and his outfit. All Jesso ever wanted was a free hand and nobody underfoot, and no smoke-blowing bug in a web was going to change that.

That's all he ever wanted, he was thinking, and then he knew there was something else he wanted. He wanted that, and a special kind....

The door opened and Lynn walked in. A special kind of woman.

"Darling! I found you!" she said.

But Lynn wasn't it.

"Do you know I was in here just yesterday, Jackie? Do you know I had a feeling you might drop in?"

He got up and moved a chair for her.

"Wanna drink?" he said. He said it nicely, because he had nothing against her. Only she'd probably give it the wrong slant, all loaded with meaning and undercurrents and inevitable love.

"Scotch, darling. But I'll have mine with water."

He drank Scotch, she drank Scotch. That was Lynn. The barkeep was eating a pickle, but he stopped long enough to bring the drink.

"Don't talk with your mouth full," Jesso said when the barkeep came up. The barkeep closed his mouth, put down the drink, and left.

"Smoke?"

"Yes. One of yours," she said.

She blew smoke, being careful to point away from the table. Then she looked at Jesso.

One thing about Lynn, she had a fine touch with feelings. She was blind when it came to loving Jesso. He could have tossed her out of a window and she wouldn't have believed it, but with everything else she was sensitive.

"What is it, darling?" She put her hand on his.

"Nothing. How's the drink?"

"Something's troubling you, Jackie."

That's another thing about Lynn, he thought. No privacy. She tries to crawl right inside you.

"Business," he said, because he knew she wasn't going to stop till she got an answer. "Just some of the usual."

"You've never talked much about your business, Jackie."

"That's because it's nobody's business. How are your stocks and bonds?"

"Jackie, don't you know I wouldn't mind anything about you? Whatever your business is?"

"Fine. So there's nothing to talk about."

"I know a little about you. Some of my friends even use your—your services."

"They do?"

"Of course. I have friends who gamble."

"Oh."

She smiled. "You say 'Oh' as if I missed something, Jackie."

"Not a thing. Another drink, Lynn? I got to go."

She shook her head. "Darling." She paused to put her cheek in one hand. She kept looking down and talked as if she had it all prepared. "Darling, I know what a strain it must be, even danger. Whatever you do, Jackie, I know you don't feel right about it."

Except for the fact that she was all wrong, she had something there.

"If something troubles you, Jackie, and I know something does—"

"Thanks, Lynn. But you're wrong."

She looked up. "Can I help?"

He wasn't even listening. He was thinking that she wasn't the right kind of woman, and if he kept her sticking around, that would be worse trouble than anything else that might happen to him.

"Jackie, if you need money—"

He made around one hundred grand a year and paid perhaps a thousand in income tax.

"I'll really help you, Jackie. Listen. Daddy's in Mexico right now, but when he comes back I'll speak to him. I can get you a job, darling, whatever you like, a real job where you'll meet new friends, have a new life, with me. I'm getting the house at Oyster Bay, any time I want it, darling, and we could ask Daddy—"

He found he'd been listening. He found he'd been thinking that there probably were no Glucks and no Kators in the world she could take him to. And for certain there wouldn't be any Snells with the fever getting too big for the man so that nothing was left but to burn up in the middle of it.

"Did you hear me, Jackie?"

"I heard what you said, Lynn." He pushed back his chair.

"Don't go, Jackie."

"'By, Lynn."

"Jackie." She held his hand.

He pulled his hand away and gave her a smile. "'By," he said, and his hand gave her a small pat. But even Lynn couldn't read much meaning into it, because then he was gone, closing the door, knowing that Lynn was not his way out of it, that what came next was Kator.

Chapter Five

He jockeyed the car through the midtown traffic as if he were beating an obstacle course. He was in a hurry now. It felt good. Jesso kept thinking about it, how Gluck had tried to cramp his style and how Jesso himself had just about let him do it. There wasn't any point in bucking Gluck the way he had felt like doing. Jesso could waste his temper on Gluck and never make a dent. But when it came to turning a fast job, that was one place where Gluck couldn't get him. That was one pitch even Gluck's organization couldn't match. And there was going to be some fancy pitching from now on. Gluck and his cronies were going to learn something. They were going to learn how Jesso could move like a one-man army.

He got to Kator's suite in a fine humor, and when he had to wait he didn't even mind that. Kator had barely nodded at him and then got busy again stuffing papers and folders into a brief case. Kator was cleaning his desk. He looked like a man in a hurry.

"That big important deal of yours, Kator. It's all wrapped up."

Kator didn't answer. He left the room with a full wastebasket in his hand, and when he came back, the wastebasket empty, Jesso tried again.

"If you're done with the spring cleaning, Kator—"

This time Kator sat down. "Did he shoot at you, Jesso? You remember, you were going to let me know whether Snell was going to shoot at you."

Jesso couldn't make it out. He cocked his head and put his hands in his pockets.

"A real clown," he said. "I get chased out on a life-and-death mission and I come back to get clowned at. What happened, Kator—the spring cleaning shake you all up?"

"It is more important than clowning." Kator stroked a pale eyebrow. "You will learn that presently."

"You sound bitter, Kator."

"Hardly. It is no longer any concern of mine. However, I am bound to tell you that you have failed."

It didn't make any sense, but Kator didn't look as if he were joking. Kator never looked as if he were joking.

"You have ignored my instructions, Jesso. I told you distinctly to take one of my men along." Kator's blue eyes were fixed on Jesso in an unpleasant stare, but it didn't impress him.

"I'm all broke up about that, Kator. So I did the next best thing. I'm back to tell you about it."

"Before you make light of my instructions, let me explain it to you this way. Did you see Joseph Snell?"

"In person."

"You were not to see him. Did you spend time with him?"

"We had tea."

"That too was to be avoided. Did you speak to him? Did he speak to you? Please answer me, Jesso."

"Look—"

"You did speak to him, contrary to my wishes. So you see, Jesso, when I give instructions, they always have meaning, they have reason, even though you do not—"

"Now shut up a minute!" Jesso leaned close enough for Kator to see the nervous twitching of his eyebrows.

"I don't go for that *Junker* stuff, Kator, so save your lessons and get this straight. I don't give one good goddamn how you like your potatoes served or your lousy reports and errands done. You sent me to find a man and I did. You don't like the way I'm doing it, so go lump it. The job's done and for all I care you'll pay for nothing."

That's when Kator started to smile; not big and sunny, but still a smile.

"You are wrong, but that is understandable. You apparently do not know what my arrangements with your Mr. Gluck really are."

"Go on. What comes next?"

"We arranged, you might say, a package deal. I am paying your Mr. Gluck a lump twenty thousand for two services. For your job and for the docking arrangements. If either service is unsatisfactory, Jesso, I do not have to pay."

Jesso was getting the drift now. He thought about it while Kator went on.

"I have no reason to believe that Mr. Gluck will fail in his docking arrangements. It is a simple matter. There are persons in my group who cannot leave this country without Mr. Gluck's special arrangements. That's why my ship is docked where Mr. Gluck has influence. As to your part of the service, Jesso, I am forced to report that you have failed." Kator paused. "Mr. Gluck will therefore not collect his fee—because of you. Do you understand now, Jesso?"

Jesso understood so fast it came like a white glare, and he couldn't see Kator, the pig smile on his face, or the small idle hands on the desk. He understood how they'd worked it and how Gluck had him good, where it hurt. Jesso cost the syndicate a fee, goofed on the simplest possible job. Or that's the way it would look when Jesso was out of the way and Gluck told the story, with Johannes Kator, the dissatisfied customer, bearing him out. It was so bad that Jesso came close to taking it out on Kator, but he let it go. There still was time and a chance. He hadn't told where Snell was holed up, and that was all he could think of right then. With Snell wrapped up, Jesso was sure there'd still be a thing or two he could do to make Gluck turn sick.

He stood still for a second, not moving. Kator sat in his chair and folded one leg over the other so that the black silk of one sock showed over his shoe. He started to dip his foot, once, maybe twice, and then Jesso took off. He took off with only one thing on his mind, so he didn't wonder about it when nobody stopped him and he didn't see when Kator uncrossed his legs, smoothed the trousers down over the black silk sock, picked up the phone, and dialed Gluck's number.

Jesso got back to Brooklyn in half the time it had taken before.

Joseph Snell was still there.

"Up, Joe, and make it fast." Jesso grabbed the man by the arm.

Joseph Snell rolled off the cot and hit the floor flat. He did not move again.

Why he was dead Jesso didn't know. There wasn't a mark on the man. And he looked almost exactly as he had looked a few hours ago, except for a thing that Jesso couldn't place right away. Then he stepped on it. A hairpiece was lying on the floor, a slick patch of dark hair that used to fit over the bald skull in the back, where the natural hair made a ring around it. The skin wasn't whole there. Somebody had ripped the thing off, and fast.

Jesso picked up the hairpiece. There was a square little patch on the fabric inside, where there hadn't been any glue.

It made sense now, why Kator hadn't been interested enough to ask where Joe Snell was holed up. Jesso had led them right to him. They had kept out of the way, watching, and after he'd gone they had walked right in, taken the thing that Snell had hidden inside his toupé, and left. Snell could have died from fright and high fever. His eyes were open, but sightless now.

It made sense. It made even more sense when Jesso got back upstairs. He ran to the back room, where he found the old man in his wheel chair. His daughter was wiping a wet rag over a welt on Bonetti's cheek, and neither of them bothered to look at him. They must have started to tussle in the store. There were glass beads and fancy buttons all over the floor, some of them broken, others just lying there and staring up from the floor, the way Snell was doing.

The thought didn't stay long with Jesso because then a hard noise jolted the back of his head and all the bright buttons came rushing up to his face.

When Jesso came around it happened slowly. It was so gradual there was hardly any surprise when he realized how bad it was.

Two men in the front, one in the back right next to him. He didn't know the kid that was driving. Every so often a light would flash by the car and Jesso could see nothing but the man's silhouette. The other two had been around since Gluck had started in his job.

Gluck had made it. Jesso was out. He felt so miserable that the thought made hardly any impression; at first, that is.

"Is he still out?" said the front seat.

"Sure. When I clip 'em—"

"Save it. We're hitting traffic. Push him on the floor so he won't sit up sudden-like and make a commotion."

Jesso heard every word of it and knew what was coming. When the man next to him pushed at his shoulder, Jesso rolled off the seat to the floor like a limp corpse. The jar to his head almost made him scream and his face contorted with pain, but it was dark down there and nobody saw it. The longer they didn't know he was awake, the better for him. The better the chance—and then he realized there was no chance. There was no chance because he'd never prepared for this, had never thought it would go this far. So at first Gluck had come along to get under his skin. Nothing important. Nothing that ever looked as if life and death were in the scales. What Jesso had forgotten was that life and death didn't have much weight.

"He still out?"

"Yeah. We almost there?"

"Almost."

"Close your window. I can't stand the smell of that river."

"I gotta get my pass ready. Here comes the gate."

He'd forgotten that a man like Gluck didn't have to ask whether anybody wanted to claim the body.

The car slowed to a stop and somebody said, "O.K. Keep left till you hit Pier Twenty-eight." Then the car moved again.

Pier 28. That was part of Gluck's section. It didn't make sense; this wasn't the way they did it. Had Kator mentioned Pier 28? The brakes squealed and then the car doors came open. Jesso could smell the stink from the river, hear it lap. They grabbed him by the arms and started to pull. His knees dragged over the concrete.

Make his move now? What move? Wait. Wait and figure this thing. He stayed limp, eyes closed, head lolling down, and listened for the lap of the river. There were other sounds: other feet walking, the chug of an engine, and a steady splashing of water that poured from someplace into the river. But all that Jesso could see, carefully, was the concrete close underneath and the legs moving on either side. When they stopped they didn't drop him, but held onto his arms.

"Grab his legs. We'll carry him up."

One man let go and Jesso swung down sideways. He caught sight of the trousered legs farther ahead, the crease sharp as a knife. That was Gluck. Jesso got his eyes closed just in time.

"You needn't bother," said the voice. "Just drop him."

When they dragged him up the ramp and Jesso saw the rivet buttons of the steel floor under him, he knew they were aboard a ship, Kator's ship. After a painful time across the deck, down the companionway, and through the dark guts of the steamer, they tossed him to the floor where the bulkhead curved up with the ship's contour. They slammed a door and then Jesso was alone.

He had stayed limp, but now he relaxed. It was safe now. He was alone, alive, and there was time to think. The pain in his head had settled down to a busy throb and his scraped shins felt like fire. But he was alive and there was going to be time. There had to be, because Gluck must have farmed out the job. Why else the delay? They could have finished him in Bonetti's button shop, out in the country, or anywhere else along the way. Not Gluck, though; not when it came to handling someone like Jesso. Jack Jesso was going to fade for good, with no one but the sharks and lobsters wise to the deal. If Gluck said Jesso was dead, the reason would be that Jesso had fouled a deal. If Gluck said that Jesso had just disappeared, the reason would be even better. Jesso took off with Kator and left Gluck behind holding the bag. No one could lose, except Jesso.

The time on his hands had stopped being a blessing. He had done all the thinking there was to be done and now the time just meant a delay, a slow wait till the end.

Jesso got up and started to pace. He didn't have far to go. It was a small hold, down low, with nothing in it but pipes along the walls and gallon cans of paint stacked in one corner. Where the ship's side curved out, the cans were stacked with more rows on top than at the bottom.

Jesso paced, and after a while the irritation became like a physical grip. The small space began to squeeze him, the sight of the top-heavy stack of cans got on his nerves, and every time he turned he had to look at them. He started to sweat and itch, with the frustration making a stone-hard thing in his throat. Like a rat, he thought; like a blind rat he was caught. In a way it had all happened so fast and with such oiled and simple ease that he hadn't really grasped the fact of his sudden fall until now. Just this morning he'd been up there where he belonged, and now— The pressure rose and Jesso felt as though the air were getting thicker. He saw the port-hole then, the small, dim circle just big enough to hold a man's head. At any rate, there was air. Cursing with a rage that made his hands tremble, he twisted on the wing nuts that clamped the porthole shut. There were four of them, four brass wing nuts that seemed to bite back at him when he strained his fingers against them. When he had them loose and had swung the port back, he felt as if he were strangling, and when he saw the concrete pier shutting off view and air and distance, he gripped the rim of the open hole with an irrational fright, reared up ready to scream—and then he held his breath. He held it so long that there was a crackling in his ears.

"A bargain's a bargain," said Gluck's voice. "Besides, there's always the police."

By twisting his head and holding very still, Jesso could see them. An overhead light made a glare from somewhere, and the top of the pier showed like a black knife edge from side to side. And on the edge, knee bent as in a lazy pose by a fireplace, was a leg with a black silk stocking showing in front of the glare of the light. That was Kator. Gluck was standing farther from the edge.

"So don't miss the tide, Kator." The head was nodding. "You're out in half an hour or hell breaks loose."

First the silk wrinkled a little and then the foot began to tap. It had the same precision as Kator's voice.

"I must delay, Mr. Gluck. I must. Your arrangements for my ship's departure could be the same tomorrow as they are today."

"Too risky. I can't buy off twice in a row. You leave now, tonight, or you take your chances with the officials."

"I'll pay you, Mr. Gluck."

"You've paid me. You're dumping Jesso for me. Besides, you've found your man. He even kicked off for you from natural causes and you're covered."

"That is the point, Mr. Gluck. As it turns out, the information I collected is incomplete. With Joseph Snell dead, I must delay departure in order to complete my mission by consulting other sources. You see, Snell's death is really a complication, Mr. Gluck."

"Sorry," Gluck said. "The ship leaves now."

"If I could stay behind, Mr. Gluck, our difficulties would not exist, but my presence is required in—in Europe. Without being familiar with the details of my business, Mr. Gluck, you must try to appreciate the importance—"

"Sorry."

That was Gluck all over. When it came right down to it, Gluck never budged; he made everything simple that way. What in hell was Kator selling?

"Twenty thousand, Mr. Gluck."

Gluck barely laughed.

"Forty thousand."

Kator's foot had stopped tapping.

"Fifty thousand."

"Pretty important, huh, Kator?"

"Fifty thousand, Mr. Gluck, for the privilege—"

"Look, you got half an hour. Call up somebody you know, tell them what you need, explain what's eating you, and don't waste your time arguing with me."

This time Kator laughed. "You underestimate the complexity of my business with Joseph Snell."

"I didn't ask you to tell me about it."

What didn't concern Gluck he didn't want to know. He was through with Kator and that's where his interest ended. But Jesso's interest was just picking up. He wasn't through with Kator, he was just starting. Nothing was clear to him yet, but what he had heard meant one thing for sure. Jesso's knuckles ached where he held the rim of the porthole with a hard, still grip, holding on as if the words from the pier were his salvation. One thing was sure: Kator hadn't got all he wanted. Joe Snell was dead when they got to him and all he could give them was the thing under his toupé. A piece of paper, most likely, a piece of paper with part of a message, and the rest had died with him. Kator was strapped.

Then Jesso's hands relaxed on the metal rim and he moved his shoulders the way a boxer does, limbering up. Kator was strapped. And nobody had seen Joe Snell before he died—except Jesso.

He wasn't interested any more in what else went on up on the pier. Kator would jack up his price and Gluck wouldn't take it. Gluck would have his way, which meant that the ship would go out with the tide. Jesso could hear the rumble of the engines somewhere nearby. He closed the porthole, stretched, and sat down where the bulkhead curved up. A nap might be good now. He leaned back, feeling the small, hard vibrations of the hull as the engines turned faster. The massage gave him a tickle around his nose and he squirmed his face to kill the itch. He smiled and settled against the steel. Once they'd cleared port and the tugs had cast off and the pilot had left, there'd be a clanking of feet and the door opening, because Kator would be ready to finish his business with him.

And that's when Jesso would be ready to start business with Kator.

Chapter Six

They came earlier than he had expected. The door clanked, waking Jesso, and he struggled against his stiffness, trying to get up. Jesso remembered the tall one by the door from the time in Gluck's office. He stayed by the door, holding a Luger in his hand, while the other one came into the compartment. Before Jesso was up, a heavy boot caught his ribs and he fell hard to the side. He stayed there, fighting for breath, while the tall one stood by with his Luger. The other one closed a solid cover that darkened the porthole. He clicked a lock on it. Then they both left and Jesso was alone in the dark.

When the pain had simmered down, he got off the floor and tapped along the wall, trying to find the porthole. It was locked, all right. There wasn't even a crack of light. If they had been far out to sea, they wouldn't have bothered to close it. Instead they would have come for him to finish Kator's end of the bargain.

The ship rumbled with a rhythmic thump. They cleared the islands, at any rate.

Jesso sat down again and waited. He tried to sleep a few times, but sleep wouldn't come. His head ached, his legs were sore from the rawness where the skin had been scraped, and with each breath a shooting pain ran up the side of his ribs. After a while he tried to think of other things, how he would handle Kator, if there was time to handle Kator, and if perhaps his whole new hope was just the crazy wish of a man the night before his death.

A thousand times he went over it in his mind. After a while a slow rage started to boil in him, and if someone had opened the door right then Jesso would have jumped up and killed him.

But nobody came. For a long while there was nothing but the steady rumble of the ship, swaying now.

Jesso was crouching by the slanting bulkhead when he heard the steps. He had been crouching for an eternity, not moving, but his breath came fast and hard. And when the door swung open there was an outlined shape standing there, but Jesso was up like a cat, out through the door, and then his balled knuckles made contact until the shape was down and moaning.

Jesso stood blinking in the dim light from the companionway. He felt all right. He rubbed his knuckles, feeling nothing but the pleasant burn where his fists had hit.

The other guy had stood back. He came out of the shadows now, first the Luger, then his long shape.

"Don't move," he said, and his voice meant that he wished he would.

Jesso waited. He put his hands in his pockets and stood still. "Bean Pole," he said. "I want to see your master."

Bean Pole maneuvered around so he had Jesso against the light. "First you're going to die," he said.

Jesso laughed. "Like hell. Show me Kator, Bean Pole. I got something to sell."

He couldn't tell whether Bean Pole was taking his word for it, because all he said was, "Up the stairs."

Before Jesso went, he turned to look at the man on the floor. It was the one that had kicked him in the ribs. Jesso went up the stairs feeling better than ever.

It was blowing strong and steady on deck, but except for the wind-ripped tips of the waves, the water seemed to move slowly; big glassy mountains of water that stood for a moment with foam like marble along their sides, and then slowly sank into themselves, becoming the dark floor of a valley.

After the airless hold, Jesso felt suddenly cold and uncomfortable. When he stopped, the gun spiked him from behind and pushed.

"Turn left," said Bean Pole, "and walk as far as you can."

Jesso was out in the wind now. He felt his trouser legs whip back against his shins.

"As far as you can," Bean Pole had said. Fifty feet ahead was the round stern of the ship, with a low railing that sank below the black line of the horizon with a lazy dip, then climbed up again to stick out into the sky.

Kator was there with two sailors. They looked very solemn at the stern of the ship.

"There's Mr. Kator," said Bean Pole, "and just on the other side is where you go. Move."

Bean Pole needn't have done that. The jab of his gun almost missed, because Jesso was already leaning against the wind and going toward Kator. When he got there the two men in pea jackets grabbed his arms as if they thought he might jump.

Kator pursed his lips, but otherwise he made no movement. Only his black overcoat flapped at the bottom.

"This is to finish my end of the bargain," he said, and he nodded to the white water behind the ship.

With the wind tearing at his words, Jesso leaned forward. "I got something for you."

Kator took an involuntary step backward. The two men held Jesso's arms more tightly.

"Since there is nothing personal in this, Jesso, you can save your breath.

All right," and he nodded at the two sailors.

It wasn't much of a heave, and they were several feet from the railing, but Jesso bucked hard.

"Kator," he yelled, "it's about Snell."

But Kator hadn't understood. They had Jesso off the floor, legs thrashing, and the low railing was almost under him.

With a powerful concentration his leg whipped out and caught one man behind the knee. The guy buckled and fell.

"About Snell!" Jesso roared. "The rest of the stuff, Kator—from Snell!"

This time Kator heard. He moved forward and opened his mouth, but the two sailors didn't catch his words. With an angry push they flung Jesso forward. He caught himself on the railing with a painful thud and balanced there until one more short push at his leg made him slant forward and down.

Suddenly the wind had stopped. Close behind the stern there was no wind, no rushing noise, just the dull hissing of the foam below, and then Jesso flailed, tossed down, and hit.

The water, cut and churned, dragged at him, twisted him, and not until moments later did he feel the icy wash of the ocean sucking at his body from all sides.

How long it took for him to surface, how hard he screamed, none of this was ever clear to him. At first there was just the great panic when he heard the murderous roar of the big screw close by, and then his head was out of water with foam bursting around him, and the tall shape of the ship sliding away in slow dips made him feel as small as a black speck.

He was fighting the water. Then, when the large swells came and the white water had died away, the ship kept him from thinking. He had to see the ship, draw it back with his last will, hold it there, hold it before the panic came back and everything was over. Then the ship was gone behind the slow mountain of a wave while Jesso seemed suddenly to fall with terrible speed. The water sucked him back and up, higher in a continuous sweep, until the ship was there again, black, and smaller.

Details meant nothing to him then, and when he saw the ship the next time, partly sideways now, it never meant a thing. The next time it was still the same, and he slid down again into the cold valley of the wave.

He started to die then. He was past the panic and ready to die, except that it came to him like a strength instead of like a weakness. He would fight the suck and push of the water until he was dead, which meant that he could fight no longer. He would never be dead until he was empty of that.

So when the boat came alongside and they tried to pull him out, he was kicking and slashing at them so hard that he almost choked in the process.

When he started to sink, they heaved him up and over the side of the boat.

Jesso woke with a strong shiver, and when he felt the warmth around him he was surprised. Then there was a cup of coffee. It was black, hot, strong: smelling strong. Right then heaven could have been that cup of coffee. It was a pleasure that gave him time to come alive again. He sipped it slowly, he remembered what he could, and he looked around without talking.

Kator was a patient man. He sat at the other end of the cabin and watched Jesso come alive. Let the man have his coffee. It was small payment for what Kator hoped to gain.

When Jesso put his cup down and sat up on the bunk, he first hit his head on the bunk above and then he saw he was naked. The blankets had fallen back. He got up carefully, cursed with concentration, then sat down again. He stopped cursing suddenly, because now was the time for the payoff.

"You mentioned Snell," Kator said. "Did you have something to tell me, or was it all a maneuver?"

Jesso picked up a blanket and made a toga. "I got something."

"Go ahead, please."

Kator picked up a cut-glass bottle and poured red liqueur into two pony glasses. He gave one to Jesso.

"How about some clothes?"

"You won't need any, Jesso. You will tell me what you know and that will be the end of it."

Except for the queer position of Kator's eyes, which gave him a fixed stare, he might have looked bored. He sounded bored.

It took a while before Jesso caught it.

"You mean I take another dive?" It came out calmly, because Jesso didn't believe it. "You mean I tell you what I know and then hop-skip-jump back into the water?"

"Certainly. More liqueur?"

Jesso nodded automatically. His mouth moved but he didn't quite know what to do with his voice.

"I can make you talk, Jesso. One way or another. And if it doesn't work the first time—" Kator shrugged. "We have nine days before making port."

They looked at each other. Kator went on. "I rarely make bargains, Jesso, except in extremities, and I grant you that I am anxious to hear what you have to say. So I will bargain. You give me the information willingly and your death will be simple; unwillingly, Jesso, and it will be complicated. There is your choice."

The blanket had dropped off his shoulders and Jesso sat bare, but the sweat stood on his skin like hot glue. He stared at the man across the table without seeing him, thinking furiously, weighing his chance. He had only one advantage. Kator wanted something and wanted it bad. A dead man was no use to him, and that's how Jesso meant to stay alive.

"Kator, I want some clothes."

It surprised Kator, and he stopped his glass halfway to his mouth.

"Bravado, Jesso, will get you nowhere." He finished his drink.

Jesso moved suddenly. He slapped Kator's hand out of the way and for good measure he grabbed the bottle and threw it across the cabin. It crashed against the bulkhead. The sound of glass breaking was just the overture. Jesso's neck started to swell, and when he talked it wasn't politely.

"Now you hear this, you bastard. I know what little Joe said and you know nothing. You pitch me in the drink or run a bullet through my head and you know nothing. You rig it up so I get scared maybe and start yelling uncle, there again you don't know from Adam. I've had my scare, Kator, back there in the white water with the screw sucking me down. That was my scare and it cured me. You scare me like that again and you won't get the time of day from me. Maybe you got some fancy notions on how to make a man remember things, a trick or two you picked up in a concentration camp maybe—"

"You're right," said Kator, who had found his voice again.

"Shutup, you sonofabitch, and hear me out!"

Kator blinked, but then he had to strain to hear the rest. Jesso's voice had dropped to a vicious whisper and he spat out the words as if they tasted too strong.

"Maybe you think you'll rattle me with little tricks or something, or peel my skin off till I crack wide open. Like hell you will, you pig-eyed bastard, because you know what'll come out. I'll even tell you why. What Snell told me takes remembering, and I'm not good at complicated stuff. You just say boo to me and I can't add two and two. I'm nervous, I get confused. I can't remember complicated stuff. You don't believe me? Go ahead and try, Kator. You're afraid of losing what I know."

He stopped there and watched Kator's face working.

"Mr. Jesso," and suddenly Kator had a heavy accent, "I do believe you're bluffing."

It was Kator's last try and it didn't work. Jesso just laughed. He said, "How do you suppose I know your information isn't all complete?"

Kator gave up then. He picked up the speaker of a phone on the wall and said, "Heinz, bring clothes for Jesso."

Chapter Seven

He got some underwear and a nice warm sweater. The pants were loose around his waist, so Jesso bunched them up with a belt. He got socks and shoes, and then had a meal. He smoked a cigarette with satisfaction, letting Kator wait, because the next thing was more complicated. Jesso wasn't worried about his life any longer. The problem now was how to swing a deal. Maybe the biggest deal he'd ever had. Kator was sitting on something hot, and Kator didn't deal in peanuts. The question was how to pull a bluff with a man as sharp as Kator.

When it came to him he laughed, it was that simple. He'd get what he wanted in the strangest way of all. He'd level with Kator. He'd pump the man and turn him inside out, and then, by God, he'd give that pig a lesson in the fine art of promotion.

Kator had watched the laugh, and turned glum. Jesso's kind was new to him. The well tried ways of his particular training hadn't worked. This man was truly from another world, with no conception of his standing, not frightened for his creature comforts, and above all he seemed invulnerable in a strange belief that there was always one more chance. It made Kator wary. While he rarely underestimated an opponent, he found in this case that his estimate needed constant sharpening, changing. This was more painful because Kator felt he knew the kind of man he was dealing with: a standard product of a gutter, born in a standard country. A country that had never learned to breed an elite. What he faced in Jesso was an insult to his background, his career. His Pomeranian family was old, producing without change only the finest and the sternest of Germany's leaders. Even poverty never changed that. The ancient tract of land where Kator had been born lay large and useless, and in the winter the dank estate house had three rooms with heat, while the rest lay cold and unused. But Kator, like the ordained, followed his mission. His special twist of mind made the Kaiser's intelligence service his proper place. And then empire and state collapsed, and a different order hardly worth the name took hold.

When Kator's special twist of mind produced his next profession, he did the same as he'd always done. There was no geographic limit to his territory; his brain was his chief tool, and Kator stayed in the invisible leadership of one of those organizations that ferret, steal, and always find the kind of information that every government conceals and every government will buy. Like Jesso, Kator was on his own. Like Jesso, Kator had no outside loyalties. But unlike Jesso, Kator had a trick of thinking that his work was a service, as if his wealth were only a side issue to his work, as if there were some extra-human dedication to his energies. It gave Kator some imaginary edge, making no one his equal. He never flaunted it, but it was always part of his stance. It always worked, because the mark of the elite was seldom questioned.

"Reach me that coffeepot, Kator, will you?"

He pushed it over.

Jesso poured and said conversationally, "First I'll tell you what I want, Kator, and then I'll try to tell you what you want. Fair enough, Baron?"

"Jesso, if you imagine that delaying tactics—"

"You said you had nine days, didn't you. Tell me, are you a baron?"

"Jesso—"

"I bet you're a Nazi, though. You a Nazi, Kator?"

There was no answer.

"A Communist?"

When Jesso made no sign of interrupting, Kator took the time to answer. "My business, Jesso, is conducted on a level where temporary political affiliations have no meaning. Not that I expect you to understand, but there are loyalties that transcend—"

"Why, Kator, you're making a speech!"

It was true. Kator appeared angry and his eyebrows went up. Kator could raise his eyebrows without ever showing the upper lids. The heavy fold of skin over his eyes stayed down, making the face emotionless and calm.

Jesso laughed again. "You're a Nazi either way, Kator, but like you said, right now we'll have some bigger kinds of loyalties. Let's talk about what I want." Jesso crossed his legs and watched his foot bob up and down. "First of all, I get safe conduct. Where are we landing, Kator?"

"Hamburg."

"I want off at Hamburg. I want five hundred bucks in one pocket and a passport in the other. And a visa. I think I need a visa. That's cheap for what you're getting, isn't it?"

It was. Kator nodded because it was so cheap. "You can make a passport and so forth?"

"Of course."

"I thought so. Well, sir, you fix me up, Baron, and once I'm safe on land I'll tell you all. Fair enough, Baron?"

"You'll tell me what?"

"I'm coming to that. Fair enough, Baron?"

"I agree."

That was that part. And that's how Jesso meant to play it. His foot stopped bobbing and he watched the tip of his shoe. Then he started to dip it up and down again.

"Now comes what you'll be getting."

Kator leaned forward a little while Jesso kept watching his foot.

"Kator," he said, "I'm going to level with you." He stopped dipping, uncrossed his legs, and leaned his arms on top of the table. "I don't know what to tell you."

The silence came down like a cloud of poisonous gas, invisible, but with a certain deathly presence. Kator's blue eyes seemed to turn colorless and the shorn part of his skull was mottled red. Then he took a breath that sounded like an animal breaking through underbrush.

Jesso didn't laugh this time and his voice was curt. "I don't know what to tell you until I know what you're after. You get my meaning?"

Kator held still. It was the tone of voice that made him listen, and he sat wary now, his fingertips feeling the tabletop with the stealth of a thief.

"I told you how I am, Kator. I get confused. Complicated stuff makes me confused. When I saw Joseph Snell, he was sick. Crazy with fear and out of his head with fever. He told me a million things that made no sense. Some he said once, and then he'd switch and talk about the moon. Other things he'd keep repeating over and over, and he'd say, 'You get it now, can you remember—you see now what I meant?' You've got to help me pick the right clue."

Jesso saw Kator relax. His fingers stopped brushing the tabletop and his shoulders came down slightly. He had him. The story made sense and Kator had to take the chance.

"Well, let us begin." Kator was sober now, just barely urgent. "Start with the first thing that occurred."

Jesso almost laughed again. Kator would like that deal. He'd just love to sit there and sift the stuff, never letting on when the give-away came along, and then good-by, Jesso, hello, lobsters. Besides, what could he say? Tell Kator about Joe Snell's first love with the village queen? About his dear old alma mater, Honeywell High?

"Kator, you've got to remember the man was out of his head. He was talking crazy. How could I remember all that? We'll do it this way, Kator. Give me a picture of what goes on. Tell me your business, tell me what Snell might have wanted to say, and that way we'll spot the gimmick in the mess. That way we'll get somewhere."

This time Kator did the smiling. He leaned back in his chair and pulled a cigar out of a leather case. The cigar was evenly round, without a band, and had a faint green color.

"My dear Jesso." The cigar waved back and forth gently while Kator sniffed. "You've done well so far. You've changed within mere hours from a corpse in the Atlantic into a forceful executor of very expensive decisions. You have done all of the talking and now you even presume me stupid. Eh?"

"What in hell you talking about?"

"I should tell you what is so important in my mission? I should hand you information for which nations, continents might wish to go to war? Eh?"

"Eh, yes," said Jesso. And he left it there.

In a short moment Kator stopped smiling. His face became a mask and the cigar held still, forgotten and pleasureless. It didn't take Kator long to see he was licked. Without the clues he asked for, Jesso might never give him the vital information. The cigar snapped in half, making a papery sound. It had to be Jesso's way. For now, at any event. Later, there were other ways; there were certainly other ways.

Kator decided fast, and he played the new role well.

"While I take another cigar, Jesso, you may begin your questions."

"Who was Snell?"

"You mean, I'm sure, what was he to me?"

"Any way you want to put it, Baron."

"Snell had worked with me for many years. But he was an American. And like you and all your countrymen, he was an opportunist. He tried to cheat me."

"How?"

"Snell was in the States to transmit information. He was my courier. He had picked up the information as arranged and then decided not to deliver. Instead he meant to sell it himself."

"That's why he was scared to death?"

Kator shrugged. "He was, like many of his countrymen, a coward. I am not including you, dear Jesso," and Kator gave a pleasant nod.

"So now we're buddies."

They exchanged smiles like two actors on a stage. "What was this hot news, Baron?"

"Jesso, that man Snell had been with me for twenty years. Not even Snell knew the meaning of the message."

"Good for you."

"What else would you like to know?"

"What's your business, Baron?"

"Very simple. I deal in information."

"Espionage?"

"Sometimes, Jesso."

"This time, Kator?"

"This time, espionage."

Kator had made a smoke ring, blue and lazy, and they both watched it float. It disappeared after a while.

"Have you found your clue yet, Jesso?"

"I don't know. I'm getting there, it's starting to make sense. Snell kept telling me of dates, dates. He meant data. He must have meant that he had data on him."

"Brilliant, Jesso."

"Now don't get snippish, Baron. I'm trying my best. Now that I know what you've told me, data makes sense. And something else makes sense. Dates in the head, he kept saying, dates in the head." Jesso looked up, making his face intent. "You got there when he was dead?"

"Yes."

"But you got his data—dates in the head. He must have carried something near his head, on his head, so that—I got it! Snell had typed information and carried the paper under a toupé!"

It sounded real hot. Kator looked impressed. But then he tapped ashes into the tray and looked bored again. "Of course, I knew this without your help."

"Sure. But I didn't. Not until you went along with me and gave out with information."

"Go on, Jesso." Kator was smoking again.

"What was it, the stuff Snell carried?"

"I told you, Jesso, my courier didn't even know that, my agent for twenty years. And I don't know you." Kator hesitated, smiled. "Or rather, I do know you."

"You're only stalling yourself, Kator."

Kator was rolling the cigar in his mouth and his lips looked like an inner tube. "You have convinced me, Jesso." He sat up with a theatrical sigh. "I'll say this once, hoping you will forget it quickly. I'll say it now so that we can come to a conclusion."

Jesso sat up too. This was the time when Kator would hand out the death certificate with the name of Jackie Jesso. Or, perhaps, the gilt-edged thing that spelled Jack's billion-dollar jackpot.

Kator got up and smoothed his jacket. His suit was dark and simple, but on Kator it looked like a uniform. He walked to the desk where the bottle had landed against the wall, and brushed some splinters to the floor. There was a locked compartment in the back, and inside it was a small green box, the kind that cashiers use.

When Kator started to unlock it, he did it in a funny way. He lifted the handle up, making it awkward to get the key in right. Then the box sprang open.

Besides the oilskin packet inside, there was a compact battery, a small thing like a stick in brown wrapping paper, and a mess of wire. The wires were attached behind the handle.

"Suspicious, aren't you?" said Jesso.

"Yes."

Kator flipped a wire off and took the packet out of the box. It seemed thick, but there was nothing in it except a sheet of onionskin. There were two columns of figures on the sheet. An ordinary typewriter had done the printing.

"You don't seem impressed, Jesso." Kator turned the sheet so Jesso could see the figures. "Do these mean anything to you?"

Jesso didn't hesitate. "No, Baron. Do they to you?"

"No." Kator turned the sheet around again and started to tap on the figures with one small finger. The gesture looked idle and indifferent. "These are production figures, Jesso. They constitute the weekly output of two integral parts belonging to a certain bomb. The bomb is being made in the United States. A most important new bomb."

"Important to whom?"

"To the highest bidder, Jesso."

"I thought the figures didn't mean a thing to you."

"I haven't finished. I said two parts are mentioned here. One is the trigger mechanism of the warhead; the other is the warhead housing."

"You're over my head, Kator. What about the bomb?"

"Yes. What about the bomb?" Kator poured himself a cup of coffee. It was barely lukewarm. "Let's say I told you how many warhead housings were being produced, a lot of five hundred, and one bomb requires one such housing. Can you tell me how many bombs are being readied?"

"Five hundred."

"No, Jesso, because the same housing is being used for a much more ordinary bomb. Five hundred housings could mean five hundred bombs of either kind, or none of one, or none of the other, or half and half. The figures for the housing mean nothing, Jesso. They leave a margin of guessing for which I cannot expect to collect a cent."

"So it's the trigger mechanism you got to know about."

"Precisely. Five hundred trigger mechanisms mean five hundred bombs, plus or minus ten per cent. In other words, dear Jesso, a salable guess with half a dozen eager takers."

The flimsy piece of onionskin started to look gilt-edged. Jesso chewed his dry lips and waited, but Kator wasn't saying any more. Perhaps he thought that Jesso knew enough, should know enough to say the next thing, whatever that might be. The onionskin looked just like paper again, and Jesso racked his brain, trying to spot the next right move.

"Shall I go on?" Kator asked.

"With what? If you know all that, Baron, what do you want from me?" It sounded brash, ignorant, and maybe Kator would think that Jesso was just hedging.

Kator started tapping the paper again and didn't raise his eyes. "One column on production of the housing, one column on production of the trigger part. Which is which, Jesso? Or which parts of the two columns go together?"

This time neither of them spoke for minutes. Only the idle tapping of the finger, a gentle, padded sound. After a while Kator began to crook his finger until he struck the paper with his nail. It sounded hard, nervous.

"Which is which, Jesso?"

"Stop scratching, damn it! I'm trying to think."

Jesso jumped up and paced the cabin. "He mentioned figures. He kept rattling figures as if they were football scores." Jesso paced, frowning, making a heavy play for just the right expression. Kator had to think that he was sifting information, that he was hard at work to find the clue in Snell's jumbled talk. "It thought they were football scores, the way he put it. Rose Bowl, you know, and then he'd jabber on and on about this high-school game." Jesso stopped, frowning. Better not bring in what Snell really said. He might have been saying a million-dollar word, the key that made the onionskin legal tender.

Kator was watching. Make up something, Jesso, make it busy and fever-crazy. "It was just figures over and over. Christ, Kator, gimme a clue. Don't just sit there."

"Of course, of course." Kator sounded soothing. "These places—Rose Bowl and so on. What other places did he mention?"

That high-school place…. What was the name? He couldn't think of it, but that was all right. He wasn't going to repeat anything Snell had said, anyway.

"He mentioned some town, but damned if I can remember the name of it."

"Underwood?"

Jesso made his voice enthusiastic.

"Underwood! He mentioned Underwood, Kator. What about Underwood?"

"It's a town in Arkansas. The factory in that town goes by the same name."

"And?" Jesso felt tense.

"They make the housing for the warhead there. You see, Jesso, this list gives the production figures from two factories. One for Underwood, the other for the production from a second factory."

It came to Jesso like a flash. He squinted once and then he said it.

"Honeywell! The other factory is Honeywell."

Kator was convinced now. Nobody could have told Jesso about Honeywell except the courier, Snell.

"Yes, the other factory is at Honeywell. They make the trigger mechanism there."

The gamble had paid off and Jesso started to breathe again. So Snell did tell him something.

"Now, Jesso, here lies the riddle. We don't know whether the Honeywell figures are in the right column or the left. And only the Honeywell figures are important for the moment." Then Kator leaned across the table. "Now, Jesso, think! Did he say right or left for Honeywell? Did he say right or left for Underwood? Which column, Jesso, which is the column?"

Jesso held still and looked as if he were thinking. Kator didn't move either, but there was excitement in his breathing.

"Jesso, think. It must be one of these columns. I've analyzed, I've searched—there is no clue. There is nothing to tell the figures apart. One column adds up higher than the other, but that tells nothing. Jesso, which did he say? Right? Did he say left?"

After a while the stiff muscles around Jesso's eyes relaxed. His face relaxed and then he smiled, slow and easy. Jesso got up and stretched. When he started to laugh it was like the first laugh he'd ever made.

Snell's alma mater? Snell never said Honeywell High School! He never even said Honeywell High! What Snell had said was Honeywell high. The high column was Honeywell!

When Jesso had poured himself a cup of the cold coffee, he held it up and looked down on Kator's head.

"How do you say it, Kator? Is it *Prosit?*" and then he drank the cupful as if it were the most delicious stuff in all the world.

"He didn't say right or left, Kator. He had another way of putting it. He said to me, 'Jackie boy, it's all in how you figure it, but whichever way, it's all right there on ye olde onionskin.'" Jesso sat down again and sounded confidential. "And then he said, 'But don't tell Kator till you get to Hamburg, because it'll take you all of nine days to figure out the complicated solution. Jackie,' he said to me—"

But Kator wasn't listening any more. He slammed the paper back into the box, put the box under his arm, and marched out of the cabin.

It wasn't until much later in the day that Kator discovered that his Luger was missing. The Luger and a box of shells weren't in the desk any more.

Chapter Eight

They stayed off the port approach for fourteen hours while the fog kept everything blank gray but brought the harbor noises close. When the fog lifted, rain stayed in the air.

Jesso leaned across the railing and watched the harbor drift close. A tug was making a lot of noise hauling the ship through the channel. Jesso watched the white water churning. He felt impatient, edgy. The wet air made his cigarette hard to draw on and he tossed it overboard. Fifteen more minutes and they would dock. He rubbed the back of his neck and stretched the muscles so they wouldn't ache. Jesso hadn't had much sleep. A sleeping man wasn't much good, even with a gun in his hand.

By the time the ship was sidling up to the mooring they were all on deck, ready to leave. There was Kator, his man Bean Pole, and two other guys who stood around in trench coats and berets, like something from the underground. Kator was in black.

"Jesso," he called.

Jesso came over, buttoning the pea jacket they had given him.

"As we pass through customs, follow with my men. I will handle the formalities."

"What about that passport and visa you owe me?"

"I have them here." Kator patted his chest. "So far, Jesso, I owe you nothing."

Jesso kept still and pushed one hand into his pocket. The Luger was there and he pulled it out. First he yanked the slide to make sure there was a shell in the chamber. There was, and while a new one slid into place the old one flew out in a short flat arc. That was one shell wasted, but Jesso didn't care. They all watched the shell drop into the water and then they watched Jesso again. He ejected the clip, pushed a new shell into the top, and slapped the clip back into the stock. Now they all knew how many shots he had and he dropped the gun back into his pocket. He kept his hand there too.

Once they were off the ship, the formalities were simple. Kator showed papers, nodded to officials, and exchanged some words. Everybody knew Johannes Kator. Then they stood on the cobbled street that ran past the long dock building. Kator was putting the papers back in his pocket.

"According to these, Jesso, your name is Joseph Snell," he said. "It makes your papers almost legitimate."

"I don't look like Snell. That passport—"

"It got you through, didn't it?"

Just how Kator had done it wasn't clear to Jesso, but it showed how well they thought of Kator here. It hadn't struck Jesso until then. He wasn't in the States any more. This wasn't a city where he knew his way around, where even his name alone could— He caught himself up in the lie. Who was he kidding? He had forgotten what he had left behind, what he had lost there. The years of his work were gone, and the big time. Jesso was a cold and tired bum, wearing a borrowed pea jacket and clamping his hand around a stolen gun. Jesso, the bum, standing on a foreign street with three punks around him, three punks posing like trained seals, and Kator there, back in home territory. The bastard was really going to move now. He was going to move with all the ease of a general surrounded by a familiar staff. And shivery stumble-bum Jesso, he was going to move along too, down the chute like a bundle of dirty laundry.

He turned his head and looked at Kator; Kator, back in home territory, silent, smug, and ready with his net of plans to catch just what he wanted and to kill what was left and of no use to him. Jesso knew that every move from now on was part of Kator's calculated trap—or Jesso's try to beat him to it. He was going to kick some holes in that net.

There had been no sign from Kator, but a big Mercedes Benz rolled up and Kator's flunkies had the doors open before the car had quite stopped at the curb. They all got in. Jesso had some plans of his own, and there was a short hassle with Bean Pole about the seats, but when the car purred off Jesso was in front with the driver. The chauffeur pulled the big car in a U turn and took off into the traffic toward town.

It looked like every other harbor town. Low dives, some cheap holes, and a dozen showy stores with tinsel gifts and the kind of novelties that sell at the county fair in Iowa as easily as in Singapore.

"Stop the car," Jesso said.

The chauffeur didn't even budge. He lifted his eyes to see Kator in the rear-view mirror. Kator barely shook his head and the chauffeur looked at the street again.

"Stop means *Halt,* Krauthead," Jesso said, and he made a swift move with his hand.

By the time he had the car keys in his pocket, the big engine had puffed, bucked, and died. Bean Pole tried to reach one arm around Jesso's neck but only got a nasty cut across his knuckles where Jesso clipped him with the gun sight of the Luger.

"Jesso."

"It's Joseph Snell to you, Kator." Jesso dropped the gun back in his pocket while the car came to a sudden stop. Then he turned around and leaned his arms over the backrest. Kator was looking at him, and the guns that had come out of the trench coats were looking at him.

"Tell your SS to put the rods away," Jesso said.

Kator hadn't figured it out yet. His face stayed blank and waiting.

"In a minute they'll shoot your million-dollar deal, Kator. Tell them!"

He sounded rough. He didn't feel like arguing and didn't give a damn just how he sounded. Kator was meeting a new Jesso; no longer rushed, impatient, as he had been in New York; no longer wary, anxious, as he had been on shipboard. Jesso was starting to tear the net and spreading one of his own.

The guns came down.

"Now I'm going across the street. I want Bean Pole along, to make with the language. Wait here." He had the door open already. "I'll only be a minute."

So they waited, because they had to, and Bean Pole came along, because he had to.

There was a little place across the narrow street that had a pair of glasses hanging over the door. There were also cameras in the window and a sign that said, "5 *Minuten.*" The sign said more, but that's all Jesso could read. They went inside and came out five minutes later. Jesso had a little bag that held three passport pictures. Then they drove off again.

"You got a guy that'll fix that passport for me?" He held the pictures out so Kator could take them.

Kator took them but looked annoyed.

"You didn't think you were going to palm that Joe Snell thing off on me without my picture in it, did you?"

It wasn't a question the way Jesso said it.

Kator gave the pictures to Bean Pole and sat back.

"When we get to the hotel, Jesso, Karl will of course rework your papers."

"Good old Karl," Jesso said. "How's he going to do it, with his fingernails?"

"We have the equipment," Kator said, and his irritation started to show.

The car turned into the Kirchenalle, a stately street with ornate old hotels on either side. Without a word from the back the chauffeur pulled up to the marquee of a place called Kronprinzen and the doorman that shot out from the hotel looked as if he were the crown prince himself. When he had the door open he made a bow as if he wanted to kiss somebody's foot, and he said, "Herr Kator," reverently.

They filed into the plush foyer, with Kator nodding at bell captain, room clerk, and elevator man. Like a general surrounded by his well-oiled staff.

"We'll try the other one," Jesso said, and without waiting for anybody to get it straight he turned on his heel and left.

The two trench coats kept on either side of Jesso but Kator almost had to run to follow. Jesso stopped a few houses down and walked into the First Bismarck. The hotel was just as plush, but nobody called Kator by name. This time he had to go to the desk and register.

There was a writing room off to the left and Jesso went there. One of the desks had a typewriter where a kid in a Little Lord Fauntleroy outfit was pecking x's and dashes.

"Beat it, kid." Jesso lifted the boy out of the chair. Then he fixed himself two sheets with carbon. For a moment it looked as if the high-heeled woman with the gold pince-nez was going to do something about her screaming Lord Fauntleroy, but then there was Jesso looking at her, his sailor clothes rumpled and two mean lines running down through the stubble around his mouth. The two trench coats stood by just in case, and they didn't look friendly either.

When Jesso had typed his piece he sealed it in an envelope and stuck the copy in his pocket. Kator was waiting at the front desk.

"If you are ready," he said, but Jesso looked right past him.

"I'm not." He stepped up to the desk. "You understand English?" he asked the clerk.

"Certainly, sir. All our—"

"Very neat. Now listen close. Here's a letter. Hold it for the next thirty minutes. If I haven't picked it up by then, open the letter, read it, call the police, and give it to them. Understand?"

Kator had stepped up, clearing his throat, and the clerk looked puzzled.

"If you won't," Jesso said, "I'll call the police right now."

Jesso hadn't been wrong. There was nothing the clerk wanted less than having a policeman come across the lobby. Jesso looked at Kator and Kator didn't like the idea either. The clerk took the letter.

"Let's go, Kator. You got thirty minutes to get my papers ready."

They went up in the elevator, looking normal enough, but when they were in the room Kator had rented and the bellhop had bowed himself out of the room the atmosphere changed. One trench coat sat down by the phone, the other stood by the door. He locked it, bolted it, then faced the room. Kator had sat down by the night stand because there was no table in the room. Jesso figured that Kator didn't mean to stay here very long and there was no reason to waste any money on a proper suite. Good enough to have four bare walls, a washstand, and a bed. Good enough for a short talk and maybe a quick death.

"I thought you'd like to know what's in that letter," Jesso said, pulling out the carbon.

Kator took the sheet. It was addressed to the police and asked them to notify the American consul of the violent death of one Jack Jesso, abducted by force by one Johannes Kator, who was described in full and whose activities for the past two weeks were listed in great detail. The whole thing made quite an impression.

Kator's words were hardly audible. "Would you mind if I burned this?" he asked.

"Go right ahead," Jesso said, "and you got twenty-three more minutes."

Kator lit the sheet with his lighter and watched it blacken and curl in the chamber pot he had found in the night stand. He closed his eyes and thought for a moment. When he opened them they looked at the man by the phone. He got up with a rush and Jesso's arms were pinned back. Then Kator leaned forward, pulled the Luger out of Jesso's pocket, and tossed it to Karl, the Bean Pole.

Jesso hadn't tried to move. When the guy behind him let go, Jesso straightened his jacket, folded his arms, and said, "You got eighteen minutes, Kator." He knew there was a reason for that quick trick, but for the moment it didn't seem to matter. "So tell Charlie to get busy with my passport."

"Karl is very adept, you will see. There is plenty of time." Kator took a leather-bound notebook from his pocket and a small silver pencil. He handed them to Jesso.

"You will write Snell's instructions down, please. It is best if my associates in this room are not burdened by any unnecessary information."

Jesso took the notebook and pencil. He flipped the pages but didn't write.

"You got fourteen minutes."

"You will write, please!" It was a voice that could have chilled an Army pro.

"Screw yourself," Jesso said.

Kator looked for one long silent moment as if he were going to burst out of his collar. Then he exhaled. Only his eyes moved when he looked at Karl, but Bean Pole scrambled to his suitcase, opened it up, and sat on the bed with the open case on his knees. Kator handed the passport to Karl, who opened it to the page with the picture.

"Where's the visa?" Jesso asked.

"Your visa is an entry on a page in your passport, and I am close to the end of my patience. Will you—"

"Why don't you shut up?"

They looked at each other like stalking cats and then there was no sound except a gentle scraping as Karl removed Snell's picture from the passport. He had a delicate touch as he worked a small scalpel under the glue of the photo.

Jesso started to write, "The upper half of the left column...."

Karl had the picture off. He picked a stamp from his suitcase, the kind notary publics use, and clamped it over the photo. A round, embossed emblem appeared on the paper.

"...and the lower half of the right column...."

Karl smeared glue on the back of the picture and pressed it to the page. While Jesso watched, Karl wrote "Joseph Snell" across the top of the picture, just the way Snell had done it.

"...combine to give the production figures at...."

There was one more job to be done. Karl had to duplicate the State Department stamp that ran across page and picture, serrating both with tiny holes. He had the stamp. It was a wide steel contraption, built like the jaws of a pair of pliers, and the job was to keep the holes on the page intact while serrating new ones into the photo.

It was a delicate job of positioning and Karl did it by touch.

"You got eight minutes," Jesso said.

Nobody answered. Karl felt the underside of the page, eyes closed, and Kator had got up to bend over Jesso's shoulder. He saw the incomplete sentence there. Jesso could hear the breath next to his ear, and he smelled the faint dry-cleaning odor from Kator's clothes.

"You got five minutes."

Karl grabbed the handles of the stamp, pressed, and held on. When he let go slowly the serrations across the picture looked neat. It read, as it should, "PHOTOGRAPH ATTACHED DEPARTMENT OF STATE WASHINGTON." Karl was an expert.

"Continue, Jesso." Kator's breath was moist on Jesso's ear.

He wrote, "Honeywell," then closed the notebook. "You got four minutes," he said, and handed the notebook to Kator.

Then they gave him the passport, unlocked the door, and walked to the elevators.

"You got half a minute," Jesso said when he leaned across the desk in the lobby. The room clerk handed the letter across as if it were soiled, and Jesso slipped it into his pocket.

"And now one final word with you, my dear Jesso." Kator noticed the look on Jesso's face and smiled. He had a smile like winter coming. "We will stay in the lobby, dear Jesso, in plain sight of everyone."

They walked to the large windows that looked out to the Kirchenalle and sat down on a wide couch, like travel companions, or like men who had time to kill.

"You realize, Jesso, there are ways of checking the accuracy of your information."

"So?"

"Simply this. The risk in accepting your information is mine, and while I have been patient, even docile with you, I warn you that I am a different man when I run a risk. Should the information you gave me prove to be incorrect, should you have lied to me, Jesso, I promise you an unpleasant end. No matter where you may be, Jesso, an unpleasant end." Kator paused and studied his frail-looking hands. "Would you care to correct the information you gave me?"

"You got the right dope, Kator."

"I am glad to hear this. And now, the matter of your payment." Kator gave Jesso an envelope. It wasn't sealed. When Jesso reached for it, the envelope dropped out of Kator's hand. So that's why Jesso doubled over, reaching for the envelope, but then he stayed that way and didn't come back up. Right in the lobby, on the couch, facing the window.

Kator had been very good. The hard edge of his hand made the slightest arch and then snapped fast against the base of Jesso's skull. It was the kind of punch that makes the victim feel he knows everything that's going on. He knows the impact, the fact that he can't move, but any minute now he will. Except no air. There was no air. But that passed too, because without transition Jesso blacked out.

Chapter Nine

It went so smoothly after that that Jesso himself would have been proud of it. But Jesso wasn't doing a thing. Kator was. He asked a bellhop to stand by and wave a handkerchief in the fainted man's face and then sent Bean Pole to the phone, because an ambulance was just the thing for a case like this. That ambulance took no time at all. It was a miracle the way that ambulance showed up. One trench coat grabbed Jesso by the legs, the bellhop grabbed his arms, and then they hoisted the body into the ambulance, ready and waiting, because the driver had jumped out, white coat and all, and swung the doors wide in the back. Kator had left before the ambulance took off. Once he had given an order, he rarely bothered with details.

The driver drove and the trench coat sat in back, smoking a cigarette. He must have thought he looked sassy as all hell with the wide coat, the beret, and the cigarette hanging down out of one corner of his mouth.

The first thing Jesso knew was smoke. It drifted past his nose and Jesso wanted a cigarette. The thought was strong but it didn't last. There was the sore neck and a blue pain below his heart. Kator must have operated like a fiend to pull this off.

It took a while of figuring, but then it all came out simple enough. There was Trench Coat, and this was an ambulance and just before that there was an envelope dropping out of Kator's hand, clumsy as could be, and then the rest not so clumsy. And there wasn't any five hundred in that envelope and this wasn't really an ambulance. But Trench Coat, he was real enough. Perhaps he'd heard something, a difference in breathing. Couldn't be. The ambulance was clattering across a street of cobblestones, and Trench Coat, crawling back where Jesso was, held himself steady with both hands. Then he leaned over Jesso to make sure of the damage. Jesso could smell the smoke again. In nothing flat the damage was one agonizing flood of pain spreading from the groin, a wicked burn where the cigarette had splashed against the nose, and one lip badly cut. Then Jesso made sure. Kator himself would have been proud of the way that hand sliced down. Trench Coat stretched out, trembled, and lay still. The ambulance was bumping badly and the driver drove.

He must have known where he was going. The ride got smooth as they crossed a bridge over the Elbe and then they turned and twisted where steep houses seemed to nod across the narrow streets. After a while the ambulance picked up speed and the tires started to sing. At first Jesso didn't realize it was a highway. He watched the tree tops shoot away to the rear, where they appeared and disappeared in the small window at the back. After a while, keeping a cautious stoop, he looked and saw the long ribbon on the black-top road. There were apple trees along both sides.

Then it started to bump again and the trees got thicker. When the car slowed down and stopped, Jesso was ready.

The driver wore an orderly's uniform but he looked more like a butcher. He had the rear door open, and then he almost stumbled, he was that confused.

"Reach," said Jesso, but the butcher didn't understand English. Or perhaps he was stupid. One hand came up chest-high, groped for the gun there, so Jesso shot him in the shoulder. The man spun and dropped.

There was a penetrating odor of wet pine in the air and Jesso breathed it in deeply. They had parked off the road, where the dark-green trees came together in a thick curtain. The soil looked sandy white, soft underfoot, and not too far away there was an open space where stone and sand made a shallow dip. Jesso noticed that the butcher had brought a shovel along. It was leaning against the side of the ambulance, ready and waiting.

Then Jesso waited. The guy in the car hadn't come around yet and the butcher was slowly rolling himself over the sandy ground. He had dropped his gun on the way, but only his shoulder interested him. Each time he rolled over he cringed with pain, but he kept rolling back and forth just the same. He was stupid, all right.

It had been close quarters in the bumping ambulance, so Jesso straightened his new shirt, new tie, new suit, and draped the big trench coat so it wouldn't bunch up in the back. He hadn't bothered with the beret. Then Jesso lit a cigarette and waited.

After a while the guy with the shot-up shoulder stopped rolling around and sat up. There was a big red stain on his orderly's uniform and it looked medical as hell. Jesso walked over to him and said, "How's the arm?" But the guy didn't understand, so Jesso waited for the other one.

When he came around he sat up with a start, but right away he lay down again. He lay that way for a while. Then Jesso didn't want to wait any longer.

"Hey, you." He prodded the man's foot. "Understand English?"

The man got up and raked his long hair back over his head.

"Come on out."

He did understand English, because he crawled out of the ambulance. He had also seen a lot of American movies, because he raised his hands over his head and waited to be shot in the belly.

"Put your hands down. Your underwear don't scare me."

The man lowered his hands and plucked at his shorts.

"What's your name?"

"Fritz."

"I should have known. And the thinker over there? What's his name?"

"Hans."

"Of course, what else? Now tell Hans to sit over there by the tree."

Fritz told Hans and then they waited for Jesso's next word.

There was a long, webbed strap on the bed in the ambulance. Jesso took it off, threw it at Fritz, and told him to tie up Hans. After that was done he waved for Fritz to come back.

"Now I want some answers. Where is Kator?"

"*Ich versteche nicht.*"

"Where's Kator?"

"I understand not."

"Look Fritz, you're getting me mad." He was going to say more when Fritz kicked up his foot and a spray of sand hit Jesso in the face. Fritz did-n't follow it up because Jesso was still holding the gun, but there was no shot. Jesso couldn't see well enough to put his shot where he wanted. For a man in his underwear, Fritz certainly had guts. He rushed to the side of the ambulance, and while Jesso blinked blindly the shovel came into view and slammed down at Jesso. It missed the head but glanced across Jesso's hand so that the gun flew down. Fritz stooped to reach for it, which was fine with Jesso. The sand trick could work both ways, and the cloud hit Fritz straight in the face. But Fritz fired just the same. With his eyes burn-ing blind he shot way off the mark, so that nothing happened except that Jesso got mad. A flying tackle took him under the firing line into Fritz's middle. One hand tore at the gun and then the two men rolled on the ground. There was one more shot, which tore through Fritz's own foot, and then Jesso let fly.

Fritz was never going to look the same. He was screaming and burbling now, and when Jesso jumped up he was out of breath.

"Enough?"

"*Genug! Genug!*"

"All right, Schmeling. Sit up."

While Fritz sat up, Jesso found the gun in the sand. He also found the one that Hans had dropped. One was an automatic; the other was a revolver. The sand interfered with the action of both of them, but Jesso was able to work the revolver free. The automatic was useless. He took the clip out, ejected the shell in the chamber, then tossed the gun far into the brush. There were shells for the revolver in the trench-coat pocket and Jesso reloaded.

All this had taken time, and Jesso figured that Fritz was ready now.

"Fritz, can you see me?"

"Yes."

"Can you hear me?"

"Yes."

"Where's Kator?"

"Ich verstehe—" He didn't get any farther because Jesso's fist caught him where it hurt. The broken nose started to bleed again.

"Where's Kator?"

"He goes home. Home."

"Where's home?"

"He lives in Hannover."

"Fritz boy, this is like pulling teeth. Give me all of it, and all at once."

"Hannover on the Leine. You drive the same road we came on and go south. Perhaps six hours' driving. In Hannover he lives in the von Lohe villa. The house is on the Herrenhauser Allee."

"He lives there, or it's his place of business?"

"He lives there and also has his business. He has his business all over."

"Fine. Get up and turn around."

He did and Jesso stepped close. The gun butt came down hard and Jesso caught the man before he hit the ground. He dragged him to the tree where Hans was, tied him up with the same webbed belt, and went back to the ambulance. After he'd slammed the back doors shut he picked up the shovel and turned to the men.

"While you're waiting for me to come back, Fritz, dig yourself something," and he tossed the shovel toward the tree.

It landed close to Hans's leg and he moved his foot over, dragging the shovel along. Jesso saw it. He was grinning when he walked over to the tree. Hans wasn't so stupid, after all. The shovel had a sharp edge and with a few gymnastics the blade could be worked against the strap. Jesso picked up the shovel and tossed it far into the brush.

"Dig this," he said to Hans, but Hans didn't.

Jesso figured that Hannover was probably a fair-sized town. There were road markers after every little village he passed. Except for the villages, there wasn't much variety on the drive. The land was flat and wet-looking, with wide potato fields and pastures where fat Holsteins were grazing. And along the road the eternal apple trees. By Jesso's habits, it was a slow drive. The highway was narrow and there were a lot of potholes. When he met a car or one of the slow teams of horses that dragged heavy wooden wagons, it helped to be driving an ambulance. Jesso cut loose with the siren and the road was his.

Still it was nighttime before he was even close to Hannover. There had been money in Fritz's pants, so Jesso stopped at a bakery in one of the towns and bought a square loaf of dark bread. He couldn't find a place that sold milk. He finally bought a bottle of beer where a sign said, *"Gasthof,"* and took it into the cab. He drove into the country and parked behind a barn in the middle of nowhere. After beer and bread he got into the back, let the ambulance bed down, and went to sleep.

It was maybe nine in the morning when Jesso hit the town. The sun had come up cold and white, never quite making it through the wet haze in the air. He drove through empty streets with bombed-out shells of houses on both sides, neat straight ruins, because the Germans were such tidy people. After a while it got busier. The streets got narrower, traffic was a mess of bicycles and tiny cars, and after several crazy corners and inter- sections Jesso figured he was in the heart of town. He pulled the ambu- lance to a curb and left it there. Let Kator worry about the ticket.

Jesso walked around the corner and found a restaurant. He would have liked a place with a counter and grill, but there didn't seem to be such a thing. The place had tables, waiters, and a sign that said "English Spoken."

The breakfast was good. There was no orange juice, but the rest was good. He had fried eggs with sausages, some thick, soft bread, a dish of cot- tage cheese, and coffee afterward. While he had his second cup of coffee he told the waiter to call a taxi. When it came he paid and left.

He told the hackie, *"Herrenhauser Allee, von Lohe Villa."* He had to pro- nounce it several times. Then the cabbie tried different versions. Finally they recognized each other and the taxi took off. The ambulance was right around the corner and Jesso saw there was a ticket on the windshield.

Traffic got less hectic after a while. The *Allee* was a broad, dark road, an open iron gate at the entrance and the branches of double rows of ancient trees forming a dim green arch over-head. It was a show place, left over from the time when the King's carriage came this way, traveling the miles to the other end, where his summerhouse was hidden in a walled park.

The taxi swung left, then followed the quiet street that paralleled the boulevard. At intervals there were large villas. They stopped at the largest.

When the taxi had left and Jesso walked through the iron gate, he thought for a moment that nobody was living there. The empty drive curved around a high-grown lawn and the rows of tall windows in the building were heavily draped. The house was as big as it was ugly. Two Atlases grew out of palm fronds to hold the porte-cochere, the house was dripping with stone ornaments.

There was a cool, watery smell in the air. Jesso looked back at the row of trees, then at the villa again. He didn't often feel like this, but suddenly it was as if he were out of place. Jesso hunched his shoulders. It sure didn't feel like home territory. Hell, there was no more home territory. There was nothing but Jesso with a two-day beard, his stolen clothes, and a half-crazy scheme that hadn't even begun to take shape. He rubbed his face and then he made a noise as if he meant to laugh but thought better of it. Christ, a real one-man operation. He always wanted a one-man operation, and now he had it; right in the neck he had it. Or it had him. A free hand and nobody underfoot. It had come true so completely that he didn't know whether to laugh or to swear. And the right kind of woman would be the next thought. At a time like this, for Christ's sake, he was going to start thinking about women.

Jesso jumped off the drive that swung under the villa's porte-cochere and stumbled over the low curbing. The long car, built like a ballroom, made just the merest hum and then stopped by the door. A chauffeur jumped out, moving as if he too were powered by a Daimler motor, and then it looked as if he were going to throw himself right up those stairs. Jesso too thought he might want to throw himself right up those stairs.

She wasn't big or sharp or anything, but she had presence. The heart-shaped face almost spoiled the impression of coolness and grace. The heart-shaped face had a full mouth and wide, light eyes that had a waiting look; and all that with live lights moving on the silk that stretched over her breasts, a blue raw silk, and hips that made a waltz out of the way she walked down those stairs. She stopped halfway down and looked at Jesso. At least, her eyes were turned in his direction. She massaged white gloves over her hands and wrists, and when she was through she got into the car. And that was that.

He stood a while, thinking about it. There are women like that. That was all that came to him. Or, anyway, there is a woman like that.

Chapter Ten

Jesso walked up the stairs. By the big door he rang a bell and waited. Then he rang it again. An old man came to the door, dressed like a butler. He cocked his head and didn't say hello.

"I want to see Kator."

The old guy cocked his head the other way.

"Herr Kator."

"I understood you the first time," said the butler. His English was precise.

There was another door behind the butler, so Jesso couldn't see very far. He felt like a Fuller Brush man.

"What is your name, sir?"

"Jack Jesso. Take my word for it."

"Your business?"

"Kator owes me money and I came to collect. Now open that door wide enough—"

"Mr. Kator is not in. If you have a private debt to discuss, his personal accounts are handled by the firm of Bohm and Bohm. You can—"

"This account is handled right here, so open up."

The door came shut but didn't quite make the lock. Jesso wasn't using any salesman's foot in the door; he hit it hard with the flat of his sole, making the heavy door fly back. It hit the wall and made a crash.

Jesso walked in.

The butler's face screwed up like a wrinkled prune. He reached for a bell near the doorjamb but thought better of it. Jesso wasn't looking friendly.

"Now open the next door."

But before the butler could get there the door opened.

What Jesso saw was a sight. The man was slim, with silky hair draped artfully across a balding head. His frail face looked like a baby's and then again like an old man's. He put his yellow hands into the pockets of his brocaded robe and looked annoyed.

Jesso didn't understand a word of what followed. There was a lot of sharp and stilted-sounding talk and every so often "Herr Baron." That was the butler talking. Jesso started to feel left out.

"All right, enough of the love talk. I'm—"

"I know," said the Baron. He spoke English with a cultivated British accent. "You are Jesso." He peered closer. "What is Jesso, may I ask?"

"Let me in or you'll find out."

The Baron had a fine, high laugh and it took a while before he whinnied out of breath.

"Jesso, so I remembered, is a paste. Something that sculptors use. It hardens into stone. Am I correct?" He put on a sunny smile.

"Why don't you try it? Where's Kator?"

"Ah, yes, dear Kator. Johannes does pick up the strangest people. Hofer, is my breakfast ready?"

The butler said yes and got waved away.

"Johannes isn't in at the moment. In fact, I understand he went abroad."

"He's back. I came back with him."

"Oh, you did? Then he must have been delayed in Hamburg. I'll ask Hofer about it. Hofer should know." He paused for a moment, then said, "Forgive me. I am von Lohe. Hofer failed to introduce me. Helmut von Lohe," and he bowed from the waist.

"Jack Jesso."

"Have you had breakfast, Mr. Jesso?"

Jesso didn't answer right away because he didn't know what to call the man. Finally he said, "Look, does Kator live here?"

"Oh, yes. When Johannes is in town he stays with me." Helmut von Lohe smiled. "Would you care to wait, Mr. Jesso? Join me in breakfast?" The smile changed from vapid to personal.

"I'll wait."

Von Lohe led the way, weaving across the large hall of the house with a rustling of his robe, then through a silk and petit-point salon and out to the solarium. There was a little fountain there, making a tinkle, and big plants standing still in the overheated air. Something was blooming with a sweet odor.

"Be seated, Mr. Jesso." Helmut swirled himself into a wicker chair. It creaked like an old gate. "You are an American, Mr. Jesso, am I right?"

"Sure."

"Would you like to know how I know?" Jesso didn't care, but Helmut told him anyway. "Because you didn't know how to address me." He whinnied. Then, with his smile, "Just call me Helmut. You'd like that, as an American, wouldn't you?"

Jesso was kept from telling him what he'd like when Hofer rolled the breakfast up. There was everything and Baron von Lohe ate like a pig.

That was at eleven. At eleven-thirty Helmut was full. He rang the bell, waved at the mess on the table, and spoke to the butler in English. Von Lohe had manners. Or maybe he wanted Jesso to understand.

"Has the Frau Baronin had breakfast, Hofer?"

"Yes, Herr Baron."

"You will tell her I am in the solarium," said Helmut, and he sat back like a king awaiting his retinue. He also gave Jesso a benign look, but that dropped off fast.

"The Frau Baronin has left for the city," said Hofer, and that answer spoiled the Baron's fun so much that he got nasty when he told Hofer to leave.

"And send her to me when she returns," he called after the butler. Then he turned back to Jesso.

"My wife, Mr. Jesso, keeps irregular hours at times. However," and he patted the yellow hair where it was draped across the skull, "she is not quite used to her new standing."

"Oh," said Jesso. "Country girl?"

"You might say so, dear Jack. In many ways, you might say so."

It sounded mysterious as hell, but Jesso wasn't much interested.

"When you meet her," said the Baron, "you will—"

"I've seen her," said Jesso. "When I came in."

"Well," said Helmut. He wasn't all pleased. "It deprives me of the pleasure of introducing her to you."

"We haven't met. I just saw her."

The Baron smiled, leaned forward. "A remarkable woman, wouldn't you say so?" He looked smug. "In my family we have always favored beautiful women." He said it as if nobody else ever favored beautiful women. The Baron leaned closer. "Her name is Renette."

Jesso looked away. Like a lousy pimp, he thought.

"Not much of a country-girl name," he said, because he didn't know what else to say. Jesso felt out of place with the Baron, and he started to wonder what had happened to Kator. He pulled a cigarette out of his pocket, twirled it between his fingers, made it snap.

"Ask Hofer when Kator is coming back, will you—uh—Helmut?"

But the Baron didn't move.

"Is your business with dear Johannes so urgent you cannot enjoy the comfort of my hospitality? How would you like some liqueur?"

Liqueur, probably with a stink like a flower perfume. The close warmth of the solarium bothered him, and the Baron, with his careful hair-do, gave him a pain. And that Renette female. He had come for Kator. He had expected Kator, cold and tricky, the kind of man who made it easy for you to act without scruples and who made it impossible to forget what you came for.

"I said, dear Jack, is your business so important—"

"Yeah. He owes me five hundred bucks."

This amused the Baron.

"Five hundred dollars!" He whinnied. "You mean you came here from out of town, broke in at an early hour, because he owes you five hundred dollars?"

"My life savings, Helmut."

He leaned forward and put one hand on Jesso's knee.

"Johannes can be unreasonable, dear Jack. But let me help you with the money. Really, it means little enough to me, and I'll speak to Johannes about—"

"I'll wait. You don't owe me a thing." Jesso moved his leg out of the way.

Von Lohe laughed. "Why should you be afraid to be indebted to me? And besides, my influence with Johannes is such—"

"So go influence him." Jesso got up abruptly. He was losing his patience.

"For example," said the Baron, and he studied his fingernails, "if you've had a quarrel with our Johannes—and how easy it is to quarrel with him—you would find that my efforts in your behalf could work wonders."

"I'll do my own promoting, thanks."

"My position, dear Jack—" Then he stopped. They both heard the front door open.

Old Hofer was scurrying across the hall and two other servants were scrambling into position.

"Send for the Baron," said a voice. Kator was there.

Helmut lost some of his baronial air, but he rose with a studied grace and walked toward the hall without another word.

"And send for my sister," said the voice from the hall.

Kator had crossed the hall with that hard click of his shoes. He turned to no one and slowed down just long enough to give old Hofer a chance to swing the library doors wide. Kator went through and the doors clicked shut. When Hofer came back to the hall, von Lohe stood by, watching the servants gather up the luggage. He was fitting a Turkish cigarette into a silver holder.

"Herr Kator wishes to see the Herr Baron."

Von Lohe placed the holder in his mouth and fished for his lighter.

"That is, immediately, Herr Baron." Hofer bowed and disappeared into a side hall. The Baron went into the library without having lit his cigarette.

The library was a room like a hall. The floor was covered with two giant rugs and one wall held a fireplace roofed like a house. There were more Atlases. They held the fireplace open. The ceiling and walls were of walnut except where the bookshelves had been replaced by locked cabinets. The cabinets were steel. They looked odd and cold in the ornate room, and the bleak light from the French windows gave them the air of a row of cells. There was a disciplined garden on the other side of the windows, a painstaking affair of different greens and thin little walks. Kator's desk faced the other way. His chair was empty. Von Lohe walked to the high-backed seat that faced the empty fireplace and said, "Good morning, Johannes."

Kator's arm waved him to step closer. "Where is Renette?"

"I don't know, Johannes. Hofer says—"

"I know what Hofer says. Sit down. When she comes back, send her to me immediately."

"But I don't know when she—"

"She's your wife, isn't she?" Kator sounded impatient.

"She's your sister, isn't she?" said von Lohe, and the spite in his voice was pure.

Kator got out of his chair and walked to the window. His back was turned when he said, "Aren't you happily married, my dear Helmut?" It sounded so casual that the Baron started to fidget. "Are you not being maintained in a style that you could otherwise no longer afford?"

Von Lohe's voice was spiteful. "And my title, I suppose, my exclusive contacts have been of no value to you? I remind you, Johannes, that without my social position to cloak your activities—"

"Speaking of bargains," Kator said, going to his desk, "have you finally managed that matter with Zimmer?"

"It so happens, Johannes, I'm seeing young Zimmer this afternoon, at the club. I think—"

"Don't think, don't make excuses, just produce! This matter has been dragging for months!"

"But Johannes, there is just so much I can do. The Zimmer family has been extremely cautious ever since the war. My good name alone cannot—"

"Remind young Zimmer," Kator said, "that I still possess the copies of patent trades that his father's company has engineered, and that the Americans have no knowledge of any of this. So far. Tell him so far! If I cannot place my men in Zimmer's American subsidiaries, I will begin to make things known."

"But they have been friends of my family for—"

"I am not concerned with your family, only with the effect of your name. Now then, I called you for other reasons. Without going into details, let me impress upon you that my trip to the States has produced complications—possibly minor, possibly dangerous. Look into the garden." Helmut went to the window and looked. "Do you see anything?"

There was nothing except the garden.

"I have stationed six men there. Several more are in front. They are here to intercept any possible danger."

"Danger?" Helmut licked his red lips and sat down.

"Yes. And until further notice you will not leave the house except in the company of one of my men."

"Johannes, please. What are we afraid of? You are making it worse with this secrecy."

Kator pulled out one of his olive-colored cigars and stroked it. "I had dealings with a man, a foreigner. The fact is, I do not know where he is at the moment. Until he is found, I must remain extremely alert. He and I have a debt of—"

"A debt!"

"What is it, Helmut?"

Helmut had started to blink with a nervous speed and he sat upright, as if suspended by the head. He opened his mouth but nothing came out.

"Helmut! Make sense."

"Is it—is it five hundred dollars? Do you owe—"

"What?"

"Just this," said Jesso, and he kicked the door shut with his foot. Hofer was with him, but couldn't keep up with him. Jesso shot his hands into his pockets and stopped.

"Forget the phone, Baron," he said, and watched Kator pull back his hand.

Kator sat still like a cat. That's when von Lohe recovered. He jumped up and started to yell.

"But I swear, Mr. Jesso, I never came near that phone. Johannes, tell Mr. Jesso—"

"Shut up," said Kator. "He didn't mean you."

Everything was still for a moment.

"I meant Superspy, here. You, Kator, you understand, don't you, Kator?"

"Of course, Jesso."

"I bet you do. So send everybody out."

Kator did. He nodded at the butler and at the Baron.

He nodded at both in the same way and then they left. The two men looked at each other. Then they walked to the fireplace and sat down on facing sofas.

"You crapped out yesterday, Kator."

"I beg your pardon?"

"You crapped out. Your two medics weren't so good."

"I know. We found them."

"Were they alive?"

"Partly, Jesso."

"You know why, Kator?"

Kator waited.

"Because I didn't half try."

"I had assumed it was sentimentality."

"Now hear this, Kator. You're going to crap out once more, and that time I'm going to be trying all the way."

"You are threatening me?"

"I'm telling you. And I'm telling you more. That message from Snell I gave you is bunk. I've got the right one, you don't. How much are you selling your merchandise for?"

Kator started to smirk, dropped it.

"Hundred grand? Two hundred?"

"That information would hardly be useful to you."

"Don't worry about that part, Kator. Just worry about how you're ever going to know if I gave you the right info. Just worry about losing your price, worry about selling worthless stuff, worry about what'll happen to your business, to you, if you should pull a boner somebody else has to pay for. Those guys you're selling to, are they gonna say, 'Forget it, Kator, dear chum, we all make mistakes'?"

Kator didn't bother to answer.

"They're gonna send out a torpedo for you. A German if you're in Germany, a Turk if you're in Turkey, and Satan himself if you should be in hell when they find out."

"I assume you have a proposition," said Kator, and the formal words came out stiffly.

"No, Kator. You're almost crapping out again. I'm giving you a chance to come in out of the rain. You show me your buyers, I show them the right dope. It'll cost you half. Half of whatever you get. That's the only way the deal is ever going to go straight. You know why, Kator? If I sell them the wrong goods, I'll be as bad off as you, and that's never going to happen to me, Kator."

Kator's success had come from the man himself; his fast mind, his unmuddled decisiveness, and his ability to dismiss his personal feelings. This made him remarkable, and he showed it now.

"Very well. I will begin my arrangements today. You may stay in this house in the meantime. Hofer will provide for your comfort."

They looked at each other without even trying to hide their thoughts. One was out for the other, and each understood the game. And for the moment neither had anything to fear from the other.

"It is customary in your country to shake hands on an agreement. But you and I, Jesso, can do without it."

"That's clear."

"Particularly since both of us cannot win, you understand?"

"I told you you'd crap out."

"You will get your money, I will make my sale. I'm not speaking of that."

"Just watch it, Kator." Jesso got up.

"I'll begin my arrangements today."

"You can start right now. You owe me five hundred."

When Hofer had taken Jesso to his room on the second floor of the villa and when he was about to leave, he was given a ten-dollar tip, which Jesso peeled off a roll of five hundred.

Chapter Eleven

Renette von Lohe looked as if she belonged in the place. There were no jewelry counters, just low little tables and wide chairs. The walls were of black glass and the ceiling was held up by bronze columns. The table in front of her was almost bare; just two bracelets lay there.

"Madame has hardly a choice," said Mr. Totanus of Totanus, Dorn, and Son. "Beauty is its own absolute, madame, and if I may be permitted—"

Renette looked up and shook her head. She smiled as a hostess would smile, with very well-mannered kindness, but Mr. Totanus stopped as if he had been slapped. Renette von Lohe, who was also beautiful in the eyes of old Mr. Totanus, gave the impression that only she might decide what was absolute.

"They sparkle too much," she said.

Her voice sounded warm, except for the way she ended a sentence. She ended it as if that were the absolute end. That can be a shock to anyone, be it Totanus trying to sell a ten-thousand-mark bracelet or someone who has long given up trying to sell anything.

"You know, Mr. Totanus," and Renette crossed her legs so that even old Mr. Totanus began to feel excited, "I think I like something warmer. Not diamonds. I like smoke opal."

The firm had smoke opal. The reason it had smoke opal was that during the war the volume of diamond trading had gone down to near zero and the firm had handled a number of lesser stones, even the semiprecious. But Mr. Totanus didn't know just where the opals were.

"Madame," he began, but then Renette put her small feet together and got ready to leave.

"I won't have to look at them," she said, "because I know you will pick the most beautiful ones for me. And set them square, as you did in this bracelet. Make the same kind of bracelet." After dangling the one she meant over one finger, she dropped it back on the velvet pad so that old Mr. Totanus quivered.

Renette smiled and stood up. She did it all in one movement, then stood to pat herself into straight lines while old Mr. Totanus looked away and fussed with the mistreated bracelet. He had started to quiver again.

"Will you send it to me?" she asked, but it was hardly a question.

Totanus rose, doing it awkwardly, because Renette hadn't bothered to step back. This was a rotten day. Smoke opals. She could afford both of those bracelets on the table, but she wanted smoke opals.

"Shall I bill the Baron?" said Totanus when he followed Renette to the door.

"No," she said. "Send the bill to my brother."

Renette got into the Daimler and told the chauffeur to drive her home. She sat back in the cushions and thought what a beautiful bracelet it was going to be. Perhaps she should have let Helmut pay for it. But that was ridiculous. Then Helmut would have to go to her brother and he would pay anyway. Besides, Johannes never argued about her bills; he only argued with Helmut.

The car circled a square with a café on the island in the middle. Renette could see the string orchestra behind the potted trees. A cherry *Torte* or perhaps some mocha ice would be a wonderful thing now. There was a large clock at one end of the traffic island and it said twelve noon. Johannes must be back. She bit her lip, decided against the café. If Johannes was home, she did not want him to wait. No, that's not the way it was. If Johannes was home, waiting, she would be afraid of offending him.

Now the square was gone. Renette looked into her purse for a cigarette but didn't find one. She tapped on the glass behind the chauffeur and when he looked she made a sign as if she were smoking. The chauffeur opened the glass, gave her his pack, closed the partition again.

Renette smoked. He has a nice neck, she thought, a nice strong neck coming out of the stiff uniform collar. With a strong neck like that, and the way he sat at the wheel, it was strange how such a man can act like a— She couldn't think of the word. Act scared, she decided. Or fluttery. It made her think of her husband, which made her laugh.

The car pulled up under the porte-cochere of the villa and Renette hoped that her brother would not be there.

She couldn't tell by the way Hofer opened the door, but by the time she had asked him Kator came across the hall.

"Where have you been?" he said.

He wouldn't care where she had been, but she saw he was in a foul mood.

"Are you all right?" he said, and this time she was surprised. It hadn't been casual and yet it didn't sound sharp.

"Thank you, Johannes, I'm fine. And how are you?"

He wasn't listening. He led her into the library, took her gloves, and put them on a small table.

"Sit down, my dear." He followed her to a couch. They sat, looked at each other, and then Kator smiled.

"In a way, it was good that you weren't here," he said. "However, it might have been just the opposite."

"I haven't understood a single word you've said so far."

"Yes, of course." He cleared his throat, changed his tone. "Renette, you are naturally free to come and go as you please. However, you must leave word where you are. In your absence a situation developed that might have been dangerous. A business associate of mine, a highly unpredictable—"

Renette interrupted. "But in the meantime you've caught him, haven't you, Johannes?"

Kator got up and stood by the fireplace. The way she took it for granted, the way she never questioned, but always admired him—it wasn't too easy to take now.

He looked down at his shoes.

"Actually, Renette, it was the other way around," and when his head came up he was smiling.

Renette smiled back, because that smile was only for her. And the confession. Only her brother could say this and not lose face.

"And so," he went on, "nothing is solved."

Renette turned to the table next to the couch and took a cigarette from a small box. She let Kator light it for her, inhaled deeply, blew out smoke with a long sound. Then she leaned back and looked at her brother.

"Are you worried?"

"No. Not for the moment."

"You don't sound sure."

"Oh, I'm sure, Renette. He's in this house."

"Here? Since when?"

"Sometime this morning."

"I remember now. The beggar. He looked like a beggar." Kator laughed, but when he sat down next to his sister she saw he was cold again, as he was most of the time. "The way you saw him, Renette, in America they would call him a bum. But in America they would also call him an operator. It means he will use anything in his favor. He has no scruples when it comes to getting what he wants or keeping what he has." Kator paused. "He has something I want."

"And why are you telling me, Johannes?"

"For a number of reasons, my dear. To warn you, and perhaps to prepare you."

"For what, Johannes?"

He got up, turned back to her. "I need your help."

When she looked back at him, she had the same look as her brother had. But she didn't talk.

"It may involve your comfort as well as mine," he said. "Or would you prefer that glorified farm, back to the empty room with a view of weeds through the window?"

"Don't be dramatic, Johannes."

"Are you forgetting that your status depends on mine?"

"You mean being the wife of a baron?"

"I don't notice that his presence is any hardship."

"Just awkward," she said. "Just one of those ridiculous situations."

"I don't notice—" he began again, but she didn't let him finish.

"What makes you think your beggar is going to give you whatever you want because I go to bed with him?"

"I'm not interested in your methods, Renette."

"Of course not," she said. Of course not. Only results. Then she had to smile. She wasn't much different from him. When he had sent for her, kept her with him and given her the things her family had long been without, she hadn't cared what the cost of the luxury was. And she hadn't cared when Kator found it expedient that she should marry the Baron von Lohe; and she hadn't cared that she and the Baron were just a showpiece together. There were other men. One would have done, she knew, but she hadn't found him. So there would be others.

"His name is Jesso," Kator said. "Jack Jesso." Then he explained what made Jesso important, that Renette had to get it out of him, whether Jesso was bluffing or whether he really knew what Snell had known.

"When do you want me to start?"

"Tonight."

"Shall I tell Helmut?"

"Suit yourself," Kator said, and left the room.

Chapter Twelve

They sat in the dining room with the high ceiling lost in the dark because there were only the yellow wall lights over the buffet and the two candelabra on the table. They all sat in their seats being formal with knife and fork and a sip of wine now and then. Kator sat looking at von Lohe and Jesso sat looking at Renette. He had a good view.

Renette might have been alone at the table or she might have been in the middle of a cluster of men, all looking at her. She sat unconcerned, just there, the way a magnet is unconcerned.

She wore a dress like a second skin, long-sleeved and naked on top. There was a very fine chain around her neck with a pearl that rolled a little each time she breathed. It lay off center on her bare skin and kept rolling there.

Hofer wasn't serving. Hofer carved and poured wine. Two stripe-vested servants did the work and Hofer just hovered.

They sat around as phony as people in an ad. Like a whisky ad showing how only the very best people drink only the very best whisky. Jesso sipped wine the way they all did and thought of whisky, even the very worst whisky. He wasn't nervous. He never drank whisky when he was nervous, but a raw drink right then would have helped.

Kator was talking to the Baron. "Any progress this afternoon?"

Von Lohe swallowed and answered as if he had just waked up. "Yes, Johannes. Oh, yes. We must discuss it. After dinner."

"Not business, Johannes." Renette gave him a smile with a question in it. "We must think of our guest." She nodded at Jesso, moving her head at him in a gesture that was beautifully done. Jesso wished she would do it again.

"By all means," said Kator, and he moved his head too. It was more like a muscled python making another slow loop before the kill. "Even though Mr. Jesso might be too polite to object," Kator was saying, "we should perhaps discuss business at some other time."

Nobody waited for Jesso to say anything, because Kator was dabbing at his mouth, which meant he wasn't through yet.

"On the other hand, as an American, Mr. Jesso might find talk about business a very fitting topic after a meal. In fact," said Kator, "his business acumen might be—"

"You mean talk about the Zimmer matter?" Von Lohe sounded surprised.

"Of course not," said Renette. "Johannes was only teasing. And besides, Mr. Jesso hasn't given his view yet. It should be his decision how we spend the evening."

She had a thought there. And the way she smiled at him, Jesso had a moment's crazy thought that she might even listen.

"Of course," said Kator. "There must be topics just as universal as business. Eh, Jesso?"

Jesso could think of one.

"I can think of one," said Helmut, and he raised his glass. "To love!" He saluted Renette, drank some wine, and looked pleased with his conversation.

"Of course." Kator leaned back, dabbing at his mouth.

"I should like to hear Mr. Jesso on the topic of love. Had you thought of the same thing, Mr. Jesso?"

"What thing?"

"Love, Mr. Jesso."

"I was thinking of women," he said.

Right then Renette became all hostess, telling Hofer to serve the coffee in the music room, and then she got up.

They all sat around her in the music room and Helmut said we must have that piano tuned. Renette nodded, and Jesso drank coffee. Kator didn't talk for a while, but then he started to toy with an unlit cigar, and when Renette was through with her sentence about Helmut's Turkish cigarettes he got up and made a small bow.

"Forgive me, Renette, but Helmut and I must discuss a few matters. We may rejoin you later."

So Jesso and Renette stayed alone. The music room wasn't large, but the chandelier and the silk on the wall made it all very cold. So did the grand piano. It was large and black and the lid was down.

"Do you play, Mr. Jesso?"

"No. Never did."

"I don't either," she said, and she smiled as if she were relieved. "I don't like to play the piano and I don't like to talk business."

"If you got any other universal subjects—" but she laughed again and he didn't have to finish.

"No," she said. "But I'm glad they're gone."

The way that room was lit up and all silk, grand piano, and glass-topped tables, there was nothing warm about it. But Jesso didn't notice it any more. She leaned over to place her cup on a table and Jesso watched the small pearl swing free. Then it lay there again, rolling a little on the curved skin.

"You needn't look so glum about it," she said suddenly.

"What?"

"My pearl."

"I'm not glum, Mrs.—Frau—"

"Frau Baronin, if you want to be formal, Mrs. von Lohe if you're just polite. Are you polite, Mr. Jesso?"

"Like the next fellow."

"Oh, no. Not like Johannes or my husband. That's why I'm glad they left."

They looked at each other. She looked back at Jesso as if she were never afraid.

"Who's Kator?" he said, because he wanted to know.

"He married us. He is my brother."

Her brother. She sat still, letting him look at her. He tried to find in her some similarity to Kator. He thought perhaps the eyes, but then that was gone too because all he saw was Renette, breathing there with that god-damn pearl winking at him.

"You don't like him at all," she said.

"Who cares?"

"I do, in a way."

Jesso sat still. It was like the moment before a jump.

"Why?" he said.

"I don't want him to get in the way." After she said "way," her mouth was still open, just parted, and nothing was in the way when the moment before the jump was gone and Jesso held her as if he had always been hold-ing her.

She had given back the kiss but she hadn't moved. Jesso sat up again. Her eyes were as they had been before, just looking at him, and then she put her hands where the dress ended on top and pulled it up. She did that while she said, "He didn't get in the way," and it sounded wrong. It made the gesture with the dress almost public, and it made Kator more present.

Now he wanted her more. Now he wanted her because she was there and not there, because he had started but had hardly started at all. And Renette looked to him as if she had waited a thousand years and all that kept him back was the puzzle of what waiting meant to her; whether wait-ing was an indifferent habit or whether it meant that the wait had grown like a fever and was searing her now, close to the end....

He moved again, but she was up.

"Jesso," she said. "Jesso, wait."

He stood next to her and held her arm.

"Wait for me, Jesso. In the next room. I'll come back and we'll sit in the next room."

Her arm moved in his hand and she was walking to the door that led into the hall.

"There's brandy in the cabinet," she said. "The one by the fireplace." Then she closed the door.

Jesso balled his hands and stared after her. She'd done it again, that trick of saying the wrong thing, of mixing things that didn't belong together.

He went to the next room, which was almost dark. The only light came from a lamp with fringes hanging down from the shade, and from the fireplace. The fireplace was busy with red flames and being cozy and intimate, and the whole thing was so completely what might have been expected that he kicked at an overstuffed chair. And brandy yet. Sniff brandy and say things into the fire and she'd probably be wearing a hostess gown. Nothing slinky, of course, because now they knew each other, but probably a heavy brocade or some such lavish thing to make it festive and also lush.

He had the cabinet door open and saw the bottles and started to reach for one, just as he was expected to do. And of course there were the snifters, a row of them with big bellies. He slammed the cabinet shut, hoping to break something, but didn't bother to check. Then he was on the second floor. There was also a third floor and another wing where the house angled about the garden, but she was probably here on the second floor. Both halls were dark. He went down the hall that angled to the right. At the end of the hallway there was light under a door. He walked in without knocking.

They both turned, the maid holding the house gown for Renette and then Renette, more slowly. She finished shrugging it over her shoulders and held the front closed.

"Send her out," Jesso said.

Renette turned to look at him. Her face was cold, he noticed, and if she had cared a little more it might have been mean. He looked where she held the gown and the damn thing was stiff, rich brocade.

"Get her out," he said, and this time Renette nodded at the maid, who left obediently. When the door clicked shut, the silence was thick.

It wasn't a very frilly room, but it was all female. Even the bed looked female.

"I'll call you Renette," he said. "Come here."

She didn't move.

He had his hands on her arms and ran his palm up and down. The brocade made a scratchy sound, feeling like tiny hooks on his skin.

"Wait, Jesso," she said.

"Call me Jack."

"I was coming back," she said. "I didn't expect—"

"Call me Jack." He had her around the back now, the brocade like the tiniest hooks on his skin, millions of them, and then he felt her relax a little. She raised her head to him and she seemed smaller. Her shoes were off. He noticed the wide eyes looking and they were still waiting, but more blank now. Her mouth held a smile that was ready to make allowances.

"I'll call you Jesso," she said, and there was nothing friendly about it.

He bent down and kissed the mouth. Then he came up slowly.

"Try again," he said.

There wasn't time to answer.

Then he held her away a little and a line grew in the middle of his forehead.

"You don't fight fair," he said.

"I don't fight."

He laughed and looked at her hands, holding the gown together in front.

"You don't let go."

"I'm not holding you, Jesso."

"You got it wrong." His hands went over her arms again, scraping. "You're supposed to give."

She didn't get it, and when he pulled her again she leaned away.

"You got it wrong," he said again, and his hands were at her front, holding the lapels of the gown. When she shrugged and dropped her hands, the gown parted with a rustling like that of the old trees in the *Allee*.

She was naked, and beautiful. And like white stone.

"You bitch!"

She couldn't answer then because his arms pressed the breath out of her, but she started to fight. It was crazy. He got her across the room, feeling the clawing of her nails, seeing her eyes, and he never knew it was fear.

When he woke the lights were still on. He got up, kicked his clothes out of the way, and turned the switch.

She lay still in the dim light from the night sky, eyes closed, but she didn't seem stone any more. He lay down again, just touching her, hearing her breath. Then she moved.

"Jesso," she said.

He could feel her heat as she turned.

"Jesso. Again."

Chapter Thirteen

There was nothing for Jesso to do until ten because nobody had come down yet. He sat in a little room facing the lawn that went down to the wall by the street and waited. Then he heard Kator. He came downstairs and Jesso stopped him in the hall.

"Made your arrangements, Kator?"

"Good morning, Jesso. Yes, I have."

"So when do we settle?"

Kator raised his eyebrows for a moment, but Jesso didn't see it.

"I made the arrangements yesterday," he said, and walked across the hall to the dining room. Jesso followed. "And there should be results today."

He sat down and watched Hofer dish up the breakfast. Jesso had coffee.

"What arrangements?" Jesso asked.

Kator finished chewing, sipped chocolate.

"The—our buyer has been informed. The next move is his."

"When?"

"Jesso, I have not seen anyone, nor has the mail been brought in."

Jesso had to watch him finish his breakfast. Then Kator rang for the mail. There was quite a pile of it. Kator found the telegram quickly.

"The answer," he said.

He put it down so Jesso could see it, but except for a date and an address, the text made no sense to Jesso. Kator looked active now. He had pulled out a cigar but laid it down by the silver pot containing the chocolate and talked in his hard, even way.

"My request for a meeting has been granted. The only difficulty is the time."

"The sooner, the better, Kator."

"Of course. We will be in Munich tomorrow." Kator paused, picked up his cigar, and rolled it between his fingers. If this guy was nervous, Jesso couldn't tell.

"It will have to be done in this manner. You take the afternoon train to Munich. It will get you there in the forenoon. I myself have a previous appointment elsewhere, so I won't go with you. I will fly to Munich early tomorrow and meet you at the hotel. From there we will meet our contact together and begin negotiations sometime that afternoon."

There was nothing wrong with it. If there was, it could only be a senseless and stupid stall, and Kator wasn't going to be that stupid.

"I'll go," Jesso. said. He was trying to remember whether he had any ammunition for the revolver in his overcoat upstairs.

"Very good." Kator gathered his mail and stood up. "It will be the time to tell the truth, Jesso." He left for his study.

Jesso went upstairs to make sure about that revolver.

It was eleven o'clock then and Renette came out of her shower. She held her hair up with both hands while the maid rubbed her with a large towel. Then the phone rang. It was a short conversation, and after Renette hung up she put on her underthings, slippers, and the heavy brocade. When she walked into Kator's study she looked awake and clean. She stopped by the desk and nodded.

"Well?" said Kator.

She shrugged and reached for a cigarette on the desk.

"You look awake, Renette, but you don't act it."

"I'm fine, Johannes." She smoked.

He got up and walked to the empty fireplace. The big hood with gargoyles and Atlases made Kator look very squat, like a bulldog.

"You look as beautiful as ever," he said. There was an edge to his voice. "Only a little wasted."

She laughed. "Wasted!" she said, and then she laughed again.

"May I point out you haven't told me a thing?"

Renette inhaled, blew the smoke out slowly. She cocked her head to watch it. "You are too anxious, Johannes."

"You mean you have learned nothing?"

"Give me time, Johannes."

"It seems to me—"

"I thought you weren't interested in my methods."

"How much time do you need?"

"Don't be obscene."

Kator kept still then. She didn't often use that tone of voice. He took a series of military steps across the room, sat behind his desk, gave his instructions. It was more familiar ground now.

"Jesso will go to Munich this afternoon, by train. Tomorrow I will meet him there. That gives you from now until about three o'clock."

"You flatter me, Johannes."

"I know you well, Renette."

She ignored the remark and looked out to the garden. She knew he was puzzled by her attitude, unable to predict what she would do next. Yesterday he would have known. Until yesterday, she would have said, "Of course, Johannes, if you say so." She might have said it with a shrug, but she would have done it. Now she said:

"Of course, Johannes, but it wouldn't be good enough. I'll go with him.

I'll have from now on, all day, and all night. I'll get ready."

She came in without knocking, the way he had done it the night before. "Jesso."

He was cleaning the gun, but after she opened the door the motion became mechanical.

"Good morning, Jesso."

"Good morning. How's yours?"

"Fine, Jesso. It's a good morning." She sat down next to him on the bed. She didn't peck a kiss or hold his neck. She just sat and smiled as if she enjoyed it.

"Something on your mind?" He still held the gun but he didn't know it.

"I'm going with you."

"Where?"

"Johannes says you're taking a trip. I don't care where."

"To Munich."

"That takes all night."

"Why? You want to get raped?"

"That won't take all night," she said, and it struck him how little it sounded like a dirty joke.

"Good," he said. "I want you to come."

She got up, ran her hand through his hair with a swift movement, and left the room.

Jesso tried to clean the gun some more but he wasn't interested in it any longer. The damn gun was clean anyway. He put six cartridges in the cylinder, took them out again, slipped them back one by one. If he had said no, she still would have come. He knew that. Like Lynn? Not like Lynn. Lynn would have tried to come. She would have asked and he would have said no. Renette hadn't asked, she had told him, and he hadn't kicked once. It stopped him for a minute, wondering how much he had changed. He had found the woman who wanted the same thing he wanted, in the same way, with the same will. Jesso felt he had found his woman.

At three the big Mercedes pulled up and Hofer carried Renette's overnight bag downstairs. Jesso had nothing to carry. He'd buy a toothbrush and shaving stuff later. Kator wasn't around when they left, but Helmut came out to the car. He said he was happy his wife had the chance for that little excursion and said he was looking forward to seeing them in two days or so. He kissed Renette on the temple and waved at the car cheerfully.

Once, on the way to the station, Jesso looked out and laughed. They were passing the intersection where the ambulance was parked near the restaurant. There were two more tickets on the windshield. Renette didn't ask him why he laughed and he didn't tell her. They hardly spoke in the car. Their hands lay on the seat between them and sometimes, with a turn of the car, their fingers touched.

They got out of the Mercedes in front of the station. The chauffeur helped with the luggage and they found the train. Kator had done it up brown this time; it wasn't any tourist- or third-class ticket. They had a compartment, and when the chauffeur was gone they locked the door, pushed the suitcases out of the way, and sat down. When the train was moving they looked out of the window. At first the landscape looked flat, industrial; even the small fields had a square mechanical look. Later the fields rolled and there were more trees. Renette sat close, with her legs tucked under her. She had the rest of her twisted around so that she leaned against him. They smoked and didn't talk. There was nothing to talk about. They looked almost indifferent, but their indifference was the certainty of knowing what they had.

She had on a wide-necked dress with a large collar. It had been made by a French designer at a time when they thought the female shape was O.K. as it was. She saw him looking at her and blew smoke in his face. He watched the pearl roll there.

"Who gave it to you?"

"Mother Nature."

"The pearl, I mean."

"No one. I got it myself."

"Lucky pearl."

"I'll give it to you."

She gave it to him and he held it in his hand. Then he put it away in his pocket. They kissed as if they had a lot of time.

It turned dusky outside. Renette put her feet to the floor and sat up.

"I'm hungry."

Jesso rang for the porter. A small table came up from under the window and there was soup, something called glazed *Wildhuhn*, potatoes, and asparagus, and a cold pudding with sour cherries in it. She told him what wine to order and they had that too.

"Helmut really your husband?"

"Oh, yes."

"He know about you?"

"What is there to know?"

He finished his wine and rang for the porter. "Plenty," he said.

"Not until yesterday," she said.

They drank coffee and brandy, and then the porter took the things away. They got up. Jesso turned her around in the middle of the small room, because the buttons were in the back. She held her breath so it was hard to get them open, and then she exhaled, laughing, and held still so he could get done. Jesso pulled down the bed and she stood by the wall grille and let the hot air blow up her bare legs. Then the dusk was almost complete and they didn't notice for a long time that it had turned night again.

Chapter Fourteen

She was asleep. The train made the same rhythm, swaying slightly, and Jesso could glimpse the moon now and then. He got up and dressed.

The corridor outside was chilly and a dim light showed the seesaw motion where the corridor met the door of the next car. Jesso walked right and stood on the connecting platform. It was even colder there. Except for a man at the other end of the car, he might have been alone on the dim train. Jesso lit a cigarette and dragged hard. It felt raw and good.

The train started to clatter across rail junctions and then a dark station platform shot by the window. They were going like hell, straight and steady. He'd been going straight and steady. There had been bumps and a couple of falls, but now, Jesso thought, he was going like hell. And it didn't feel like rushing and panting, not since Renette, but straight and steady with nothing in the way to make any difference. Almost too easy. Tomorrow the Munich deal and then Kator was out. Kator had been almost too easy.

Jesso left the clanking platform and crossed into the next car. This one had a corridor too. They all did. They had a corridor squeezed to one side and glass-doored compartments on the other. Everyone was asleep. When Jesso came to the club car he smelled tobacco smoke but the place was empty. He sat in an easy chair and looked to the other end. The door opened and a man came in. He sat down by the door. Jesso noticed he was smoking a pipe.

"Got a match?"

He jumped around and there was the other one. The cigarette in his mouth was lit.

"I know, I don't need one. Just wanted you to turn around. And take your hand away from your pocket."

Then the one with the pipe stood there too.

"Been waiting for you ever since Hannover," said the pipe. "Been busy, huh, Jesso?"

"American?"

"Sure," one of them said.

"But not tourists," said the other.

"You were hanging around at the other end of my car," Jesso said.

"Right. And the name's George."

"And Ralph," said the pipe.

They sat down, George opposite and Ralph next to Jesso.

"You're nervous, Jesso. And you got a lot to be nervous about."

"Keep talking, Ralph boy."

"Keep your hand away from that pocket, Jesso. We don't carry no guns."

Just for that, Jesso had the revolver out and was up on his feet. The two men just sat. George had his hands between his knees, big hands, and Ralph, who was small and sandy-haired, kept sucking his pipe.

"Now what, Jesso?"

"Now this," and he waved the gun for them to get up. "You guys know my name, so I guess you know who I am."

They got up this time and kept their hands where he could see them. He frisked one, then the other. They were clean.

"Park yourselves. And talk."

"That's what we've been waiting to do, Jesso. Christ, ever since Hannover we've—"

"So shut up and talk." Jesso sat down too and looked at George, the big one.

"We're in the same game like J. Kator," said George, "only a different outfit."

"Fancy that."

"I knew he'd be suspicious," Ralph said. "I just knew—"

"We are," said George. "And we're buying."

"Right now you're just talking."

"We're buying. You got the key from Snell and we're buying."

"Who told you, Kator?"

"I knew—"

"Will you keep your cotton-pickin' mouth clamped shut on your cotton-pickin' pipe, if you please?" George sighed and turned back to Jesso. "He's a pain."

"Not to me."

George stuck his long legs across the aisle and put his hands in his pockets. "Look, Jesso, we can't prove a thing, so we won't even try. It would take a lot of time, and time we don't got. We got money, though."

"So buy yourself something."

"I'm trying to, Jesso. I'm trying to."

"What George means," said Ralph, "is we want the key. Snell's dying words, if you know what I mean. Now you wonder how do we know so much? Simple. Kator wasn't the only one after that info. To wit, Snell was going to jump off Kator's wagon and sell elsewhere."

"That's us. Elsewhere," said George. "But you know what happened. We missed the boat. So right now we're trying to catch up is all." George got up. "Wanna come and look at some money, Jesso?"

Jesso kept sitting. "You haven't said a thing yet."

"Money talks, Jesso."

"What good's it to you? Kator's got the figures."

"We don't need 'em. We got later ones."

"Look, Jesso." Ralph sounded serious now. "Let me tell you the whole thing. We got figures, Kator's got figures. Together they'd give a much more reliable score for estimating bomb production than either of the lists alone. With your information in our hands, we can argue with Kator. We can get together, make a combine."

"You're giving me ideas," Jesso said.

George made an exasperated swing with one arm, sighed. "Jesso, you talk like an ass. There are some deals too big for one man to handle. You'd be twisted out of shape."

"I've been doing all right."

"Have you got your dough?"

"No."

"So don't talk."

Jesso thought about that.

"Jesso, there are details to this deal that you as one man, or me, or Ralph over there, couldn't handle alone. You didn't know, for instance, that your info isn't any good after a couple of months, did you? You didn't know the plants change models, that they produce in periods instead of at a steady rate—all things that you never heard of, that I only know by name, and that I mention just to impress you. Then there's the problem of getting bids for the merchandise. You don't know under what phony company transactions these deals are handled, how the money is moved without attracting attention."

"I'm impressed. Come to the point."

"The point is simple. Sell to our combine and your troubles are over."

"How much?"

"Fifty thousand."

"I can't even hear you."

"Cash, Jesso. Cash in small bills, right here on the train, and we can make it seventy-five. Whaddaya say?"

"I say crap."

"I told you," Ralph said.

George leaned over to Jesso and sounded tired. "Look, Jesso, you know how it is. We're supposed to argue. We're just hired to do a job. But we're authorized to go to one hundred grand. That's all we got, Jesso, honest."

"Go back where you came from. Kator pays me more."

"Have you got it?"

Jesso thought about that.

"You don't know Kator very well, do you, Jesso?"

They waited while Jesso just sat and they gave him all the time he wanted.

"You got it here?"

"Right on this train."

"Show me."

Ralph sighed around his pipe and George looked relieved.

"Honest, Jesso, you won't regret this. Grab your swag and get out of a field you know nothing about." They walked down the corridor. "We know your rep and everything in New York and so forth, but this is different. Christ, you don't even know any languages, I bet, except Brooklynese."

"He don't sound Brooklynese," said Ralph.

"Ralph, your mouth. You're gonna hiccup one day, and fall in. Look, Jesso, I'm just making a figure of speech. I'm trying to show you—"

"You know what you can show me, so stop bending my ear."

They kept still, both of them, and Jesso followed George down the corridor. Ralph was behind him.

They had a compartment too. It was just like the one where he and Renette were staying, and it made things nice and familiar. Jesso watched George unlock the door and waved Ralph to step through. He himself went in last.

"I'll lock this door," he said, and made a noise with the slide. His other hand pressed one of the buttons that kept the bolt from locking.

"I told you he'd be suspicious," Ralph said, but he was grinning this time. He pulled a suitcase out from under the seat. "Come here and count it."

"Put it on the seat. I'll count it from here."

George spoke up and his voice was apologetic as hell. "Jesso, look. I know how you feel, and you got every right. But let's play it even. We got all this dough and you got a gun. Your hand's in your pocket again. So let me get my cannon, see, right here in my coat, and I keep it in my pocket and you keep yours there. You know how it is, Jesso, so don't misunderstand. If we knew each—"

"I get it." He made a noise in his pocket.

"So I'll just get my—"

"Never mind. This is crazy enough as it is. Here, take mine, and keep it till I leave." He tossed his gun over to George, who caught it, grinned, and dropped it into his pocket.

"No hard feelings, Jesso. You know how it is."

"So open the suitcase."

Ralph hefted the two-suiter onto the seat and clicked the locks open. He threw back the cover, lifted the underwear off, and there were the bundles.

They were tens, twenties, and a row of fifties, some dog-eared and held by a rubber band, some stiff and clean, still with the bank wrappers around them. It was a sight.

"Count them out on the seat," Jesso said.

"In bills?"

"In bundles is good enough."

Ralph did, and there was one hundred thousand. Jesso grinned and shook his head. "I never saw such a bunch," he said. "Believe me, fellers, I never saw such a bunch."

They grinned and nodded too. Ralph put the bills back in the suitcase.

"So whaddaya say, Jesso?" George folded his arms over his chest.

"My, my," said Jesso. "Myomy."

Ralph made a laugh. "Guess I can close it, huh?" He closed it.

"You'll take it, huh?" George was laughing.

"I guess I will," laughed Jesso.

"So pick it up," said Ralph, and they all laughed at each other.

When they stopped, it was almost as if on cue.

Jesso said, "Push it over here," and his voice was different.

Ralph looked at George. He was refolding his arms, "You forgot to tell us your story, Jesso."

"So I did."

They waited.

"Push it over here."

"Your story, Jesso."

There was the silence again, except that they all heard the singing and clacking of the train. It hadn't occurred to Jesso before, but this train made a constant clack on the tracks. American trains didn't clack like that. They must join the rails differently.

"The story," he said. "Do you know the story I told Kator? The wrong one?"

"No."

"If I told you the same one, you'd never know."

"Not until later. We'd find you and you'd end up dead."

"I can see that."

They heard the clacking again and the wind rushing by the window.

"The right story, then," and he told them the one he had fed to Kator. "The upper left half and the lower right half of the two columns of figures give the production of the thing they make at Honeywell."

And they did nothing. Ralph didn't kick the suitcase over because he knew Jesso was lying. George kept his arms folded because to shoot Jesso would keep them from ever knowing. They couldn't have figured any of this, except that Kator had told them.

"I was kidding, fellows." Jesso looked at his shoe. He lifted his foot and rubbed the shoe against his pants leg. Then he looked at the shine he'd made. "You know how it is, fellows." He laughed, looked at the shoe again. "If you'll kick the suitcase over, like security, sort of—"

Ralph pushed it up to Jesso's feet and George unfolded his arms.

"We understand, Jesso. I'll even toss your gun over there." He took it out, threw it on the seat.

"You understand," said Jesso, and he looked apologetic. He held it on his face for fear he'd break up and laugh. He still looked that way when he told them, "The upper halves of both columns make up the figures you want. Honeywell."

He bent down then, slowly, and picked up the suitcase. It wasn't heavy. He still moved slowly when he straightened up and caught Ralph reaching over for the gun. When it came around, pointed, he couldn't hold it any longer and burst out laughing. Then the gun went click and click and click. Jesso was still laughing when he threw the suitcase at Ralph, and even though it was light there was force behind it and Ralph stumbled back so that George had to catch him. The door was open and they heard Jesso laughing down the corridor.

But he didn't keep it up. By the time he was racing through the next car there was only the fast clack of the wheels and his own breathing. You don't know Kator much, George had said. He should know and he had been right. Kator had figured there'd be these two jovial fellows, countrymen, all ready with the pile of real live money. And that's one thing Americans can't resist, Kator must have figured. And then when he'd told them the right story they'd shoot. Kator had tried that one before and figured wrong, but he wasn't going to be wrong about the part with the money.

There's one thing about those German trains, they all have a catwalk along the side, so when George came clattering through the platform between the cars he didn't see Jesso because Jesso hung outside the door. Then Ralph came by. They went the way Jesso had gone, down the long end of the train. Jesso got back in and walked to the stateroom where the dough was. He didn't even run. The suitcase was there, and they had left his gun because without bullets there wasn't much point to it. Jesso took the bullets out of his pocket and reloaded the cylinder. Before he picked up the suitcase he thought about leaving a note, something like "You know how it is. The right combination is tick-tack-toe diagonally across the list, honest," but then he let it go because it came to him where they'd be headed first. He went out into the corridor.

He held the revolver in one hand and the valise in the other, and kicked the door to his stateroom open.

"Drop it," Jesso said, and they did.

"Honest—" George said, but he saw Jesso didn't look conversational.

"I got a proposition." Ralph's voice was squeaky.

"Shut up. You'll wake up the girl."

Renette hadn't even opened an eye. She'd got to be a heavy sleeper. They all turned to look at her in the bed and she looked sexy as hell.

"Turn around."

They did.

"To the other wall, you bastards."

They turned.

"Now lean."

They knew what he meant, and they leaned against the wall with their hands out. Jesso kicked the door shut, put the case down, and started to wake Renette. It took a while. She didn't ask any questions because she was still half asleep, but then her clothes weren't handy.

"George," Jesso said.

George started to turn.

"Face front, you sonofabitch, or you've taken your last look."

George looked front.

"Those clothes on the seat under you. Throw 'em back here."

George reached down and tossed the dress back. Renette held the dress and looked at Jesso.

"The other stuff first, damn it. What's the matter with you!"

George threw the other stuff and Renette got dressed. Then she went to the bathroom and combed her hair. She did it as if she had all the time in the world, as if there were nothing on her mind but combing her hair. There wasn't.

The three men waited. After a while Ralph started to moan because of his arms and George hissed something at him. But Ralph kept moaning.

When Renette came back, Jesso told her to keep out of line of his gun. She turned and went back to the mirror to put on some lipstick. Then she came back.

"Ralph."

Ralph didn't answer, but he stopped making his noise for a moment.

"You can turn around and sit. The lady's presentable."

Ralph did and sighed deeply. Then Jesso told George to do the same.

"Ever hop trains, you two?"

They shook their heads.

"You'll learn."

"God, Jesso, this thing's going ninety."

"Next curve you jump."

They came to the next one and the train never slowed down.

"Open the window."

They sat with the icy blast coming in and listened to the black roar outside. Then came the grade, with the clacking getting slower all the time.

"Next turn you jump. George, on your feet."

George stood by the window and waited.

It had got cold in the compartment and Renette shivered. Jesso sent her to the bathroom, where her coat hung on a hook.

"Out, George."

George climbed through the window, held on, found the catwalk with his feet.

"You're next, Ralph."

When they both were outside, Jesso stood by the window holding the gun on them. At the next curve, on top of the grade, they jumped.

The train took half an hour to the first stop on the run. Jesso carried the suitcases. They got off and headed for the round booth that said "Information" in German, English, and French. It was the middle of the night but somebody was ahead of them. They waited and then Renette looked up at Jesso. She had to blink her eyes in the light.

"Where are the other two?" she said, but Jesso figured he'd explain that one later.

Chapter Fifteen

Jesso went to the ticket window and pronounced the name of the town he wanted. The man at the information desk had told them the name; the earliest train went there. Renette stood by the train gate and waited. She was awake now. Jesso had told her what had happened and she had said only, "I'll go with you." Even if she had said no she knew he would have taken her.

They took a train with short, high cars, and once they were inside they saw that the whole car was one compartment. They rode and every few miles they stopped. Then a gray light started to come, showing fields outside and long stretches of wood. A conductor came through turning off the gas lights in the ceiling.

After a while a woman came in carrying two crates with live hens. She put them on the floor. A farmer wearing a blue shirt that hung down to his hips sat in the seat next to them. He smelled of animals and held a sack of seed grain between his knees. The train made a slow clatter, stopped for a while, clattered again.

"No joy ride," Jesso said.

She shrugged. "It won't last long," she said. Then she looked at the two women across from them, who kept staring at her, and then she looked someplace else.

The market town was Bad Brunn. They got off and walked to the bus terminal across the square. The sun was up now, and the air was clear, without moisture. Not like Hannover or Hamburg, with the constant dampness blowing in from the North Sea. This was a warmer climate, with country smells; the houses looking small and busy.

They climbed into the yellow bus and waited for it to fill up. The motor started to shake the bus, they took a slow turn around the fountain in the middle of the square, and then came the country road. This time it was cherry trees along both sides, cherry trees and every so often a dead one. It was a very old road. They took twenty miles of it and then they got out; over egg baskets, apple crates, and tools lying in the aisle, they finally got out, they watched the bus hobble off with blue dust behind and stood in the gravel where the two streets of the village crossed.

"This is it," Jesso said.

Renette looked down both streets. She laughed but didn't say anything. She smelled a cow odor in the air, and when she looked at the rutted dirt roads again she was reminded of Pomerania. Except that the low houses had slate on the roofs, or wood shingles. In Pomerania they used swamp grass.

"The whitewashed job over there, with the balcony," Jesso said. "That must be the one that rents rooms." He picked up the suitcase. "At least, that's what the information guy said."

But Renette wasn't listening. She was still looking at the village street. It had been a bad moment, seeing it. Not that there was swamp grass on the roofs; there wasn't. But the streets with the spaced, squat houses, with the dirt ruts and a chicken walking across, had suddenly felt like the desolate time, like the dank and poor time before Johannes had helped her and she could leave her home. And all this in spite of the sunshine on the street and the peaceful warm smells in the air. Jesso hadn't noticed, of course. She saw Jesso crossing the road ahead of her and for a moment she felt like running.

Then she followed him. Suddenly it was easy, because everything was different now, as different as having left the rotten estate and having joined Johannes. Now she could even be through with Johannes and it would not turn bad again. She had lost poverty. First, through Johannes, who had given her the comforts of his money. Then she had done with another poverty, now that Jesso had come. It was a freedom.

He was waiting on the other side of the road and they went to the whitewashed house together.

The room had a balcony. Inside was the low ceiling of the peasant house, a tile stove in one corner and a monster closet against one of the walls. The rest of the room was mostly bed, and the bed was mostly feather blanket.

"Let's lie down," she said.

Jesso put the suitcase in the closet and stepped to the bed. "Like rolling in dough," he said.

"Good."

She stretched herself out and sank into the feathers. "Watch your clothes," he said. "You haven't got any others."

"I'll take them off," she said.

She got up and stood with her back to him so he could get at the buttons. He undid them.

"Come," she said. She lay on the feather bed and he sat down beside her.

"Soft," he said. "Better than that lousy ride on——"

"Your clothes are still on," she said.

"Yeah. Sure." He undressed.

"Jesso," she said.

The sun was going higher outside and the village street was empty because the men worked in the fields and the women worked in the gardens. None of that meant a damn to Jesso or Renette, and later they went to sleep.

Renette had to borrow a pair of shoes from the landlady because her high heels weren't any good outside. And Jesso bought a clean shirt from her, a heavy linen thing that smelled of lavender because the landlady had been widowed for almost ten years and since that time there had been no call to take her husband's things out of the trunk.

They went to the Gasthof, where the bus had stopped. Inside there was a sweet odor of freshly ground flour and the smell of beer. The wet beer stink was strong, but after a while they didn't notice it. They ate at a long wooden table—boiled potatoes, boiled beef, and boiled cabbage, and then coffee that was gritty on the tongue because it had been boiled too. Only the beer was good. Jesso had some, but Renette just smoked and sat by.

After a while they took a walk past the last houses and through the fields. The evening air was full with hay odors and the spice of herbs. It was very quiet. Only insects were singing in the air. They thought of walking a piece farther, to the bridge over the creek ahead, but the mosquitoes got thicker and they turned back.

It was better on the small balcony. They sat in the dark and smoked.

"Sleepy?" he asked.

"No. I slept during the day."

"I know."

She laughed and then her cigarette glowed. When it went down again she leaned close, toward his chair.

"Are your legs on the railing?" she asked.

"Yeah."

"I bet nobody has sat here like that for years."

"Ten years, maybe."

"Yes," she said.

Jesso stretched in his chair, recrossed his legs.

"For a while that's going to be the news around here."

"For a while?"

"A week. Maybe two weeks."

"Make it a day. Maybe two days."

"We don't show that soon. A couple of weeks is better."

"I was in Carlsbad once. Why don't we go to Carlsbad?"

"What's Carlsbad?"

"It's a resort on the Rhine. It's full of retired professors and old ladies with rheumatism. I'd like to go there, Jesso. Just for the contrast."

"Just for the contrast this'll do the same thing. Better, even."

"Let's go to Carlsbad."

"Listen, Renette. You and me, from now on, we gotta stay out of sight. Then when I see Kator, after that we gotta stay out of sight. You don't know your brother much, do you?"

"You hate him, Jesso?"

"No. But I want to stay alive."

"You're with me now."

"Boy!" he said. "You sure don't know your brother much."

"But I do. I've known him longer than you have."

Jesso laughed. "You don't count. Besides, you like him too much."

Her cigarette glowed again and she exhaled. "I have great respect for him, Jesso."

"Me, too," he said.

His tone of voice wasn't pleasant and Renette tried to see Jesso's face in the dark.

"We are not talking about the same kind of respect. Yours is more like dislike."

Jesso let his feet come off the railing and it made quite a racket. Then he leaned over the arm of his chair. He sounded harsh.

"Now you listen to this love story, Renette. First he hires himself out to do a killing, then he tries putting the screws on a guy already half dead. Next comes a double cross to make a corpse, then another one of the same, and I'm the guy he was doing it to every time. So don't tell me to love your brother, kid, because he's the one I'm going after, and when I go out for a hit I don't do any loving."

When he was through she could still hear the sharp ring of his voice, and for a moment she sat thinking about it, to get clear what he had said. A while back, just days, there wouldn't have been any reason to think about it. There had been no Jesso. There had just been Johannes. And now the strength of Jesso was taking the place of her brother's.

But she said, "I don't excuse him. He needs no excuse."

"I didn't ask for excuses. Just don't sit there and tell me the sonofabitch is the end. He isn't. Or else I'd be dead!"

The strength of Jesso.... Or else there would be no Jesso, she thought.

"Whose side are you on, anyway?" he said, and he was out of the chair now, standing before her so she could see his black shape against the sky. She didn't know what to answer and then he did it for her. "You're on mine. That's why you're here and that's why I'm keeping you."

"Jesso," she said. "Do you know why I'm here?"

He was listening.

"Johannes sent me."

He still didn't move.

"To make you talk, maybe to make you weak."

Then she waited for whatever would come next, but his shape against the sky didn't move for a long time. At first, the way it started out, she didn't know what it was, but then it was Jesso laughing. He laughed so hard that when he stopped she didn't know how he had done it. He moved and sat down again.

"That poor sonofabitch," he said. "That stupid sonofabitch." He laughed some more. He lit two cigarettes, gave one to her. "So that's why you're here."

"No. That's why I came."

"You stayed because of Kator?"

"Because of you," she said.

"You know he's through with you, don't you?"

And then Renette laughed, because what Jesso had said didn't mean a thing any more. What meant something was the way she felt, the way she suddenly felt that she was through with Johannes. He was out of her fear, her need, and her hopes.

"Jesso," she said, "I can forget Johannes."

"Good for you. But I can't. He's crapped out before, but I won't forget him till he craps out for good."

"Forget him, Jesso."

"Why? Because he's your brother?"

She felt he needn't have said that. It was nasty, the way Helmut might have done it. But Jesso needn't have.

"I don't understand you," she said, because she didn't.

"Don't try. Just watch me forget him once I'm through with him. Pretty soon I'm going to be through with him."

But she still thought of Johannes the way she had thought of in the past, so she didn't see what Jesso meant, what he was up against. She herself was through with Johannes, not needing him any more, but not being concerned with him didn't make him her enemy.

"What you said before, Jesso, about hiding. You mean we run, from now on, we keep running and hiding?"

"That's a crazy way to put it. And maybe we won't. Maybe Kator will drop dead."

She didn't think he would. She was through with him but he was as strong as ever.

After a while she threw her cigarette over the railing. "Jesso," she said.

He sat still for a minute. Then he flipped his stub and watched it sail across the road.

"Jesso," she said again.

He got up, took her arm, and they went inside together. Nothing had changed and she wanted him as before. So far, nothing had changed.

Chapter Sixteen

It stayed that way for two days, but after two days the dullness of the place started to get her and something was getting Jesso too. It felt unfinished. If he hadn't been with Renette, it occurred to him, he might not have thought of waiting. He might have taken the train straight back, hit Kator in the head with his hundred thousand bucks, and asked for the rest of it. But there was Renette and it was just as well to let Kator sweat for a while—but not any more. He had Renette, and now, for the last time, Kator was going to pay.

They caught the once-a-day bus back to Bad Brunn and when they passed the white house with the balcony they laughed at each other because they both, for their reasons, were glad to go.

"And after Hannover, Jesso, let's go to Carlsbad."

"How about the Riviera?" he said.

"Or the Riviera."

"Or we can hit out to Africa. I've never been in Africa. Maybe big-game hunting, or whatever you do in Africa."

"I like the Riviera better," she said. "I know people there. We can stay there as long as we want, Jesso. I have a small chalet in Menton, from Johannes, and many friends who—"

"They'll keep. For a while we keep moving."

"Where, Jesso?"

"Just move. Out of the way, for a while, until—"

"Jesso," she said. "I don't like places out of the way. Did you live out of the way?"

"Now and then."

"What do you mean?"

"Just that. Now and then. The way I live, I gotta watch where I step, and that's part of it."

She smiled at him and for a moment it looked half like a frown, but then she shook her head and said, "It sounds too much like running, Jesso. I don't run any more. I just look and see what I want."

"What do you want?"

"You," she said, and she gave him a kiss so that the peasant woman across the aisle made a movement as if she were thinking of crossing herself.

After the local from Bad Brunn they took the through train back to Hannover. They had a compartment and during the warm afternoon Renette slept. Jesso sat by and smoked. He had started to smoke too much. It had started right after deciding to go back to Kator, not to wait any more, because the longer he waited, the more unfinished the business was. He wished Renette would wake up and talk to him. About Kator, for instance. There were a lot of things he might learn about Kator.

He went to the club car, had a drink, and came back. Renette was awake. Her clothes were all over one seat and Jesso could hear the shower behind the door of the tiny bathroom. Then it stopped.

"Jesso?" she called.

"None but."

"Dry me, Jesso."

She came out as she was, holding her hair up.

"The big towel," she said. "See it?"

He saw it. He got the towel and dried her.

"My back red yet?"

"Not yet."

"Harder, Jesso."

She turned for him and after a while she was dry. She lay down on the wall bed and after she stretched she said, "It feels good."

"You look good."

"So do you."

"That's because I'm dressed," he said.

"No. Because I'm undressed," she said, and when he started to get up and come to the bed she said, "No. Stay there, Jesso. Stay there a while longer."

He sat down and grinned at her.

"Talk to me," she said.

He played the game and talked.

"Nice weather," he said. "Looks good on your thigh, that sun there."

She moved her leg and smiled.

"Say something else. Just as brilliant."

"Well, like Helmut would say, how about love?"

"Helmut would," she said. "He always talks about love, one form or another."

"How did that creep ever get to you, Renette?"

"He never did. We're just married."

"Was that another one of Kator's plans?"

"Yes," she said, and there was no feeling in it. "It worked, too."

"What's von Lohe got that Kator wants?"

"Position. A special kind of position. I don't know if you knew it, but Johannes has a title, too. But it's out of touch. Poor and very secluded. The von Lohes know a different set, the industrialists, the families who got rich under the Nazis."

"Nice friends."

She shrugged and stretched her arms over her head.

Jesso had a hard time listening right then.

"Not nice, but Kator needs them. And Helmut can help with the introductions. Like the Zimmer matter."

"Who?"

"Zimmer. I thought you might know."

"What's Zimmer?"

"Oh, an industrial combine. One family runs it. They have holdings or plants all over the world, and that's what interests Johannes."

"In America too?"

"There too. Why are you interested?"

He thought he might be, but when she asked him she rolled on her stomach, which was a beautiful movement, and Jesso didn't feel any interest in plants or Zimmers. He went over to the bed and ran his hand down her spine.

"Now I'm hungry," she said, and she jumped up from the bed. He let her jump and watched her dress. There was time. She wanted to eat in the diner, and after that they sat in the club car instead of in the compartment, and that wasn't bad either. Jesso had never seen her except alone or at von Lohe's place, and she was good to watch anyplace. When they went back to the compartment it was almost dark, which was all right with Jesso, but as soon as he had the door shut the conductor came through the corridor calling something or other. He went by and kept calling.

"What's he want?"

Renette smiled, sat down by the window, and said, "Hannover Station, fifteen minutes," and then she cocked her head at Jesso, and he thought that if she had known the expression she would have said, "So do me something; go ahead."

"So you're safe," he said, and they both had a laugh.

It changed by the time they were in the taxi. The thought of Kator had started to irritate him, his beef and the stance like a Buddha and the mind like a machine. When they passed the intersection where he had left the ambulance he saw it was still there, with more parking tickets. But even that didn't amuse him. For once he wasn't eager to see Kator or to think out the next step before Kator took it. Jesso leaned back in the seat and put his arm around Renette. She leaned, took his other hand, but he sat up again, watching the traffic.

The row of villas had dots of light all along, but the von Lohe place was lit up as if for a coronation. Jesso paid the cab driver and took Renette up the drive. They carried no suitcases. They passed long cars all the way up and Hofer was at the open door, ready with a guest book.

"Evening, Hofer. Don't bother. We're not seeing anybody."

That shindig wasn't for him, anyway, so Jesso turned to the stairs. Kator could wait. Renette was ahead of him, but then she stopped on the stairs.

"Up with you," said Jesso.

"He wants you, I think," and she nodded toward the hall.

Jesso turned and saw Kator. He hadn't heard the sharp little steps because of the party noises.

"I've been expecting you, Jesso."

That bastard had gall. Not a hair out of place, soup and fish as if they had been invented for him, and looking cool as ice.

"So you got what you wanted."

"Hardly," Kator said. He made a stiff smile.

"And that's the way it'll be till you start playing it my way."

"You're not complaining, are you, Jesso? It paid well."

"And I'm keeping it."

"The wages of war," Kator said, bowing briefly.

Jesso turned to go but Renette hadn't moved yet. She started to go when Kator stopped her.

"After you have changed, Renette, please see me in my study."

"She's going upstairs," Jesso said.

"Naturally. And after she has changed—"

"Why, Johannes?"

Kator seemed to need a moment to collect himself, but then it came out as smoothly as ever.

"I will wait for you in the library, Renette. Afterward, there is the party."

"But Johannes, I'd rather—"

"She'll see you in the library," Jesso said. "Without changing. And no party."

Kator seemed to swell out. When he didn't say anything, Jesso told him, "And I'll wait here. So don't be long." Then he stepped aside and waved Renette down the stairs.

"And tomorrow, Kator, you and I talk turkey."

Kator heard it but turned on his heel, following Renette.

She was waiting for him by the desk. He stopped in front of her, looked her up and down, told her to sit.

"I'll stand, Johannes."

"Very well. I suppose you are bursting with information, my dear."

"You mean about Jesso?"

"I was thinking of Jesso, yes. What have you learned?"

"I've learned this, Johannes. He doesn't talk about business, but after a while he talked about you. He has no illusions about you, Johannes, and it does not frighten him."

"This much I knew."

"He is dangerous, Johannes."

Kator sat down on one of the couches, crossed his legs, and spread his arms along the backrest. The pose made him look more bull-necked than usual.

"You stand there, Renette, and find it necessary to warn me?"

"You are my brother."

Kator gave one short hard laugh. Then the big nostrils seemed to move up between his eyes.

"And Jesso, what is he to you?"

"A lot."

"You love him?"

It surprised Kator when she just shrugged.

"He means a lot, Johannes."

"And the wedding, my dear. When will I announce the wedding?"

"I don't think I'll marry him."

"And when will you return to us, my dear, to resume your proper functions?"

"If I leave him it will have nothing to do with you. Not any more."

Kator stopped playing. He understood how she had changed, and more, he understood something that Renette herself might not yet know; that she would now be capable of leaving Jesso just as she had left her brother. It was a fact that pleased him, a fact that he understood. She had become like himself, in a way. She had gained his kind of freedom to choose and discard. So for the moment he left her alone. He made it light.

"Would you like me to tell Helmut about this?"

"Suit yourself," she said, and went upstairs.

Chapter Seventeen

When Jesso heard Renette pass his door, he gave her a few minutes and then went to her suite, behind the bend of the hallway. Downstairs there was music and polite laughter, but Jesso hardly heard it.

The first thing Jesso saw was the maid leaving, and there was no argument about it this time. She was carrying Renette's dress and a few other things, and she left the door ajar for him when she saw him coming.

The big light was on in the room, so Jesso turned it off. Just the faint one by the bed was left. Renette was humming behind the door where the dressing room was. Jesso didn't go in. He went back to his room and got himself pajamas. He hadn't noticed before, but there was a small crest on one pocket; the von Lohe brand, most likely.

She was waiting for him. He could see her through the milky white thing she was wearing, white where it gathered and live skin tones where the thing stretched.

"Don't come any closer," she said. "Your suit scratches."

Then she turned for him, wanting him to look. "I've done all the looking I'm going to," he said.

"I'll yell," she said.

"I know you will." But he didn't go any closer. He went to the bathroom and took a shower. When he was through they pulled the quilted seat she had in the bedroom to the window and sat there looking out over the garden. The watery moon sent shafts of light here and there, and glittered on the cut glass of the decanter by the seat. It was a sweet liqueur with a curled gold leaf floating along the bottom, the kind of drink Jesso didn't even know. He watched how she tasted it, and he had some and thought it was good too. They had more and sat on the seat.

"Turn some," he said. "You're poking me."

"I have big hips."

"Good."

"If I turn I'll just poke you somewhere else."

"Good."

She turned and they sat still.

"You know, I've never seen that garden at night."

"I haven't either."

"Look at it sometime."

"I will."

"Not now."

"I'm not looking now."

"I know, Jesso."

"Done with your glass?"

"Put it down for me, please?"

"Just drop it."

She dropped it and looked where it rolled. "I might step on it in the dark."

"You won't. I'll carry you."

"Carry me now, Jesso."

And then the door made an oiled movement, swung wide, and the big light overhead came on like an explosion. Jesso let go and jerked around just as Helmut closed the door. Then Jesso's voice came like a bellow.

"What in hell do you want?"

It shook the Baron. It was an insult to which there was no answer. A moment later he drew himself up and sounded cultured.

"I'm sorry the light startled you. It must have—"

"It did. So turn it off."

This made another pause and when the Baron found his voice again it was edged.

"Actually," and he smiled with his mouth, "I came to see my wife."

"Scram, Helmut."

"Renette," and he looked past Jesso, "I would like you to come now."

She had turned in the seat and made a face. "But Helmut, I don't understand your—"

"As your husband I demand—"

"Shut up, Helmut. You interrupted her."

Renette frowned. "Just what do you mean, Helmut?"

"I know what that sonofabitch means!" Jesso was barking. He jumped up from the seat and watched the Baron take a step back. The Baron fiddled with his cuff links and his voice had a slice to it.

"Do not take my leniency for granted, Jesso." He started a thin smile. "I will overlook your intrusion. However, at the moment I desire the presence of my wife. I assure you she is well able to forego your—"

"Get out." It wasn't very loud.

"Why, Jesso. You have affrontery—"

Then Jesso roared again. "You think you can talk like that just because she's your wife? Now scram!" Jesso went across the room fast, but by the time he got to the door it had closed again and the Baron was gone. He was bolting down the hallway like a puppet on too many wires, even forgetting about his hair, which had flapped out of place, showing the skull.

Chapter Eighteen

Jesso was down at eight and Hofer served his breakfast in the long room next to the solarium. He would eat till eight-fifteen, smoke a cigarette, take a walk in the garden. He would walk in the garden like a gentleman, because Kator never showed till after ten, when he had breakfast and read his mail. He wouldn't be ready for business till close to eleven. That was two hours anyway, two hours to walk in the garden like a goddamn gentleman and maybe think everything over again.

Hofer came back.

"I don't want anything and I'm not done, so stop popping in here or whatever you call it."

"Herr Kator is waiting for you in his study."

Jesso jumped up and made for the door.

"There is no need to interrupt your—"

"You finish it, Hofer."

Kator looked cold and impersonal. He got up from his desk. He was ready for business.

"Get your coat, Jesso. We are leaving for Berlin."

"Another dry run?"

"I am going with you. Please get your coat."

The airport was far out of the city and the plane was Kator's. It was a two-engine with a separate pilot's cabin and the outside was painted gray, a thick gray, as if there used to be some other paint underneath. They climbed aboard and took off almost immediately.

Neither of them talked. Kator read papers that he took out of his brief case and wrote on a pad. Jesso looked out of the window. Once Kator went to the front and handed the pilot a message he wanted radioed, then sat down again as before. Jesso looked out of the window again. There wasn't much to see. He'd got used to the constant overcast over Hannover and was almost surprised when the plane broke through the layer and there was sun. Underneath there was nothing but clouds.

That changed after a while. Occasionally the sun broke through underneath, and when the plane entered the traffic pattern over the Tempelhof airport the country below had a glassy brilliance.

The car that waited for them was Kator's and the chauffeur wore the same livery as the one in Hannover.

"The Klausewitz address," said Kator. "But go down the Charlottenburger Chaussee."

"It's out of the way, sir."

"Just the same."

When they came out of the Tiergarten the wide street ended on the Potzdammer Platz. Jesso recognized it from newsreels he'd seen.

"Take a slow swing past the gate," Kator said. He leaned toward his window and looked across to the Russian sector.

"Homesick, Kator?"

"Historical interest, Jesso. Actually nothing has changed."

"Where was your office, Kator—Unter den Linden? War Department, maybe?"

"No. A much smaller building. Not far from there."

"And what a beautiful uniform you used to wear."

Kator turned slightly, looked almost bored. "I never wore a uniform, Jesso."

"That figures. And if you're through sight-seeing, I'm dying to meet your friends. We going across?"

"I arranged the meeting in this sector. Your passport is hardly good enough for the East Zone—at this short notice."

"How about yours?"

"I manage. Erich, the Klausewitz place," and the big car slid off, back toward the West.

Kator turned in his seat, ready to talk. It turned out to be the briefing voice.

"This will pain you, Jesso, but for both our sakes I advise you to remain— uh—polite. In view of the stakes, you should be able to manage it. The man we shall meet does not have my leniency, nor can he be forced to adopt it. For the sake of our business and your well-being, please be warned."

"I'll be like a mouse."

The Klausewitz address was nothing special, one of a row of clean-looking, modern apartment buildings. The apartment itself was on the top floor. There was no name on the door, just a number. And there was nothing unusual about the inside, just an apartment with several rooms. The only remarkable feature was a compact switchboard in the small entrance hall. The girl who had let them in sat down again and then one of the doors opened.

The man was nothing extra, either. He was small, dressed in gray, and if Jesso had tried to pick him out of a group of ten the next day he wouldn't have been able to do it. The man bowed and closed the door behind them. He sat down on a metal chair next to a steel desk and waved at the couch by the wall. His desk chair stayed empty.

"Von Kator, I am pleased to see you."

They bowed to each other. Jesso didn't think they were friends.

"And Mr. Jesso?"

"Mr. Jesso, Mr. Delf."

That was all, and then Mr. Delf put out his hand and took the folded sheet of onionskin that Kator held out. While Delf looked at the figures, a pencil in his right hand made monotonous spirals on a pad of paper by the edge of the desk.

"Have you microfilmed this?"

"No."

"I admire you, von Kator. If it should be seen by someone else, who would worry about a piece of onionskin with rows of meaningless figures? But you will supply the meaning, yes, Mr. Jesso?" The left hand let the paper slide on the desk and the right hand kept making spirals.

Jesso frowned. "Look, I came to sell, but what are you paying with?"

Delf just kept spiraling.

"Money, of course. In the usual way."

Kator said, "A detail I have not explained to Mr. Jesso. Mr. Jesso requires a lot of explaining."

Jesso looked at Kator. With Delf in the room for contrast, Kator suddenly looked colorful and vital.

Kator went on: "You deliver the correct information and Mr. Delf will sign over the agreed amount. That completes the transaction."

"How much is he paying?"

"I am paying five hundred thousand," said Delf, "in dollars."

Nobody batted an eye, so Jesso didn't either.

"Who decided that?" Jesso sounded gruff.

There was a pause this time while Delf and Kator looked at each other as if they had never met.

Kator was hoarse. "Are you quibbling, Jesso?"

"I'm asking. I want to know how you got that price."

"It is my price," said Delf. He had stopped making spirals, and for the first time since he had said anything he had an identity. Jesso kept still for a moment, stuck his hands in his pockets.

"Where's the money? I don't see any suitcase of money standing around."

"I mentioned this earlier, Jesso." Kator's voice was getting sharp. "The money will be signed over."

"I don't even see any checkbook lying around."

"Perhaps I might explain it," Delf said. "You can see, Mr. Jesso, that an amount of this size would attract attention. It would do so if I drew the money in cash and it would do the same if you cashed my check for five hundred thousand. This is to be avoided at all costs."

"Just a minute. There's no check for five hundred thousand. There's one for Kator and one for me and they are both for two hundred and fifty."

It wasn't news to Delf, but even if it had been he wouldn't have acted differently.

"I mentioned that figure as an illustration only. Actually, we proceed in an accustomed manner. There will be some stock transfers, there will be diverse payments for services rendered to a number of companies with which Herr von Kator is affiliated, and your little personal arrangement will be settled between you two."

"Like hell it will!"

This time even Delf looked human.

"You are new to this," he said after a while. "My advice—"

"I don't need it. I'm new to this, but not green."

"Your idiom is not clear to me."

"I want cash. Clear enough?"

For a while Delf's spirals got blacker and tighter. The pencil made a thin sound. When Delf suddenly coiled the spirals the other way, everybody noticed it.

Even Jesso felt relieved when Delf gave a deep sigh and looked at Kator. Then Delf spoke to Kator as if they were alone in the room.

"Have you tried everything, von Kator?"

"It's no use. He's in."

"We used to be very clever with this sort of thing, you remember?"

"I remember. The quick methods are self-defeating in this case. His information seems complicated."

Jesso got it then. He listened as if they were discussing somebody else's operation. An operation without ether, maybe.

"And the long methods defeat our time schedule," said Delf.

"I know Mr. Jesso quite well by now. I suggest you pay me as in the past and make different arrangements for him."

"What have you tried, von Kator?"

Jesso remembered what he had tried. He had tried frightening him to death, shooting him to death, tempting him to death. The only thing he hadn't tried was giving in. Even now. And Delf was worse. Delf could sit there and make tired doodles while going over in his mind to break a man's arm so it took half an hour, how to kill him while keeping him alive.

Jesso's fingers were painfully clenched and a thick sweat was growing over his skin. Everywhere. Except on his face. He rarely sweated on his face. That was good. His hands were in his pockets, so they couldn't see that. His face was dry, and nothing showed there. Only his jaw had started to set with a grip like murder and any moment it would show, it would show with a crazy jumping and trembling as if he had some nervous disease.

"Your judgment must do in this case, von Kator. Mr. Jesso?"

He hadn't heard any of it, but now the tone was different and the room was just a room, with Kator looking correct and Delf making a simple doodle.

"Mr...."

"I hear you."

"While cash is out of the question, Mr. Jesso, I can agree to make deposits in your name in any bank."

"O.K.," he said. "O.K., do that. Do it now."

"What banks, Mr. Jesso?"

"I got an account at Chase. Put it there."

"Only one bank?"

He was right. One bank was no good. The bulge would show too much. Jesso sat up. He was just getting to be himself again and it made him sit up.

"How do I know you're depositing? How do I know this finishes it off and—"

"Mr. Jesso. I don't see Herr von Kator behaving in this stupid, suspicious manner, and I also fail to see why you—"

"That's because you and Kator are buddies, but Kator and me aren't such good friends any more. I'm going by that, Delf, because with you I don't know what to go on. Now, figure me out how to make a deposit and I know about it."

"What banks, Mr. Jesso?"

"What banks, what banks! I give a damn what banks? The one in Hannover, right after the square where you leave the villa for town."

"He means the Handelsbank," said Kator. He had a smile on his face.

Jesso didn't see it because he was getting impatient. "All right, the Handelsbank near that square. Fifty thousand."

This time Kator laughed out loud.

"And what are you hee-hawing about?"

"It's von Kator's bank," said Delf.

"So maybe they haven't got room for another depositor?"

Kator wasn't laughing any more; just sort of a grin was on his face.

"He owns it," said Delf.

Jesso was going to yell again when Kator made a wave with his hand.

"It's a legitimate bank, Jesso, and you are quite safe there. Just the thought struck me as amusing. I pay two per cent."

"One buck to the Handelsbank," said Jesso.

"You're being ridiculous. I told you the bank is legitimate, and when I am legitimate, Jesso, I am completely so."

Jesso believed that.

"Fifty thousand into Kator's jug, and let me see how you do it, Delf."

"I'll call the bank by phone and—"

"*I'll* call the bank by phone."

"Certainly. And request the confirmation by wire. That is, if the phone isn't enough for you."

"It isn't."

After ten minutes Jesso was fifty thousand richer. "What other banks, Mr. Jesso?"

"Give me a Berlin directory."

Delf coughed lightly and shook his head. "Fifty thousand is the total amount I will deposit for you in this country. I explained to you that our transaction must appear as unimportant as possible. I would suggest you pick American banks. I can make payment there through local sources that cannot be identified with me at all."

"I'm here, Delf, not in the States."

"I have compromised with you; now you compromise with me."

Jesso thought about it for a moment, then let it go.

Gluck wasn't going to find him any more easily in the States than in Europe, and this deal was coming to a head. It wasn't worth the delay.

"Chase National, fifty thousand."

"Will you speak to them for confirmation or do you require a cable?"

"Both."

It took half an hour while Jesso listened to the operator on the second phone on the desk. Then Delf started to talk and the man across the ocean answered.

"Is this Mr. Troy? Mr. Troy, this is Delf. Yes, thank you, quite well. You have an account in the name of Jack Jesso. Please deposit fifty thousand dollars to Mr. Jesso's name and charge it to the Antwerp Gem Importers account.... Yes, if you please.... Indeed, indeed, she is as well as ever.... I will, Mr. Troy, and the same to Mrs. Troy."

That was that, and Jesso was one hundred thousand richer.

"Manufacturer's Trust, New York."

"Very well. However, the further deposits will be more complicated. The Antwerp account is the only one in the States with which my name is associated."

"Manufacturer's Trust, twenty thousand."

Then came three others, ten thousand each, all of them in New York, and Jesso was worth one hundred and fifty thousand. He figured on putting the rest into places on the Coast, but that didn't make sense. The less time he spent in the States collecting his loot, the better. His plans for the future had nothing to do with that side of the globe. But he had run out of banks, so he put fifty thousand in the Bank of America, Los Angeles, then American Express, New York, twenty thousand, and since he couldn't think of anything else, another Los Angeles Bank, thirty thousand.

Jesso was worth a quarter of a million. Not counting the hundred thousand that he had stashed at Express in Hannover. Then Delf said, "And now for your part, Mr. Jesso" They looked at each other. "Which of these sets of figures shows production of the trigger?"

It didn't occur to Jesso to stall. The deal was on, half of it finished, and he was next. Delf must have known that about Jesso. He had paid first. Or he had known that Jesso wouldn't talk unless he was paid first. In any case, Jesso was next.

"Joe Snell kept saying, 'Honeywell high.' The high column of figures shows production of the trigger."

Delf nodded, stopped making the spirals, and went over the columns. He checked it, folded the paper, and slid it into his pocket. That was all. Then he spiraled again.

But Kator wasn't so calm. The slow rage grew on his face like an attack of the hives, and when his mouth came open as if it hurt, Jesso thought that the man would scream. Only a croak came out, a breathy, articulate croak.

"'Honeywell high'! That's all—'Honeywell high'! A complicated bit of remembering, a complex piece of instruction that saved you all this time from—from—" His eyes shone as if he were seeing some swift, sharp torture that would have dragged anything out of him and now it was lost. He sat by when Jesso started to laugh, long and loud, and he sat by while Jesso got it out of his system because he was through with waiting and free to laugh. If Kator hadn't been convinced before, he knew it now. This time Jesso had told the truth. That's the way that laugh had gone.

From now on it was an easy kind of waiting for Jesso. They sat around to wait for the cables to come, the last formality that would put the touch on the deal. They came one after the other, until four in the morning, and each time Jesso folded one and stuck it away, it was one more step into one great big future.

Chapter Nineteen

He didn't really come back down to earth till they got outside. A blank sun was over the street, and the early morning looked anesthetic. It made Jesso feel dirty. He ached in the back and his shirt felt old. He could feel the socks in his shoes and it made him nervous.

"Where's that damn car of your's, Kator?"

They stood at the curb where the sprinkled asphalt started to steam in the sun. They sprinkled the streets. They glazed them early in the morning so that the poor bastard who had come out on the street real early in the morning could feel his eyeballs get sore in the sun.

"Didn't you hear me?"

Kator had heard. He turned slowly, and when Jesso saw the look on that face he really came to. Kator was just getting ready. Kator wasn't through by a long shot. The hate on Kator's face was distilled.

So Kator didn't have to say a word for Jesso to see it all.

"You're ready to fight?"

Then the car rolled up.

"I shall see you, Jack Jesso." Kator opened the door.

For the moment it threw him. He had to blink and remember that Kator did things in a different way.

"You see this street, Jesso? It is empty," Kator said. "Good-by, Jesso, and run as fast as you can."

But when he got into his car Jesso pushed after him, sat down, slammed the door.

"Sporting chance, huh?" Jesso tried laughing. He gave it up quickly and talked. "I'm sticking close like a Siamese twin. I'm gonna sit on your back or in your pocket and watch you move. And if you move down a dark alley to get me so I can catch a slug, I'll be so close, Kator, you'll catch it in the same place I do, only first."

"Get out of my car."

Jesso leaned back, crossed his legs. "I left my toothbrush at your house."

Kator wasn't ready to laugh, and above all not on Jesso's terms.

They drove to Tempelhof and they flew to Hannover and each wished the other was dead. They tried it quiet at first, but the tension between them was too close to the surface. It bound them together like steel wires so that Kator's tight collar became Jesso's discomfort and Jesso's throat became Kator's pain. And the next move perhaps would be big enough, would be enough of a shock to break things wide open. Each was the other's disease as they sat scratching at time, straining to find the place where the cut could be made.

"You can stop chewing that lip of yours, Kator. You'll eat yourself up."

"It annoys you, Jesso? I hope it stays with you each time you face a meal."

"You know, when I can't think of a dirty word from now on, I'll say Kator."

"It is remarkable. I have never felt like this before, Jesso. The thought of you does not make me hate *you*. It is more like hate of myself, and that is the worst state of all."

But it never broke, just got tighter. They probed each other for the clearest pain and each winced when his own strikes struck where he wanted it.

"Your toothbrush, you say. Might that be my sister?"

"They never made a thing that was related to you, Kator."

"You think she is yours, then?"

"It wouldn't mean anything to you."

"You are right, Jesso. It is the other way around."

"To her you're just a whoremaster."

"And she doesn't mind it, Jesso."

"That's good. It's good she doesn't really know you, Kator."

Both of them stopped at the same time. They left the plane and found Kator's limousine waiting. Kator stopped talking about his sister and Jesso stopped talking about his woman. But he had to think about her. He thought about her as the only sane spot in the strong twist of his hate, the only spot where hate had no meaning, and so he really thought of Renette for the first time. He found it was hard to think of her. He remembered the tone of her voice, the feel of her skin, the way she stood, but all those things were parts only and the whole woman was hard to think about. As if he knew her so well that there was no point in thinking of it. If he were questioning her, any part of her, it would be different. But there was nothing to question, nothing to think, because she was all his and no doubts.

They crossed the square with the Herrenhauser Allee opposite and both of them had the same thought. It was a hope. It was as if the end had to come now, and the tight pull between them soon had to crack.

But when it happened it didn't crack and there was no drama. Neither wanted to think about it, so it happened as if nothing happened at all. The car slid up and stopped by the door. Hofer was there. They saw Hofer stand there in his striped pants and frock coat, and they didn't fit, because no clothes are made to fit an old man.

Hofer opened the car door and Kator got out. He said, "How are you, Hofer? It is good to be back."

Then Jesso got out and said, "Good to see you, Hofer."

Hofer followed them into the hall, where he took Kator's coat. Jesso wasn't wearing any.

"Your mail is in the study," said Hofer, and Kator went there.

The dim hall was big and clean. Jesso thought of going upstairs, to the end of the corridor maybe, but then he stayed downstairs and went to the kitchen. They gave him a cup of coffee and he had it there leaning against the long pantry shelf. The maid was putting a tea service away.

"How's Frau von Lohe?" Jesso asked.

"Quite well, sir. She is resting."

Quite well, sir. Jesso gave up and lit a cigarette. Then he asked for another cup of coffee. He had it finished before he knew how, and he stamped his cigarette out on the saucer. He kept crushing the butt as if he were trying to burn through the porcelain.

What was he waiting for? He pushed himself away from the pantry shelf and made for the door. When he found himself still holding the cup, he almost threw it against the wall. He went back to the pantry, put down the cup, and got out.

She was resting. She was lying on the bed, wearing a house thing that went down to her feet, and when Jesso came in she didn't turn at first because she was sleeping.

"Renette," he said, and he stood looking down at her. Then he said her name again, low this time, but his voice was much more urgent because suddenly waiting was almost like pain.

She had a nice way of waking up. She opened her eyes slowly, saw him, and smiled, and then she lay there a while longer.

"Renette, do you hear me? It's done. We've got to move fast."

"You're back," she said. "You didn't take long."

"Renette, did you...."

He stopped then because she sat up and yawned. But she had been listening. She sat up and took Jesso's hands.

"I'm happy for you," she said. "It's over now and you have what you wanted."

"Almost. Listen, Renette. I've got to go to the States. They paid off through some banks in the States. So before something goes sour, we got to jump."

She got up, fully awake now.

"You have to leave, Jesso?"

"I said the money is in the States."

"You have no money at all? I can—"

"Listen, Renette. Most of it is over there, so here's what we do." He sat down on the bed and pulled her down next to him. "I'm going to ask your brother for a passport. The one I got now couldn't get across the street without his help, and I want him to fix me a good one."

"He will. He can—"

"He will like hell. Not unless you help me, Renette. You've got to pressure him some way so he gets me a passport quick, because the longer I wait from here on in, the more time he has to figure himself an angle."

"Stay here," she said. "We'll go somewhere and you send for the money. You know, Jesso, we can—"

"Damn it, listen to me. We got to get to the States for this thing. There are angles you don't know a thing about. Tax, immigration, and a dozen others. Your brother can play any one of them if he's got the time."

She got up and pushed her hands into the big pockets of her gown. It almost looked to Jesso as if she were suddenly twice as far away.

"Of course I'll help you. Johannes will give you that passport." She turned, leaned against the satin couch by the window. "How long will you be gone?"

"Perhaps—" Then he got up too. "What in the hell are you talking about?"

She just looked back at him. Jesso came closer.

"You're going along, don't you hear?"

"You don't really have to go there, do you?"

He got very patient then. "Look, Renette. You're arguing about something you don't know a thing about. Pack something, get me that passport. I'll get the tickets, and in a few days we'll come back to—to whatever you had in mind. But don't argue with me about this thing. It's too big. You hear me?"

"Of course, I see what you mean." She took her hands out of the pockets and started to hold her arms. There was a rare indecision in her posture. "Perhaps I mean this, Jesso. Over here, Jesso, I know you, I want you, we are what I know now. You and I. But over there you must be somebody else. I've never known you over there and your life is perhaps quite different. Perhaps not, Jesso, but I don't know. I want you now, here, and not later and somewhere else. You must not start to think of me as something you own, keep around wherever you happen to be. It would not be the same. What we have between us is just the opposite of that. It is the very thing you have given me, Jesso, and it is freedom." She put her hands on his shoulders. "I want you here. So I'll wait for you here, Jesso."

"Renette—"

"You said a few days only."

She wasn't going to budge and he knew it. So just a few days. She'd wait and he had to wait. But it didn't feel right to him.

"You can't stay here. Dear Johannes, you know, isn't going to—"

She just laughed and started to turn. "I'm safe here, Jesso." She walked to the dressing room.

He followed her and watched while she changed to a dress. He lit a cigarette and watched, leaning against the doorframe.

"Just one thing, Renette." She looked up. "Stay close to the house, stay away from Helmut, and watch Kator like a hawk. When I get back here I don't want any damage."

"Yes, Jesso."

"Now come along."

He took her downstairs and Kator was in the library. One of the files was open and Kator was leafing through a folder. He stopped when he saw them and shut the drawer. It clanked like a metal door.

"You are overstaying your welcome, Jesso."

"I'm leaving."

"Good-by, then." Kator carried his folder to the desk.

"I got something for you," Jesso said, and he tossed Snell's doctored passport on top of Kator's folder. "And from you I want a going-away present."

"Johannes, I want you to give Jesso a passport. A good one."

Kator was leaning back with his hands across his front and there was no way of telling what he thought. For that matter, Jesso couldn't even figure why Kator hadn't made his move yet. Or perhaps he had, only the trap hadn't sprung yet. Or maybe Kator was really through. The deal was closed and paid for and that was it. Kator might be that sort.

"When do you want it?" Kator asked.

If this was bluff, Jesso would play it the same way. "Tomorrow. At eight."

"Very well," Kator said. "I still have your pictures."

Jesso felt flat. Kator had been easy before, but not that easy.

"Provided one thing," Kator said.

Here it came.

"My sister remains behind."

If that was his angle, he was welcome to it. Jesso looked at Renette and she looked back. She played it well and made the right kind of face. It had been easy.

"Have the passport ready," Jesso said. "She'll stay." Then he took Renette's arm and they left the room.

When they got out to the hall they didn't know where to go. They didn't know why they felt that way, because everything had gone all right and in only a few days Jesso would be back. They walked into the garden and for a while they leaned over the stone ballustrade of the terrace and looked at the winding walks.

"He didn't even make a stir," Jesso said.

"I told you he wouldn't," Renette said.

"But he meant to. What if we were going together? That's how he meant it."

"I know," she said. She took some gravel and tossed little stones at a flower bed. "But it doesn't matter."

Jesso said nothing and Renette tossed some more stones.

"Renette. It does matter."

"What he did?"

"No, you. That you won't come."

"That doesn't matter either. Because you agreed."

"You make it sound easy," he said, and hearing his own voice, he wondered at the change in it.

"Jesso," she said. "You sound like good-by."

"Like hell."

But when they stood there longer, not speaking, the damp air, maybe, or the lead in the low sky got to him, and Renette too didn't feel the ease any more and the sure sense of herself, and when he said, "Come," she followed him, very eager, and they went upstairs without saying anything and closed the door behind them.

Then they made love as if it were the only time, with no before and no after.

Chapter Twenty

He watched the runway fall away and then the city where it lay flat below with a green park spreading at one end and factory chimneys at the other. It disappeared after a while as they entered the overcast. Jesso pulled out his passport again. The green cover was properly worn and inside there were his name and his picture and his signature, and there was nothing wrong with any of it as far as he could tell. He stuck it back in his pocket with the envelope and the airplane tickets. One of them said Hannover to Frankfurt-am-Main and the other one hadn't been used yet. It said Frankfurt-am-Main to New York. There was a return ticket too. A week at the most and he'd be back. Everything was running so smoothly that he would be back even sooner.

Jesso sat in his seat and didn't feel right, even though the feeling made no sense. Renette? How could he feel uneasy about something he wanted so much and had altogether? Helmut? Why waste time thinking about a thing like him? Perhaps Kator. He thought of Kator when the plane went down at Frankfurt, when he got off and went along the airport corridor to the other ramp. His connecting flight was there. Jesso stood in the line that went through customs, and if there was any reason to think of Kator, this was it. Maybe the passport wasn't as good as it looked. Almost Jesso's turn in line. Maybe they'd take one look, pull him out, and that was Kator's play. Jesso could see the two guys in green, customs officers. Two German policemen with those crazy shakos on their heads, like flowerpots. And two M.P.'s. They wore khaki and white for the occasion.

The line moved and Jesso stepped closer. He had a very calm thought and it was that he'd kill somebody if they tried to pull him out. *"Pass, bitte,"* and Jesso handed it over. Then he got it back and walked through the gate. Then the plane, the stewardess who was a living doll from Cleveland, Ohio, and the seat. The seat. The plane took off and that was that.

He didn't take a deep breath of relief, because he hadn't been holding his breath. It was a weird state to know that nothing was right and to find nothing wrong that he could do anything about; and weirder still to know that even inside of him nothing was happening. They shipped eels that way, curled inside a block of ice in suspended animation. The whole trip went by without any real passage of time. He didn't come out of it until the pilot invited everyone over the loud-speaker to look down below, the United States coast was coming up. Jesso thought it was the weirdest yet to be going in one direction in order to go in the other.

Jesso had only one suitcase and got through customs fast. He took a taxi from Idlewild and they made the Queens Midtown Tunnel in less than an hour. It was five in the morning. He knew a nice family hotel on Forty-fifth Street and he took a room at $7.50 with bath. Then he went to sleep until nine. He woke up the way he rarely did, with a quick, wide-awake jump, but there were just the Chinese mandarins on the wallpaper and the thing with the house rules on the door. He showered and shaved and wanted breakfast. There was a hamburger place across the street and he had an English muffin with jam and drank coffee.

That was at nine-forty-five. He smoked a cigarette in the taxi and from nine-thirty till three in the afternoon he kept the same cab going from one bank to the next. He got some cash and a lot of traveler's checks. They cost a fortune, but that was the least of his worries. He was stepping out of a bank stuffing an envelope into his brief case when he came awake as he hadn't been since the trip had started. Manufacturers Trust Company, it said next to him on the brass plate. That time in Delf's office with nothing on his mind but racking up a list of New York banks, that's when he had picked Manufacturers Trust. He would; he knew it well enough. He should-n't have, because Gluck's office was in the building right across the street.

Jesso hefted the brief case and made for his taxi at the curb. It was dou-ble-parked, so all he saw was the rear fender, and then the fender started moving. Jesso made it to the curb, ran out between the cars that stood there, and yelled, but the hacky either didn't hear or didn't want to, because the cab was off, moving with the traffic.

"He stood there twenty minutes, bud. At twenty minutes even I draw the line," said a cop, coming out from between the cars.

He didn't look mean, he didn't look as if he were part of a plot, or maybe planted there, maybe no cop at all. Jesso was wide awake now, so much so that he felt he was going to shake any minute.

"He'll be back," said the cop. "Just making a circle around the block." He turned and walked across the street.

Jesso watched him leave, knowing it was just that, a cop moving a cab that was double-parked too long and nothing more, but Jesso felt the sweat creep out even though it was all over. Till then he hadn't known just how much asleep he'd been, hiding his fear that something would go wrong under a thick blanket of nothingness. He yanked at his tie, wiped a hand across his face, and looked down the street. He felt like a fool for the way he'd taken that business with the cab. Any more of this and it wouldn't need any Kator to trip him up. Just keep stumbling along with almost a quarter of a million under his arm, just keep goofing the way he'd picked a bank right across from Gluck's place, and he wouldn't have to wait for any monster mind like Kator's to spring a trap for him.

Jesso didn't see the cab right then, so he looked elsewhere, alert now. He saw the guy in the Brooks Brothers suit across the street and the way he watched the backside of the girl in front of him. He saw the same cop down by the fire plug, and this time he was pinning a ticket on a car. And when the two-tone Buick pulled out of the basement garage opposite, Jesso saw that too. He saw Murph behind the wheel before Murph saw Jesso, but then he didn't jump back to the curb behind the cars, because first he took another look down the length of the street. No taxi yet. Jump, Jesso. The subway, two blocks down. That damn taxi....

"Hey! Jackie!"

That's when he jumped.

The Buick had swung around and Murph slowed down. He blinked at Jesso at the bank, trying to get the door open, but it was past three-thirty so Murph got a good look.

Jesso had seen him too. Gluck sat in back, spread out, and when Murph started his yelling Gluck had looked up, but he was looking at Murph. There are millions of Jacks. Jesso didn't see him by the bank, turning away from the door, not knowing whether to run or stand right there because his taxi was coming down the street. That taxi was going to pull up right behind Gluck's Buick. And Murphy, stopping the car to crane his neck— was that idiot ever going to catch on and move? Then Gluck looked up again. He said something and Jesso could imagine what it sounded like. If Gluck looked down again.... Gluck lowered his head and Jesso made his sprint. And that's when Gluck looked up again.

There wasn't any turning back, and if this was going to be the end, it was going to be full of action. There wasn't going to be any more waiting around for dreamed-up traps to spring, because there weren't any. And no more clouts on the head in some Brooklyn button shop, because from now on Jesso had a pair of eyes in the back of his head. He slammed the taxi door shut and yelled, "Drive like hell." Just for good measure he threw a bill next to the cabbie to make it legal. Forty-five bucks was the fare so far; the rest was tip. The cabbie grabbed the C note and took off. Jesso sat behind him and the cabbie hadn't missed a thing; how Jesso sat and how he held that gun. The taxi took a wild swing around the Buick to get clear, because one door had opened and Gluck had scrambled out. Through the rear window Jesso saw Gluck taking the wheel. Good old trusty Murph. Gluck didn't trust him.

They could have made it easy the way the cabbie started to roll except that soon all of Manhattan would have known about it. About one crazy cab, one crazy Buick, and traffic scattering itself into a snarl wherever they went.

"Pull up," Jesso said, "and then keep going."

He jumped near the corner and ran. Going down the subway stairs, he caught a glimpse of the Buick roaring by and the taxi up ahead turning into a one-way street.

The subway was good. He could barrel along underground and like a mole come up just about anywhere. He took the first train coming through and then watched for the stations. He could come up anywhere, today, tomorrow—and then he remembered about Gluck. That bastard wasn't one man, he was a thousand. And any place Jesso would come up there'd be a subway station, and in that station would be one of Gluck's gorillas. Unless he got out now.

He passed two more stops, just for the distance, and then he got out. It looked good. It wasn't far from Beekman Place. He was fingering for a dime while he was still running up the stairs, and then he was inside a drugstore, dialing a number.

"Bard residence," said the maid.

"Get me Miss Bard."

"Who shall I say—"

"Get Miss Bard!"

It took a while and then her voice said, "Hello?"

"Lynn, listen close and don't talk."

He heard her gasp.

"You alone, Lynn?"

"No, but—"

"Out of earshot?"

"Yes, Jackie. My God, Jackie, I heard—"

"Shut up. Is your place on Long Island empty?"

"Yes, Jackie."

"And nobody coming out there?"

"It's closed. Daddy is in—"

"I'm two blocks away. Get your car out, roll by the drugstore, and I'll meet you on the curb. And keep the motor going."

"Right now, Jackie?"

"Who's in the apartment?"

"Winnie, but you don't know him. He's just somebody I know and when I heard about you—"

"Never mind. Can you leave?"

"Of course, Jackie."

"Ten minutes. And bring the keys for that house."

He hung up, waited five minutes, and Lynn's convertible pulled up. She had the top down. She looked anxious and beautiful.

"Lynn. Now don't talk. Let's have those house keys and get out of the seat. In two days you can come out to the place and pick up your car. I've—"

"I'm coming along," she said, and she looked at him as if she weren't ever going to let go again.

He bent over the door, talked fast.

"This is trouble. Lynn. Stay away and I'm sorry I had to call you. Thanks for the car. I'll—"

He didn't have to finish. There wasn't any point to it unless he was going to toss her out of the car and leave her lying in the street. She had moved over, wanting him to drive, but that's as far as she was going.

Jesso jumped in and slammed the door. They sat like that while he made the top come up, and when he pinched his finger putting the catch on the top he swore as if nobody were listening. Then he drove. Once she tried to ask him questions, but it didn't work. He took the Queensboro Bridge and headed out Northern Boulevard.

They weren't far from La Guardia. Why sit around in Oyster Bay when he could take off for California, three thousand miles away from Gluck, pick up the rest of his dough, and then head back for Germany? The only trouble was he didn't know about the flight, had no reservation. Better yet, forget about that loot in L.A., head back for Europe, leave Gluck and Lynn and all of it behind.

He made a sharp turn south and headed for Idlewild. His ticket back to Frankfurt was good any day, there was a good chance of getting a reservation at short notice, and it was seven-thirty. The Stratoliner was due to leave the same time every day, nine P.M.

"Darling, Oyster Bay is the other way. You shouldn't have turned off."

"I changed my mind. We're going to Idlewild."

She didn't answer. She didn't know where he was going from Idlewild, but she thought she was going along.

"It's better that way all around. You won't get involved any more."

"Jackie—"

"Give up, Lynn. I'm just using your car."

Then they both kept still. When he approached the airport he could recognize it by the lights. It was dark by now. The traffic tower glowed with a bluish light and the building below had a long bright line of windows that looked like teeth. Almost by instinct he swung away from the drive leading to the gates and cruised the parking lot first. Take it slow, check how it looks, because maybe Gluck has notions about airports and railway stations and maybe not.

He didn't see a thing. He cruised the entrance once, didn't dare try it twice. Park a while, maybe? And let the reservations get used up. Or maybe do some necking in the front seat just so time would pass and he wouldn't have to risk it out there, risk the trip, the dough, Renette, and his life.

"I'm getting out." He braked the car past the entrance. He gave it one more look, picked up his brief case from the floor. "Lynn, now hear me good. I'm going out there and maybe nothing happens." He paused, reached to his belt. "See this?" She saw the gun. "And this?" She watched him cock the hammer. "I'm going out there with this thing in my hand. Here, in my pocket. And maybe you'll hear about it from where you're sitting. So sit, don't move, and if I'm not back ten minutes later, take off and be glad you're rid of it all. So long." He got out of the car.

And then he was by the bright entrance. There were cars parked along the curb, one was empty, one had an old couple in it, the other one a G.I. and his mother. Nobody looked like a gorilla or like Gluck.

When Jesso had his hand on the glass door he didn't freeze, he almost died. The man's voice said, "Wait, Jackie!"

Chapter Twenty-one

He snapped around like a spring and would have had the gun out if the couple hadn't come through the door and bumped his arm.

"Jackie, your left," and then he saw Murph. He ambled toward the door, past Jesso, and while he passed he said without moving his mouth, "There's a nest of 'em inside. Blow fast."

Jesso was off. He sprinted to the convertible down by the curve. Lynn had the door open and he almost jumped into her lap.

"Hold on," he said, and the car tore off.

He almost went crazy at the Cross Boulevard intersection, but then he was twisting the car through the clover leaf and along the freeway that went across Jamaica Bay.

"Darling, are they chasing us?"

"Shut up a minute."

He looked back, but all the cars looked alike. He was cursing under his breath till the lit highway stopped swimming and then he felt better. He was at the toll gate before he knew it and Lynn was ready with the money. Good, smart Lynn. And when he twisted down the ramp to Channel Drive, going out the length of Long Island he felt for a second the way he and Lynn had felt a long time ago. But then only Lynn felt that way any more.

"Jackie? Can I talk now?"

"Sorry about this thing, Lynn."

"I'm glad I helped you, Jackie."

"Yeah. It's not over yet."

"Bad, Jackie?"

"No. Just business."

She slid closer to him. "It's the first time you've taken me on one of your business trips."

"Hope it's the last, kid. Just hope that."

"But I remember another one," she went on. "That was business, too, you said. And I waited for you at Lake Tahoe and then you came back from Reno and joined me. Remember, Jackie?"

He sat up and made it hard for her to lean up against him. "I told you to lay off that stuff, Lynn. I told you it's no good."

She sat up too. He caught her profile and the line of her suit where the dashlight showed it, and even though she wasn't like Renette, she reminded him of her. She wasn't built like Renette, she was slimmer, but there was an expression about her face that reminded him. Lynn, too, used to look much colder.

"You told me," she said. "You told me, you told me. You think it's as easy as that?" But she didn't sound mean about it; her voice was pleading.

He didn't answer.

"You think you can ever hurt me enough so I'll let go?"

"I've never tried to hurt you."

"I know," she said. "Perhaps you should."

"Perhaps I should," he said.

They came to Cedarhurst and Jesso slowed down. He pulled the car up, put it in neutral, and turned toward her.

"Listen to me, Lynn. You know what I've got to say about you and me, so I won't say it again. But here's something new. This time you hang around and I think you might get killed."

She looked at him, but only her eyes moved.

"So get out."

She sat still.

"Get out of the car. Give me two days and report it stolen."

"I won't," she said.

"Or I'll clip you and throw you out."

"Clip me," she said, and it sounded funny in her finishing-school diction.

He almost hauled out, but when he saw how she closed her eyes and put up her chin, he couldn't do it. At first he thought he wanted to laugh, but that wasn't it. He thought that if she meant something to him she wouldn't look pitiful sitting there like that.

Her eyes were still closed and she started to tremble.

"For God's sake, open up and relax," he yelled at her. He felt like an idiot, but she didn't seem to notice.

"You could have done it, Jackie." Jesso put the car into gear, held it.

"If this kills you, Lynn, I won't give a damn."

"I won't either," she said, and he knew she meant it more than he did. He turned the car toward the North Shore of Long Island and didn't talk the rest of the way.

They got to the house around two in the morning. A wall and a plot of trees hid the place from the road, but Jesso remembered where to turn. Inside, Lynn switched the lights on and turned up the heat. Then Jesso went to the bedroom. It faced the water and had a plate-glass window for one wall. The whole house was plate glass on the water side.

"Turn the light off," Jesso said.

Lynn had her jacket off and was sliding the blouse down one arm. Her bra made sharp points.

"I don't mind, darling. Even if the bay were filled with boats."

"Turn off that light. You can see it for miles the way this place is lit up."
She worked the switch and came back to Jesso.

"You can't see me," she said. "You won't have to see me."

She was so close he thought he could feel the warmth of her naked skin through his clothes.

"Go to bed. I'm sleeping on this—this damn love seat or whatever it is."

"We have a double bed, Jackie. One side for me, one side for you, if you want."

They went to bed, he on one side and she on the other.

By morning she had caught on that this was business, and she even remembered the part about getting killed. She made sure that the gate was closed after she came back with the groceries and pulled the car into the bushes by the side of the house. She didn't make a fire in the round pit under the copper hood so that there wouldn't be any smoke coming out of the chimney. And when she saw the revolver in Jesso's belt she didn't say a word. They ate something and then Jesso looked for the phone.

"You know how to reach Murph?"

"I've called him often enough, Jackie."

"Call him once more. Call him the way you always do, because he doesn't know where I am and neither do you."

"What do I say?"

"Ask about me. He'll do the rest. And get him to tell you what Gluck's doing."

She picked up the phone and gave the operator a number. She knew it by heart. She held the phone so Jesso could hear both ends of the conversation.

"Is Murph there?" she said, and then she waited. "Murph, this is—"

"I know, Miss Lynn, but I got no news for you."

"Murph, he wants to know about Gluck."

"You know where he is?"

"No, Murph."

"Fine. Tell him to stay there."

"You don't want to see him?"

"Not for a while, Miss Lynn. They got the town staked out, the airports, and all the rat holes I can think of."

"Oh, dear," she said. "Oh, dear. He'll get killed. I know he'll get killed."

"Don't you worry none. Jackie knows what he's doing. Besides, that ain't the pitch."

"What did you say, Murph?"

"That ain't the pitch."

"I know. What does it mean?"

"It means, Miss Lynn, they ain't gunning for him. Gluck wants him alive."

She gave a real sigh and was ready to hang up. But perhaps Jesso wanted to know more.

"Where did you say they're looking for him, Murph?"

"Everywhere. Every rat hole—"

"You mean here in New York, in other cities, all over the country?"

"They don't figure he's got far. They're looking just in New York. Everywhere."

She sounded concerned some more and then she hung up and turned to Jesso.

"Well, it isn't so bad," she said. "They don't want to kill you. They just want to talk, Jackie. Can't you go and talk it over and get clear of all this? Jackie, you've never said much about your work, but there must be a better—"

"I never have, you're right. So you don't know what they mean by talk."

He got up and walked to the window. She followed him. She leaned her back against the big glass, hands behind her, and it almost looked as if she were floating.

"Where will you go from here, Jackie?"

"Why? You want to go along?"

"I didn't ask," she said.

"You never ask."

He hit the glass with the flat of his hand as if he didn't care whether it broke or not.

"Enough now, Lynn!" Then he paced to the round fireplace and back. "I want you to cut it out. I want you to shut up about that old and gone business but for good. You know why I'm here and it isn't you. It was but it won't be again and you never catch on. Did you hear? I want you to lay off!"

"You want, you want," she said. It was almost a mumble.

Then she said, "All right, Jackie. I will," and it looked as if he was rid of her.

"Now back to normal. Remember your friend at Tahoe, that—that Jill whatshername—"

"Jill Timerlane, from Pasadena, Jackie."

"That's her. You still friends with her?"

"Of course, Jackie. I wrote—"

"Never mind. You got her phone number?"

"Not here. In the apartment."

"Can you phone there and get it?"

"Of course, Jackie. Right away."

She called and the maid answered and she gave Lynn the number.

"Now call up that Jill there. Call her long-distance and tell her about this joke you're having with a buddy of—with a friend of yours, and that she has to send a telegram for you from L.A. to New York. You got it?"

Lynn nodded.

"Now write this down. The telegram says, 'Dear President.' Yeah, yeah, it's President. All right now, 'Dear President, sorry about mix-up. L.A. rainy and no smog. Sit tight.' And sign it 'Jack Jesso.' Got that?"

She said yes and read it back to him. He told her to send it to C. Gluck and gave her the address.

He smoked two cigarettes and kept pacing around the crazy fireplace in the middle of the room while Lynn got the connection and tried to break through the small talk. Then she explained about this game she was playing and dictated the telegram. There came more chit-chat and then she hung up. She asked Jesso if she'd done it all right and Jesso said yes, that was fine. She went to the bedroom and lay down. When he looked in a little later she was asleep. He went in and put a blanket over her shoulders. She was asleep so she couldn't make anything of that.

Jesso went back to the room with the round fireplace and stood by the plate glass. Two more days. He'd look at the bay for two more days and then he'd crawl out of his hole forever. He'd make one more dash, run just once more, and that was going to be the last. Then Renette would be there. The thought of her made the two days seem like standing still forever, but then there would be Renette forever. He had never thought that way before, but he was already used to the thought. Anything else hardly mattered—New York, Lynn, Kator—and if they got in the way, they and their lives would matter little enough.

He held on for the two days, talking little and pacing the room. Then came one more call to Murph, who said the heat was off, mostly, and they were looking for him in L.A. And Lynn. Without saying much, just by looking the way she did, she told him to take her, do anything, and if not she'd always be there. He had nothing to say to her and on the second day the big Stratocruiser barreled off the Idlewild runway and Jesso watched Jamaica Bay shoot by underneath.

Chapter Twenty-two

The room was lit as always, two candelabra and the yellow bulbs over the buffet. It kept the tall ceiling in the dark and made the three figures around the table look like decorations. They ate in silence. In itself, this wasn't anything unusual, except what they made of it. Kator made a waiting out of it. He'd laid his trap and all he had to do was wait. Jesso would be back, Kator had made sure of that. Jesso would be back because Renette was here and this was Kator's simple trap. To spring it shut would be even simpler. Kator was on home ground and all he had to do was wait. He chewed his meat, drank his wine. Jesso hadn't sat at this table more than once, but it almost felt to Kator as if he missed him.

Von Lohe didn't have a thing to say for once. He sat, not tasting anything and to him the room was like a prison. And Kator had the key. Not Kator, Jesso! If Jesso were here now, then von Lohe would know what to do. Somehow his hate would find direction and all it needed was the moment—and Jesso. It almost felt to von Lohe as if he missed him.

Renette waved at Hofer and had another glass of wine. She tried to pay no attention to the room, the mood, and the two men. It wasn't really hard. Another fifteen minutes and she would leave. Her plans for the evening had nothing to do with Helmut or with Kator, and both had learned that it didn't make much difference to her any more what they might say. She still had her old suite behind the bend in the corridor, but that was all. She didn't live there as von Lohe's wife and Kator hardly felt that she was still his sister. She looked across the table, past the bouquet, and thought of Jesso, the way he had sat behind the flowers. She thought of him with pleasure; a pleasure without regrets and in the past. She tasted her wine and didn't miss him.

When von Lohe looked at her she was pulling her napkin through the silver band and placing it next to her plate.

"Johannes," said von Lohe, "if you are going to follow my suggestion, better speak to her now."

Kator looked up, trying to understand.

"She's leaving, I believe." Von Lohe sounded peevish.

"Oh, yes." Kator wiped his mouth, looked at Renette. "Before you leave...." and then he waved at Hofer.

Hofer waved at the two servants by the buffet and followed them out of the door.

"Helmut had a suggestion," Kator said. "A rather good one."

"Helmut?" She smiled at her husband as if she hadn't known he was at the table.

"It seems," Kator said, "that his friend Paul Zimmer is proving difficult. I have not obtained the concessions I want, and Helmut found it hard to apply the pressures on the Zimmer family that are at my disposal. Traditional loyalties, he calls it. But no matter." Kator sighed. "I'm giving you the assignment, Renette."

Kator watched her turn her head and for a moment he had the uneasy feeling that she had just noticed him at the table.

"I know nothing about the whole affair," she said. "Nothing that would help."

"That's not the help you are supposed to give," said von Lohe, and his smile was angelic. His mouth was lewd.

"I see why you didn't get anyplace," she said to him.

"Nevertheless, in a way Helmut is correct," Kator said. He said it without inflection, made it cold and businesslike. Maybe that way he would get Renette back in line. "Zimmer—that is the one we're after—is only slightly older than you. I'm sure, Renette, there is very little about you that he wouldn't like."

"I'm not interested," she said. "I know him."

Kator had expected something like that, even though the reason for her refusal confused him. "Nevertheless," he said, "I am giving the assignment to you."

Renette wet her lips with her tongue and her wide eyes seemed to go bland.

"Johannes," she said, "your insults no longer work. I have other plans."

"She means that—that—Jesso!" Von Lohe waved his arm. He never noticed when he wiped his sleeve through the gravy on his plate.

"Of course, Helmut." Kator turned back to his sister. "Listen to me, Renette."

"You're wrong," she said.

Nobody believed her.

"Listen to me. I feel I cannot force you, Renette, but as your brother—"

"I know. You'll try anyway."

He took it in his stride. His voice got soft, as if he were saying something sad. "Your Jesso, Renette, is like something from another world, a world where your tastes, your kind of life, mean nothing. You understand?"

She did. She knew it.

"To attach yourself to him is like eating the wrong kind of food, Renette. I say this as a warning, as a threat. But not from me. From Jesso."

She listened because she understood. Her brother hadn't talked to her, come close, since— It didn't matter. She understood him and the old attachment was still there. Not like a chain this time, but simply there.

"I'm sure you think he's done nothing but good where you have been concerned," he went on. "I'm sure you think that no matter how perverse, how rotten this man is, somehow he had it in him to be for once, with you, only good." Kator made a tired gesture and smiled as if he weren't sure. "You know, Renette, I like to think you feel that way about your brother, because I, I truly live two lives, Renette. One for my work, and one for you." He suddenly frowned and his face turned to stone. "But I was talking about Jesso. With him you are part of his schemes. Tell me," and Kator suddenly jabbed one finger at Renette, "did he ever ask you about me?"

Jesso had, and Renette knew that Kator knew it. She had told him. But now the question was ominous.

"And has he ever asked about my business? We both know he has and I refrain from guessing at what moments of your intimacy he has asked. Now more. Did he make you promise to help him get a passport? And finally, Renette, did he not leave you behind?"

"I didn't want to go," she said.

"I'm proud of you. But you see, my dear, he didn't try to force you, did he? A man like Jesso, and he did not insist!"

Kator stopped, as if at the end of a triumphal march, and then he summed it up, making it casual. "You see, my dear, from your first meeting to the very last, each thing he did served one purpose only. It served Jesso. Anything else he might have done was nothing but the bait to serve the moment of his advantage. And you, Renette, have been his tool." There was silence and he was through. He stopped because he knew the spell of his words was there, Renette had heard, and, judging her by himself, he knew he'd given her the clues that she might need to break with Jesso. One thing he didn't know: that Jesso had not been a man to her, a person, but a force; that she had gained by that force, made it her own.

"And now, Johannes?"

"What do you mean?"

"Before you advised me about Jesso, it was the Zimmer affair you talked about."

"Oh, yes." Kator thought the switch was very rapid, but so much the better. "Young Zimmer will be at a party. I'll give you the details. I want you—"

"Johannes," she said, "I told you no," and when nobody answered she got up, excused herself, and left the room.

Kator did not see how he could have failed. Nor did he know that Renette had been impressed with many of the things he'd told her. They meant to her that Kator was a cold and clever man. They also meant that Kator was trying to be kind. They meant that Jesso had set her free from both those things, and even from himself, and that her brother did not see any of it. No one did, only Renette.

Chapter Twenty-three

Jesso kept watching the torn clouds race by because it made the movement faster. But not until they circled Paris did it all become real to him. A few more hours and Renette. Perhaps Kator was waiting like a cat that knew there was just one way out for the mouse in the corner, but even that worry turned simple. Jesso got out in Paris, let the rest of his flight go chase itself through the wild blue yonder, and changed to an Air France liner that went straight to Berlin. It had one halfway stop, Hannover. That's how Jesso got to town.

The villa still sat behind the wall like an ornate tomb and the only sound was the constant rustling of the trees in the *Allee*. The light was failing and pretty soon the damp day would be a damp night. Jesso sent his taxi off and for a moment the sound of the old motor was the worst noise in the world. Then just the villa again and the mumble from the old trees.

He didn't ring the bell and he didn't wait for Hofer to do any honors. He walked through the two front doors, and he was halfway across the hall when the library door opened and a shaft of light cut toward him. And there stood Kator.

Each knew the other as if he had expected it this way. The door came shut, the light was gone, and very slowly Kator came across the hall. It took Jesso a while to place the queer thing, but then he realized that Kator walked without the sharp click of his heels.

"You're back."

"The last time, Kator."

"I know that, Jesso."

"So move," but nothing moved.

As once before, after Delf, when they had held each other with a grip that meant one of the two had to break and die, nothing happened. A door opened upstairs and they both turned. Then the door shut again, the moment went. Jesso didn't know about Kator, but Jesso had to move right then. He turned toward the stairs and took them two at a time. Neither corridor showed a light. He went right, turned the bend, and then he opened the door to Renette's rooms.

The bed was there, her clothes, and the decanter with the liqueur stood on a little table where the seat faced the window. She hadn't moved the seat since that time. There wasn't any noise from the shower, but he went in there just the same. If he hadn't maybe the noise from the corridor might have reached him.

That same door had clicked again, only this time it flew open, hit the wall, and stayed there. Then Renette came out. She walked so that her hair bounced and dipped over the back of her neck, and there was nothing calm or gracious in her face. The eyes seemed to slant with anger and her parted lips showed her teeth. She headed for the stairs. Helmut von Lohe was close behind her, looking sharp in his riding clothes and making a tinkle with the spurs on his polished boots. His hair was combed over the skull the way he wanted it and his small red mouth had a new sharp cut to it. He followed Renette down the stairs.

So Jesso missed them. He saw that the bath was empty, the bedroom, the sitting room, and nothing in the dressing room. Her clothes were there; he checked her coats and furs, and it looked as if she had to be somewhere in the house. He started for the stairs as if he felt she had been calling.

It turned out there were plenty of rooms he hadn't seen before. They were furnished for different moods with different doodads, but all Jesso saw was that they were empty. Once he passed Hofer, but Hofer was just a moving doodad, and then another room with furniture, walls, windows, portraits.

He saw them across an angle from one part of the house to another, behind the glass of the solarium, where the fat plants stood in the heat. Jesso couldn't hear a word where he stood by the window, but the Baron's face was working and his hands were making quick flutters. Then Jesso saw Kator. He stepped into sight, looked stolid. He reached out with both hands, seemed to talk in the same back-and-forth rhythm with which he pulled and pushed with his arms whatever he held there. That's when Jesso saw Renette. Because of the plant Jesso never saw all of her, but the plant was shaking.

The only way to the solarium was back through the rooms that made the angle of the house. Jesso was breathing hard when he hit the salon with the silk and needle point, but racing to get there had taken none of the temper out of him. It made it worse, worse than in the plane with Kator, worse than in the hall a while ago. There wasn't just Kator. There was Helmut, there was Renette, and Jesso slowed down when he got to the silk place because he didn't know which way to jump first.

"He's lying!" he heard Renette say. "Johannes, he's making it up from spite. I said nothing to Jesso to cause this thing. His own failure—"

When Jesso burst through the door, they all turned.

"You all right?" he said without looking at her. He had stopped and was looking at Kator, feeling the same harsh pull come back, and it was only a question of five, six steps along the passage between tall plants and they would lock into each other like traps that couldn't let go.

"Stay there," she said. "I'm all right, Jesso."

He walked around the little fountain and stopped.

"Did you touch her, Kator?"

"Jesso, leave," she said.

Helmut had swiveled around. "You intrude!" he said, and there was a screech in his voice. "We will deal with you later!"

Jesso watched him flip a riding crop against his boot, and it might have looked funny at any other time. Now Kator folded his hands behind his back, legs wide, and suddenly it was as if they had all waited for him. When he opened his mouth the voice was like that of the commanding officer at a courtmartial.

"He stays. He's the important one."

"You're damn right I'm staying." He said it to Kator.

Kator didn't move his head, only his eyes. He looked at Renette and said, "Was it on the train? Did he get it out of you on the train, Renette?"

"I told you!" She said it loudly, stamping her foot. "He knew nothing to cause this thing. Helmut botched it!"

Kator's words flew into Jesso's face like slaps. "What did she tell you? What did you make her say?"

"I don't get it."

It was so true and so simple that it caught Kator short. Then he bunched up all the poison and spat, "I can only guess how you worked her over so well, on the train to Munich, but you managed to do what my sister has never permitted. She informed on me, on her brother, and once again, Jesso, you have cost me a fortune."

"Don't deny it," screamed Helmut.

"He will," said Kator. "How did you do it, Jesso? What did you do on that train?"

"What did you do?" said Helmut, and his face was like filth.

Jesso didn't get any of it, but nothing showed.

"I don't talk about what I do in a bedroom," he said, and he watched Helmut jerk back.

"Do you deny it?" Helmut yelled.

"Comb your hair, Helmut. It's slipping."

"I will ask you," Kator said. "How did you ruin the Zimmer affair?"

"What's a Zimmer affair?"

"Zimmer, you idiot!" and for once Kator was bellowing. "A year of delicate preparation! Thousands in expenditures, and when the time comes for the final closing, you step in, you worm it out of my sister, you give the tip to—to the others, and everything fails."

Jesso let the sound die down. He looked from Kator to Helmut and said, "Who told you, Kator? That creep?"

"I told him," said Helmut, "as it was my duty. No one knew of the arrangements with Zimmer except we three, and no one could have told you except poor Renette. Under what fiendish pressures—"

"Stop dreaming, Helmut. There's spit on your chin."

"Dreaming! You swine! My wife came back to me after you left, she confided to me as I suspect she was made to confide by you. She—"

"My God," she said, "he's out of his mind. Johannes, don't you see his game? He wants to make you do it for him, set you against me, make you fight with Jesso."

It made sense. It would be something like that and it would be somebody like Helmut to do it that way.

"I never heard of Zimmer or whatever it is, and Renette never said a word," Jesso said, but the words were only a sound. They weren't big enough or soon enough to catch up with the tension. From now on it hardly seemed to matter what was said. The big plants stood motionless and seemed to get darker. And under them, motionless like the plants, the three stood waiting in the half-light, waiting for the spark to blow it up.

"You're lying, Jesso." Kator moved his arm. He reached around, found Renette, and jerked her to his side. "And you, Renette, you lie."

Kator had sounded quite still. His eyes never left Jesso, but suddenly his hand slammed against Renette's face.

She hadn't finished staggering when Jesso made his dash. His foot caught in a flagstone, and when he was half up there was Kator behind the gun.

"Get up."

Jesso got up. This was it.

Kator knew this was it, but he wasn't rushing. "Do you see the fountain, Jesso?"

He didn't. The fountain was in back of him.

"Turn around and look at it, Jesso. I won't shoot."

Jesso knew that. Kator wouldn't shoot without seeing the face.

"There is a cupid on the fountain, Jesso. Do you see it?"

He saw it. A small copper cupid, looking wet and green, and no larger than a toy dog.

"He is raising one hand, isn't he, Jesso?"

He was. He was sort of waving one baby hand.

"Now you see it, now you don't," Kator said, and behind Jesso's back the gun went off with a sharp crash and Kator was right. The little hand was gone.

He was good. He had shot right past Jesso's middle, with maybe inches to spare, and the cupid's arm had a shiny end where the metal hand had been ripped off.

"And now turn around again."

Jesso turned around.

"I knew this would impress you," Kator said. "Helmut, what else did she tell you?"

The Baron straightened himself as if he were going to give a speech at graduation.

"Once Renette began to confide in me, she held back nothing. He wanted to take her away from us—from me—set her against you, dear Johannes, and—"

"Stop him, Johannes!" Renette's voice was sharp. "Send him away, or you'll never stop playing it his way. And the gun, Johannes."

"You are wrong, Renette. This is my way. And Jesso's way. Isn't it, Jesso?"

"No, Johannes, don't! Neither of you will win. Leave each other, let it go!" She reached for Kator's arm and flinched.

He had snapped up his arm, ready to hit again, but he did not strike. His gun was steady and a slow thing came over his face like an ugly grin. Jesso had moved, Kator saw that. And when Renette had stepped away Jesso relaxed.

"It's time, Jesso." Kator's face did not change. He kept staring at Jesso, daring him, and there was a constant triumph on his face.

"Come here, Renette." He waved at her without turning. "Jesso," he said, "for a while I thought you were very much like me. A man without a flaw. Look, Jesso." Kator reached around, taking Renette by the arm. He pulled her and she winced.

"Look, Jesso," he said when she stood next to him. "Look!"

Kator's hand came up in a fist, slowly. He held it in the air, very still, so that Jesso could see the knuckles turn white. One of his tricks, one of his intelligent tricks, to give it a stretch before tearing it. Jesso held still, not believing that Kator would do it when the fist blurred, stopped with a jar that made a sick sound, and Renette stumbled back. And Jesso charged. And the gun exploded.

Kator had played it his way, for the sport. He hadn't meant to kill, and he hadn't. And that's how he played it Jesso's way.

The gun went off again, but the bullet went wild because first the target was gone and then the target had turned attacker with the gun snapping out of Kator's hand and a fist exploded in his right eye.

Helmut was gone. Spurs tinkling, he had dashed from the room, and only Renette stood there. Her face was cut but she seemed not to know it. She stood and looked, and when she cried her shoulders did not move.

It was a while before Jesso and Kator stopped rolling like one mass of evil strength while the fat leaves shook, large plants dipped, leaned, and slowly toppled to fall with a sound like a splash—but that wasn't how it went. It was like an instant spasm with beginning and end all in one while they cut at each other, the cut that was going to kill one or both. That's how it was to Jesso, and it was the same to Kator. He never knew when he didn't see any more. He never knew when he changed from a man to a mass and was dead.

Jesso didn't know either. He might have stopped sooner. As it was, he sat under the broken leaves of the dark-green plant long after it was still.

Chapter Twenty-four

"You haven't changed since yesterday. Since then." Renette looked at his spurs.

"No," said Helmut. "I've been too busy."

"I know. They came very fast."

"I was on the phone when it happened, my dear. I was not standing there, being sentimental."

"No. You were clever, for once."

"And now you, dear Renette. Now you must be clever. The crime was murder, first degree. Remember, Renette. First degree, and Johannes fired in self-defense."

"You know that is false."

"What was it, my dear? *A crime passionnel?*"

"You know what it was, Helmut."

"Yes, and what will happen if you say so?"

"Maybe he will go free. Soon."

"And come back, like a leech and a disease. Is that what you want?"

"You should talk of disease."

"Ah! So you admire it, all of it."

"It was useless and ugly. And it killed Johannes."

"How sentimental of you! Johannes left us everything."

"Not *us*, Helmut. Me."

"And you don't resent the gift, do you? The wealth, the freedom."

"No, I don't."

"Then be clever, Renette. Cold-blooded murder, you understand? Anything else and it might take years. Years in litigation, from one court to the next—"

"And you couldn't wait that long, could you, Helmut?"

"So you love him."

"I do not despise him, as I despise you."

"Be clever, Renette. I want nothing from you. I don't interfere with you one way or the other."

"You won't."

"But I will. If you don't share with me what he left."

"Helmut, listen to me—"

"I might even get it all, if you do not act as I say."

"Listen to me, Helmut. Have you thought of this? You killed Johannes. You attacked him, Johannes fired, and Jesso, trying to pull you apart, got shot."

"You're being absurd!"

"Jesso will say the same thing. We had just a moment before they took him. He explained it to me."

"You must be insane, Renette!"

"So don't threaten me, Helmut. Nobody threatens me any more."

"No. Johannes is dead. But Jesso isn't."

"He doesn't threaten me."

"I forget. You love him. Do you love him enough to go to prison, too? Not in the same one, my dear, not with him, but just a prison?"

"Now you're absurd."

"Perhaps, but it's worth a try. Like your trying to implicate me. I could say you engineered the whole thing, the murder, the passport. Even—"

"None of this would stand up in court. And I would never murder my brother."

"Of course. But it might take years. We would lose everything in the meantime. My name, which means nothing to you. Your money, which means a great deal to you. And your freedom, Renette. For a long time—your freedom."

"You are clever, Helmut."

"Of course."

"But you're wasting your time."

"You don't believe what I said?"

"What I believe I believed before you came."

"Three o'clock," said Helmut, and he got out of his chair. "The police *Präfekt* will be waiting."

Jesso looked at the bars in the window, and at their shadows, stretching big across the wall. When he stood up they reached across his face. He sat down, facing the wall where the washbasin stood, because that corner looked least like a prison. He wasn't trying to get used to the bars. There was no point in that. Ten minutes, five minutes, maybe, and she would be here. In five minutes the testimony, and then he would be free. Kator was dead and he was free. Renette was outside and he was free. Five minutes perhaps.

He got up and moved carefully. His arm was in a sling and the wound where the bullet had cut through felt hot. When he got out he would go to a real doctor, he would pay a real doctor and not leave it the way some underpaid prison quack fixed it up, with iodine and some stinking ointment. Jesso could smell the reek of it through the bandage. Or perhaps it was the reek of the prison. The whole place stank, and if he were staying he would go crazy. He'd go out of his mind without trying to stop it. He walked the length of the room a few times, walking as if he were crossing a street. It wasn't impatience and he didn't feel he was waiting. He was hardly there any more. Then the door opened.

The guard waved and showed him the way. It was behind the bend in the corridor. The door was paneled wood and inside he saw wallpaper and curtains on the windows. He saw Renette. He saw also the guard, a stenographer, the *Präfekt* with his gray mustache, and Helmut. Behind the curtains on the windows there were bars. But for Jesso there was only Renette.

"Please be seated," said the *Präfekt*.

"Hello, Renette."

She didn't say, "Jesso." She nodded and they sat down.

"This need not take long," said the *Präfekt*, and he swiveled his mustache around. "Baron Helmut von Lohe, you have given your formal statement?"

"I have."

"Premeditated murder, you stated," and the *Präfekt* shuffled papers. "Now then, the corroborating testimony. Frau Baronin?"

Renette was looking at Jesso and once she smiled at him. He needed no more. There would be more, but right now...

"Frau Baronin?"

She turned toward the old man behind the desk but she looked out the window. Jesso saw how the sun lit her face. She was looking through the bars, past the wall where the head of a green tree was showing. Jesso sat back, crossed his legs. He had forgotten his arm, so when it touched the back of his chair it made him wince. Renette looked back to him.

"Does it hurt?"

"Hell, no."

But the cigarette had dropped out of his hand and Renette got up, gave it back to him. When she had straightened she put out her hand. Just a short gesture. She ran her hand quickly over his hair, where it looked like velvet.

"Frau Baronin," said the *Präfekt* again. "Your testimony."

"Yes," she said, and Jesso saw she was not hesitating. She looked at Jesso, and her eyes were clear and almost far away. "He killed my brother," she said.

The cell was black and the sky was black, so Jesso couldn't see the bars any more. It was as if there weren't any. As if it didn't matter. His good hand felt the pocket and the fine chain with the pearl. He couldn't see it in his hand and only remembered how it was. Then his fingers clamped and the delicate shell made a sound. The broken pearl cut his finger. He knew it had cut, but there was no pain. Because he felt he was dead already.

THE END

PETER RABE
BY DONALD E. WESTLAKE

Peter Rabe wrote the best books with the worst titles of anybody I can think of. *Murder Me for Nickels. Kill the Boss Goodbye.* Why would anybody ever want to read a book called *Kill the Boss Goodbye?* And yet, *Kill the Boss Goodbye is* one of the most purely *interesting* crime novels ever written.

Here's the setup: Tom Fell runs the gambling in San Pietro, a California town of three hundred thousand people. He's been away on "vacation" for a while, and an assistant, Pander, is scheming to take over. The big bosses in Los Angeles have decided to let nature take its course; if Pander's good enough to beat Fell, the territory is his. Only Fell's trusted assistant, Cripp (for "cripple"), knows the truth, that Fell is in a sanitarium recovering from a nervous breakdown. Cripp warns Fell that he must come back or lose everything. The psychiatrist, Dr. Emilson, tells him he isn't ready to return to his normal life. Fell suffers from a manic neurosis, and if he allows himself to become overly emotional, he could snap into true psychosis. But Fell has no choice; he goes back to San Pietro to fight Pander.

This is a wonderful variant on a story as old as the Bible: Fell gains the world, and loses his mind. And Rabe follows through on his basic idea; the tension in the story just builds and builds, and we're not even surprised to find ourselves worried about, scared for, empathizing with, a gangster. The story of Fell's gradually deepening psychosis is beautifully done. The entire book is spare and clean and amazingly unornamented. Here, for instance, is the moment when Pander, having challenged Fell to a fistfight, first senses the true extent of his danger:

Pander leaned up on the balls of his feet, arms swinging free, face mean, but nothing followed. He stared at Fell and all he saw were his eyes, mild lashes and the lids without movement, and what happened to them. He suddenly saw the hardest, craziest eyes he had ever seen.

Pander lost the moment and then Fell smiled. He said so long and walked out the door (page 47).

Kill the Boss Goodbye was published by Gold Medal in August of 1956. It was the fifth Peter Rabe novel they'd published, the first having come out in May of 1955, just fifteen months before. That's a heck of a pace, and Rabe didn't stop there. In the five years between May 1955 and May 1960, he published sixteen novels with Gold Medal and two elsewhere.

Eighteen novels in five years would be a lot for even a cookie-cutter hack doing essentially the same story and characters over and over again, which was never true of Rabe. He wrote in third person and in first; he wrote emotionless hardboiled prose and tongue-in-check comedy, gangster stories, exotic adventure stories set in Europe and Mexico and North Africa, psychological studies. No two consecutive books used the same voice or setting. In fact, the weakest Peter Rabe novels are the ones written in his two different attempts to create a series character.

What sustains a writer at the beginning of his career is the enjoyment of the work itself, the fun of putting the words through hoops, inventing the worlds, peopling them with fresh-minted characters. That enjoyment in the *doing* of the job is very evident in Rabe's best work. But it can't sustain a career forever; the writing history of Peter Rabe is a not entirely happy one. He spent his active writing career working for a sausage factory. What he wrote was often pate but it was packed as sausage—those titles!—and soon, I think, his own attitude toward his work lowered to match that of the people—agent, editors—most closely associated with the reception and publishing of the work. Rabe, whose first book had a quote on the cover from Erskine Caldwell ("I couldn't put this book down!"), whose fourth book had a quote on the cover from Mickey Spillane ("This guy is *good.*"), whose books were consistently and lavishly praised by Anthony Boucher in the *New York Times* ("harsh objectivity" and "powerful understatement" and "tight and nerve-straining"), was soon churning novels out in as little as ten days, writing carelessly and sloppily, mutilating his talent.

The result is, some of Rabe's books are quite bad, awkwardly plotted and with poorly developed characters. Others are like the curate's egg: parts of them are wonderful. But when he was on track, with his own distinctive style, his own cold clear eye unblinking, there wasn't another writer in the world of the paperback who could touch him.

The first novel, *Stop This Man,* showed only glimpses of what Rabe would become. It begins as a nice variant on the Typhoid Mary story; the disease carrier who leaves a trail of illness in his wake. The story is that Otto Schumacher learns of an ingot of gold loaned to an atomic research facility at a university in Detroit. He and his slatternly girlfriend Selma meet with his old friend Catell, just out of prison, and arrange for Catell to steal the gold. But they don't know that the gold is irradiated, and will make people sick who are near it. The police nearly catch Catell early on, but he escapes, Schumacher dying. Catell goes to Los Angeles to find Smith, the man who might buy the gold ingot.

Once Catell hides the ingot near Los Angeles, the Typhoid Mary story stops, to be replaced by a variant on *High Sierra*. Catell now becomes a burglar-for-hire, employed by Smith, beginning with the robbery of a loan office. There's a double-cross, the police arrive, Catell escapes. The next job is absolutely *High Sierra*, involving a gambling resort up in the mountains, but just before the job Selma (Schumacher's girlfriend) reappears and precipitates the finish. With the police hot on his trail, Catell retrieves his gold and drives aimlessly around the Imperial Valley, becoming increasingly sick with radiation disease. Eventually he dies in a ditch, hugging his gold.

The elements of *Stop This Man* just don't mesh. There are odd little scenes of attempted humor that don't really come off and are vaguely reminiscent of Thorne Smith, possibly because one character is called Smith and one Topper. A character called the Turtle does tiresome malapropisms. Very pulp-level violence and sex are stuck onto the story like lumps of clay onto an already finished statue. Lily, the girl Catell picks up along the way only to make some pulp sex scenes possible, is no character at all, hasn't a shred of believability. Selma, the harridan drunk who pesters Catell, is on the other hand real and believable and just about runs away with the book.

An inability to stay with the story he started to tell plagued Rabe from time to time, and showed up again in his second book, *Benny Muscles In*, which begins as though it's going to be a rise-of-the-punk history, a *Little Caesar*, but then becomes a much more narrowly focused story. Benny Tapkow works for a businesslike new-style mob boss named Pendleton. When Pendleton demotes Benny back to chauffeur, Benny switches allegiance to Big Al Alverato, an old-style Capone type, for whom Benny plans to kidnap Pendleton's college-age daughter, Pat. She knows Benny as her father's chauffeur, and so will leave school with him unsuspectingly. However, with one of Rabe's odd bits of off-the-wall humor (this one works), Pat brings along a thirtyish woman named Nancy Driscoll, who works at the college and is a flirty spinster. At the pre-arranged kidnap spot, Pat unexpectedly gets out of the car with Benny, so it's Nancy who's spirited away to Alverato's yacht, where she seduces Alverato, and for much of the book Nancy and Alverato are off cruising the Caribbean together.

The foreground story, however, remains Benny and the problem he has with Pat. Benny doesn't know Pat well, and doesn't know she's experimented with heroin and just recently stopped taking it because she was getting hooked. To keep Pat tractable, Benny feeds her heroin in her drinks. The movement of the story is that Benny gradually falls in love with Pat and gradually (unknowingly) addicts her to heroin. The characters of Benny and Pat are fully developed and very touchingly real. The hopeless love story never becomes mawkish, and the gradual drugged deterioration of Pat is beautifully and tensely handled (as Fell's deterioration will be in *Kill The Boss Goodbye*). The leap forward from *Stop This Man* is doubly astonishing when we consider they were published four months apart.

One month later, *A Shroud for Jesso* was published, in the second half of which Rabe finally came fully into his own. The book begins in a New York underworld similar to that in *Benny Muscles In,* with similar characters and relationships and even a similar symbolic job demotion for the title character, but soon the mobster Jesso becomes involved with international intrigue, is nearly murdered on a tramp steamer on the North Atlantic, and eventually makes his way to a strange household in Hannover, Germany, the home of Johannes Kator, an arrogant bastard and spy. In the house also are Kator's sister, Renette, and her husband, a homosexual baron named Helmut. Helmut provides the social cover, Kator provides the money. Renette has no choice but to live with her overpowering brother and her nominal husband.

Jesso changes all that. He and Renette run off together, and the cold precise Rabe style reaches its maturity:

They had a compartment, and when the chauffeur was gone they locked the door, pushed the suitcases out of the way, and sat down. When the train was moving they looked out of the window. At first the landscape looked flat, industrial; even the small fields had a square mechanical look. Later the fields rolled and there were more trees. Renette sat close, with her legs tucked under her. She had the rest of her twisted around so that she leaned against him. They smoked and didn't talk. There was nothing to talk about. They looked almost indifferent, but their indifference was the certainty of knowing what they had (page 93).

The characters in *A Shroud for Jesso* are rich and subtle, their relationships ambiguous, their story endlessly fascinating. When Jesso has to return for a while to New York, Renette prefigures the ending in the manner of her refusal to go with him:

Over here Jesso, I know you, I want you, we are what I know now. You and I. But over there you must be somebody else. I've never known you over there and your life is perhaps quite different. Perhaps not, Jesso, but I don't know. I want you now, here, and not later and somewhere else. You must not start to think of me as something you own, keep around wherever you happen to be. It would not be the same. What we have between us is just the opposite of that. It is the very thing you have given me, Jesso, and it is freedom (page 131).

And this opposition between love and freedom is what then goes on to give the novel its fine but bitter finish.

Rabe kept a European setting for his next book, *A House in Naples,* the story about two American Army deserters who've been black market operators in Italy in the ten years since the end of World War II. Charlie, the hero, is a drifter, romantic and adventurous. Joe Lenken, his partner, is a sullen but shrewd pig, and when police trouble looms, Joe's the one with solid papers and a clear identity, while Charlie's the one who has to flee to Rome to try (and fail) to find adequate forged papers. In a bar he meets a useless old expatriate American drunk who then wanders off, gets into a brawl, and is knifed to death. Charlie steals the dead man's ID for himself, puts the body into the Tiber under a bridge, then looks up and sees a girl looking down. How much did she see?

In essence, *A House in Naples* is a love story in which the love is poisoned at the very beginning by doubt. The girl, Martha, is simple and clear, but her clarity looks like ambiguity to Charlie. Since he can never be sure of her, he can never be sure of himself. Once he brings Martha back to Naples and the vicious Joe is added to the equation, the story can be nothing but a slow and hard unraveling. The writing is cold and limpid and alive with understated emotion, from first sentence ("The warm palm of land cupped the water to make a bay, and that's where Naples was" – page 7) to last ("He went to the place where he had seen her last" – page 144).

A House in Naples was followed by *Kill the Boss Goodbye,* and that was the peak of Rabe's first period, five books, each one better than the one before. In those books, Rabe combined bits and pieces of his own history and education with the necessary stock elements of the form to make books in which tension and obsession and an inevitable downward slide toward disaster all combine with a style of increasing cold objectivity not only to make the scenes seem brand new but even to make the (rarely stated) emotions glitter with an unfamiliar sheen.

Born in Germany in 1921, Rabe already spoke English when he arrived in America at seventeen. With a Ph.D. in psychology, he taught for a while at Western Reserve University and did research at Jackson Laboratory, where he wrote several papers on frustration. (No surprise.) Becoming a writer, he moved to various parts of America and lived a while in Germany, Sicily and Spain. His first published work he has described as "a funny pregnancy story (with drawings) to *McCall's.*" The second was *Stop This Man.* In the next four books, he made the paperback world his own.

But then he seemed not to know what to do with it. Was it bad advice? Was it living too far away from the publishers and the action? Was it simply the speed at which he worked?

Fortunately, with his twelfth book, *Blood on the Desert,* Rabe gets his second wind, goes for a complete change of pace, and produces his first fully satisfying work since *Kill the Boss Goodbye.* It's a foreign intrigue tale set in the Tunisian desert, spy versus spy in a story filled with psychological nuance. The characters are alive and subtle, the story exciting, the setting very clearly realized.

My Lovely Executioner, is another total change of pace, and a fine absorbing novel. Rabe's first book told completely in the first-person, it is also his first true *mystery*, a story in which the hero is being manipulated and has no idea why.

The hero-narrator, Jimmy Gallivan, is a glum fellow in jail, with three weeks to go on a seven-year term for attempted murder (wife's boyfriend, shot but didn't kill) when he's caught up in a massive jailbreak. He doesn't want to leave, but another con, a tough professional criminal named Rand, forces him to come along, and then he can't get back. Gallivan gradually realizes the whole jailbreak was meant to get *him* out, but he doesn't know why. Why him? Why couldn't they wait three weeks until he'd be released anyway? The mystery is a fine one, the explanation is believable and fair, the action along the way is credible and exciting, and the Jim Thompsonesque gloom of the narration is wonderfully maintained.

And next, published in May of 1960, Rabe's sixteenth Gold Medal novel in exactly five years, was *Murder Me for Nickels,* yet another change of pace, absolutely unlike anything that he had done before. Told in first person by Jack St. Louis, righthand man of Walter Lippit, the local jukebox king, *Murder Me for Nickels* is as sprightly and glib as *My Lovely Executioner* was depressed and glum. It has a lovely opening sentence, "Walter Lippit makes music all over town" (page 5), and is chipper and funny all the way through. At one point, for instance, St. Louis is drunk when he suddenly has to defend himself in a fight: "I whipped the bottle at him so he stunk from liquor. I kicked out my foot and missed. I swung out with the glass club and missed. I stepped out of the way and missed. When you're drunk everything is sure and nothing works" (page 164).

Nineteen-sixty was also when a penny-ante outfit called Abelard-Schuman published in hardcover *Anatomy of a Killer, a* novel Gold Medal had rejected, I can't think why. It's third person, as cold and as clean as a knife, and this time the ghostly unemotional killer, Loma and Mound, is brought center stage and made the focus of the story. This time he's called Jordan (as in the river?) and Rabe stays in very tight on him. The book begins,

When he was done in the room he stepped away quickly because the other man was falling his way. He moved fast and well and when he was out in the corridor he pulled the door shut behind him. Sam Jordan's speed had nothing to do with haste but came from perfection.

The door went so far and then held back with a slight give. It did not close. On the floor, between the door and the frame, was the arm.

...he looked down at the arm, but then did nothing else. He stood with his hand on the door knob and did nothing.

He stood still and looked down at the fingernails and thought they were changing color. And the sleeve was too long at the wrist. He was not worried about the job being done, because it was done and he knew it. He felt the muscles around the mouth and then the rest of the face, stiff like bone. He did not want to touch the arm.

...After he had not looked at the arm for a while, he kicked at it and it flayed out of the way. He closed the door without slamming it and walked away. A few hours later he got on the night train for the nine-hour trip back to New York.

...But the tedium of the long ride did not come. He felt the thick odor of clothes and felt the dim light in the carriage like a film over everything, but the nine-hour dullness he wanted did not come. I've got to unwind, he thought. This is like the shakes. After all this time with all the habits always more sure and perfect, this.

He sat still, so that nothing showed, but the irritation was eating at him. Everything should get better, doing it time after time, and not worse. Then it struck him that he had never before had to touch a man when the job was done. Naturally. Here was a good reason. He now knew this in his head but nothing else changed. The hook wasn't out and the night-ride dullness did not come (pages 7-9).

It is from that small beginning, having to touch a victim for the first time, that Rabe methodically and tautly describes the slow unraveling of Jordan. It's a terrific book.

There was one other novel from this period, a Daniel Port which was rejected by Gold Medal and published as half of an Ace double-book in 1958, under the title *The Cut of the Whip*. Which brings to eighteen the books published between 1955 and 1960. Eighteen books, five years, and they add up to almost the complete story of Peter Rabe's career as a fine and innovative writer.

Almost. There was one more, in December of 1962, called *The Box* (the only Rabe novel published with a Rabe title). *The Box* may be Rabe's finest work, a novel of character and of place, and in it Rabe managed to use and integrate more of his skills and techniques than anywhere else. "This is a pink and gray town," it begins, "which sits very small on the North edge of Africa. The coast is bone white and the sirocco comes through any time it wants to blow through. The town is dry with heat and sand" (page 5).

A tramp steamer is at the pier. In the hold is a large wooden box, a corner of which was crushed in an accident. A bad smell is coming out. The bill of lading very oddly shows that the box was taken aboard in New York and is to be delivered to New York. Contents: "PERISHABLES. NOTE:

IMPERATIVE, KEEP VENTILATED." The captain asks the English clerk of the company that owns the pier permission to unload and open the box. The box is swung out and onto the pier.

They stood a moment longer while the captain said again that he had to be out of here by this night, but mostly there was the silence of heat everywhere on the pier. And whatever spoiled in the box there, spoiled a little bit more.

'Open it!' said the captain (page 11).

They open it, and look in.

'Shoes?' said the clerk after a moment. 'You see the shoes?' as if nothing on earth could be more puzzling.

'Why shoes on?' said the captain, sounding stupid.

What was spoiling there spoiled for one moment more, shrunk together in all that rottenness, and then must have hit bottom.

The box shook with the scramble inside, with the cramp muscled pain, with the white sun like steel hitting into the eyes there so they screwed up like sphincters, and then the man inside screamed himself out of his box (page 12).

The man is Quinn, a smartass New York mob lawyer who is being given a mob punishment: shipped around the world inside the box, with nothing in there but barely enough food and water to let him survive the trip. What happens to him in Okar, and what happens to Okar as a result of Quinn, live up to the promise of that beginning.

But for Rabe, it was effectively the end. It was another three years before he published another book, and then it was a flippant James Bond imitation called *Girl in a Big Brass Bed,* introducing Manny deWitt, an arch and cutesy narrator who does arch and cutesy dirty work for an international industrialist named Hans Lobbe. Manny deWitt appeared twice more, in *The Spy Who Was 3 Feet Tall* (1966) and *Code Name Gadget* (1967), to no effect, all for Gold Medal. And Gold Medal published Rabe's last two books as well: *War of the Dons* (1972) and *Black Mafia* (1974).

Except for those who hit it big early, the only writers who tend to stay with writing over the long haul are those who can't find a viable alternative. Speaking personally, three times in my career the wolf has been so slaveringly at the door that I tried to find an alternative livelihood, but lacking college degrees, craft training or any kind of useful work history I was forced to go on writing instead, hoping the wolf would grow tired and slink away. The livelihood of writing is iffy at best, which is why so many writing careers simply stop when they hit a lean time. Peter Rabe had a doctorate in psychology; when things went to hell on the writing front, it was possible for him to take what he calls a bread-and-butter job teaching undergraduate psychology in the University of California.

It is never either entirely right or entirely wrong to identify a writer with his or her heroes. The people who carry our stories may be us, or our fears about ourselves, or our dreams about ourselves. The typical Peter Rabe hero is a smart outsider, working out his destiny in a hostile world. Unlike Elmore Leonard's scruffy heroes, for instance, who are always iron-ically aware that they're better than their milieu, Rabe's heroes are better than their milieu but are never entirely confident of that. They're as tough and grubby as their circumstances make necessary, but they are also capa-ble from time to time of the grand gesture. Several of Peter Rabe's novels, despite the ill-fitting wino garb of their titles, are very grand gestures indeed.